HONEY
AND HEAT

TITLES BY AURORA PALIT

Sunshine and Spice

Honey and Heat

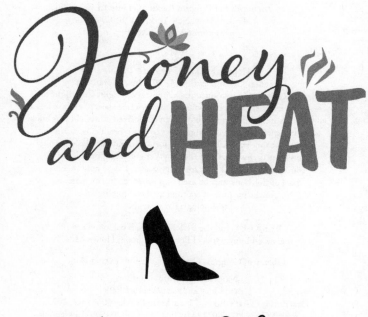

Honey and HEAT

Aurora Palit

BERKLEY ROMANCE

New York

BERKLEY ROMANCE
Published by Berkley
An imprint of Penguin Random House LLC
1745 Broadway, New York, NY 10019
penguinrandomhouse.com

Library of Congress Cataloging-in-Publication Data

Names: Palit, Aurora, author.
Title: Honey and heat / Aurora Palit.
Description: First edition. | New York: Berkley Romance, 2025.
Identifiers: LCCN 2025007123 (print) | LCCN 2025007124 (ebook) |
ISBN 9780593640203 (trade paperback) | ISBN 9780593640210 (ebook)
Subjects: LCGFT: Romance fiction. | Novels.
Classification: LCC PR9199.4.P3427 H66 2025 (print) |
LCC PR9199.4.P3427 (ebook) | DDC 813/.6—dc23/eng/20250307
LC record available at https://lccn.loc.gov/2025007123
LC ebook record available at https://lccn.loc.gov/2025007124

First Edition: September 2025

Printed in the United States of America
1st Printing

The authorized representative in the EU for product safety and compliance
is Penguin Random House Ireland, Morrison Chambers, 32 Nassau
Street, Dublin D02 YH68, Ireland, https://eu-contact.penguin.ie.

This one is for all the fierce, intelligent, and hardworking women out there who try to do it all.

And for Chelsea, who is all of the above and more.

HONEY
AND HEAT

CHAPTER 1

"Y ou must be Cinderella . . ."

Cynthia Kumar didn't bother suppressing a disgusted shudder seconds before knocking back her tequila shot and swiveling her barstool to face whoever had delivered that tired remark. It was the fourth pickup line she'd received tonight and despite the beer commercials of her youth, the speakers were *not* looking more attractive with each additional ounce of alcohol she welcomed into her body.

This particularly terrible opener had come from a guy with droopy blue eyes who was sporting a floral Tommy Bahama shirt in the dead of winter. In Canada.

". . . because I see that dress disappearing at midnight," Droopy finished, his lips stretching into a sluggish grin.

Cynthia needed another shot.

"Not interested," she replied, tone clipped and precise, before turning back to the bar and signaling to the bartender. She could practically feel the man bristling under his awful shirt.

"What? I'm not good enough for you, sweetheart?" Droopy sneered.

When she didn't respond, his shoulders jerked in an uneven shrug. "Just so you know, I wasn't *actually* interested. I was just trying to be nice because you're sitting here all alone on a Sunday night."

Typical. She was attractive to them until she stood up for herself. Every guy who'd approached her that night had trodden a similar path: an embarrassing attempt at flirting followed by a level of hostility that spoke volumes of their fragile masculinity. Cynthia kept her eyes trained on the bartender assembling her drink and pretended she couldn't hear him. The choice words he muttered before scuttling away barely broke skin—*rude, stuck-up, bitch*—she'd heard it all before, whether here, in this sticky bar, or at work, aimed at her retreating back after she pointed out a miscalculated risk in someone's project proposal.

She'd long ago given up trying to solve the age-old question of why men continued to run the world and was now much more focused on her next shot, sliding cleanly across the bar to stop right in front of her.

With a wrinkled brow, the bartender watched Cynthia toss it back—without even bothering with the salt or lime this time—and cleared her throat. "Everything okay?"

Cynthia shrugged and signaled for another. She was so *not* the type to spill her woes, especially to a stranger, however well-meaning they were. This whole night, really, was not her usual scene; she'd had to google the nearest bar for the under-fifty-but-definitely-not-twenties crowd.

And as a new dose of tequila slid into view, Cynthia wondered if it would even do the trick. The alcohol was not softening the bitter disappointment congealing in her stomach since earlier in the evening, after her weekly dinner with her parents.

Up until the end, it had been a predictable evening of rice, roti, and curry simmered in *Cynthia-why-are-you-not-in-a-relationship* sauce with a side of *boys-prefer-long-hair* vegetable pakoras. Her mother had done the cooking while her grandmother, whose wrinkled face via video call had been propped up against a vase for the main course, had spiced the meal with her not-so-unique blend of complaints over the rising cost of living and jabs directed at her single—and *not* looking—granddaughter.

Cynthia didn't care much about fulfilling her family's ridiculous expectations of what constituted a good, obedient South Asian daughter, but even she knew better than to argue with her grandmother. Still, her dad nodding his agreement with every one of Grandma's critiques combined with her mother clearing her throat purposefully every time Cynthia tried to change the subject had been enough to make Cynthia sprint for the exit as soon as the last spoonful of kulfi had passed her lips.

But three words, overheard from the hallway outside the dining room, had stopped her in her tracks, her white, down-filled coat hanging limply from the one arm she'd shoved through the sleeve.

"About your retirement . . ." Her mother's voice trailed off.

During dinner, it had been a welcome respite from marriage and baby-making when Grandma had switched gears and brought up the subject of her son's retirement. The family matriarch rarely broached the subject even though she called from India multiple times a week, undeterred when she often missed her son, who had usually already left for the office. Or a site visit. Or a meeting with prospective clients. Or drinks with one of the men on his senior leadership team.

Rich Kumar loved to work.

Cynthia hadn't thought twice when her father didn't bother to address the topic of his retirement over the dinner table. She'd worked in her father's office since high school and he didn't seem eager to slow down anytime soon, but the slight edge to her mother's tone, somewhere between annoyance and stubbornness, perked Cynthia's ears right up. And it wasn't because Sipra Kumar rarely weighed in on the goings-on of her husband's business.

Like Cynthia, Sipra was more than a little interested in Rich's retirement plans.

At the prolonged clinking of her father's spoon against his crystal ice cream bowl, Cynthia quietly slid her second arm through the other sleeve of her coat but made no move toward zipping it up. Instead, her teeth clamped down on her bottom lip, her breath hitching when the creak of wood alerted her that Rich was leaning back in his chair, his hands likely folded together on his abdomen.

Cynthia knew her father *that* well, had been studying him her entire life. The soft squeak of velvet upholstery against a handcrafted oak chair spoke volumes: he had something important to say. And Sipra must have sensed it, too, because the room fell silent. If Cynthia's industrious mother was abandoning clearing the dessert plates, then News—capital *N*—was forthcoming.

"I think I've finally found the right person to take over the family business," her father announced.

A shiver of apprehension raced through Cynthia, but she stood as still as the coatrack in the drafty hallway. Since attaining her diploma in marketing—before then, even—she'd been working her ass off at Kumar Construction, trying to prove that she, as her father's only child, was a worthy successor to the multimillion-dollar legacy he had built. From toiling away between file cabinets as a high school intern to bringing in lucrative clients as an up-and-coming interior designer and brand consultant, she'd done everything in her power, and then some, to prove that even though she was not the son Rich Kumar had hoped to mentor and mold in his image, she was qualified to inherit his empire.

She could have stepped out of her father's far-reaching shadow years ago, set up her own business that was more than equipped to stay afloat without people knowing her last name. But she'd stayed on at Kumar Construction as an interior designer and tried to establish herself within her father's company to prove herself.

Maybe her efforts were finally paying off.

Sipra snorted at her husband's retirement announcement. "I'll believe it when I see it. For years you've been talking about finding the *right* person, someone that reminds you of yourself, someone with the exact qualities to take on everything you've built."

It took all of Cynthia's self-control not to burst forward into the dining room, to remind them—especially her father—that she was *right here*. After years of watching her father in and out of work, she'd modeled herself after him, mimicked his ambition, decisiveness, and confidence so that anyone with half a brain could see that their genes ran deeper than their shared pin-straight black hair and mild intolerance to lactose.

But Rich was a man who believed actions spoke louder than words. Besides, even had she made her presence known, he would likely see right through her, as he had every day since she'd turned fifteen.

Until her sophomore year in high school, she'd been Rich's side-kick and, likewise, he'd attended every single track meet and debate competition. He'd always been first in line to tell anyone within yelling distance that the tall, gawky preteen collecting the top student trophy on awards night was *his* little girl. Ever since she'd learned to walk without face-planting every third step, Rich had dragged her to construction sites, hoisting her on his broad shoulders so together they could watch him build his legacy from the ground up—figuratively and literally.

Funny how the hormone-driven mistakes of a teenager in the first throes of love could shatter all that. With a grandmother constantly badgering her to get married and have babies, and a stay-at-home mother who never once considered entering the workforce, her father strictly came to see her as just a girl. One impulsive, silly mistake and she became, in her father's eyes, a daughter who belonged at home, raising (if she was lucky) a brood of sons.

Yet the topic of her father's retirement watered the tiny seed of hope taking root in Cynthia's chest. She'd long ago given up on the Vancouver Canucks ever bringing home the Stanley Cup and had zero faith that Remi Matthews would ever forgive her for kneeing him in the balls when he'd spread rumors of her taking steroids after she beat him—and all the boys—in a long-distance race on track-and-field day in the sixth grade. But when it came to the future of Kumar Construction, the seed had always been there, waiting.

"Trust me, Sipra," her father said with the calm assurance that secured investors and made good on the bottom line. "This person reminds me of me."

In the space of a heartbeat, that tiny seed germinated.

"How so?" Sipra asked. Cynthia tilted her head back and smiled with relief. After years of being on the receiving end of countless interrogations about her unexceptional wardrobe, her disinterest in meeting "a nice boy from a good family," and her ineptitude in the kitchen, finally—*finally*—her mother was asking the right questions.

"Hardworking, ambitious, aspirational . . . I'm telling you, this kid might be the whole package."

Forget fertilizer and water. The seed shot up, blossomed. Likewise, a wide grin was flourishing across Cynthia's face.

But everything shriveled when Rich spoke again.

"He might be the one."

That one little pronoun sucked all the oxygen from Cynthia's lungs.

She hadn't stuck around to hear more, to listen to her father wax poetic about Kumar Construction's Chosen One—a *male* Chosen One, of course. Some unremarkable dude who didn't have to worry about stupid things, like biological clocks and underwires and smiling through business meetings while period cramps ate his insides with razor-sharp teeth, was going to receive the keys to her father's empire in his big, dumb, hairy hand.

She'd scurried out of her parents' home, into the biting cold of a starless January night. Her brain bypassed the practical need for calming breaths as well as the pathetic urge to shed angry tears. And she absolutely would not dwell, as she had so many times before, on how much simpler her life would be had she not given in to the reckless whims of her first crush so very long ago.

Instead, she'd opted for the worst cliché possible to dull the ache spreading rapidly like thistle weed in her gut: alcohol.

Cynthia examined the straw-colored contents of her shot glass, irritated that it was failing to wash the all-too-familiar pain away. Kumar Construction was supposed to be her future, not the reason she was sitting in a dive bar that, on its best days, would still be described as dank. She couldn't remember the last time she'd had a shot, never mind the last time she'd tried to get drunk. Did she even like tequila?

"Fuck it." Cynthia downed the drink as someone slid into the seat next to her.

CHAPTER 2

Rohit Patel couldn't help tapping a jaunty, rhythmless beat on his steering wheel as he grinned at his phone perched against the dashboard of his rental car. Nothing could get him down—not the lingering smell of marijuana wafting from the upholstered seats nor the fact that springing for a rental would set him back a student loan payment.

"I know you're excited that you landed a new job," his sister, Maisa, teased from the video call on his phone, "but could you tone down the goofy smile a notch? Your teeth are practically glowing in the dark."

Rohit slid a glance at his watch. "Give me a break. It gets dark early here."

"Hashtag expat struggles."

"Expat?" Rohit raised his eyebrows. "That's a fancy word for a sixteen-year-old."

Maisa ducked her head. "My tutor and I are working through Ernest Hemingway."

Fluorescent teeth be damned, Rohit couldn't hide his proud

smile or the burst of warmth in his chest when Maisa's answering grin matched his. She'd been diagnosed with a learning disability last year, and it was more than a point of pride that Rohit—living almost twelve thousand miles away in Canada—could pay for the tutors his sister needed to keep up in school. It was the *least* his expat ass could do, living so far away in a country whose social services were a dream come true compared to the ones offered in India. Especially when, at the start of his second year pursuing an MBA, his mother had slipped and fallen at work, badly injuring her wrist.

Her broken radius bone had been a wake-up call for Rohit, a persistent ringing between his ears that had only intensified when he'd been unable to physically care for his mother during her twelve-week recovery in a cast. He'd been forced to look after her—of all of them—from afar, and so he did it the only way he knew how. Financially.

Maisa now went to a private school with international teachers and smaller class sizes; his mother had quit her backbreaking job in a garment factory permanently; and while his father still worked at a bank, the deep worry lines bracketing his mouth had faded considerably.

Working multiple jobs to foot their bills hadn't been easy over the last year, but things were finally, *finally* looking up. The universe had just gifted him with a great job with a hefty salary *and* benefits included.

His sister would have to deal with his glow-in-the-dark teeth.

"So, you'll be moving to Kal-hona?" Maisa asked.

"Ke-*low*-na," Rohit corrected her even though the name of the new city seemed strange to him, too. When he'd left the MBA program, giving up his convenient but bare-bones student housing in Toronto to move to a cheaper—and draftier—living situation hadn't been easy, but an on-campus apartment was a luxury, not a necessity. It would be no hardship leaving his shady apartment on an even shadier street in Hamilton, Ontario.

Checking his bank account balance was dicier than playing roulette at a Vegas casino. Maisa's educational needs and the little extra he sent home to make up for his mother's unemployment were one thing, but along the way he'd also taken on his grandmother's medical care after she'd suffered a stroke, somewhere between his mother requiring physiotherapy for her wrist and a distant cousin coming out of the woodwork looking for help to finance his daughter's wedding.

But it was Rohit's duty to give; he'd always been taught that family came first. It was then that he'd decided to look to the west, seeking what so many eastern Canadians did when money was tight: a job that paid and a lease that wouldn't land him in collections. The universe had cut him a break because he'd found an employer he liked who seemed to like him back.

And didn't seem too bothered with fact-checking his sparse résumé.

Desperate times, Rohit reminded himself. There was no room for guilt, not with so many people relying on him, and anything was worth the new brightness in Maisa's eyes after years of shifting uncomfortably whenever someone asked her about school. Besides, his new employer hadn't seemed too interested in discussing his MBA at the interview and Rohit planned to prove himself, twice over. This job had the power to solve so many of his problems—he wasn't going to take the opportunity for granted.

"Sorry." Maisa rolled her dark eyes. "*Kelowna.*"

"Kelowna," Rohit repeated, the word rolling more easily off his tongue. The more he said it—and thought about the influx of much-needed cash this new job would bring him—the sweeter it tasted.

His sister cocked her head to the side. "It's a great opportunity, but are you freaking out at all? You don't know anyone there and it's a big move."

"I'm feeling really good about this, actually. I . . . I can't describe it." Rohit closed his eyes, trying to find the right word to describe the determination, hope, and excitement zinging through his chest like Diwali fireworks ricocheting into the sky.

Maisa clucked her tongue. "'I know you can be overwhelmed, and you can be underwhelmed, but can you ever just be whelmed?'"

Rohit's eyes popped open as his sister laughed at her own wit. "I can't believe *10 Things I Hate About You* is your favorite movie," he said.

"Oh, stop pretending it's not yours, too. You introduced me to it, after all."

"Well, regardless, it was the perfect line at the perfect time."

As his sister sketched an overdramatic bow, Rohit's chest clutched and for a nanosecond, it was hard to breathe. With each passing year since he'd left India to study abroad, he missed less and less about his country of birth. Some things, like celebrations that shut down the entire city in a blaze of color and noise and happiness, still pricked at his heart, but nothing reached in and hollowed out his chest cavity like thinking about his family.

Especially Maisa. Rohit's acceptance to the University of Toronto for his undergraduate degree had been the ultimate gift for a young guy with big dreams and a desire to see the world. His sister deserved the same.

"I miss you," he said.

Maisa's eyebrows quirked. Despite the grand gestures of the

rom-coms they both loved and knew too well, their common ground was exchanging quotes from said movies, not discussing feelings. Still, her face softened. "I miss you, too, big brother. You should do something fun tonight. Whenever we talk, you're on your way to or from work or sitting in your apartment watching television. Boring."

Rohit forced a careless smirk. She didn't need to know that his shoestring budget didn't allow for much else.

"Where are you now?" Maisa asked.

"I'm in my rental car."

"No, you fool." Maisa closed her eyes in exasperation. Although his family loved loudly and freely, they never shied away from ribbing one another. "I mean, where are you in Kelowna right *now*?"

Rohit squinted through his driver's-side window at the building across the street. He'd parked here before his interview because it was free and had ignored his surroundings as he rushed, on foot, to beat his interviewer at the agreed-upon meeting location. "In front of a bar, I think. The Leprechaun Trap."

"Perfect! Leprechauns are lucky! Go inside and have a drink. Get to know your new townsfolk. Have some fun."

It sounded like a good idea to Rohit, but he couldn't help but tease his little sister. "Encouraging me to drink and party? Does Ma know that your tutor is debauching you?"

"'Debauching'?" Maisa pursed her lips. "What does that mean?"

"Keep studying Hemingway and you'll find out. I'll talk to you later."

The inside of the Leprechaun Trap was like all the Irish-style pubs Rohit had frequented as a student. There was no cover, it was dimly lit, the sticky floor squelched beneath his feet, and the mostly male patrons nursing pints of beer were clearly regulars. It was too dark to see the framed black-and-white photos scattered across the peeling walls properly, but they weren't the focal point—the rectangular bar in the center of the room was.

It was kind of a sad place for celebrating, a Sunday-night stop for someone who did *not* want to go home. Everything inside felt a little dull and worn out.

Except her.

A woman in a red dress sat at the far corner of the bar, seemingly oblivious to the dreariness around her as she contemplated the shot glass on the counter in front of her. Now *she* was the true focal point of the pub whose name Rohit could no longer recall. His brain was buzzing, his senses both alert and overloaded at the same time.

It might've been the red dress she wore, conservative in cut and length but wonderfully seductive, hugging the slender curves of her long, lithe body. It could have been the glossy shine of her chin-length hair that Rohit somehow knew would feel like silk against his skin. Maybe it was the perfect curve of her back—her spine was straight, regal even, bowing only a little at her smooth, bare shoulders so she could rest her elbows on the bar. In this dingy, near-empty bar, she projected strength and grace and something else that Rohit couldn't quite name but that tugged him forward like a magnet's south pole seeking its north mate.

She didn't glance his way when he took a seat on the stool next to her, nor did she seem to notice when he ordered a beer. She appeared to be talking to herself and Rohit swore he heard her murmur "fuck it" before tossing back the shot.

Nothing about her invited him to speak and yet, for the first time maybe ever in his life, words fell from his mouth before his brain could properly polish them.

"I can't hold my tequila worth a damn," he said, "but can I join you?"

CHAPTER 3

can't hold my tequila worth a damn," someone beside Cynthia said, "but can I join you?"

The faint beginnings of a tequila-induced fog in Cynthia's brain parted like the Red Sea for that voice. The smooth, rich timbre was satin against her auditory nerves, but when his words sank in, she rolled her eyes and turned to face bachelor number five. Or was it six?

Lively dark brown eyes, brimming with amusement and humor, met her gaze. Cynthia's eyes widened as she took in his warm, golden skin and playful half smile on *really* nice lips that no man deserved in a fair world.

Huh. Maybe the beer goggles were finally kicking in.

Cynthia gave her head a shake. "Okay, let's hear it."

"Hear what?"

She gestured at herself with an impatient wave of her hand. "Your lame pickup line about how good I look. Or how nice I smell. Or if you can 'see my keys because I'm turning you on.'" With a sarcastic laugh, Cynthia spun back to the bar and rolled the empty shot glass between her hands. "Go ahead, tell me I'm beautiful and then toddle off."

He was silent at first, prompting a thin, cold sensation that felt suspiciously like disappointment snaking down her spine. When she risked another glance at him, he was watching her with a thoughtful glint in his narrowed gaze.

"What?" Cynthia asked, tugging at the left strap of her dress self-consciously.

"Well, obviously I need a second. I don't want to waste the opportunity." There was zero sarcasm or defensiveness to his tone, and Cynthia swiveled on her barstool to face him properly.

"Give me the best you can do," she said. To her ears, the words played back harsher than she had intended, a depressing indication that when it came to flirting, she was woefully out of practice. Teasing and coy digs were not the mark of an aspiring CEO who relied on working overtime and detailed project charters to get what she wanted. But, to her relief, he responded to her challenge with a low chuckle that rasped like the wrong side of crushed velvet against inquisitive fingertips, and Cynthia found herself leaning forward.

"Okay, fine," he said, clearing his throat. "'I'm also just a boy, standing in front of a girl, asking her to notice him.'" With a lopsided smile, he added, "I had to wordsmith it a bit."

The words were so familiar that the last of the buzzy mist clouding her mind cleared away. "Wait . . . Where have I heard that before . . . ?"

He accepted a beer from the bartender and tipped its open mouth toward Cynthia. "Would you prefer 'To me, you are perfect'?"

Cynthia's head tilted to the side as the words rolled through her, just unfamiliar enough to be out of reach. Or perhaps it was the speaker's darkly fringed gaze upon her that was throwing her off, the sparkle in his deep brown eyes that was shifting the ground underneath her. He met her stare head-on with humor and blatant curiosity, which sent a new feeling through her, hot on the heels of her confusion.

Exhilaration.

"You did not come up with those yourself," Cynthia said, pleasantly surprised to hear the note of playfulness lacing her words.

He made her wait as he took a long pull from his beer bottle, leaving her nothing to do but trace the arch in his throat with her eyes. Long, graceful muscles worked with every swallow and Cynthia's mouth dried, suddenly parched.

Ordering another drink, however, was the last thing on her mind.

When he met her eyes again, his smile was blinding. "It feels too soon for 'I wanted it to be you. I wanted it to be you so badly,'" he said.

Cynthia let out a delighted gasp. "You stole those from movies!"

Their shared laughter faded as his eyelashes lowered, his eyes sweeping down her red dress before lingering where the hem had ridden up several inches above her knees. Heat and appreciation flared in his eyes when he raked them back up to her face. His perusal was so direct and so unapologetic that Cynthia's cheeks flushed, but she had zero desire to look away.

"It was worth a shot," he said, his smooth voice dropping to a husky pitch.

"It was a good try . . ." she murmured, submitting him to the same once-over he'd given her. He was wearing a charcoal-gray suit that hugged wonderfully broad shoulders and even broader thighs, a welcome change from baggy Tommy Bahama and other atrocities she'd borne witness to that night. The white shirt he wore beneath his suit was a little rumpled where it was loosened at his throat, like he'd gratefully tugged off a tie after a strenuous day.

The thought of him loosening his collar, the tension in his body as he worked to pull the confining material away, stirred a tight, delicious heat in the pit of Cynthia's stomach. He had sexy collarbones.

"I might be willing to let you try again," she finished.

He grinned and tipped his drink to his mouth again. Cynthia's eyelids lowered to half-mast as she tracked the path from his pursed lips to the sharp line of dark stubble along his jaw. His beard was short and shaped with angular precision, and the skin on the pads of her fingers tingled. Whether it was the neatly trimmed roughness of his facial hair or the alluring texture of his voice, she suddenly itched to touch something.

Him. The realization hit her like an electrostatic shock and with it came just the right hit of endorphins to send a tingle into her core and pull her inner thighs closer together. *I want to touch him.*

"'As you wish,'" he said. "I'm Rohit, by the way."

The reference to one of her favorite childhood movies pulled Cynthia off her seat so she stood between his spread legs, loving how he immediately leaned a fraction closer. He smelled good, too. "Cynthia."

Rohit cocked his head at her empty shot glass. "So, can I buy you a drink, Cynthia?"

She let her gaze flit to his slightly parted lips before settling on his eyes again. His pupils dilated, laser focused on her with a hunger that charged Cynthia with the confidence to pull the near-empty bottle from his hands and place it on the bar with a resolute *clink.* The disappointments from earlier that evening tucked themselves into the deep recesses of her brain as a slow, catlike smile curved her lips. For the first time that night, she felt like herself. Or perhaps, a heightened version of herself: bold to the point of dramatic, assertive and unafraid.

She was surrendering to her primal instincts, and it felt damn good. Cynthia leaned forward, dropping her voice, careful to not let any part of her body touch his. There'd be time for that later, and the anticipation sent another wicked jolt through her.

"It's my turn," she said. "How about I show you my keys and we get out of here?"

AT ANY OTHER time, Rohit's modest choice of hotel accommodation would've given Cynthia pause. The cozy, bumblebee-inspired lodgings of Marta's Honeycomb Inn seemed far too wholesome for a man whose slow, precise hands seemed hell-bent on exploring Cynthia's body until every square inch of skin transformed into an erogenous zone that practically sparked under his hot, curious touch. In that quaint room of old-fashioned, heavy wood furniture and soft, lemon-yellow wallpaper, he made no move to discard his suit, no matter how urgently she pressed herself against the firm planes of his body.

Cynthia palmed the lapels of his suit. "Take your clothes off." The urgency underlying the breathless command surprised her. There was no mistaking the want in her voice, but the note of neediness was one she'd never heard slip from her lips before.

Rohit's hands moved from where they'd been caressing the underside of her jaw to her waist in a firm grip, as if he was grounding himself. "No," he said, softening the rebuff with a sweeping brush of his lips against hers. "If I take them off, it's going to be all over for me, and I want to make you come first."

At that dark promise—laced with such honesty and frankness—the cloying décor of Marta's Honeycomb Inn faded away completely. It was a first for Cynthia, tuning out her surroundings and thinking only of the sweet, thrumming ache building deep in her core, demanding relief. How could she not slide closer to the man whose intense, full-blown pupils drank in the sight of her—and only her—with a reverence that promised to meet her every demand between the bedsheets as effortlessly as he had in the bar? The tequila buzz had worn off, but Cynthia's brain hummed with a new kind of intoxication she'd never experienced before.

She pushed onto her tiptoes so her lips brushed his soft earlobe as she whispered in his ear, "But I want you inside me now."

Rohit's body went still, his hands becoming dead weight against the curve of her waist, prompting a jarring rush of blood to pound against her eardrum. Suddenly, Cynthia's neediness embarrassed her. What had prompted her to say that? She had no idea what she was doing, had never hooked up with a near stranger like this, never mind one she'd just met at a bar. A bar! What was she doing?

Although she'd never been particularly talented at reading people, Cynthia tried to search Rohit's face, but his chin had dipped downward, his eyes on the sliver of space between their chests. Great. She'd ruined the moment. Cynthia shifted backward, ready to pull away, but Rohit's fingers tightened at her waist, anchoring her to him, and with that one little act of resistance, heat—and hope—crept forward again, spiraling outward from the delicious burn building in her core.

Slow and achingly careful, Rohit's hands dipped to the hem of Cynthia's dress, and the rustle of the soft, red fabric hiking up her hips was the most erotic sound Cynthia had ever heard. She rarely wore color—certainly nothing as bright as this—but it had seemed like the only logical choice when she'd found the dress in the back of her closet. She'd wanted to feel different tonight, to shed the disappointment of never feeling like she was enough.

When she'd stepped into the Leprechaun Trap's less-than-impressive interior, her clothing had felt like the wrong choice, but not anymore, especially when Rohit touched her bare thighs and uttered a rasped curse. It was the first time, all night, that Cynthia had witnessed him losing his composure. Confidence sizzled through her, burning all her former uncertainty to a crisp.

She felt so powerful yet so full of want in his hands, now moving insistently over her—almost clumsy but still worshipful—to push the crotch of her panties aside. He slipped a long, questioning finger inside, her slick wetness welcoming the invasion as her hips canted upward.

He takes direction well, Cynthia acknowledged faintly to herself before her thoughts splintered in a million different directions as he pumped once, his gaze riveted on her face. She could only stare back, her left leg rising by its own volition to curve and hook around his waist, eliminating the last bit of space, and doubt, between them.

It also served to push his finger more deeply inside her and she shivered.

"Like this?" he murmured in a hushed voice, only slightly audible over the lush, wet sound of his finger meeting the rhythm of her eager hips.

"Yes." Cynthia's leg tightened around Rohit and her forehead dropped to his shoulder, letting him bear the burden of her weight as she practically writhed against that talented, seeking finger. She hardly recognized this version of herself, following someone else's lead and blatantly eager for where he might take her next. She only cared for the exquisite sharpening inside her. It was coming so fast, and for once in her life, she would welcome the sense of chaos building inside her with open arms.

She didn't want to think—she wanted to come. Now.

"Can you handle more?" Rohit asked.

She loved that he asked as much as she loved how his other hand had snaked around to cup her bottom and hold her firmly against him, and she nodded against his shoulder.

Rohit added a second finger and the new fullness—coupled with his discovery of a particularly sensitive bundle of nerves inside her— jolted a hot flash behind Cynthia's eyelids, and she closed her eyes and did something she couldn't remember *ever* doing before during sex.

She moaned.

She moaned *loudly*, from a place deep in her chest. The raw, primal sound was such a far cry from her usual calm reserve that it was almost too honest, too desperate.

But she didn't fucking care, especially when Rohit pressed his mouth to her damp temple and whispered, "You are so sexy."

The ache sharpened inside her and Cynthia focused all her attention chasing this wonderful high as Rohit, still fully clothed, scraped his teeth against the sensitive skin behind her earlobe. The gentle bite was enough to push her over the edge and she clung to him as heat burst through her, liquefying her bones in its wake.

His arm tightened around her as she shuddered against him, and even though she'd met him only a short while ago, Cynthia knew, without a doubt, that tonight he'd hold her up. Rohit wouldn't let her fall.

When her orgasm subsided, Rohit's hand retreated from between her thighs. Like her, he was breathing hard, and with his other hand, he gently tucked a lock of her hair behind her ear before cradling her jaw gently.

"I feel like the luckiest man in the world right now," he said in a low voice that was equal parts thunderstruck and adoring.

His words caused a lovely little tug in her chest, but it was more than the pleasure of receiving such a compliment. Her feelings felt too big and baffling in this moment and she couldn't resist leaning her cheek into the palm of his hand, nuzzling like a spoiled, contented cat.

She felt too bashful to say anything particularly profound or appropriate, so she settled on another truth instead. "I want you inside me again."

Eagerness lit Rohit's eyes, and his hand moved down her body once more, but Cynthia shook her head. "No, not like that," she said, reaching for the front of his suit pants and giving him a bold squeeze. He was rock-hard.

Rohit's groan sounded pained and his head dropped to her shoulder. "Damn it," he said.

"What?" Cynthia asked, slowly unhooking her leg from around him. Her hands, though, were loath to let go, but the realization didn't make her feel clingy. It felt right.

"I don't have protection." Even though his voice was muffled, Cynthia could hear the regret seeping through his words. "I didn't think I'd be doing something like this tonight." He jerked his head up and looked at her. "Not that we have to do anything else. I'm not assuming that we're going to—"

Cynthia clapped her hand over his mouth, delighting in the little thrill that ran through her when his soft lips parted against the sensitive skin of her palm. "We're definitely going to do more," she said. "I have condoms." The night might've been unexpected for her, too, but she was always, *always* prepared for anything. Had he asked, she could've supplied floss, lip butter, disinfectant wipes, and ibuprofen, too.

When she pulled her hand away, Rohit's neck corded. "You have condoms?" he asked in a strangled voice.

She couldn't help but stiffen, preparing herself for the worst. She knew all too well that some men couldn't handle a woman who took charge, who stayed a step ahead with more than enough slack to make up for a man's shortcomings.

But Rohit leaned forward until his breath brushed against her parted lips. "You're so . . . fierce," he said. Awe coated his words. "It's such a fucking turn-on."

She turned him on. Impulsively, Cynthia curled her fingers into Rohit's soft hair and closed the distance between them, pressing her lips against his, not caring if her tongue stealing into his mouth seemed desperate or if the arch of her back pushing her breasts into his chest betrayed the feelings of gratitude and relief coursing through her. It was an unfiltered, almost sloppy kiss, and Cynthia threw every part of her being into it.

Her enthusiastic tongue against his seemed to be the last straw for Rohit's self-control. His hands tore at their clothing, first his and then hers, and before her brain could catch up with the lick of fire awakening every last nerve ending, Cynthia found herself flat on her back on the honeycomb bedspread, Rohit's chest and stomach firm and defined under her palms, condom rolled on by both their hands, his skin warm against her greedy hands. He smelled incredible—faintly fresh, and vibrant, like tangerines, and so very male—and with each ignited touch, Cynthia breathed deep as the heat in her rose higher and higher, eager to engulf them both.

And, once again, Rohit welcomed her flame. Under his solid

weight, there was no room to feel self-conscious of the whimpers building in her throat or the beads of sweat gathering at the nape of her neck, dampening the pillowcase beneath her. Rohit worshipped her body so thoroughly, there was no room to think or plot her next move.

Cynthia could just *feel*.

And, God, she wanted to feel this forever. He was tuned to every one of her bodily reactions. When Cynthia bit her bottom lip, he lapped her nipple with the flat of his tongue again. When she raised her hips, his thumb happily set up camp in that special, secret place just left of her clitoris that sent a delectable shock wave through her.

He sank into her with a groan that matched the hunger unfurling at her core. It was tight and full, and when he'd reached the hilt, he studied her face and tenderly brushed a lock of hair from her forehead. "This okay?"

Cynthia responded by lifting her hips and palming his lower back, drawing him tighter to her. "I think I'm close again."

Rohit slid his hand between them to work her clit, and her body responded almost immediately by squeezing his cock tight. Satisfaction crossed his face as her inner muscles fluttered around him, and he scraped his teeth over the skin behind her ear again.

This man read her body like a book and Cynthia spread her legs wider as her second orgasm subsided, wanting him to memorize each and every subtle nuance hidden between the pages. She'd slept with only two men prior to Rohit—one of which had been a year-long relationship—and never once had it felt like this. Never had she been worshipped from head to toe, every gasp and whimper chronicled and bookmarked for later.

Cynthia couldn't blame the tequila for what came next: she sank her fingers into the thick, silky hair at the crown of Rohit's head, pulled him down for a long, messy kiss, and said to him words she had never, ever said to anyone, whether naked or not:

"I need more."

"More of this?" he asked, pumping hard and eliciting a moan from them both.

She kissed him again, sighing into his lips. "More of *you*."

A look of wonder crossed his face. "Who *are* you?" he murmured before giving her exactly what she needed.

CHAPTER 4

Rohit shifted in his seat from where he sat across from his new employer the next morning. He tried to look attentive as the endless cerulean sky stretched outside the window of the CEO's thirtieth-floor office as his new boss squinted at his computer screen, single-finger-typing every few minutes and muttering under his breath.

Some of the mutterings were discernible and it was all Rohit could do not to laugh when he heard the words *damn technology* and *font is too damn small* and *what did I click on now?*

"Sir, maybe I could do a quick search for you?"

"No, no. I emailed Gayle last night—it should be here."

"Gayle?"

"From human resources."

Rohit's brows shot up but, wisely, he refrained from commenting. He'd always considered messaging an employee on the weekend for nonurgent work-related matters to be inappropriate, but if that was how things were run here, he'd keep his mouth shut and get on board.

He had too much riding on this not to.

Rohit sat back in his chair for what looked like a long wait and let his mind drift. There was a lot to think about. Like signing the lease on the apartment he'd found yesterday after being offered a new job and calling his parents to inform them he'd officially accepted.

But all Rohit really wanted to do was think about Cynthia.

He'd awoken alone in his motel room this morning, the empty sheets beside him rumpled and cool but smelling so sweetly of something he couldn't quite place that for one quick, mortifying moment, he'd rolled over and inhaled deeply.

Rohit couldn't fault Cynthia for sneaking off in the dead of night—he had no idea where she worked or what time she started her day—but even he was a bit surprised at how optimistically he'd taken her absence in stride. In her wake, he was left with a strange sense of satisfaction—a peculiar, intense kind of rightness sitting deep in his chest. A certainty that what had happened was meant to happen, like a down-on-her-luck single mother finding a winning lottery ticket in the street.

There was no other way to feel after the night he and Cynthia had shared together. He'd always had a thing for strong, assertive women, but Cynthia . . .

Cynthia was on a whole other level.

She was sharp, fierce, and intelligent, with a confidence that ran hot, drawing him closer to the flame, addicted to the burn. She'd been so honest and uninhibited in bed last night; hell, she'd been nothing but fearless and challenging, from the moment he'd spotted her in the bar.

She was regal and commanding. Sexy as hell.

The memory of her fingers fisting a greedy handful of motel

sheets while her other hand dug into his hair, tugging at the roots, would be imprinted in his brain forever. Rohit wanted her again—in bed, at the bar, or wherever she'd have him.

From the outside looking in, Rohit was well aware that these feelings for a woman he had known for less than twenty-four hours were unhinged. But he was a big believer in fate, and one did not ignore a chance meeting with a woman who tempted every single one of his senses. Besides, she'd left her phone number on the hotel stationery pad by the cheap coffee maker on top of the mini fridge. No name, no cutesy hearts, just ten boldly scrawled digits as if she knew he would call.

And fuck yes, he was going to call.

"Well, son, you'll have to wait until HR arrives, I guess," his boss announced with a sigh of defeat.

"Gayle," Rohit said.

The older man nodded approvingly, clasping his hands together on the desk. "That's what I like about you, Rohit. You seem like a people person and that's exactly what we need around here. This company is like a family."

A sliver of self-assurance threaded through Rohit. He'd always found it easy to get along with others, decipher their body language, and react accordingly. "That's great. It sounds like an excellent work culture." Except for possible lack of boundaries when it came to after hours, but who was he to judge?

When the older man stood up, Rohit followed suit, his eyes catching on a framed photograph sitting beside the printer. In the picture had to be a younger version of his new CEO. Beside him was a little girl with a big grin on her face as she clutched at his hand with her two smaller ones. The pair of them wore matching outfits and yellow construction helmets on their heads.

"Is that your daughter?" Rohit asked.

"Hmm? Oh, yes. She was a very focused little girl, always wanted to be number one in everything she did."

As Rohit's gaze slid away, he couldn't help but linger on the large expanse of the polished cherrywood desk between them. Everything in this office—from its location on the thirtieth floor to its gleaming surfaces and expensive-looking furnishings—fed Rohit's determination. If he played his cards right, this place was going to help turn his life around, he just knew it.

He looked at the framed photograph again. "Her excitement reminds me of my sister," Rohit said.

"The one you're sending money home for?"

"Yes, sir." It was a topic they'd covered yesterday, and he was glad he'd been honest about his financial responsibilities. They'd stumbled onto the topic by chance after Rohit had learned that his new boss was an immigrant, too, and was well acquainted with helping support family back home. By no means was this an uncommon trend for expats living overseas, but the common ground had bonded the two men almost immediately, allowing Rohit the ability to ease off the desperate need to land this job and enjoy getting to know Rich.

"I like your attitude, Rohit. You're going to fit in just fine here."

"Thank you, Mr. Kumar."

His boss chuckled. "No need for the formality, son. We're going to be working very closely together. You can call me Rich." A new gleam entered Rich's eyes. "You're going to be glad you joined Kumar Construction, Rohit. I see a very bright future for you here."

Rohit didn't bother to subdue the grateful smile spreading across his face. He couldn't believe his luck. Looking for a job in western Canada had been the wisest decision he'd ever made. "Thank you for this opportunity, Rich. I won't let you down."

Truer words had never crossed his lips. Rohit was going to be the best damned employee Rich had ever seen. He wasn't going to squander this. For his family's sake, he was going to make every moment count.

"I know you won't," Rich agreed. "Why don't you head over to your office and get settled? I'll send a quick note to Gayle to find you as soon as she gets in. And close the door behind you if you wouldn't mind. I have to make a phone call."

Rohit quickly grabbed his messenger bag and did as Rich asked. But when he looked up after gingerly closing Rich's heavy office door, he almost stumbled into a very familiar body in the hallway.

"Cynthia?" Rohit blurted as a prickle of delighted shock danced down his spine. Cynthia, on the other hand, didn't look at all surprised to see him, and when her shrewd, amber eyes flicked over his shoulder and narrowed on Rich's closed door, Rohit realized that she had overheard at least some of the conversation that had taken place inside only moments ago. Perhaps she had even spied them through the cracked door.

The burgeoning suspicion wrinkling her forehead couldn't quell his pleasure, nor did it diminish the too-wide, too-telling smile stretching across his face. It was fate.

"What are you doing here?" He was powerless, too, against the teasing note in his voice. "Besides skulking in the corridors."

Cynthia's face hardened and the adrenaline thrumming through Rohit dulled to an uneasy crawl. None of last night's drugging playfulness glinted in her beautiful eyes, nor was there any give in the lithe, supple body he'd eagerly explored between the swish of starched sheets. This wasn't the cool flirtation he'd first encountered at the Leprechaun Trap the night before. She looked remote. Withdrawn.

Wary.

"You were just in there with my father," she stated flatly.

"What? I was in there with my new boss—"

"My name is Cynthia Kumar," she interrupted with an impatience that might have embarrassed him had he not seen her naked only hours ago.

"I—I didn't know . . . We didn't exchange last names."

"And now?"

The challenge in Cynthia's voice gave Rohit pause. He was reminded of when, as a child, he'd seen a lion tamer at a traveling circus. The lion and the tamer had circled each other for endless seconds, the audience on the edge of their seats as they waited for the human, so small and insignificant, to misstep. Even then, Rohit had known it wasn't real, that the entire thing—right down to the dramatic music piped through surround sound speakers—was part of a well-rehearsed show.

But Cynthia's feline glare felt very real, and something about the tension around her eyes warned Rohit that she rarely missed a thing.

He softened his tone. "This doesn't need to be a problem, Cynthia. I think your father really likes me, so—"

She rolled her eyes and jerked her thumb over her shoulder toward the hallway of office doors. "I work here, too," she said as if he should have already known.

"Oh. Well, we can just . . ." Rohit trailed off. He wasn't entirely sure what solutions were available to them; Rich hadn't been able to procure the employee handbook after all. Maybe intraoffice dating was frowned upon at Kumar Construction, although if that was the case, Cynthia's antagonism was still puzzling. "We'll find a solution," he finished firmly. They would have to—she was worth it.

"Here's a solution," she replied. "Quit."

Incredulous, Rohit shook his head. "Are you—are you serious?"

"Deadly."

She *looked* deadly and Rohit shook his head again. "I . . . I can't quit, Cynthia. I need this job." There was no way he was going to explain about his family, not now with Cynthia glowering at him, ready to tear the flesh clean away from his bones.

Even with her snarling at him, Rohit had no doubt Cynthia was worth many things, but his family's current situation—Maisa's education, his grandmother's medical bills—was incomparable. And not a topic of discussion.

Rohit straightened. "I *need* this job," he repeated firmly. "My future depends on it."

For less than a split second, Cynthia looked taken aback and her face faltered, her jaw going slack as a shadow clouded her eyes. But it wasn't regret that Rohit saw there; it was hurt. Disappointment. And, he realized with a sharp pinch in his heart, a fair amount of distrust.

Rohit chanced a step forward and then winced when she immediately stepped back. He fought the impulse to reach for her hands, to hold her. Funny how just last night, she had melted against his touch, leaning into his caresses with a seductive, raw kind of grace that had made his head spin.

"Cynthia," he said in a careful voice while shuffling backward half a step to give her space. "What exactly is this about?"

Cynthia's face hardened again and whatever vulnerability Rohit had witnessed in that heartbreakingly fleeting moment was erased into nothingness. "That's none of your business," she snapped.

"But—"

"This isn't going to work," she said, her voice downright frigid, and this time Rohit had no idea how to proceed. Oxygen deserted him, and he focused on calming the strange panicky feeling building in his chest as they stood staring at each other in silence while the sound of cheerful voices floated from the direction of the elevators.

When Rohit had walked into Kumar Construction at seven this morning, the office had been empty. He had no idea when Cynthia had arrived but this, he realized glumly, was obviously where she had disappeared to after one of the best nights of his life.

Lucky me, he thought grimly. They now both worked for her dad and, for some reason, that angered her. *She* was the girl in the framed picture in Rich's office, Rohit realized now. Once upon a time, Cynthia had been an excitable little girl whose doting father had built an empire to, presumably, offer her the world.

And Rohit's sister deserved the same.

"I'm not going to quit," he said quietly. "And you're just going to have to deal with it."

Cynthia's eyes narrowed into slits, and she shot him one last frostbite-inducing glare before turning on her heel and walking away.

CHAPTER 5

Over a year later . . .

*P*hone, check.

    Reports, check.

    Cynthia Kumar paused at the front doors of the Desmond Business Center and glanced down at the top of her favorite black pumps—Kate Spade, pointed toe, no scuff marks in sight—and nodded to herself.

    Don't-fuck-with-me heels, check.

    At her usual brisk clip, she breezed through the front entrance. Everything about the professional downtown space that housed Kumar Construction, with its gleaming floor-to-ceiling windows and bustling lobby of harried-looking tenants, was meant to project a sense of power and class. Most of the building was home to law firms, financial advisors, and, if the rumors were true, a collaboration of private medical practitioners that catered to the one percent. The elevator required a special fob to gain access to that floor.

    Even though Cynthia's workday often commenced long before she stepped into the building—usually in pajamas and slippers in the comfort of her bed—the polished marble floors always served as a reminder to compose herself. This was Kumar Construction's home, and she was a Kumar. Sure, the Desmond Business Center was snooty and elitist, but it was also a testament to everything her father had built, of his achievements as an ambitious, hardworking immigrant.

The city of Kelowna knew the Kumar name, had read about its many accomplishments in both newspapers and publications from the surrounding towns. *Kumar*, as far as Cynthia was concerned, was synonymous with *success*.

She stood up straighter. *Shoulders back, check.*

"Afternoon, Ms. Kumar," Malik, the security manager, greeted from his post at the front desk.

"Malik," she returned, placing an unmarked brown paper bag in front of him.

Clad in a black Hugo Boss suit—the mandatory uniform for the building's security guards—Malik responded with a curt nod as she flew past. The exchange was so brisk and devoid of any emotion that no one would suspect that Cynthia had just delivered a cinnamon raisin bagel with extra blueberry cream cheese, Malik's favorite.

They'd become friends, of sorts, in an unremarkable way that meant nothing to the average passerby and everything to Cynthia. One late afternoon, the hulking, stoic security guard hadn't hesitated to help her gather the fabric samples that had spilled from a cardboard box she'd been lugging to her car when the bottom dropped out. People had sidestepped around her to avoid the furiously blushing girl scrambling to clean up her mess, but Malik was different.

He'd stooped right down to the floor in his pristine black suit to help her.

In the five years since Kumar Construction had started leasing the thirtieth floor in the business center, Cynthia had learned of his incorrigible sweet tooth and always tried to swipe him something on her way in. But she never lingered at his desk, nor did she crack a smile when his wrinkled hands tore open the treat with childlike haste. She had places to be and too much to do.

And a reputation to uphold. Her father, too, doled out kindness with the same kind of fluidity—often unnoticed and behind the scenes.

At the elevator bay, Cynthia's assistant was waiting and from the restless way Jilly shifted her weight, it was clear she'd been situated there for some time.

"Jilly, you don't have to wait down here for me," Cynthia reminded her. "You can leave messages for me on my desk. Or send me a text if they're urgent."

Jilly responded with a nervous nod. With her wide-eyed stare and tendency to twitch, she often reminded Cynthia of a frazzled squirrel and had the short-term memory to match. "Right, Ms. Kumar."

"Cynthia."

"Wh-what?"

"You can call me Cynthia." Cynthia kept her tone level and polite, even though this was also something she'd reminded Jilly of several times in the past. She jabbed the elevator button a little more forcefully than necessary and reminded herself to be patient. She'd hired Jilly two years ago as a favor to her father because some cousin of a friend's daughter was having trouble holding down a job. And thus, Jilly the assistant was born.

And despite Jilly's tendency to accidentally hang up on clients when receiving two or more calls at once, her inability to decipher the carefully honed color-coded filing system Cynthia lived by, and her penchant for long lunch breaks, Cynthia kept her on because that was what her father would do. He hired people, not skill sets, and had infinite patience when it came to giving employees the benefit of a doubt. If her father treated the staff at Kumar Construction like his second family, then she must, too.

In the crowded elevator, Jilly was a silent ball of anxious energy at Cynthia's side, which did nothing to tame Cynthia's own growing apprehension as the elevator glided upward. She dreaded the first and third Tuesdays of the month, when the senior leadership team at Kumar Construction—plus her—met to discuss business operations. These meetings were the only days that she seriously considered faking sick, and yet, every first and third Tuesday, she forced herself out of bed, shoved her feet into a pair of shoes that made her feel confident, and showed up, nary a hair out of place.

There was no taming her uneasiness, though, and by the time they reached the top floor, where the conference rooms were located, Cynthia had forgotten that her assistant was still with her until she spoke.

"Uh, Ms. Kumar?"

Cynthia didn't bother to lift her eyes from the email she was scrolling through on her phone in her left hand. "What is it, Jilly?"

"The owner of Kashmiri Dining called and wanted to set up a meeting for tomorrow afternoon."

"Fine. But I have a presentation to the Batleys at noon, so make sure I have time to manage the commute." Cynthia paused midstep, causing Jilly to gasp as she came to a teetering halt next to her. "Wait, I have a meet-and-greet with a potential client at two. See if you can reschedule Kashmiri Dining for Thursday and, if not, I can squeeze them in toward the evening."

It would mean a twelve-hour day, at least, but that was nothing new.

Protein bar for dinner, check. With a firm nod, Cynthia resumed her swift pace.

"And the quote . . . for the fabrics . . . you ordered . . . came through." Several inches shorter than Cynthia's five-foot-seven frame, Jilly was panting to keep up, but Cynthia couldn't bring herself to slow down. The steady click of her four-inch heels on the natural stone floor was like the beat of a battle drum, urging her to march forward as she hung a sharp right to the conference room. Whether it was the soothing repetition of her footfalls or the sharp precision of each heel drop, this sound had the power to carry her through even the most grueling day.

With a dexterous thumb that had long ago mastered the art of singularly crafting concise responses to the truckloads of messages she received daily, Cynthia punched out a quick response to a vendor and hit send as she came to a stop in front of a set of double doors.

CONFERENCE ROOM B, the gold-plated sign read. ENTER AT YOUR OWN RISK, it should have said instead.

Cynthia took a moment to suppress her fluttering nerves. She loathed this stupid mahogany door with its shiny chrome handle. She detested these meetings, especially since on the other side of this ostentatious, oversized door was the worst—

"Uh, Ms. Kumar?"

With a sigh, Cynthia slipped her phone into the pocket of her tailored gray shift dress and maneuvered the small stack of folders from under her arm into her hands. "Cynthia."

"What?"

"You can call me Cynthia," she said, her irritation bubbling to the surface. She tamped down the kernel of guilt that popped to the exterior as well. After all, hadn't she seen her father, many times before, resort to curtness to get his point across when people were slow on the uptake? He was not the kind of man who beat around the bush.

Yet the world had a lot less admiration for a direct woman.

"Oh, okay," Jilly replied uncertainly. "But Ms. Kuma—I mean, Cynthia . . ." When Cynthia finally trained her sharp, whiskey-brown eyes onto Jilly, the shorter woman cleared her throat. "Ms. Kumar, you have a bit of . . ."

As Jilly trailed off, Cynthia leaned toward the conference room door ever so slightly, her ears straining to hear the voices of the half a dozen or so men who lounged inside. It was unlikely she'd pick up anything, not with Jilly's labored breathing in the same vicinity.

Cynthia gestured at the messy stack of Post-its in Jilly's hands. "You can leave any other messages on my desk." *As I've instructed you to do countless times before.* "Thanks."

"Okay. Um . . ."

"Yes?"

"Well . . ."

"What is it, Jilly?"

"You have some toilet paper stuck to your shoe," Jilly blurted out, her pink cheeks darkening to crimson.

Cynthia glanced down, more curious than embarrassed. Sure enough, three squares trailed from her left shoe where the stiletto had speared the single ply.

With a wry smile, Cynthia freed her heel and met Jilly's eyes again. "See, *that* you can text me about."

From the confusion wrinkling Jilly's brow, it was obvious the joke was lost on her as she slowly backed away. Cynthia had long ago stopped hoping their working relationship might give way to friendship, and perhaps it was her fault. Impatient by nature, she found it near impossible to slow down and match Jilly's pace.

I'll slow down when Kumar Construction is mine, Cynthia acknowledged. *Then everything will fall into place.* As expected, the reminder served its purpose. She smoothed the front of her dress, no longer caring that she might have to forgo a real dinner to keep her clients happy, and notched her chin upward before entering the conference room with a confidence that belied the nervous tumble in her stomach.

Or so she hoped.

As usual, all chatter ceased abruptly as she stepped inside and made her way across the plush, forest-green carpet to where six men sat around a long conference table. If only the floors here were marble like the lobby so she could draw strength from the tapping of her heels. But no, the room had been specifically designed and decorated to humiliate her, soundproofed and carpeted so she was hyperaware of the stony silence that greeted her entrance. Some of the men averted their eyes as she pulled out a cushy executive chair for herself, while others offered tight but polite smiles before deferring their gazes to the tall, salt-and-pepper-haired man seated at the head of the table.

Her father was a commanding presence, thin-lipped and sporting the deep forehead lines of a gentleman who furrowed his brows often. Cynthia knew he was similar in age to the other men in the room, all over the age of fifty, but unlike most of them, his energy was entirely different: simmering, driven, boundless. He would turn sixty-three this July and Cynthia was certain that her mother would plan an opulent birthday party in his honor. For all his workaholic tendencies, her father loved those parties, and everyone at Kumar

Construction, from the office staff to the foremen and their crews, would be invited.

"As I was saying," Rich said, his voice steady under the rapt attention of six sets of eyes, some adoring, others curious, and, in Cynthia's case, irritated. She was mad at herself for allowing Jilly to tardy her arrival and more than a little chafed that her attendance was, as usual, treated as if she had stumbled in here at random.

Since insisting her way into these meetings a few months ago, she'd never felt welcome among the stale male departmental leaders at Kumar Construction. Deep down, Cynthia knew her father had only granted her access because she was his daughter, even though she'd made a solid argument for including a marketing and brand specialist in the room where strategic decisions were made. The others were less tolerant, but that didn't stop Cynthia from showing up, ready to have her say.

It would *never* stop her.

"If we're going to expand into Vancouver competitively," her father continued, "we need to do so with the future in mind." Immediately, the grizzled heads seated around the table—as well as the reflective, bald ones—nodded in unison.

Expansion into such a large city would open a lot of doors for Kumar Construction, and Cynthia tried not to dwell on her already full work schedule spreading even thinner for a whole new market.

She'd have to reevaluate her color-coding system. *Poor Jilly*.

"And so," Rich added, "we're going to buy out Feirhair."

Cynthia cocked an eyebrow. "Feirhair is a motel chain from the seventies."

"It is." Her father nodded in her direction once before addressing the others. "I've been in contact with their vice president and I'm getting the impression that they'd be willing to sell quickly for a reasonable offer."

"Are we sure Feirhair is the best option?" Cynthia asked. Someone across the table exhaled noisily, but Cynthia was not about to let some guy's sinus issues deter her. "The quality and reputation of their motels are not up to the standard of what Kumar Construction has come to represent in Kelowna," she added. Her father's lifelong legacy consisted mainly of modern architecture, sleek lines, and polished metal design. Cynthia, who had also handled the interior design and décor of many of these buildings, liked to think she'd left her stamp on the Kumar legacy, too.

And, when Kumar Construction was hers, she'd brand the organization properly so it could exist beyond name recognition and her father's familiar face.

The finance director, Keer—or as Cynthia privately referred to him, Klepto Keer for his tendency to hoard donuts whenever someone brought in a box—cleared his throat. "Vancouver is a highly competitive, oversaturated, and expensive market," he said. His condescending voice contained none of the sugary sweetness of the Timbits she was certain he'd devoured earlier. "A motel chain is a sensible option. Risk averse."

With little discretion, Klepto shook his head at the man sitting next to him. Leering Larry, who headed sales, rolled his eyes back. *Here we go again*, they seemed to be telepathically admonishing. *This is above her head.*

Thankfully, Cynthia was a master of resisting the burn of frustration gathering behind her tear ducts. She had conditioned herself against unnecessary displays of emotion years ago, knowing that, in her father's eyes—and everyone else's in here—they were a sign of weakness.

In a room full of men, there was never any space for a crying female.

Cynthia unclenched her teeth. "I know what the Vancouver market is like," she replied to Klepto Keer. *As does everyone who works in business in this country, you asshole.* "Is the plan to tear down existing motels and rebuild?"

Her father shifted in his chair and glanced around the table, exchanging long looks with the other men, as they often did when Cynthia's point of view went against the grain. Which was most of the time.

Their reaction always made her feel like a child trying to play grown-up at the adult table, where everyone had previously agreed to tolerate her until a nanny whisked her off at bedtime. The squeak of Rich's tall, sturdy frame shifting restlessly in his leather chair made Cynthia want to claw her sharp, manicured nails into the mahogany conference table. She'd drag them downward, splinter the wood, and carve her fucking name in its smooth surface if she had to.

"Well, we'll have to see . . ." her father finally answered, which a few of his decaying stooges took as permission to bestow their patronizing smiles on her.

Not for the first time, Cynthia asked herself the eternal question: *How many men does it take to get things done?* Too many, in her opinion. When *she* took over, she'd . . .

She was getting ahead of herself again. Thinking about future plans for Kumar Construction was dangerous territory, especially since Cynthia was fairly certain that her reserved and careful father had not divulged any information regarding his retirement and succession plans with any of the members of this sausage fest. No one but she and her mother knew about his plans for Rohit, the Chosen One. She was also *completely* certain that no one in this room would ever put her in the running for the next head of the company. The men her father had chosen to sit around this table treated her with varying degrees of dismissiveness: she was too opinionated, too radical, too headstrong.

Too female.

Regardless of the fact that her father had quietly earmarked a certain someone to take over his company, Cynthia knew there was still time. There was no way her meticulous and hardworking father would drop what he had spent his lifetime building in a near-stranger's lap and go buy a yacht to sail around the world or whatever he planned to do with his retirement.

She had time to change his mind, to show up the Chosen One and prove that Kumar Construction belonged to her. After all, Cynthia had devoted *years* to doing exactly that and she wasn't defeated enough to think that, at thirty years old, she'd failed to seal the deal and should throw in the towel.

Cynthia ignored the tightness in her throat as she gestured at the files she'd brought in, stacked neatly on the table. Her arguments were right in front of her, thoroughly researched and proofread twice the night before. Although she always tended to go about her work with this level of commitment, she felt it was especially important that she present herself in this way at these infernal meetings. For the only woman in the room, overprepared never seemed quite prepared enough, even though the most anyone else brought with them was little more than a pen with paper and, for one gentleman in particular, a pocket full of stolen donuts.

Cynthia had no choice but to go above and beyond all the fucking time. The city of Kelowna and its surrounding areas might be familiar with Kumar Construction's legacy, but she worked overtime to make sure they knew about her, too. She was *not* planning on riding anyone's coattails to get what she wanted. Sure, her father's connections had opened doors, but *she* had singled herself out as a reputable brand consultant and interior designer. More and more, her portfolio contained clients outside her father's illustrious network, business owners who sought her expertise because of a desire to work with the best to help build their livelihoods.

But the men in this room didn't see that. Here, she was Rich's too-nosy, too-young daughter. She'd be thirty-one years old next January but in her father's eyes, she knew what he saw: a girl who should be more concerned with family planning.

Her ovaries puffed a huff in disgust. *No thanks.* At least her dad's yes men had stopped asking her when she was finally going to give her father grandchildren; curtailing that insipid form of small talk had felt like a victory for all womankind.

Cynthia's nails skimmed their way to the opening of the folder at the top of her pile, but before she could make her case for business expansion into Vancouver, the door swung open and everyone's heads swiveled at the interruption. Most of the men grinned and a few actually clapped.

Nausea, check.

The Chosen One had entered the room.

CHAPTER 6

With the sole of his shoe, Rohit shut the door to Conference Room B before shifting his tablet under his left arm. Amid the cheerful chorus of "Hello" and "How you doin', son," he dutifully made his way clockwise around the long boardroom table, shaking some hands, fist-bumping others, high-fiving a few. Every senior leadership meeting started this way for Rohit, and he was careful to take note of every person's face as he made the rounds, cataloging each interaction to ensure his position in everyone's good books.

Only two people in the room kept their hands in their laps: his boss, Rich, who watched him make the rounds with a small, approving smile, and Cynthia, who scowled down at the gleaming tabletop, likely conjuring curses to unleash upon him.

Her glower came as no surprise. If anyone could summon the wrath of demons in an otherwise innocuous conference room, it was the Ice Princess. For that reason alone, Rohit was forced to complete an entire circuit around the table to avoid sitting beside her, lest she was armed and inspired to drive something sharp through his balls.

"Sorry I'm late," Rohit said as soon as he found his seat. "I was dealing with an issue at one of the sites."

Keer, the finance director, nodded. "Taking care of the essentials leads to excellent credentials." Besides a quick, courteous smile, Rohit kept his face carefully blank. Keer might be a spreadsheet wizard, but in all other areas, he was prone to spouting gibberish and Rohit didn't want to offend him.

Or anyone. As the men fell into quiet side conversations around the table, Rohit cast a furtive glance around him. Would he have accepted the job had he known it would entail fifty-hour workweeks of tiptoeing on eggshells and making sure he was helpful, charismatic, and indispensable to every single person at Kumar Construction?

Yes. There was no question about it, not with Maisa filling out college applications much to everyone's surprise and delight, and the doctor upping the dosage of his grandmother's medication. It was worth the odd long-winded lunch break with Keer; showing Olufo, head of operations, how to convert a file to a PDF for the tenth time; or, that one time, filling in for reception when Baljinder's daughter went into labor.

Knowing that he had become the guy everybody could trust filled Rohit with an ironic sense of satisfaction that he never allowed himself to dwell on.

Across the table, the Ice Princess cleared her throat, prompting Rohit to sit up straight in his chair. He could imagine how much his tardy entrance grated on her nerves, how waiting for him to greet everyone frayed her patience to its last threadbare inch. He'd learned very quickly that when it came to business, Cynthia meant, well, business. She was the most focused and driven person he'd ever met, and nothing seemed to irritate her more than distraction.

Especially when it came to him. Unlike everyone else, she had no use for him.

It was for this reason that Rohit always tried so damn hard, even though the general environment at KC was fairly laid back. Rich was known for employing people from all walks of life, and while everyone put in the effort, it was obvious that not everyone was stellar at their jobs. And that was okay. Once you were in with Kumar Construction, you were part of a work family, and while Rohit couldn't help but admire Rich's loyalty to his staff, he sometimes wondered if a business was meant to be run this way.

The view from the top wasn't much different, either. Upper management behaved more like a frat club than a brain trust. Most of the men around the table wore untucked, wrinkled golf shirts or outdated, ill-fitting blazers. From the number of times he'd been summoned to their offices, Rohit knew which of the men in the room rolled in late every morning and which were prone to dozing at their desks after lunch.

But not Cynthia. She was a machine. Rohit had chosen a three-piece suit specifically for this meeting, knowing that *she* would be in attendance. But looking the part was just the tip of the iceberg where the Ice Princess reigned supreme.

If Rohit brought a new, potential stakeholder to the table, Cynthia already knew everything about them, from their business history to the CEO's dietary restrictions. If he'd discovered new land for development, it was likely that she'd already secured the permits and held focus groups with the surrounding businesses. If Rohit built a damn rocket ship, he'd probably find Cynthia hanging out on Mars, on the brink of mastering the alien language while redesigning their homes for them.

She ran circles around him—around everyone, really—while wearing high heels that did fantastic things for her legs and nothing for Rohit's peace of mind.

Even now, as she straightened the folders in front of her, she leveled him with a look that left no doubt in his mind that he was wasting her time. "As I was saying," she said, "there are several boutique hotels in Vancouver that might be a wiser investment for us."

When Keer opened his mouth to object, Cynthia turned her glare on him, daring him to interrupt. Keer pursed his lips and shoved his hand in his pocket, where Rohit was fairly certain he always stowed a handful of donut holes. From his vantage point sitting beside him, Rohit could see flecks of sugar in his mustache.

"I've found several, including a few smaller chains, that align better with our brand," she continued before snapping her folders open and pulling out reports. She was so assertive and sure of herself that Rohit could not deny that he was a little turned on, even though common sense informed him that he should be a little afraid of her.

Unfortunately, that turned him on, too.

"I've run estimates and looked into sales histories," Cynthia said. "It might cost us more up front, but the long-term gains far exceed the initial investment." With a polished black nail, Cynthia tapped a graph on one of her reports for emphasis, and it took all of Rohit's willpower not to let his gaze linger on her elegant fingers.

Or imagine the slow, sweet burn of those onyx nails scratching down his back when she'd come apart for the second time, sandwiched between his sweat-dampened body and faded honeycomb sheets. Rohit gave his head a rueful little shake. On a cerebral level, he knew that the past—theirs especially—belonged *in* the past, but his hypothalamus lived for the replay.

Cynthia's words were met with silence. This was often the case, as it was for any of the new or creative ideas she brought forward to this group of traditionalist, risk-averse men. From the blank looks on their faces, Rohit could see the rusted gears struggling to turn in their heads, could practically *hear* the clang of metal on metal as they tried to process what Cynthia was proposing.

"We've already discussed this," Larry finally said with a sigh. He turned to Rohit and shrugged, as if to say, *Women, amirite?* Rohit averted his eyes and subtly wheeled his chair a few inches away in case Cynthia decided to throw something at the director of sales.

Larry shook his head at Cynthia. "The Feirhair chain of motels . . ."

"Are old-fashioned and outdated," Cynthia finished, her jaw tight.

Rohit glanced at the head of the table, where Rich sat with a furrowed brow. When the older man's gaze roved the faces around the table, obviously waiting for others to speak, Rohit cleared his throat and leaned back in his chair, purposefully adopting a casual, personable tone.

"The Feirhair chain of motels are a safe choice," he said, "but I think it would be rash not to consider *all* our options, especially since it looks like Cynthia has done a fair bit of legwork."

With his warmest smile, Rohit extended his hand in Cynthia's direction so she would pass the reports his way. She made no move to do so, forcing Rohit to lean, belly down, across the table like a toddler reaching for his toy.

No one else seemed to notice the immature power play, nor how the wicked little upturn of Cynthia's lips sent a shot of awareness straight to Rohit's groin despite the discomfort of his shirt buttons pressing into his stomach as he dragged the bulk of the reports across the table. Yet when he passed the papers around, the men cooperated by taking their respective copies and studying them.

Rohit couldn't help but offer Cynthia a tentative glance. *See?* he tried to communicate with an affable shrug, *I can be on your side. You don't have to hate me.*

In response, Cynthia's eyes frosted over, and she subtly flashed him her middle finger before using it to tuck her glossy, chin-length black hair behind her ear. Unfortunately for her, her snark had the opposite effect as Rohit's attention was drawn to her earlobe. He'd love to bite the sensitive tissue there, as she had let him do once before.

But from the way she was avoiding his gaze again, that wasn't going to happen anytime soon. Or *ever* again, at this rate. Everyone at the office knew of their antagonistic relationship, and the knowledge that it was *he* who received the majority of sympathetic pats did little to soothe the sting. Cynthia didn't seem to have any friends at the office, and Rohit wasn't expecting to be her first.

He still couldn't figure it out. Maybe mixing business with pleasure was Cynthia's ultimate taboo. Maybe she'd woken up, realized that she'd gotten naked with the man whose idea of intellectual foreplay involved stolen lines from romantic comedies, and bolted. Perhaps he'd been wrong that night, that he'd falsely convinced himself that under the cool exterior of a regally composed, striking woman was a vulnerability as real and enticing as fresh, raw honey. Maybe the baffling, soul-shattering, *unbelievable* night they'd spent together had been entirely one-sided.

Rohit winced—maybe it was better he didn't know. It was easier to focus on what mattered: do his job, stay in Rich's good graces, and send money home.

And yet Rohit couldn't help his eyes straying to where Cynthia's fingernails drummed against the tabletop, and despite it all—the murmured conversations around them, Keer sneaking a donut hole into his mouth—Rohit's entire being was drawn to those restless fingers as if he and Cynthia were the only ones in the room. It took considerable effort to pull himself away and rejoin the meeting.

"These projections seem far-fetched . . ." Keer was muttering to Larry.

"I always say, leave the math to the men and—" Larry's mouth immediately snapped shut midsentence when the CEO stood, signaling the end of the meeting.

"Thank you, Rohit and Cynthia, for bringing this new information to our attention," Rich said. "We will discuss this further at our next meeting."

In a flurry that belied her usual grace and poise, Cynthia swept the folders and remaining reports into a messy pile and stood. She kept her eyes firmly on the floor as she stormed out. And despite his best interests, and the fact that only a few minutes ago she'd flipped him off, Rohit leaped to his feet and followed her.

He caught her at the elevator in classic blockbuster romance style: he thrust his arm between the doors just before they closed and shot her a rueful smile before stepping inside. Under normal circumstances, it might have been a boss move, but from the look on Cynthia's face, it was clear that he wasn't the hero of her story. She looked like she'd love nothing more than to see the metal doors clamp down and shatter his arm.

Thankfully, the oversized elevator car made it easy for Rohit to keep his distance as he stepped inside. Even though he had moved to Canada from India seven years ago, his brain always marveled at the difference in space. Everything in this building was oversized:

the doors, the tables, the hallways. Even outside, from the giant SUVs crowding the streets and the double-wide sidewalks, the people here seemed to take up more space simply because they *could*.

Sometimes Rohit missed the crowds back home, where the constant layering of voices, traffic, and life infiltrated one's ears with a comfortable kind of dissonance. But more often than he liked to admit, he preferred the overabundance of space in this cold, dry country with its obsession for chain restaurants and maple syrup. Possibilities here seemed endless.

Possibilities he could only hope to offer his family with every wire transfer home.

"So . . ." he ventured, shooting Cynthia a sidelong glance. When she didn't acknowledge him, he coughed and tried again. "It looks like they're going to consider your idea."

Only the Ice Princess could make a derisive snort sound somewhat royal.

With a helpless shrug, Rohit turned to face the elevator doors. "You're welcome, by the way," he muttered under his breath.

On Cynthia's sharp intake of breath, Rohit could have sworn the temperature dropped a solid ten degrees. "*What* was that?"

Rohit stuffed his fists into his pockets and swallowed his smile. Despite the real risk of first-degree frostbite in the elevator-turned-icebox, he couldn't deny the tiny thrill he felt whenever he got a rise out of Cynthia. It was stupid, and immature, but also so . . . *easy*. She rose to every occasion and never pulled her punches.

He admired that about her, but he was also fond of *not* getting kicked in the shin with a pointy-toed shoe and so he forced himself to backpedal. "What I mean is, at least they're considering your proposal now."

"'At least'? Are you serious? This is a multimillion-dollar company on the brink of expanding into a competitive market, but my extensive and methodical research is dismissed unless I get the golden boy's vote?" Cynthia's scorn whipped through him, punctuated by her jamming her thumb against the main-floor button as if doing so would make the elevator move any faster.

She was practically seething, and Rohit eyed the elevator dashboard nervously. Suddenly, the oversized elevator seemed half its size, and Rohit was very aware that he was alone in here with a furious Cynthia.

"I was just trying to help—" he said.

"Oh, right. You passed out my report like a kindergarten teacher showing off his student's art project and somehow managed to steal the credit."

"Whoa." Rohit lifted his hands defensively. "I wasn't looking for credit. I don't want it. If that's what you're so mad about, I'll clear things up with your dad right away—"

"The *last* thing I want is for you to talk to my dad about this. And next time you want to swoop in and save the day, don't."

As the numbers above the doors illuminated in descending order, Rohit's temper rose. *Typical Ice Princess. Never gives an inch, impossible to please, and independent to the point of rudeness.* He knew better than to try with her: she was thorny at her best but spiked with poison whenever he was near.

Rohit knew that he was overly cautious about choosing the appropriate time and place to speak up, but he would *never* not give credit where it was due. Besides, everyone knew Cynthia worked hard and delivered results. But would it kill her to admit that he did, too? That he was busting his ass to keep his seat at the table? She wasn't the only one working long hours, treading through office politics, and trying to go above and beyond.

He didn't know the reasons behind her relentless ambition, but he sure as hell knew his own and they were not insignificant.

"I don't need this," he muttered as the doors finally slid open, ending what must've been the slowest elevator ride known to human existence. But when Rohit brushed past Cynthia and made a beeline for the doors leading outside, *she* trailed *him* now. Rohit could practically feel her frosty breath on his neck as he worked his way through the moderately crowded lobby of the Desmond Business Center and stepped outside into the glare of the afternoon sun.

There were quite a few people outside enjoying the cool May weather, sipping coffee, and scrolling on their phones. Rohit might've joined them, but when he chanced a backward glance and caught Cynthia's stormy face, he veered to the right side of the building, where the wheelchair ramp was deserted and partially secluded behind a row of large shrubs.

Rohit walked a few steps down the incline before leaning against the guardrail, arms folded across his chest, and tipped his head back. "Okay, let me have it."

Cynthia skidded to a stop at his side. "What? What are you talking about?"

"You trailed me out here to yell at me, didn't you?" Rohit closed his eyes and let the sun warm his eyelids. His traitorous lizard brain aside, he'd long ago given up on the hope that she'd corner him for something more enjoyable. Like making out.

Whether it was the resignation in his tone or the effects of global warming, the Ice Princess sighed, her voice thawing somewhere between annoyed and weary. "You just don't get it, do you?"

Rohit's head snapped downward, and he met Cynthia's level glare with one of his own. Likely on purpose, Cynthia had situated herself a few steps upward on the ramp, so they stood at eye level.

Briefly, Rohit wondered how many moves Cynthia required on a chessboard before declaring checkmate and demolishing her opponent.

Probably less than five.

"What don't I get?"

Her full, burgundy lips pursed and, combined with the sun sparking fiery amber streaks in her eyes, Rohit was struck, not for the first time, at how seductive this woman could be without even trying. He should've been disgusted with himself for being as attracted to her now as he had been that first time he'd laid eyes on her . . . and as soon as he tore his attention away from her mouth, he'd remind himself of that.

"You've got everything and everyone in your pocket at Kumar Construction," her perfect lips said. "Whatever Rohit wants, Rohit gets, and it's just handed to him on a silver platter."

Rohit opened his mouth to protest but Cynthia lifted an imperious finger. "Since you started, you've been welcomed with open arms into the fucking members-only frat club. You've been given the best portfolios, and my dad treats you like the son he never had." Cynthia shook her head. "It's *revolting*."

"You don't know anything about me," Rohit argued. "I'm putting in the same hours, in case you hadn't noticed."

"I know you have your fancy MBA, but you have no idea what it's like to hustle every damn second around here and not . . ." Cynthia trailed off and, for a moment, seemed to forget Rohit. She braced her hands on the railing and stared off into the building's parking lot, her lush lips falling into an unhappy, stubborn pout.

A part of Rohit wanted to defend himself; he was no stranger to the hustle. He was an immigrant living in Canada with no financial support, wasn't he? Like her, he was making every second count—

impressing Rich, staying in the senior leadership team's good graces, promising clients the world and then figuring out how to deliver . . . Rohit had plenty to throw back in Cynthia's face.

But at the mention of his credentials, Rohit shut his mouth and averted his eyes to the side of the building instead. To everyone he worked with, he represented the wholesome immigrant success story turned box office hit. He'd come to Canada to study and make a life for himself, working hard to find his place among the white-collar community so he could send money back home and build a name for himself in the land of opportunity.

Too bad his life wasn't a movie. He'd *love* to be the underdog that rises above the odds, gets it all—and the girl—in the end. Instead, with his grandmother's declining health and Maisa's looming postsecondary expenses should she get in—Rohit's happy ending seemed a long way off.

Rohit turned to Cynthia and risked nudging her forearm with his elbow. It was a bold move, but when Cynthia turned her head to look at him, he saw something he'd never seen before clouding her beautiful eyes.

She looked exhausted and it made his chest hurt. "You did an amazing job with those reports. I was only trying to help."

"Yeah, I know. You love being the good guy at work."

Rohit lifted his eyebrows. She was right, but was that so wrong? Aside from constantly chasing job security like a gambler chasing a win, he liked being part of Kumar Construction, enjoyed exchanging small talk and pleasantries and seeing the same familiar faces every day. Many of his coworkers had become his social and support system in Kelowna, where, even though people were generally friendly, Rohit hadn't ventured too far away from KC's corporate office thanks to the long hours and obsessive need to prove himself as indispensable.

Why would that bother someone like Cynthia, whose confidence fit her like a second skin?

Cynthia misunderstood his puzzled expression and continued in a sarcastic voice. "Mr. Popular. Rohit the White Knight. Everybody's favorite neighbor, Mr. Rogers himself."

"Wait, who's Mr. Rogers?"

"Forget it." Cynthia folded her arms on the railing and stared off into the parking lot again, her face unreadable. "It must be nice to be everyone's hero."

Except yours, Rohit thought. He wanted so badly to move closer to her in that moment, so much so that his shoulders actually bunched forward, his arms flexing on their own accord to do something really stupid like pulling her into a hug or tucking the stray lock of black hair that had come loose from behind her ear. He settled for gripping the safety railing instead. "I'm sorry the KC guys didn't give your reports the respect they deserve," he said in a low voice.

"They never do."

"Are we talking about respectful workplaces?" The question came from a woman sauntering up the ramp toward them, and though she'd sounded jovial, the dark green eyes behind her oversized glasses were disturbingly shrewd. She wore a well-tailored pantsuit and clutched a small notepad and pen in her hands.

Rohit cocked an eyebrow. "I'm sorry?"

Almost imperceptibly, her lips lifted in the hint of a smug smile, and she began flipping through her notebook. "Because according to my sources, Kumar Construction doesn't care about respecting their employees."

CHAPTER 7

Cynthia watched as Melanie Burgos made another exaggerated show of flipping through her notepad as if she were one of the Olsen twins starring in a made-for-TV mystery from the nineties.

But because it was Melanie Burgos, Cynthia didn't dare roll her eyes. Instead, she shuffled backward, using the broad expanse of Rohit's back to hide her expression as she studied Melanie. She looked the same, sharp eyes magnified by large, statement eyewear, reddish-brown hair smoothed back in a tight French braid, and a wrinkle-free pantsuit paired with brown, square-toed loafers complete with tassels.

The woman had terrible taste in shoes.

But it wasn't the ugly shoes that kept Cynthia partially shielded behind Rohit, who, for all his annoying prom-king tendencies, provided excellent cover. The corners of Melanie's thin lips lifted in a smile that was so knowing and sly that the hairs on Cynthia's arms stood to attention. As the self-proclaimed lead writer of *The Watch*—a local Kelowna newspaper whose staff, if Cynthia remembered correctly, boasted three writers and one editor—Melanie was always looking for an angle. If anyone was going to uncover that a biannual traveling dog show was a front for a mafia-run drug cartel, it would be Melanie. In every edition of *The Watch*, her name appeared in multiple bylines as if all her waking hours were devoted to running around town and sticking her nose in everything.

Cynthia risked a quick glance at Rohit's profile. His face was stretched into the trademark good-guy smile Cynthia knew too well. She'd seen it plenty of times in the last year, had been on the receiving end when he tried, unsuccessfully, to disarm her.

Once was enough to fall for that smile, that charm.

But now, the fact that he could switch it on and off like a desk fan didn't irritate her. In this rare moment, it felt nice to be standing on the same side as him.

"Come again?" Rohit asked. "Are we talking about the same company?" His voice straddled that fine line between humorous and teasing, and when Melanie's lips quirked in what could be read as flirtation, Cynthia bristled.

"Let me check my notes." Melanie continued thumbing through her notebook. "Oh, there we go," she said, pointing to a page that was probably blank. "My sources claim that Kumar Construction lacks progressive workplace policies and is detrimentally hierarchical."

Cynthia winced, and when Rohit inhaled sharply, she laid a gentle but warning hand on his lower back. When he spoke again, his voice was cheerful.

"I think you might have the wrong place after all."

Melanie's eyebrows lowered and her smile widened. "Can I quote you on that?"

Cynthia scoffed and nudged the back of Rohit's biceps. He immediately stepped aside. "Hello, Melanie," she said, her voice loud and purposely drawing out the syllables in a chiding, singsong fashion that she usually reserved for Leering Larry when he hovered over her assistant's desk a little too long.

"Cynthia."

Rohit's head whipped between the two of them. "You two know each other?"

Cynthia wasn't going to waste any time explaining to Rohit that if he deigned to spend a fraction of the time she did networking with local business owners and getting her card in people's hands, he likely would've run into Melanie a time or two as well.

But if he was choosing to put on a cheerful, friendly front in the face of Melanie's accusations, so could she. *For now.*

"Melanie is a reporter from *The Watch*, which, correct me if I'm wrong, Melanie, is the second *smallest* newspaper in the city?"

Well, she'd tried. Killing someone with kindness had never been Cynthia's style. At Melanie's answering glare, Cynthia's shrug was somewhere between innocent and indifferent.

"Uh . . ." Rohit coughed. "Okay."

Had the circumstances been different, Cynthia might have indulged in a gleeful chuckle for throwing Rohit off-kilter for a change, but she pressed her weight into the heels of her feet instead, steeling herself as Melanie's fingers tightened around her notebook.

"Allegedly, CEO Rich Kumar cares only about the bottom line, and employee morale is low," Melanie spat, her gaze locked on Cynthia.

"*Allegedly*," Cynthia repeated with a condescending smile.

"The word *chauvinism* was tossed around," Melanie added.

Cynthia's breath caught as if a handful of dry leaves were stuffed in her windpipe. When she failed to respond, Rohit took a small step forward.

"Well, that's a load of bullshit," he said, ever the ray of sunshine. When he glanced over his shoulder and caught sight of Cynthia's face, he quickly added, "Off the record, of course. Who are your sources, exactly?"

"They've asked to remain anonymous," Melanie replied.

Of course they have. Cynthia tucked her hands into the pockets of her dress and tried to adopt Rohit's easygoing, loose-limbed stance, well aware that she'd feel more comfortable riding a horse backward while blindfolded. A small part of her had to admit, in this at least, Rohit had her beat. It wasn't just dumb luck, either, because although his body language and tone belonged to a seniors-only cruise director, Cynthia didn't miss the assessing gleam in his eyes. Rohit might've been welcomed into Kumar Construction by her father with open, patriarchy-driven arms, but his popularity with every single staff member was not just a coincidence.

Much to her chagrin, he was genuinely likable and sharper than most of the senior leadership team.

"You can't blame staff for seeking anonymity," Melanie said, cutting Cynthia a smirk. "Given Kumar Construction's influence in this town."

"Well then, off the record, I second that it's a load of bullshit," Cynthia said, inwardly cringing when her attempt at cheerful sounded constipated at best.

Melanie raised a beautifully microbladed eyebrow. "Are you sure you don't want me to quote you?"

Cynthia straightened her shoulders and dropped the pretext that she could handle this with an ounce of Rohit's charm. That wasn't how things were done in her world—acting deferential and magnanimous did little for women in business but attract unwanted attention or, worse, a pat on the head. If she could learn to stop apologizing when *other* people bumped into *her*, she could deal with this gnat in human form.

Leveling Melanie with a firm stare and the cool smile that convinced clients to up their budgets and service providers to lower theirs, Cynthia stepped in front of Rohit and lifted her chin. "No, but here's your direct quote: those allegations are unfounded and do not reflect Kumar Construction's organizational values." The words left behind a gritty layer of sawdust in Cynthia's mouth, but she forced herself to nod, in hopes that doing so would project confidence for Melanie's benefit while convincing herself that her own shattered morale after her meeting only moments ago was an independent event. Her father might be a ruthless competitor and developer, but he was a teddy bear when it came to his beloved company.

Except with her. But that was different: that had nothing to do with the bottom line or the hierarchy and everything to do with the absolute shit luck of being born as Rich's imperfect daughter.

"Well, I'll be curious to see what other employees have to say," Melanie mused, tucking her notebook away. She turned to look at the office tower, a tenacious hunger in her eyes that Cynthia recognized immediately. That same fire burned within her, often defying logic and rationale and being told *no*.

But this confrontation had diminished something inside Cynthia, and she couldn't resist taking a small step closer to Rohit, seeking what exactly she wasn't sure. When her shoulder bumped into his biceps, she realized that he, too, had moved closer to her and she tried not to pay attention to the pleasant feeling flaring in her chest.

Not a spark, certainly.

"No one is going to talk to you," Rohit said, his voice confident. "Kumar Construction is a great place to work."

Cynthia forced another nod when Melanie glanced at her for

confirmation. Whatever Melanie saw on her face brought a quirk to her lips before she turned and headed down the ramp toward the parking lot.

"Whatever you say," she called over her shoulder, swaggering away in those terrible brown shoes. "But if anyone is talking, *I'll* be listening."

IT WAS JUST not Cynthia's day. Not even the sweet, savory smell of Korean barbecue could improve her mood.

But bitching about Rohit might.

"And he just *sat* there, with that annoying smile, all 'no problem, boss,' and 'whatever you need, boss,'" she complained later that day as she transferred a generous helping of bokkumbap to her plate. Her hand paused in midair when her friend and fellow brand consultant, Naomi Kelly, raised an incredulous eyebrow.

"He actually said that when your dad gave him credit for your work?"

"Well maybe not those *exact* words. But he was thinking it."

Naomi's lips twitched.

"He was!" Cynthia insisted.

"How do you know?"

"I just know. You can tell with guys like him."

Naomi added a few more beef short ribs to her plate, and it was Cynthia's turn to cock her brows. After befriending each other several months ago, the two of them had begun a weekly dinner, and their shared love for locally owned holes-in-the-wall had quickly cemented a surprisingly easy friendship between the unlikely pair. Where Cynthia was intense, hard, and prone to see the world in black and white, Naomi was an empathetic and forgiving optimist.

And prone to hogging the galbi, Cynthia had quickly learned. Whenever they visited their favorite Korean restaurant, A Little Seoul, Naomi always hoarded more than her fair share of ribs. But Cynthia couldn't bring herself to hold it against her friend, not when, for the first time in forever, Cynthia had an inkling that the bond of sisterhood might be in reach.

She'd always been too driven and competitive as a child, earning her jealousy and cold shoulders rather than friendship bracelets. It had been worth her father's adoration, though—seeing him cheering her on the front lines had driven away the loneliness.

Or so she'd chosen to believe. Because hanging out with Naomi was . . . nice. Unexpected, too, like wearing fake eyelashes for the first time. With Naomi, Cynthia could let her guard down and relax a little. She could drop the professional front and whine about Klepto Keer and Leering Larry. Unlike everybody else, Naomi wasn't put off by Cynthia's dry, pointed sense of humor, nor was she intimidated by her ambition. Cynthia could lament, complain, and despair to her heart's content and Naomi never acted like it was a sign of weakness or that Cynthia was in over her head at work.

She just listened and dished it right back out.

"And what kind of guy is Rohit exactly?" Naomi asked before taking a bite of a perfectly grilled short rib with a ferocity that spoke to a friendship that had long ago transcended the need for polite table manners and portion etiquette. It warmed Cynthia from the inside out to watch her friend eat like a starving dinosaur and, in turn, be able to do the same.

"You've met him before."

"I have? When?"

"The first time was when you came to my office at Kumar Construction." When Naomi's forehead wrinkled in concentration, Cynthia sighed and threw down her fork. "He's . . . He's that guy that everybody likes right away. The one who's all smiley and cheerful for no particular reason at all. The kind who doesn't need to earn respect or impress people because it's just *given* to him. He's a 'dude' but in a good way. Rohit is . . ." Cynthia's mind wandered to the night she'd met him, how his wit had slid under her skin and nestled there in the most intoxicating way. "People are drawn to him, and I have no idea why. It's annoying." Cynthia nabbed a few of the ribs onto her plate before Naomi devoured them all. "You don't remember?"

Naomi cocked her head as she wiped her fingers on a napkin. "Vaguely. I've only seen him a handful of times and always briefly." Her lips tilted in a mischievous grin. "He has great hair."

Cynthia glared and, in a fit of spite, grabbed the last short rib on the platter. "Seriously?"

"Oh yeah. Thick and silky. It looks really soft, too."

Dropping her gaze to her plate, Cynthia tried to ignore the heat rushing to her cheeks. It *was* really soft, which Cynthia knew firsthand, having felt the tickle of those satiny strands against her cheek when he'd leaned down to whisper in her ear, his fingers buried between her thighs.

She'd never revealed that part to Naomi, had never been able to admit to a screwup she hadn't even realized she'd been making at the time. Even now, more than a year later, the memory of that night gave her mental whiplash: feeling invincible and sexy under Rohit's worshipful touch, the baffling tenderness tempting her back to his side as she'd glanced at his sleeping form while scrawling her phone number on the hotel stationery.

And then the sharp, bitter disappointment a few hours later when she realized he was her father's Chosen One. Sixteen months had failed to clear the air, and aside from acting like it never happened, there was nothing Cynthia could do about it now except look forward and secure the future she wanted.

Thinking about that night always left her unsettled. And irritated with herself, not to mention Rohit. Cynthia hated feeling uncomfortable, abhorred how the memory of his slow, steady hands sliding down her body to revel in her slick heat made her shift in her seat.

Cynthia resisted the urge to press her glass of ice water against her neck and settled for a sip instead. "Sexy or not," she said tightly, "I don't trust him. And I don't like him."

"Sexy?" Naomi's voice was innocent. "Who said anything about sex appeal? I thought we were talking about his hair. Do *you* find him sexy, Cynthia Kumar?"

The bonds of sisterhood could kiss her ass. "Don't even go there, Naomi. He's all wrong for me."

"How so?"

"Oh, I don't know," Cynthia replied sarcastically. "How about the entitled-frat-boy thing? The social-butterfly-on-steroids behavior? Or the fact that he's my competition at work?"

"Last I heard, opposites attract. Look at Dev and me."

At the mention of her friend's fiancé, Cynthia leaned her chin on the palm of her hand with exaggerated confusion. "I don't even know how you two function as a couple."

"Don't try to change the subject, Cynthia." As an added rebuke, Naomi forked a short rib from Cynthia's plate and moved it to her own. "I don't understand why you consider Rohit your rival at work. As your father's only child, aren't you kind of set up for life?"

Cynthia dropped her eyes down to her plate and fiddled with her fork. While Naomi knew she hoped to run Kumar Construction one day, she never divulged the full extent of what an uphill battle she was facing. It felt disrespectful to her father, and while Naomi would never judge, Cynthia didn't want to admit that most of the time, she felt like she was losing the fight.

When she didn't respond, Naomi shrugged good-naturedly. "Okay, fine. Let's move on to a different topic. How was the rest of your day?"

Cynthia contemplated the table of near-empty plates. Although her friendship with Naomi still felt new and shiny, there were often times Cynthia surprised herself with how well she felt she knew Naomi. She was aware of Naomi's wedding planning frustrations thanks to the critical eye of a too-involved and too-enthusiastic future mother-in-law; she knew of the complex but protective relationship Naomi shared with her own mother; and she sympathized with Naomi's uncertainty, as someone who hadn't been raised with a strong connection to her Bengali roots, with finding her place in the Desi community.

She also knew, despite all their differences, that Naomi was smart, loyal, and compassionate. Yet Cynthia struggled to bare herself to the same degree that Naomi had done with her. A childhood of pretending she didn't care that the other girls called her snobby or that, more often than not, she'd eaten lunch alone in the library, Cynthia was a pro at keeping people at arm's length. She could only bring herself to feed Naomi bits and pieces of her challenges at work, her strenuous relationship with her parents, her hurt feelings after those Tuesday meetings.

Hell, Cynthia could barely acknowledge to *herself* how lonely she sometimes felt, climbing an impenetrable mountain with no view of the top.

It was for these reasons that Cynthia, even as Naomi patiently waited with a smile as open and warm as the sun, couldn't talk about Melanie and the horrible claims she'd made. The information was lodged in the back of Cynthia's throat like a swallowed fish bone and had led to her cutting out of work early—something she rarely did—and hitting up a kickboxing class at the gym, where the subwoofer had drowned out her ability to think.

Besides, Melanie's stupid claims would amount to nothing. Probably.

"Hey," Naomi said, gesturing at her phone. "My ride showed up early. Can he join?"

"Is it your fiancé?" Cynthia sang back in a teasing voice.

Naomi rolled her eyes. "Yes."

With a nod, Cynthia relaxed back in her chair. Naomi's fiancé, Dev Mukherjee, whom Cynthia not-so-secretly found awkward and hilariously pessimistic, would be a welcome distraction. "Sure."

A few minutes later, Dev slid into a seat and didn't resist as Naomi heaped what was left of the bokkumbap onto a plate for him. It was such an innocent gesture and yet, to Cynthia, another stark difference between them: with Naomi, there was always enough to go around, and everyone was welcome. She doled out kindness and warmth so easily. Cynthia, on the other hand, always felt she had to keep everything close to her chest lest someone snatch it away.

"So, uh, what were you two talking about?" Dev said in his graceless way. He looked embarrassed and was obviously attributing the lack of conversation at the table to his interrupting a dinner for two.

"Period products," Naomi replied with a straight face, and Cynthia smothered a chuckle. She'd come to appreciate how much her friend loved to give her fiancé a hard time.

But Dev, obviously used to Naomi's teasing, looked unperturbed. "No, seriously."

Naomi grinned at Cynthia. "Oh, nothing much, just this and that." The grin turned evil. "Like the people Cynthia works with . . ."

Cynthia shot her friend a dark glare.

"Like Rohit," Naomi continued, nudging Dev's arm. "Do you remember him? You met him once when we ran into him at the grocery store."

Cynthia's dark glare turned murderous. So Naomi *had* known whom Cynthia was talking about when she had mentioned his name.

Dev frowned for a moment before recognition lit up his brown eyes. "Oh yeah. That dude—" Dev stopped himself and ducked his head. When Naomi prodded his arm again, he cleared his throat before adding in a reluctant voice: "That guy has really nice hair."

Reaching for the menu, Cynthia groaned over Naomi's cackle. "Shut up and order more galbi."

CHAPTER 8

As Rohit slid the red-and-white Tim Hortons coffee cup across the desk to Rich, he could have mouthed his boss's next words along with him.

"Rohit, son, you're a godsend."

Rohit grinned to himself as he took his seat on the other side of the large cherrywood desk. It blew his mind that a millionaire like Rich would consider a simple double-double from Tim's, of all places, an indulgence, but his boss expressed his appreciation in this exact way every morning. It didn't matter that the drink cost two dollars and was charged to Rich's company card, or that Rohit brought him the exact same thing every day for their twenty-minute "strategy meeting" to start the day. Rich was just that kind of guy. Humble but very set in his ways.

This time together was usually spent shooting the breeze, but Rohit didn't mind. Rich seemed to relish the opportunity to contemplate his life in Canada with Rohit, reminiscing about his experiences as an immigrant and how he had gotten to where he was now. He did most of the talking, repeated many of the same stories.

Any time Rich's mind wandered to his first-time navigating ice-crusted streets, mistaking orange dish soap for juice, and the wonder of riding a gondola between snowcapped mountains, his voice thickened with sentimentality despite having immigrated over thirty years ago.

For Rohit, the twenty-minute touchpoint was a gentle reminder of a life he'd left behind that, he was slightly ashamed to admit, he only felt connected to through video chat these days. His parents' family room, although sometimes fuzzy depending on the strength of their Wi-Fi that day, triggered nostalgia, but the world outside their walls was beginning to blur for Rohit.

"Did you ever visit Vagator Beach in Goa?" Rich was asking, his face taking on a faraway look.

When Rohit shook his head, Rich launched into his story about his favorite family vacation as a child, oblivious to Rohit's eyes dropping to his hands, which were clasped tightly in his lap. Rohit came from more modest beginnings. His family was part of the struggling middle class, and while his parents had scraped together enough to send him to a credible private school as a child, there hadn't been vacations much farther than a relative's house in a nearby town.

Unlike his boss, whenever Rohit thought about home, his thoughts revolved around money. His entire life revolved around keeping the roof from caving in on his family, and only when he achieved a fraction of what Rich had done for himself in Canada could he break free of those shrinking walls and carve his own path.

If that day ever came, of course.

"How's your family?" Rich asked, as if he had read Rohit's mind.

"They're great, sir," Rohit said, trying to remember the last time he'd spoken to them. Had it been Saturday? Thursday? The calls had been so frequent when he'd first moved to Canada seven years ago as an eager twenty-three-year-old undergraduate student. Even then, Rohit had known he wouldn't return to India, making it easier each year to burrow deeper into his newfound identity as an aspiring South Asian Canadian. As homesickness shed, so had the need to see his father's cheerful, quiet face and take comfort from his mother's recount of day-to-day activities that seemed impossibly far away.

"And you've been able to keep up?" Rich asked.

Rohit knew what Rich was *really* asking, and he slouched a little in his seat. He wasn't ashamed of his family's financial situation, and his boss—who, as the eldest son and dubbed the "American Success" by his family—was all too familiar with the burdens placed upon the younger man's shoulders. But to Rich, caring for one's family was a point of pride.

For Rohit, it felt like something else. Something heavier that made him want to hunch forward and scrub his hands over his face. He could never admit to Rich that since his mother's accident— when the responsibility of providing for his family had shifted from a shared endeavor to resting mostly on his shoulders—what had felt like pride and love now felt, at times, like a burden.

One that came with consequences he had failed to anticipate when he'd jumped to the task of helping his family. It wasn't just sending a hefty portion of his paycheck at the end of every month, but knowing that his future was mapped out by his family's needs.

Prior to everything back home falling apart, Rohit had wanted to pursue a second degree in architecture after his MBA. It hadn't seemed that fanciful at the time, not for a young guy who'd moved out for the first time into a world much less conservative and traditional than the one he'd left behind. Before he'd known the weight of financial obligation, he had been pleasantly overwhelmed with the idea of staying in Canada to study architecture, or maybe even venturing elsewhere, like London or Singapore. He had been disgustingly idealistic, excited to take on the world and find his place in it. Studying the points of intersection where art and engineering met technology and sustainability . . . It would've been worth the countless hours spent laboring over a drafting table, fingers blackened by graphite.

But he had let go of those dreams a long time ago.

"I'm doing fine," Rohit replied even as a tight little pinch took up residence between his shoulder blades. "I mean, I'm taking care of them."

Rich shot him a long look. "You know, you can come to me if you need help."

"No." Rohit's voice was firm; it wasn't the first time his boss had put that idea forward. "I'm fine. We're fine."

"Well, the offer is always there."

Rohit opened his mouth to answer, but this was always the hardest part of his relationship with Rich. He had no idea where to find the right words to express his gratitude, how he didn't take this opportunity for granted. How Rich had, unwittingly, saved him and his family. Rohit owed his boss more than fetching his coffee every morning could ever repay.

He was saved from mumbling something inane by a firm knock at Rich's door.

"Ah, yes," Rich said, with a wink that Rohit couldn't begin to decipher. "Come in."

The door swung open to reveal Cynthia, severe in a flattering black suit like she was on her way to a celebrity's funeral. She was by far the most formally dressed person at the office, not that Rohit would ever complain. In the last year, he had developed a deep appreciation for powerful women who dominated every room they walked into wearing perfectly tailored pants with pleats so sharp they could cut glass.

Well, one powerful woman, anyway.

As usual, nothing escaped Cynthia's quick, amber eyes. Not the heavy and expensive furniture or her father, relaxed in his cushy executive chair, ankle crossed over his knee. It was only when her shrewd gaze landed on Rohit that a hint of uneasiness flickered over her face.

It was barely a nanosecond before Cynthia's cool, confident mask was back in place, but Rohit never missed these moments. The sharpening of her gaze, the slight downturn of her full lips. Even her body appeared to tighten, resorting to a tension that existed between wariness and suspicion, yet always primed for a fight.

But for once, it didn't feel like deep-seated hostility . . . Well, not *entirely.* There was something else there, too: enflamed but not enraged. Dark but not murderous.

If he had to put a word to it, Rohit would say she looked *bothered.*

Her gaze narrowed onto the coffee cups on her father's desk, but she didn't look surprised. It was Cynthia, after all. She always knew all the goings-on at Kumar Construction, sometimes before they happened. Rohit never was able to figure out how, since she didn't seem to have any in-house alliances or gossip networks that he'd observed.

"My assistant said you wanted to see me?" she said in greeting.

"Have a seat," Rich replied, gesturing to the empty seat next to Rohit.

Cynthia's body moved to obey, but the set of her jaw told Rohit that was the *last* place she wanted to sit. Then again, she'd spoken with him yesterday outside the business center by her own free will *without* clawing his eyes out, and for that reason alone, Rohit aimed a tentative smile her way.

"Good morning, Cynthia," he said.

She didn't spare him a second glance. "Rohit."

He didn't know if it was her barely suppressed desire to flip him off at every opportunity or that by the simple act of producing carbon dioxide, he was able to grate on her nerves, but whenever he was around her, Rohit felt like a younger version of himself. Carefree, a little obnoxious, and receiving a light rush of pleasure from getting a reaction out of her. It was a heady enough combination that prompted him to add in a sly voice, "'Make anyone cry today?'"

Cynthia's shot him a long, sidelong glance, her face impassive. "Sadly, no. But it's only eight thirty." Rohit's heart leaped, backflipped, and somersaulted but before he could respond, Rich spoke.

"I'm sure you're wondering why I called both of you in here today," he said.

Cynthia made a noise in the back of her throat that sounded like a strangled *duh* and Rohit had to swallow the chuckle rising in his throat. It was nice leaving his overloaded adult self behind occasionally. Besides, every uncharacteristic emotion Cynthia failed to rein in, as brief as it might be, felt like a gift. Like he'd earned something, discovered something new just for himself.

The Ice Princess would drive an icicle through his chest if she knew that a part of him lived for glimpses of her rare, vulnerable moments—that they tugged at that little corner of his heart he'd kept stowed away ever since running into her for the first time at Kumar Construction.

"I got a call today from a reporter at *The Watch*," Rich continued. "Are you two familiar with that local publication?"

Rohit and Cynthia traded quick, panicked glances. Cynthia's

was a little more controlled, however, and she punctuated hers with a subtle, wide-eyed shake of her head before turning back to her father.

"It's a local newspaper," she said calmly. "Owned by Tim Parker, I believe."

"Yes, correct," Rich said. "Apparently, there have been claims of unscrupulous policies at Kumar Construction and they're working on an article exposing them."

Rohit watched as Rich sat back in his chair and steepled his fingers. He seemed a little too calm about the threat of negative press lurking in the distance, and Rohit wasn't sure how to react. He shot a quick look at Cynthia for guidance, but she was studying her father in an identical fashion: alert but composed. Not for the first time, Rohit was struck by how alike the two could be, not to mention how terrifying they'd be in an interrogation room.

"What do you think about all this?" Rich asked, staring at Rohit.

Rohit sat forward in his chair, his hands glued to his thighs so he wouldn't give in to his nervous habit of cracking his knuckles. Cynthia had seemed so unbothered by the confrontation with Melanie outside the business center yesterday afternoon that Rohit had almost completely shrugged it off. For all he knew, Melanie's claims were unfounded and would amount to nothing—they certainly seemed overblown and a product of maliciousness rather than the truth.

But under Rich's steady gaze now, Rohit felt like he was sitting down for an exam in a subject he knew nothing about. Should he admit that he and Cynthia had gotten the heads-up about the article yesterday? Should he trash the local newspaper's credibility in a show of solidarity for Kumar Construction?

Thankfully, Cynthia took the lead. "I'd be curious to hear what *you* think," she replied, "seeing as you called *both* of us in here this morning."

Damn, she was smart.

Rich nodded. "Obviously, I don't think these claims reflect what Kumar Construction stands for and how we operate. I think we need to get on top of it."

"'On top of it'?" Rohit repeated.

"'We'?" Cynthia blurted out at the same time.

Rich turned to Rohit. "If there is any truth to Kumar Construction being a poor work environment—whether idle gossip or not—then actions must be taken to rectify whatever issues people are having around here. We need to fix it." He then turned to his daughter. "I'm putting you two in charge of fixing it."

"Why both of us?" Cynthia asked.

"Surely you've noticed how well-liked Rohit is around here. He's the best person to tap into what's going on at the ground floor, and if you want to change minds about this organization being a great place to work, Rohit is the man for the job. He's a natural leader."

Rohit ducked his head a little, both flattered and a little flustered to have his boss praise him in this way. He couldn't help but say a silent prayer of thanks that Rich had given him a shot. Whatever Rich asked of him, he would do.

Everything, and everyone, depended on him succeeding here.

"If you've got *Rohit* on the case," Cynthia said flatly, "then why do you need me?"

"You have that background in public relations," Rich said.

"Marketing."

Rich nodded. "Right, right. And aren't you well acquainted with the staff at *The Watch*?"

Cynthia cleared her throat. "Somewhat."

"You two seem like the most well suited to tackle whatever is happening with staff morale," Rich said.

Out of the corner of his eye, Rohit caught sight of Cynthia's fingers tightening over the armrests of her chair in a white-knuckle grip, and his heart flatlined. She must really loathe the idea of working closely with him to attempt choking the life out of her chair in lieu of what she'd like to do to his throat. She hated him that much.

"I want this to be a priority for both of you," Rich added.

"These are allegations," Cynthia pointed out. "For all we know, it's just *one* employee blowing off some steam to the wrong person."

"Kumar Construction is a family." Rich's voice was stern. "All it takes is one. This will be your top priority." He tilted his head at Rohit and added, "I know you've got the Jenkins Lot on your plate. I'll reassign." Rich waited for Rohit's nod of confirmation before turning to his daughter. "Your projects, too, will need to be delayed."

Again, a strangled sound rasped from the back of Cynthia's throat, but this time it sounded more like a growl. Although Rich didn't seem to notice, Rohit risked a quick glance at her profile and immediately shook his head to clear it. Now was not the time to dwell on how the fire in her eyes ignited something hot and tempting in the pit of his stomach. Or how the long, graceful line of her neck and the proud tilt of her chin made his skin feel two sizes too tight.

He must be seriously hard up if a woman's *neck* could turn him on. There should be nothing erotic about a few inches of bare skin above a stark white shirt. Skin that looked incredibly smooth and soft to touch. And a buttery, earthy scent he hadn't had the chance to get close enough to again.

Who was he kidding? He'd relinquish his bank card PIN to get close to that intoxicating smell, and the realization made him more uneasy than the prospect of working alongside Cynthia for the foreseeable future ever could.

"I expect results," Rich said, turning his attention to his computer screen. "And soon."

"Yes, sir," Rohit replied.

"Is that all?" Cynthia asked.

At Rich's distracted nod, Cynthia jerked up to her feet and, for the second time in two days, Rohit watched Cynthia storm out.

And, like the worst kind of fool, for the second time in two days, Rohit chased after her.

CHAPTER 9

It took all of Cynthia's self-restraint not to sprint back to her office. A faint tingle prodded the back of her eyelids, but she refused to let her chin drop. But when the framed pastel landscapes dotting the walls started to blur, she picked up the pace.

Don't cry, don't cry, don't cry, she coached herself. There was no comfort to be had in the rhythm of her clipped footfalls today. Once upon a time, the fact that Kumar Construction was one of the few businesses in the Desmond Business Center to occupy an entire floor had filled Cynthia with pride, but now the sprawling office seemed endless. A cruel joke when the last thing she wanted to do was laugh.

Or maybe it was actually her father's words, echoing inside her head, that made her destination feel so far away.

Rohit is the man for the job. He's a natural leader.

Cynthia reached into the dark, hot recesses of her brain for *anything* that might help stem the flow that was building in her eyes. Mentally reciting her jam-packed schedule for the week, maybe. Or the video clip Naomi had sent her earlier that day with some guy in suspenders splitting wood in the forest. Or—

An errant tear dotted her left lower lash line and she wiped it away impatiently, wincing when she saw the black streak left behind on the pad of her thumb. She tried to rally anger instead—the predictability of her father gushing over the fucking Chosen One always unsheathed her claws. Or the mortifying revelation that her father had no idea what projects she was balancing at the moment? He thought she had a degree in public relations, for God's sake. She should be *ferocious.*

But all this only drove home one cold, hard truth: her heart hurt.

"Ms. Kumar, you have someone—" Jilly's voice was a blur, too, as Cynthia flew past her assistant's desk.

"Later, Jilly." It came out harsher than Cynthia had intended, but she was unable to focus on anything other than sealing her tear ducts shut by sheer force of will. *Don't cry, don't cry, don't cry.*

Cynthia barged into her office, carelessly swung the door shut, and then almost fell over when she saw her mother sitting in one of the guest chairs, a manicured finger momentarily pausing over the screen of her cell phone.

"Too loud, Cynthia," Sipra intoned without looking up.

The familiar admonishment, coupled with the sight of her mother's signature salon blowout and Louis Vuitton purse tucked neatly beside her on the chair, knocked against Cynthia's resolve not to cry, and her gait became unsteady as she lumbered her way to her office chair.

"Must you always stomp around like a caveman?" her mother added as Cynthia seated herself behind her desk. "Honestly, Cynnie, it's so masculine."

Cynthia plopped into her chair and tipped her face toward the ceiling. It wasn't uncommon for Sipra to drop by unannounced—especially since her husband was prone to forgetting his blood pressure medication on the kitchen counter—but her presence was especially unwelcome today.

"Not today, Mom."

Sipra's eyebrows snapped up. "Are you crying?" she asked, her tone sharp.

Cynthia closed her eyes, silently willing the sheen in her eyes to retreat. "No. *Jesus.*"

Her terse reply subjected her to one of Sipra's greatest strengths: a long, thick silence that spoke volumes. Cynthia's prim, proper, and chic mother was the queen of silence. She never argued in public or behaved in any way that would raise eyebrows, but in silence she could command armies and win wars.

But had a war been won, it was Rich they would hail on the battlefield. Throughout her childhood, Cynthia had witnessed the accolades showered upon her father, the community awards and letters of thanks that were displayed in *his* study at home. Rich, the self-made immigrant. Look at what he's done for himself, for the community. What a success, what a role model.

Not once did anyone attribute his accomplishments to his wife, who, in the silence of their home, raised their daughter, cooked their meals, and made sure all the bills were paid on time. Her lamb biryani was praised far and wide, but that paled in comparison to Rich's wealth, which people talked about in hushed, reverent voices. Her mother was capable, but it was her father who was powerful, and while her mother didn't seem to mind toiling away behind the scenes, it made Cynthia want to *scream*. Even as a young girl, she'd known exactly the kind of life she *didn't* want.

Still, because it was her mother, Cynthia lowered her chin with a resigned sigh and met her mother's amber gaze. "Sorry," she mumbled.

"Hm." The low-pitched noise was as close as her mother ever got to acknowledging an apology. "Learn to endure with grace, Cynnie. It's the only way to get through."

When Cynthia met that useless piece of advice with a blank stare, Sipra changed tactics.

"Maybe you should invest in a good waterproof mascara," she said, her voice returning to the mild dulcet tone she reserved for charity events and personal shoppers at the high-end stores she loved.

Equally unhelpful. And yet the unintentional reminder for Cynthia to straighten in her chair and compose herself plugged her tear ducts instantly. Kumars did not cry at work.

Actually, Kumars did not cry *period*.

"I just have some dust in my eye," Cynthia said as she snapped a tissue from the box aligned perfectly to the upper left corner of her desk. Her mother wouldn't ask about the tears. Sipra could talk about decorum until she was blue in her Botoxed face, but she wasn't the kind of mother who talked about *feelings*.

As far as Cynthia could see, it was the only thing they had in common. Raised to be a devoted housewife, Sipra seemed perfectly content living within the confines of that role. For the most part, she deferred to her husband in all things, was well-versed in South Asian cooking, and played the part of a rich businessman's wife perfectly, down to the biweekly manicures and understated designer outfits. As far as their families overseas were concerned, the only thing lacking in Sipra's immigrant success story was the failure to birth at least one son, but everyone knew Rich and Sipra had tried for years after Cynthia.

Besides, their wealth made up for it, especially since Rich was more than generous when it came to sending money back home to family members—and good friends—in need. He also never said a word against his wife's passion for ordering Desi couture online, paying the tab for expensive lunches with her wealthy friends, and needling her husband to retire so he'd finally take her on a luxurious European cruise. Sipra never seemed concerned about the day-to-day operations at Kumar Construction and had only recently given up on trying to convince Cynthia to do the same, to find a husband instead.

Because that was what good South Asian girls did: they married and had babies. They were docile, obedient creatures who wouldn't be caught dead in an unaccessorized straight-cut black pantsuit, interrupting powerful men in the workplace.

With another sigh, Cynthia tossed her soggy tissue in the garbage underneath her desk. She couldn't win. Her father wanted a son to take over his empire while her mother longed for a girly girl she could take on spa dates.

Their one child was neither.

"Have you ever considered adding some color to your wardrobe?" Sipra asked, gesturing to her own blush-pink cashmere sweater. "This shade would do wonders for your skin tone."

"I like neutrals."

"You always wear black or white. It's unflattering and too severe."

Cynthia's jaw tightened. She could think of more depressing things, like organizing one's day to cook for a preoccupied husband and watching soap operas.

"At least come with me to see Antonio later today," her mother suggested, referring to her hairstylist. "He told me about these hair extensions from—"

Lucky for Cynthia, she was rescued from her mother's unsolicited beauty—and fashion, etiquette, and lifestyle—tips by a subtle tap outside her office door. With his broad shoulders and coal-black hair, Rohit was a dark blur through the frosted glass, but, for the first time, Cynthia welcomed his uncanny knack for popping up, uninvited, in her life.

With her thumbs, Cynthia swiped under her eyes and, finding them dry and makeup free, cleared her throat. "Come in."

Rohit pushed the door open gently and shuffled in. When he noticed Cynthia's mother, he hesitated. "I'm sorry, is this a bad time?"

Sipra glanced between her daughter and Rohit. "Not at all, Rohit," she said, gracefully standing and shouldering her bag. Everything about Cynthia's mother was the slide of a gentle stream—cool, controlled, and elegant—and Cynthia wondered how this conversation might have gone differently had Sipra not given birth to a daughter who charged forward like wild rapids in a storm. She could admit that her mother was a force of nature in her own right and even now, in front of her husband's protégé, Sipra didn't fawn over him like everyone else in this stupid office, nor did she act like she knew anything about him other than his first name.

Rohit shifted on his feet. "Please don't leave on my account."

"Nonsense. I should find my husband, anyway." Sipra offered Rohit a polite smile as she studied him. "Your hair is so thick. What kind of conditioner do you use?"

Cynthia rolled her eyes as Rohit blushed. "I . . . don't?"

Her mother raised her eyebrows, and, once she had moved past him toward the door, she shot her daughter a pointed look. *Extensions with Antonio*, she mouthed.

When Rohit caught Cynthia's curt but venomous head shake, he looked over his shoulder at Sipra, whose face had neutralized again. "I'll see you Sunday night for dinner," she reminded her daughter before flowing out the door.

As soon as she left, Rohit walked toward the chair Sipra had vacated, words tumbling from his mouth as if he had rehearsed them.

"Listen, I know you're not thrilled about this assignment," he said, gripping the back of the chair and leaning forward.

"Oh, really?" Cynthia didn't mask the bitterness in her voice. "What gave it away?"

"Could you just drop the Ice Princess act for, like, two minutes and"—Rohit gestured with his hands—"I don't know, thaw out?"

"Chill out."

"What?"

"The expression is 'chill out,'" Cynthia said, feeling a little stupid about the turn of the conversation. It was one of the very rare occasions she wished she had kept her mouth shut.

Rohit's forehead crinkled. "The expression 'chill out' implies I want you to *cool off*, which is the opposite of—"

"Forget it." Cynthia cleared her throat. Under the desk, she gave the skin above her kneecap a little pinch—there was absolutely *nothing* endearing about the confusion on Rohit's face. "Why are you in my office right now?"

While Rohit rambled on about strategy and working together and other feel-good crap, Cynthia took a moment to sort herself out. Unfortunately, pretending to pay attention to whatever Rohit was saying meant she had to look at him, where he stood braced against the chair. He'd forgone a suit jacket this morning and Cynthia wasn't entirely opposed to how his olive-green shirtsleeves pulled tight against his strong forearms. Her eyes didn't need to linger there too long to remember the firm curve against the palms of her hands.

She'd gripped them tight while on top of him, urgent as he'd palmed her breasts. His hands had been slow and attentive the second time she'd reached for him that night, fingers tracing the dips and peaks of her body with the devotion of a harpist learning the pitch and nuance of each individual string. The concentration etched across his face as he chronicled every stuttered breath and soft moan had gone straight to her head, making her uncharacteristically uninhibited and carefree, not worried in the slightest that she'd likely been sporting raccoon eyes and serious bedhead.

"Cynthia."

They'd just met and yet her name had fallen so easily from his flushed, swollen lips.

"Cynthia!"

Startled, Cynthia sat upright. "Right."

Rohit crooked an eyebrow. "Were you even listening?"

A fiery blush scalded Cynthia's face. First tears, now daydreaming. What was wrong with her today? "Of course."

"So, you agree with me?"

"Um . . ."

"Are you okay?"

Cynthia scrambled for a tart response, but Rohit continued, his eyes intense and watchful.

"Twice now I've seen you stomp out of a meeting," he added.

"If you were to ask my mother, all I do is clomp around," Cynthia said dryly before thinking better of it. She cleared her throat and straightened an already tidy pile of papers on the desk. "I'm fine."

But Cynthia couldn't shake the events of the last thirty-six hours; they seemed to be festering in the back of her mind, gathering mold. From the senior leadership team dismissing her hard work for the umpteenth time, to Melanie's claims about Kumar Construction that were surely exaggerations but maybe also not entirely untrue. And, most cutting of all, her father's obvious preference for Rohit over his own daughter. None of this would have fazed her a month ago—she would have used them to drive her climb up that proverbial mountain, kept her clawing for the top.

But now she kind of wanted lie down in the cool, gritty dirt and take a break.

Perhaps Rohit read exactly that on her face because in a gentle voice he asked again, "Are you sure you're okay?"

Cynthia pushed her fatigue aside. She wasn't about to admit any weakness in front of the Chosen One.

"I'm fine," she said in a firm voice. "What is it that you were rambling about earlier?"

"We need to find some time to meet and discuss a plan for how we're going to tackle this." Rohit shot her a cautious look. "It's not ideal given our . . ."

Would he bring up the fact that, once upon a time, they'd fucked? With a small smile, Cynthia leaned forward in her seat, waiting for what Rohit had to say.

". . . our workloads," he finished, averting his eyes.

Coward. But something that felt alarmingly like disappointment threaded through Cynthia. God, she must *really* be off her game if a small part of her relished the idea of flirting with him.

"But I think your dad is right about us being the best team," Rohit added. "This isn't going to work without your expertise. No one knows this place as well as you do."

"Except you, apparently."

"We both know that's not true. You run circles around me."

"Yes, well . . ." Cynthia's lips twitched. "Try to keep up, would you?"

"'The man who embraces his mediocre nothingness shines greater than any.'"

When Cynthia stared back in silence, Rohit dropped his eyes sheepishly and Cynthia felt a strange little tug underneath her breastbone. "It's a quote from a rom-com," he said, addressing the surface of Cynthia's desk. *Always Be My Maybe.*"

"I haven't seen that one."

Rohit's head snapped up. "You should. It's in my top ten."

"You have a top ten?"

"Doesn't everyone?"

"I've always been more of a true-crime kind of girl."

Rohit shot her a long look that was anything but cowardly. "Why doesn't that surprise me?" he murmured before clearing his throat and adding, "Believe me, I've been trying to keep up with you for the better part of the last year."

Cynthia feigned disappointment. "And this is the best you can do?"

"Careful," he said in a low voice, and an actual shiver skipped up her spine. "Let's not forget what happened the last time you told me to give it my best shot."

Careful, a voice in the back of her head echoed, and Cynthia forced herself to relax in her seat. She wasn't going to get anywhere at this rate, not if she lost sight of her end goal. She needed to impress her father, convince him that she had the right qualities to take over his company. And she needed to do it on her own. Now was not the time to give in to Rohit's charm and that stupid smile with perfect, straight white teeth that seemed to dazzle everybody.

Everybody but me, she vowed.

When she didn't respond in kind, Rohit's face shifted back to cautious. "So, shall we meet in my office after work and come up with a game plan?"

Cynthia lifted her chin but in the face of Rohit's earnestness, the hot press of guilt crept up her neck and she reached back to their meeting with her father earlier that morning to subdue it. *Remember how invisible you felt? And how invisible you always feel in this boys' club hell while Rohit "Aw Shucks" Patel soaks up all the attention as if he doesn't receive it all the time for doing the bare minimum?*

Deep down, Cynthia knew she was being unfair to Rohit, who was far more competent and hardworking than half the old codgers her father surrounded himself with. But why should she bother with fair? She'd worked so hard to crack through her father's indifference and underestimation long before the Chosen One had ever set foot in Kumar Construction and started sucking up all the glory.

"Cynthia?" Rohit repeated, "do you want to meet up after work to talk about next steps?"

She didn't owe him anything. "Count me in," she lied.

CHAPTER 10

"Count me in," Cynthia murmured mockingly to herself that night, her strained eyes burning as she slouched against the headboard of her bed. She gave the laptop propped crookedly on her lap a glare before pushing it aside. She was loath to admit it but it was quite possible she'd bitten off more than she could chew.

Possibly. Even after hours of fruitlessly combing the internet and scavenging through her large network of local business owners for team-building activities, she couldn't allow herself to admit total defeat. Not after she'd lied outright to Rohit's face *and* stood him up.

Cynthia ignored the nagging little flutter at the base of her sternum when she thought about the downturn of Rohit's lips, the disappointed crinkle in his forehead when he realized she wasn't going to show. Hopefully he hadn't waited long.

Not that I care, she quickly reassured herself. For all she knew, maybe one of the women who hung around his office all day, like that long-legged Darcy or Lavinia, with her cutesy, breathy voice, had run into Rohit on her way out of the office and offered to cheer him up without her pants on, or something.

Great. Now she was annoyed with herself *and* grumpy. With a huff, Cynthia reached for her laptop again and kicked the covers off her legs. Working late into the night in bed was not an unusual occurrence for her, but coming up empty-handed was new and she didn't like it.

"Stupid Rohit," she murmured to herself, well aware she was being irrational. Reluctantly, Cynthia reached for her cell phone and unlocked the screen. She wasn't sure what she was looking for until her eyes fell on the contacts icon.

"Stupid Rohit, who probably has hair plugs," she added, glaring at the screen as her finger moved, as if of its own accord, to place a call. Her muttering continued as the phone rang.

"Cynthia? Is everything okay?" Naomi asked.

Pushing herself off the bed, Cynthia jammed her feet into a pair of thick-soled slippers. "Of course everything is okay," she grumbled, padding toward the kitchen. "Why wouldn't I be okay?"

"Because it's half past ten on a Wednesday night."

In the midst of opening her pantry cupboard, Cynthia paused to glance at the stove timer and grimaced. "Oh my God, it is."

"Is everything all right?" Naomi's voice was gentle.

It was the second time someone had asked this exact question in the last twelve hours, and Cynthia wasn't sure if the new lump in her throat was from embarrassment or something else. Something that made her stare into the neatly organized interior of her pantry and feel overwhelmed by the choices.

"I . . . I was stuck on a problem at work," she said, closing the cupboard door and turning to lean against it. "And I called you without even looking at the time."

"That's okay," Naomi said in a reassuring voice that made Cynthia's chest tighten. "I'm glad you called. What can I do? What's the problem?"

Cynthia kicked her slippers off. Put them back on. She'd spent all evening combing through her contacts, messaging corporate trainers, wellness coaches, and influential speakers, but so far, none of them could commit to delivering some kind of team-building activity on such short notice. When that hadn't panned out, she'd even hit up local boutique owners, mediation lawyers, and even a bookseller because, with the right ambience, group story hour could be healing, right?

No dice.

She'd been coaching herself to not lose hope all night, but now, with Naomi on the other end of the line—likely in pajamas and getting ready for bed—Cynthia felt heat climbing up the sides of her throat. Had she *ever* felt this way when tasked with a work project? Even in her current state of embarrassment and panic, the answer was clear: no, she *always* delivered perfection.

Alone.

"You know what, don't worry about it," Cynthia said, making her way back to her bedroom. "I can figure this out."

"Cynthia, if you need help, I want to—"

Help. The word made her shoulder blades tighten. "No," Cynthia said hastily. "I mean, no thank you. I hadn't realized it was so late. I shouldn't have called."

"But . . ." Naomi paused.

In the background, Cynthia thought she heard Dev's quiet murmur, and it was enough to strengthen her resolve. She could fix her own problems. "I'm sure. Forget this whole conversation."

"Okay," Naomi said slowly, "but you can call me anytime."

After a quick goodbye, Cynthia tossed the phone near the foot of her bed before crawling back in. She wouldn't let herself dwell on this baffling moment of weakness—garbled cries for help were *not* her style. Somewhere along the way, her ambition, independence, and grit had become something more than a suit of armor. It was all she knew, all she had to depend on to get her to where she wanted to go. If her father could work his way to the top all by himself, then so would she.

In the dimly lit confines of her tidy, uncluttered bedroom, Cynthia pulled her laptop back onto her lap and pressed her palm on its cold, flat surface. If only things could be different. She'd be lying to herself if she blamed everything entirely on being born a girl because, once upon a time, it hadn't mattered. *My little spitfire*, her dad used to call her when she presented her straight-A report card or beat out her entire track team in the eighth grade.

Back then, her father had doted on her, pushing her to be the best in everything she tried. And she'd risen to every occasion, much to his delight. Often, Cynthia would hear her mother, who watched them from afar with a faint crease in her forehead (this was before the Botox, obviously), telling friends in a fond voice that their daughter was definitely *Daddy's* little girl. It had been a point of pride in Cynthia's life, making it easier to ignore whispers from the other girls that she was stuck-up and keep a stiff upper lip when the insecure little boys refused her entry onto the soccer field at recess.

She hadn't needed anyone in those days, either. But then Jimmy Reilly had walked into fifteen-year-old Cynthia Kumar's life, and she had fallen *hard*. Hard enough to barely register that her grades were slipping, to stop caring if she showed up for track practice. She'd stopped spending time with her father, too, unaware that the growing distance between them was pushing him away. How could she have known the irreparable damage that infatuation over a sixteen-year-old boyfriend *with a car* and a *real* job at the sunglass kiosk at the mall could do?

That first misguided shot at love had ruined everything.

With a deep breath that was more self-admonishing than cleansing, Cynthia opened her laptop. It was time for a plan of action.

What she needed was to find a vendor—*any* vendor—who was enthusiastic and passionate enough about their product that staff wouldn't question how something irrelevant like flower arrangements or Fabergé egg painting could have any influence whatsoever on low morale. She needed someone desperate for business. Someone who—

Aha. Gotcha. Buried deep in her direct messages was a long-forgotten note from a girl she'd gone to high school with, one that Cynthia had barely talked to, who occasionally sent her messages about her business with the offer to co-host small- or large-group parties to share whatever her organization did. Cynthia's eyes bounced to halfway down the screen and found the organization's name: TeamStart. Perfect. And while Cynthia wasn't *entirely* sure what TeamStart was, the words sounded exactly right for the situation at hand.

Cynthia skimmed the rest of the message until she found the one sentence in Sahara McMillan's last message, unread and sent over five months ago, that clinched the deal.

Sahara: Contact me anytime and I'll make myself available!

Cynthia's fingers hovered nervously over the keyboard. It was almost eleven o'clock . . . but Sahara had said contact her "anytime," hadn't she? Besides, a quick late-night message over social media was nowhere as desperate as calling someone in full-on panic mode.

> Cynthia: Hey, Sahara. I'm really sorry for the late notice, but I'm looking to co-host one of those events you've mentioned in previous messages tomorrow morning for a team-building type of activity. Is that something you can accommodate? I know it's last minute.

Cynthia's eyes flicked to the clock at the bottom corner of her laptop screen as she waited for Sahara to answer. After a few minutes, the most wonderful words appeared before Cynthia's eyes.

> Sahara is typing . . .

All traces of fatigue flitted away as Cynthia waited for Sahara's message. Impatiently, she began closing the dozens of tabs she'd opened as she waited for the response that could potentially seal her fate.

> Sahara: Omg, Cynthia Kumar!!!!! What a TREAT to hear from YOU. YES I can accommodate your request! IT WOULD BE MY PLEASURE! TeamStart just introduced a new line of HEALTHY, ORGANIC, and INVIGORATING breakfast smoothies and I could arrange a TASTING for you and your coworkers!!

Relief ebbed through Cynthia's limbs, and any lingering panic cooled from simmering to tepid. She relaxed back against the headboard, snuggling down in her bed. This newfound calmness was like a sedative, potent enough to allow Cynthia to overlook Sahara's weird use of capitalization and exclamation marks. Had she been that enthusiastic in high school?

It didn't matter. The only thing that Cynthia cared about as she sent Sahara the address and number of employees to expect was that she'd gotten the job done—and all by herself, at that.

Rohit is the man, my ass, she thought smugly.

After dashing a quick email to the junior and entry-level staff at Kumar Construction requesting their presence at an impromptu team-building activity the next morning, Cynthia put her laptop away and sank into her Egyptian cotton sheets. They felt especially soft against her skin in this moment, the perfect amount of crispness and comfort. Somewhere, in the back of her mind, was the echo of a nudge that she should probably do a quick search for StartTeam or whatever Sahara's company was called for the sake of due diligence, *blah, blah, blah*, but the thought trickled away in the waterfall of freshly washed cotton hugging her everywhere.

She couldn't *wait* to see Rohit's face tomorrow. What she wouldn't give to be a fly on the wall when he read her email and realized she'd single-handedly conquered the task her father had assigned them. Maybe he was sitting in his apartment—surrounded by douche-bro things like a pyramid of beer cans in the corner—shirtless and wearing worn-in gray sweatpants, his long muscular legs propped up on some tasteless coffee table, opening her email right now.

Cynthia snuggled into her pillow and pulled her lavender—and *very* tasteful—comforter up to her chin. The weight of satisfaction sank her into the mattress, the tension around her shoulders uncoiling for the first time all night. But despite her exhaustion, Cynthia's legs shifted restlessly underneath the blanket.

Rohit, shirtless in gray sweatpants. Warmth stirred in Cynthia's belly.

It's the heat of victory, she assured herself, and she turned onto her side and welcomed the coolness of her pillowcase against her cheek. But her mind's eye was locked several inches below Rohit's crest-fallen face in the mental image she'd idiotically conjured for herself. He had a great chest. Her hands remembered the firm planes against her palms, the delicious ridges of muscle bumping along her finger-tips when she'd trailed her hand down his stomach. A light dusting of chest hair had teased her nipples when he'd thrust into her for the first time, the subtle musk of citrus and amber from his cologne sharpening the toe-curling frissons of pleasure shooting through her as he slowly stretched her out in careful, wonderfully painstaking inches.

She'd been frantic for release that night, perhaps even a touch desperate, but Rohit had welcomed her energy, met her head-on in ways she hadn't expected. In the dark of that damn motel room, his eyes had glittered with reverence and desire. *Wrap your legs around me*, he'd whispered, pumping deep, as if he, too, had felt that weird, exhilarating surge crackling in the air, urging them closer. Binding them.

"Oh, for fuck's sake," Cynthia said out loud now, flipping onto her back and glaring at the ceiling. It wasn't the first time her trai-torous mind had stumbled back to that night, had replayed the too-perfect sequence of events from the moment he'd thrown stolen pickup lines at her in the bar to him gently gathering her against his chest after their first round, as if they hadn't just met only hours ago. He had lulled her to sleep drawing light patterns on her arm as if he couldn't stop touching her—as if he'd been searching for her his en-tire life.

More than a year later and her mind—and body—wouldn't let her forget.

Rolling onto her side again, Cynthia curled into a ball and closed her eyes tight. She didn't want to linger on the tender way he held her afterward; it was always easier to focus on the heat. The roll of writhing bodies, her leg hiked over his shoulder as he sank deep. Cynthia reflexively touched the skin behind her earlobe with a shiver. He'd scraped his teeth numerous times over that sensitive spot, and the nip of pain had ignited a fiery path down her body, arching her hips on the soft mattress, spreading her legs wider to accept everything he had to offer.

And he'd given it to her. Four times.

Once again, Cynthia kicked the blanket off her overheated body and tentatively traced the sliver of skin exposed just above the waistband of her silk pajama shorts. She didn't need to venture lower to know she was wet and achy. Ever so slightly, the fingers on her other hand flexed against the soft sheets and Cynthia bit her lip. No one would know—*Rohit* would never know.

With a defeated sigh, Cynthia reached over the side of the bed and grabbed her vibrator from the bedside table.

CHAPTER 11

"That'll be seven dollars even, Rohit."

The words vibrated between Rohit's ears in a faint, nonsensical buzz, and he blinked at the credit card hanging limply between his fingers.

"Seven dollars, Rohit?"

Rohit knew he was supposed to do something now, but the heavy, bitter scent of roasted coffee beckoned his senses, the familiar, soothing aroma urging his eyelids to lower over dry, tired eye sockets. Hadn't he read somewhere that coffee was a lot like alcohol in enhancing one's present state of mind?

"Allô, Rohit? Rohit!"

With a little jolt, Rohit's eyes popped open to find the barista, Camille, staring at him from behind the cash register at Tim Hortons, amusement flitting across her face. He didn't blame her for laughing at him—he probably looked as good as he felt. He'd hit the snooze on his alarm too many times this morning, forcing him to settle for a thirty-second, cold-water rinse in the shower and skip ironing his shirt.

And it was all the Ice Princess's fault.

"Rohit?" It wasn't so much Camille's prodding voice that snapped Rohit to attention but the gentle pressure of her hand on his wrist as she guided his credit card to the tablet so he could pay. When his gaze lingered at where her palm touched his skin, she welcomed his attention by grazing her fingers over the back of his hand before pulling away.

Startled, Rohit lifted his eyes to her face to find that the hint of amusement on Camille's face had transformed into a curiosity that was so obvious that Rohit's sleepy stupor fled, leaving behind a dumbfounded corpse whose ears were turning red under the bold attention of a pretty barista.

Camille was always friendly when Rohit dropped in every morning for a cup of coffee. No matter how crowded the restaurant was, or how harried the staff behind the counter looked as they hustled to fulfill drive-through orders, Camille always had a kind word for Rohit. She was perky and welcoming and unbelievably cheerful before eight A.M. and yet she wasn't—

No. Rohit would *not* let his mind wander into that dangerous, glacial territory. Not after he'd been stood up last night. It had been foolish to believe that he and Cynthia had reached some kind of understanding yesterday, that their last few conversations had laid the foundation for civility and, just maybe, friendship. Of course, Cynthia was cold enough to engage him in a little light flirtation before lying through her perfect lips about putting their differences aside to work as a team. She'd rather drink snake venom than collaborate with him.

And, knowing Cynthia, she was likely immune to poison and could run a marathon while it worked its way out of her system.

"Rohit, did you hear what I said?" Camille asked.

He grimaced again as he tucked his card away and palmed the coffees. "Sorry, Camille."

"You're working too hard," she mused. "N'est-ce pas?"

Everything in Rohit's being, right down to his leaden feet, felt like one long, groaning complaint, but he forced a chuckle instead. "Who isn't hustling these days?"

Camille slid him a wink. "Well, if you ever decide you need a day off for something more . . . fun . . . let me know."

A part of Rohit wanted to be taken in by Camille's wide, clear blue eyes. It would've been easy to be charmed by the light dusting of freckles across the bridge of her nose or the flash of dimple in her left cheek. Like him, she was an immigrant to Kelowna, kind of. From Quebec, she'd told him once, to study at Okanagan College's Kelowna campus. A master's in . . . anthropology? Or was it art history?

His brain couldn't be bothered to remember; unfortunately, his mind was already at the office with *her*, wondering what she might say to him, especially after last night . . . and what she might be wearing today and—

Stop it, he admonished himself. *You idiot*.

And yet one thing was clear this morning. He wouldn't be taking Camille up on her offer.

With a friendly and somewhat apologetic smile, Rohit stepped away from the counter. "Thanks for the coffee," he said.

It must've been crystal clear to Camille, too, because her voice was considerably cooler when she threw a parting "à bientôt" at his retreating back.

The smell of prosciutto greeted Rohit when he stepped into his office at Kumar Construction, but he couldn't add that to Cynthia's growing list of transgressions. He'd been so damn stupid, ordering a small spread of Italian sandwiches for the two of them last night. How foolish he'd felt, shoving the uneaten food in the office fridge at a quarter after nine, two and a half hours longer than any self-respecting person would've waited. It had been even more pathetic to believe that Cynthia would see the offering as a token of good-will, that a humble offering of deli meat and gourmet cheese might pave the way for more of the things his baser instincts craved from her.

Banter. Her fiery, razor-edged intelligence. The way her eyes burned hot liquid amber when she was about to deliver a parting shot.

Rohit leaned back in his chair and rubbed his eyes with the heels of his hands. He should've stayed in bed. When he leaned forward to turn on his laptop, he spied Nancy from operations shuffling past his open doorway.

"Good morning, Nancy," he called, his greeting punctuated by a poorly suppressed yawn. "Sorry," he added with a sheepish smile.

The petite woman managed a nervous half smile and a tight little wave before scooting away. Weird. With five rambunctious grand-children, Nancy rarely wasted the opportunity to show off their pictures on the phone she barely knew how to use.

But she was in a hurry this morning, as was the small-scale stampede that followed in her wake. It wasn't so much the volume of people lumbering past that caught Rohit's attention but the vary-ing degrees of nervousness on everyone's faces. No one bothered to wave or pop in with a quick hello as they normally would.

They moved like animals being led to slaughter. When Jilly, Cynthia's anxious assistant, trotted by, she looked downright scared.

"Yannis," Rohit called when the crowd began to thin. "Come here for a second."

"What's up, man?" the junior sales rep asked, his gaze on the departing crowd as he planted only one foot into Rohit's office as if afraid to lose his spot in the death march.

"You tell me. Where's everybody going?"

Yannis was already moving back into the hallway. "There's a mandatory staff meeting."

"There is?" Rohit furrowed his brows. He didn't recall being invited to any such meeting, nor had Rich mentioned anything when Rohit had popped his head into the CEO's office to deliver his usual coffee and apologize for missing their morning chat.

"Check your email," Yannis advised before hurrying away.

Rohit opened his inbox and cracked his knuckles as he waited for it to load. Sure enough, a message had been sent to all the junior and administrative staff at 11:22 last night from Cynthia:

```
You've been selected to attend a staff meeting in
the lunchroom at 9:00 a.m. tomorrow morning, May 3.
Attendance is mandatory.
```

No wonder people were on edge this morning. The formal, abrupt tone was classic Cynthia, but to a random staff member, it sounded like an invitation to a mass layoff. Rohit could just picture Cynthia waiting for the antsy livestock to arrive, sawed-off shotgun cocked and ready to put them out of their misery. Rohit glanced at the time—9:03 A.M.—before standing and hurrying to join the rest of the staff.

What he found there triggered a symphony of alarm bells.

Unlike the rest of Kumar Construction's corporate office, the lunchroom was nothing to brag about. The kitchen was small with one rickety, linoleum table surrounded by four equally uncomfortable chairs. The dining area gave way to a medium-sized sitting area complete with old, mismatched furniture and a television that was missing its remote.

Aside from using the fridge for their food, staff rarely hung out here, and right now they looked like they'd rather be anywhere else as they stood huddled in the space between the eating and sitting areas. Their collective gaze was riveted on the sole table, which was covered with rows of sample-sized drinks arranged by color. On the other side of the table stood Cynthia in deep conversation with a woman Rohit didn't recognize.

Rohit offered the staff a reassuring smile before slipping into the narrow kitchen space to stand behind Cynthia. The woman she was talking to was like a cartoon art teacher brought to life. She wore a flowy, ruffled orange dress underneath a tie-dyed denim jacket, and her neck was adorned by at least four necklaces ranging from home-made to fine silver. A dozen or so bracelets rattled around her wrists, tinkling the jittery percussion of an animated hand talker.

"The health benefits have been amazing," the woman was gushing. "One month of TeamStart and I swear, my night terrors have all but disappeared! And my bowel movements—"

Rohit cleared his throat. "Sorry to interrupt. Cynthia, what's going on?"

Cynthia shot him a smug smirk over her shoulder. "Watch and find out." She then turned to address the staff, many of whom were staring at the exit. They stood to attention when Cynthia began to speak. "Thanks, everyone, for attending this last-minute staff meeting. We appreciate your time."

At the mention of "we," Rohit's jaw clenched and he took a small step backward.

"As you all know," Cynthia continued, "Kumar Construction is committed to providing staff with a positive and enjoyable work environment. Team building is very important to us."

Rohit eyed the faces in front of him, trying to catch any guilty faces in the crowd, but whoever had complained to Melanie Burgos from *The Watch* was not incriminating themselves today. The staff gave away nothing, save for Cynthia's assistant, Jilly, who appeared ready to shit a brick, but, then again, she always looked that way in her boss's presence.

When Cynthia smiled, Rohit couldn't help but inwardly wince. The smile seemed practiced and forced. "As part of this commitment to ensuring that staff look forward to and appreciate what Kumar Construction has to offer, we thought you might enjoy a little perk today," she finished.

Rohit could tell from the dip in Cynthia's voice that the words were heartfelt, but they didn't sound like the right ones. Whatever had possessed Cynthia to go rogue with the task Rich had given them was one thing, but colorful freebie drinks did not feel like a step in the right direction. Judging from some of the employees who were now eyeing the refreshments dubiously, Rohit had a feeling he wasn't the only one who felt this way.

Still, whether Cynthia had been referring to the royal *We* in her little speech or their failed tag team, Rohit also attempted an encouraging smile.

"Looks great," he added, his voice sounding hollow to his own ears.

The lady next to Cynthia stepped forward, her smile a much more convincing combination of excitement and warmth.

"Good morning, everyone!" she sang, raising her hands as if addressing the congregation. "My name is Sahara, and I am your party rep today!" Sahara held up her phone, dramatically tapped its screen, and bobbed her head as the opening bars of the Black Eyed Peas' "I Gotta Feeling" began to play.

Over the heads of the baffled, uncomfortable staff, Rohit's eyes met Yannis's in disbelief. *What in the actual fuck?* his friend mouthed. Luckily, after fifteen or so seconds, Cynthia stepped forward and placed a hand on Sahara's shoulder just as the woman was starting to sway her hips to the beat. "I think that's enough."

Undeterred, Sahara silenced her phone and slipped it into her pocket. "Now that we're all in the right mood, let me introduce myself! I'm a sales representative from TeamStart, where we provide healthy, organic products that will Change. Your. Life." Sahara paused to nod, and Rohit felt like he was watching a very bad, very low-budget late-night infomercial. "Our selection of snacks, meal replacements, supplements, and energy drinks are all you need to jump-start your dreams."

Jump-start your dreams? Out of the corner of his eye, Rohit caught Cynthia's wince, and he fought to keep a straight face.

Sahara grabbed a stack of papers from the counter and began arranging place cards in front of each row of drinks. "Today's flavors include Citrus Mistress, Strawberry Fields of Serenity, Tropical Turn Up, and Ginger Vigor." Sahara winked and shimmied her shoulders. Although the staff looked confused, she continued, oblivious. "If you like what you taste today and are interested in learning more about our line of health products *and* receiving a complimentary coupon to use toward your next TeamStart purchase, leave your name and email on my sign-up sheet." Sahara pointed to a clipboard on the counter behind her before straightening her jacket and raising her hands again. "Enjoy and get ready to Change. Your. Life!"

From somewhere in the back of the group, someone let out a

nervous giggle, but no one made a move toward the table. Rohit glanced at Cynthia—that practiced smile was back on her face, but when the edges began to tremble, Rohit shot Yannis a meaningful stare until he shuffled forward and grabbed a few cups with a mumbled "Thanks." Slowly, a few more staff followed suit and within minutes, everyone in the room held at least one cup of TeamStart's life-changing refreshments in their hands and were conversing quietly.

Sahara didn't waste any time and moved throughout the small groups, chatting animatedly. After the third time Rohit heard her exclaim the words *change your life*, Rohit pulled Cynthia aside.

"You couldn't have given me a heads-up about this?" he asked in a low voice.

Cynthia busied herself with leftover contents on the table. "It was a last-minute decision," she said, avoiding his gaze. "My dad said this project was urgent and I wanted to get a jump on things."

"By yourself."

"Well, as was pointed out in our meeting yesterday, you're *so* busy with big clients."

Although Rohit ached to sink down to her level and throw back something equally immature, a more embarrassing sentiment surfaced instead. *You stood me up*, he wanted to say, but as he watched Cynthia bustle around the table, her hair falling forward to shield her face from him, he couldn't bring himself to say the words.

She didn't need to know how pathetic he was, how he'd waited for her until after nine o'clock last night, his office reeking of deli meat.

In the corner of the room, Sahara's enthusiasm was reaching new heights as she flapped her arms to punctuate whatever she was telling a smirking Yannis.

"Where did you even find her?" Rohit asked Cynthia.

"Who?"

"Sahara. TeamStart. These products that will 'Change. Our. Lives.'"

A smile flickered across Cynthia's face and Rohit hated himself for catching it, for how his chest expanded in response. Even now, despite his hurt feelings, a small part of him was wistful for her. She must've cast some kind of spell on him that night, blinding his common sense with a seductive red dress and witchcraft.

"I went to high school with Sahara," Cynthia replied. "She's reached out a couple of times in the last few years about her job at TeamStart and how she co-hosts group taste-testing experiences." Cynthia shrugged. "I never replied, or even really read her messages too closely, but she was willing to accommodate last minute and did this whole thing for free."

Rohit's eyebrows lifted. "Wait. This didn't cost the company anything?"

Cynthia nodded. She looked so proud and sure of herself that Rohit had to fold his arms over his chest to smother the unwelcome flutter behind his breastbone.

"Not a dime," she confirmed.

Forty-five minutes later, the room had cleared out and only a few cups of TeamStart's life-changing drinks remained. Rohit was about to reach for a Citrus Mistress when Sahara let out a squeal of delight.

"Seventeen emails!" she said, waving her clipboard in the air. Her eyes were slightly misty as she looked up at Cynthia. "Thank you so, so much, Cynthia."

Confusion splashed across Cynthia's face. "Oh no, *I* should be thanking *you* for coming on such short notice."

"Girl, you have no idea what this might mean for me," Sahara replied, shooting back the remaining leftover samples with impressive gusto. "TeamStart is going to be so pleased with me. I am three sign-ups away from a promotion! Really, thank you." Sahara glanced at the clipboard. "Your name isn't on here, Cynthia. This could be your opportunity to Change. Your. Life."

"No, I'm good," Cynthia murmured, sounding as perplexed as Rohit felt.

Sahara shrugged. "Well, you know where to find me," she said before shooting them a wonky little salute. She grabbed the handle of her rolling cooler and marched out, her clipboard tucked tightly underneath her arm.

Rohit watched her go as Cynthia grabbed a sponge to wipe down the table. It occurred to him that he should just leave without a backward glance—it was her victory and her mess to clean up. But instead, he grabbed the handful of chairs that had been scattered near the fridge and pushed them back into the table, aware that Cynthia was watching his every move.

"We were supposed to tackle this together," he said above the squeak of her sponge's efficient swipes across the table.

"Yeah, well, I decided to handle it by myself."

"Right, but—"

"I'm capable, you know. I didn't need your help."

"I never said you did."

"Then what's the big deal, Rohit?" Cynthia tossed the sponge into the sink and planted a hand on her hip. The pose accentuated her supple form and, combined with the stretchy midnight-black dress she wore, it was almost lethal. Dealing with Cynthia would be so much easier if Rohit didn't know the subtle curve of that hip so intimately, the imperfect triangle of beauty marks just above the crease where her hip met her long, shapely leg. In moments like this, he almost wished they hadn't met the way they did, hadn't shared that unforgettable, perfect night together.

Almost.

"The big deal is that Rich is counting on me, too," Rohit said, shoving the last chair back into the table a little more forcefully than necessary. "We're supposed to work as a team."

"And you'd hate to let my dad down." Cynthia rolled her eyes. "God, you're like a golden retriever. Maybe you should thank me because now you have time for all those clients Rich hooked you up with." The words were biting, but something else sizzled behind her voice as she jerked open an overhead cabinet and grabbed a fresh roll of paper towels. The metal holder clattered on the counter as she replaced the empty one.

"You think some free drinks are going to fix the problem?" Rohit asked in disbelief. "Do you really believe this taste-testing thing is actually going to 'change people's lives'?" He would regret using air quotes later but right now, lowering himself to Cynthia's childish level felt pretty damn good.

"It's a perk. People love free stuff."

"These aren't just random people, Cynthia. We should be thinking long-term and researching why the turnover—"

"Please," Cynthia drawled with a dismissive wave of her hand. "Melanie was probably exaggerating the claims against Kumar Construction. So what if *one* person around here is disgruntled?"

"That's not the point. We need to come up with a strategy. Your dad said—"

"You told my dad I stood you up, didn't you?" Cynthia scoffed. "*Of course.*"

"What are you talking about?" Rohit shook his head.

"You guys are so—"

"Uh, excuse me?"

"What?" Rohit and Cynthia snapped in unison, turning toward the door where Yannis stood, discomfort stamped across his face for walking in on Mom and Dad fighting in the kitchen.

"Um." Yannis cleared his throat and directed his gaze at Rohit. "I ran into the TeamStart lady in the elevator? Sarah?"

"Sahara," Rohit and Cynthia corrected at the same time before cutting glares at each other.

"Right. Well, Sahara was telling me a little more about Team-Start and . . ." Yannis shot Cynthia a nervous glance.

"And . . . ?" Rohit prodded.

"Are you aware it's an MLM?" Yannis asked.

Cynthia's eyes widened. "What? No, it's not."

"What's an MLM?" Rohit asked, racking the special corner of his brain he reserved for filing away Canadian acronyms. Learning them was a feat he took seriously, a cultural trademark he felt was his duty, as an immigrant, to know.

"A multilevel marketing scheme," Yannis explained. "My cousin is into them. It's where . . ."

An icy bead of sweat slid down Rohit's spine as Yannis explained the finer details of TeamStart. He'd heard of these before, had received a few messages from Canadian university friends exalting the perks of their side hustle. They always concluded with an invitation for him—and his family and friends—to learn more.

Suddenly, Rohit had a very good idea what Sahara's messages to Cynthia must have looked like.

"Are you sure?" Cynthia asked, her voice weak.

"That's what she said." Yannis hesitated before adding, "She also said that she's never been to a more successful recruitment event."

"Recruitment . . ." Cynthia shot Rohit a look of horror.

"You know how it goes: they come in, show off the product, see if people are interested in signing up to sell it and make their dreams come true. The whole 'be your own boss' and 'financial freedom' schtick." Yannis snickered. "It's pretty obvious when you think about it, but I did a quick search on my phone to confirm."

"Oh, God." Cynthia covered her face with her hands.

Rohit turned to Cynthia. "We should've added our names to the sign-up sheet," he said dully, "because we'll definitely need a fall-back when Rich finds out about this."

CHAPTER 12

T hank you, Samuel, for that update on purchasing. Now, from finance . . ."

As the senior leadership team of Kumar Construction continued their standard roundtable of departmental updates, Cynthia allowed herself the luxury of sitting back in her cushy executive chair for the first time all meeting.

Actually, it might've been the first time she'd *ever* let down her guard in these stupid meetings and quite possibly while in the same room as her father, period. But, more surprising to Cynthia, was the reason *why*.

Her father was paying zero attention to her, and she didn't care.

In fact, she *loved* that he'd barely spared her a glance all meeting, given that, a little under two weeks ago, she'd accidentally orchestrated an MLM takeover of Kumar Construction. At this rate, her father could go right on ignoring her for the rest of the month and that would be just fine with her.

Cynthia couldn't remember ever feeling this way before. Even when she'd gotten drunk at Dennis Jackson's graduation bush party, she'd half wished her father would catch her drinking while under-age, if only to acknowledge that screwups happen but they didn't need to define the rest of her life.

But today, with every minute she escaped his notice, the air circulating through her lungs felt clearer. Tasted sweeter. The thirteen days since Sahara had been here had been a hangover ten times worse than a long, boring night drinking straight Sour Puss around the fire.

It seemed she was in the clear: Cynthia had heard exactly zero complaints about how the CEO's daughter, under the guise of a mandatory staff meeting, had tried to lure unsuspecting staff into a pyramid scheme.

"With investments like these . . ." A slow grin spread across Klepto Keer's face, signaling that he was nearing the end of his report. He *always* ended with an awful finance joke. Cynthia's gaze zeroed in on the remnants of donut sugar crusting the edges of his smile while she waited for the punch line.

"We'll be laughing our *ass*ets off right to the bank!" Keer finished.

Only a few men around the table attempted half-hearted smiles; those whose interest had already waned didn't even bother. Leering Larry was busy rooting around the inside of his ear with his pinkie finger. Cynthia glanced toward the ceiling and shook her head. *This* was her father's crack team and had been for the better part of the last decade. She had no ill wishes against them, but they didn't represent the team she wanted behind her when she took over the helm. Cynthia didn't want yes men—she thrived on fresh, modern perspectives and working with people whose passion for their work led to lively debates and creative problem-solving. Kumar Construction was none of those things . . . yet.

Cynthia's gaze landed on Rohit as Olufo, the senior leader in operations, began the last and final report. Rohit, she mused, was an outlier. He might not push boundaries to the same extent as she did, but this musty gathering of corpses needed him. Like her, he came to these meetings with more than sleepy-eyed interest, but, unlike her, the tomb came alive when he opened his mouth. The Chosen One's new ideas were met with contemplation, not haughtiness, and his methods of introducing these ideas never failed to charm her father's decrepit henchmen. When Rohit spoke, they responded with encouraging platitudes and promises to mull things over.

It was always puzzled Cynthia how Rohit seemed to take their final decisions—whether in his favor or not—in stride. He never lost his temper or grew churlish when things didn't go his way. He just . . . rolled with it.

Maybe she didn't have him completely figured out. After all, *he'd* been the most easygoing about the whole MLM ordeal, keeping quiet and graciously refraining from rubbing her face in it. Granted, he'd kept his distance since then, but even so, he'd chosen to be kind to the one person in his life who probably least deserved it.

Cynthia wasn't quite sure what to make of that.

As if he'd heard the direction of her thoughts, Rohit suddenly whipped his head up to look at Cynthia, his long, sooty eyelashes now framing wide eyes bright with caution.

What? she mouthed.

Rohit tipped his head toward the head of the table, and when Cynthia followed the line of sight, six pairs of eyes stared back at her. Her father's gaze was the sternest. How long had they been staring at her while she had been staring at *him*, as if enthralled by the curve of his thick eyelashes and the sharp edge of his meticulously groomed beard along his strong jaw?

Not that she had been noticing those things about him.

"S-sorry, what was that?" Cynthia asked, aghast by the hesitancy in her voice. This wasn't a room for timidity. This was a room for strength and conviction and never, *ever* getting sidetracked by someone's cut jawline.

"I said, 'Cynthia, are you listening?'" her father said.

"I'm sorry, I missed that last note."

"Care to share what could possibly be more important than our meeting today?"

The faint *crunch* of Rohit cracking his knuckles caught Cynthia's attention, but she didn't dare glance at him again. "No."

"Then I'll ask again: do you or Rohit have anything to report back about the task I assigned you two?"

"Task?" someone farther down the table murmured. "What task?"

But no one replied—no one would dare to. There was something darkly foreboding in her father's tone, a barely leashed note of anger bubbling near the surface.

Cynthia couldn't resist risking a peek across the table. Unlike everyone else, Rohit wasn't looking at her. His attention was locked on her father, his face so still and devoid of any emotion that Cynthia's heart began to pound.

She was on her own with this one. "N-no. Nothing to report," she said.

Rich frowned. "Are you saying that you two have failed to take action after receiving direct, high-priority orders from your CEO?"

Don't say it, don't say it, don't say it. But with years of speaking up—and committing tooth and nail to following through—the words spilled forth anyway.

"Well, we didn't do *nothing* . . ." Cynthia trailed off, her mind racing to spin her recent disaster in a positive light. There had to be some merit to *trying* at least, right?

Wrong.

"Oh, yes," Rich drawled. "Let's not overlook the day your efforts at team building conned your coworkers into joining a multilevel marketing scheme. My receptionist mentioned that she received several emails from a Ms. Sahara McMillan spamming her into joining something called TeamStart."

In her peripheral, she saw Larry lean toward Keer. "Darcy gave me a sample of Ginger Vigor. Tastes like trash but I am a *lot* more regular," he murmured.

"Get me some," Keer whispered back.

Cynthia could feel the dampness gathering at the back of her neck, and she folded her hands tightly in her lap so she wouldn't swipe at it and give herself away. "Well, to be fair—"

Her father cut her off. "You are aware that bringing an MLM on company time and demanding your coworkers attend such a presentation goes against company policy."

Don't say it, don't say it . . . "We don't have an *official* company policy," Cynthia argued, only to wince immediately afterward. For once in her life, she needed to keep her mouth shut.

Her father must've agreed because he sat forward, his nostrils flaring. "If we did, don't you think that would be on there? Where's your common sense, Cynthia?"

Cynthia shrank back. "I . . . I . . ." Her lips felt frozen, her throat tight. Out of the corner of her eye, she caught several members of her father's leadership team shaking their heads, and something uncomfortably thick worked its way up her chest. It was worse than the inability to find the right words. Worse than vomit, even.

Tears. The tears were coming. Cynthia's brain flew into panic mode and without second-guessing herself, she immediately turned to where Rohit sat, aware that her eyes were wild, her cheeks flushed, and that she had no right to turn to him.

But Rohit was already standing up to face her father, his hands splayed on the table in front of him. She was done for. Rohit's pronouncement would seal her fate; everything she'd worked toward this last year—and her entire career—was out the window. There would be no coming back.

"It's my fault," Rohit announced. "I invited TeamStart to the office."

Cynthia's shocked gasp was drowned out by Larry.

"What?" the director of sales blurted out. "*You're* the reason I now have a two-year subscription to the Ginger Vigor Wellness Package?"

Rohit ignored him, his unblinking stare trained on Rich.

"This is a very surprising lapse in judgment," Rich said after a moment, sitting back in his chair, bushy eyebrows raised. "I'm disappointed, Rohit. What on earth possessed you to do this?"

Cynthia stared at the side of Rohit's face, willing him to look at her, but for what reason she wasn't exactly sure. She knew she should take responsibility for her actions, but one glance at her father, whose piercing eyes and hard frown broached little room for apology, and the confession shrank in on itself.

Her cheeks burned and she bit her lower lip. Deep down, Cynthia knew, had the tables been reversed, Rohit wouldn't have looked at her for support or reassurance. On more than one occasion, she'd made it all too clear that they weren't a team, that he couldn't trust or rely on her. Cynthia couldn't imagine standing up for him like he was doing for her now, voluntarily accepting the brunt of her father's displeasure and disappointment.

Shame knotted tight and hot in her stomach, making Cynthia wonder if she'd been wrong—tears were the lesser evil compared to losing one's breakfast in front of their superiors.

"I take full responsibility," Rohit said, his voice quiet but firm. "I didn't research TeamStart closely enough. I panicked, tried to get things done quickly, and made an error in judgment."

Somewhere down the table, someone let out a long, low whistle, but when Cynthia made to speak, Rohit shook his head in her direction with such severity that her mouth snapped shut.

"I'm not going to sit here and pretend like I haven't made mistakes in the past," Rich said, "but I expect better from you, Rohit. This is a serious matter, and it should have been obvious to you that it deserves serious consideration. Attempting a quick fix was stupid and an embarrassing representation of this organization's values." Rich paused and Rohit lowered his head. "I assigned this task to *both* of you," Rich continued, his gaze seeking Cynthia's across the table, "and so not only do I expect *both* of you to work on this, but it should be your top priority!"

"Uh, sorry to interrupt," Martin said from Rich's left, "but what exactly is this 'task' you keep referring to?"

Rich's frown deepened and he reached under his seat before tossing a copy of *The Watch* onto the table. It slid dramatically before coming to a rest near the center of the long boardroom table, its front-page headline startling the room with its big, black letters:

LOCAL BUSINESS'S SUCCESS BUILT ON THE BACKS OF DISGRUNTLED WORKERS

Cynthia couldn't help but roll her eyes. Typical Melanie Burgos: long-winded and dramatic as hell.

"'Disgruntled workers'?" Keer read out loud. "What is this non-sense? Where did it even come from?"

"This 'nonsense' is a task I gave Cynthia and Rohit to take care of. The editor of *The Watch* owes me a favor and was kind enough to pass this advance copy along," Rich said, his eyebrows slamming down on a tight glare. "And considering they're running this in the paper tomorrow, I think it's clear that Cynthia and Rohit have failed."

MOMENTS LATER, CYNTHIA and Rohit stood in the elevator, staring at the shiny reflective doors as they silently slid shut.

Cynthia couldn't bring herself to look at Rohit, so she focused on his blurred, motionless reflection on the door instead. Tucking her hair behind her ears, Cynthia forced her chin up and addressed the reflection.

"Are you . . ." She wet her lips. "How are you feeling?"

A short laugh puffed from Rohit's blur. "About what, exactly? About my boss handing my ass to me in front of the entire senior leadership team? Or that *The Watch* is running the story and now we're in deeper shit than we were before? Or about being dismissed from a meeting like a naughty child being sent to bed without dinner?" Rohit turned to lean against the side wall, his fingers massaging the bridge of his nose. "What a mess."

Cynthia followed suit, leaning against the opposite side and bracing her arms behind her on the safety rail. Rohit's shoulders were hunched forward, all traces of the charismatic, confident Chosen One wiped clean.

Because of her.

A part of Cynthia wanted to blow up at him, charge him for

taking the fall like some kind of altruistic wannabe knight. She hadn't forced him to do it. It was his choice to step in and play the hero.

But she knew that was the guilt talking. She owed him gratitude, and an apology for everything that had led up to this horrible moment. But when she opened her mouth to scrape out the words, Rohit spoke, too.

"Thank you for—" she started.

"Listen, I'm sorry—" Rohit said before his eyes widened. "Wait . . . What?"

"I'm trying to say thank you," Cynthia snapped, and then flinched when she heard how defensive she sounded. "For what happened back there. Why are *you* apologizing?"

Rohit ducked his head. "Habit, I guess? Even with the best intentions, I usually fuck up when it comes to you."

A reluctant laugh escaped Cynthia's lips, and she leaned into it for the sheer pleasure of basking, just for a moment, in the unfamiliar warmth blooming within. Her chest cavity felt full of something sweet and special that she'd never felt before and couldn't name.

And it made her feel bashful, God help her.

This man had stood up for her. And now he was apologizing. He looked like he wanted to say something else, but the elevator doors slid open to the lobby, surprising them both. They'd forgotten to select their floor. Yet, as if by some unspoken agreement, they made their way to the front doors and simultaneously veered for the ramp where, together, they'd confronted Melanie just two weeks ago.

It was in that quiet place, alone with Rohit, that something settled in Cynthia's stomach and the words that had deserted her in the face of her father's disappointment became startlingly clear. Suddenly, she wasn't embarrassed to admit them.

"I shouldn't have ditched you that day," she said. "I thought I could fix things myself. I wanted to take care of everything without anyone's help, but . . ."

Rohit folded his arms over his chest, a dubious look shadowing his handsome face. He was clearly expecting her to qualify her apology and try to defend herself.

Cynthia swallowed hard. "But I was wrong."

"Why did you feel the need to go at this alone, anyway?" Rohit asked. The question was kind considering she *always* went at everything alone and they both knew it.

"You probably don't see it, but everything is an uphill battle around here for me," Cynthia said, but there was no heat behind her words. For once, she wasn't angry with Rohit's obliviousness. "I guess I'm just . . . used to standing on my own."

"It sounds lonely," Rohit said, his voice quiet.

Cynthia bit her lip. Strange how, only a few weeks ago, she would've choked on these painstaking confessions. Maybe it was the earnestness in Rohit's brown eyes or the seclusion of their spot, but the admission didn't make her feel weak or lacking. She just wanted him to understand.

"Well, you don't have to do it alone," he added. "I wish you didn't feel like that."

Cynthia couldn't help lifting a skeptical eyebrow. "Didn't you notice that the blame of what happened fell upon me first? My dad was so quick to hold me responsible even though he didn't actually know that the idea to bring in Sahara was mine."

"Yeah, I did," Rohit murmured, his eyes searching hers, his face unreadable.

Whether it was compassion or regret flitting across his gaze, Cynthia wasn't sure, and she shook her head, still bewildered over

Rohit's decision to take responsibility for her actions. "And now he thinks the idea was yours. Why did you cover for me?"

"I've thought about our conversation the last time we were here . . ." Rohit trailed off and stared into the crowded parking lot in silence for a few minutes. When he turned back to her, there was a new softness just shy of tender in his eyes that was both hypnotizing and made Cynthia want to look away. For a brief, silly second, she wondered if this innocuous wheelchair ramp, lined with bright green shrubs, was beginning to mean something to Rohit, too. If, like her, this smooth, cold cement transported him to a different place, made him feel vulnerable and safe at the same time.

"I saw how everyone was looking at you and, I don't know. I wanted to help you, Cynthia," he finished.

He wanted to help me. She'd always viewed that four-letter word with a degree of loathing; needing help was weak and she had never, ever considered herself a damsel in distress.

But with her insides still battered and bruised from her father's chilling disappointment, she couldn't summon an ounce of disgust for what he'd done. She hadn't asked nor had she made it easy for him, but he'd scaled the wall and slain the dragon anyway.

Cynthia glanced at Rohit's left hand on the safety railing. A part of her wanted to cover it with her own, feel the warmth of skin and the strength of bones under her hand—maybe she'd draw a little of it for herself or, perhaps, offer her own.

But that felt like too much; he'd probably jerk his hand away in shock.

"I still don't understand why," she murmured softly, mostly to herself.

Rohit let out a long sigh. "Cynthia, I'm on your side."

The words, so simply said, overwhelmed her body. Her chest felt full, her throat tight, and her eyes suspiciously moist. *To hell with it.* Before she could talk herself out of it, Cynthia placed her hand on the railing next to Rohit's, their pinkies lightly brushing against each other, hoping he'd understand the gesture. Hoping he'd realize that for her, it was a big step.

That, for once, she didn't feel alone.

CHAPTER 13

When Cynthia arrived at the Pipe and Straw at six o'clock on the dot that same evening, Rohit was struck by how different she looked. The same silky, jet-black hair swept feathery kisses against the nape of her neck, and she wore her standard work dress, always in a neutral color and always sliding around all the right curves.

But a vertical wrinkle split the smooth curve of her forehead, and her stride lacked the strength of a woman who could, and would, run the world.

She appeared uncertain. Out of place. Which made Rohit feel uncertain and out of place and, like an idiot, he blurted the first words that came to mind as she approached his table.

"Thanks for not standing me up this time."

Cynthia took her seat and fiddled with the edge of her napkin, turning it this way and that so it sat angled on the table just so.

She wasn't the only one who was nervous. Since he'd arrived a half hour earlier than their agreed-upon meeting time, Rohit had been tapping an unsteady beat against the scarred tabletop with a metal spoon until a neighboring table had asked him to stop. Had Cynthia shown up five minutes earlier, she would've caught him checking out his appearance in the back of said spoon like an upper-primary boy on his first date.

Not that this is a date, Rohit hastened to remind himself as he cast a furtive glance at Cynthia, now half-hidden behind a laminated menu. Her eyes, however, were anywhere but the Pipe and Straw's British pub-style offerings; her long, graceful neck swiveled side to side as she glanced around the room. When she tucked her hair behind her ear, Rohit's body tightened as he remembered the softness of those strands brushing teasingly against his cheek as his tongue explored the sensitive skin behind her earlobe.

"I didn't realize so many people from work hung out here after hours," she said.

Rohit cleared his throat. "What?"

Cynthia lowered her menu and shot him an impatient glance. Just like that, she looked like herself again. "I said, I didn't realize so many people from work hung out here."

With a shrug, Rohit followed her gaze to where Yannis and several staff members from various departments had taken over the family-style high-top in the back corner. "Oh, sure. It's kind of a casual standing-invitation thing for everyone at the office."

"Not everyone," Cynthia muttered, rearranging her napkin and cutlery set again before picking her menu back up. "What's good?"

"Oh! You're staying for food?"

Cynthia eyebrows shot up. "I thought that's why you wanted to meet here around dinnertime?"

"Yes! I mean, sure. Food is good. I love food. I just . . . I didn't know if . . ." Rohit rubbed his hands against his thighs, knocking his spoon onto the floor in the process. He automatically dipped to retrieve it, thought better of it, and jerked upright again while clearing his throat. "Yeah, let's eat."

It was Rohit's turn to take cover behind his menu, and he ducked his head for good measure so Cynthia wouldn't catch the heat of mortification searing across his face. Rohit had dated plenty of confident, ambitious women before, but he'd *never, ever* stumbled over the right thing to say. The ability to find the right words was the one thing he always had at his disposal, allowing him to fit in seamlessly in any kind of situation, social circle, or country.

But Cynthia was not those women. She was an ethereal force of nature whose siren call Rohit had long ago succumbed to. It wasn't just because of the unforgettable night they'd shared, either. It was more than that. Being with Cynthia did strange things to Rohit's gray matter. Her presence heightened all his senses, and it overwhelmed him; all cylinders were firing but at the same time turning his thoughts to gibberish.

And yet, in this moment, there was no other place he'd rather be. Rohit peeked over the top of his menu and caught Cynthia's lips lifting in a genuine smile complete with adorable little crinkles at the corners of her eyes, and he gripped the menu a little tighter as if holding on for dear life.

He should've known better than to pick the Pipe and Straw for this meeting—bars were dangerous places with Cynthia in near proximity. For good measure, after they'd ordered, Rohit steered them to safer ground: work.

"I think we need to present staff with some kind of engagement survey," he said. "I've given this a lot of thought, and if we want to get to the root of the issue and make lasting, meaningful changes at KC, we should probably hear from the people."

Cynthia's lips pursed as they often did when she was thinking something over and Rohit reminded himself not to stare at her perfect Cupid's bow, which became even more pronounced when she pouted.

"When you say, 'the people,' are you referring to your little boys' club, too?" she asked.

Rohit's brows furrowed. "Are you talking about the senior leadership team? No, of course not. This should be for entry to midlevel staff only. I had Gayle pull some HR records for me, and our junior staff turnover is a little startling."

"A survey could invite trouble," Cynthia mused. "There's a chance that there are more disgruntled staff than Melanie let on . . . or that Melanie even knows about at this point. Maybe we should focus on finding who said what and nipping that in the bud."

"If we start a witch hunt, morale is going to plummet even lower than it already is. Besides, our concern is fixing the problem, and pointing fingers rarely does anything to help move toward a solution."

"That's . . . smart." Cynthia frowned and tilted her head to the side. "An engagement survey might open the floodgates, though."

"A lot of organizations do annual staff surveys as a means of building positive office culture. We can focus on head office for now, but in the long run, this could—and should—be a regular, organization-wide thing," Rohit said, leaning forward in his seat. "And it needs to be anonymous."

As Cynthia nodded, a sense of pride flooded Rohit's senses. It wasn't so much that for once he was a step ahead of Cynthia, whose brain seemed to work triple time compared to everyone else's, but there was respect in her eyes and maybe even a hint of admiration.

It was intoxicating having her look at him like that.

"Someone came prepared," she said. "But I think we should be careful with how we conduct this survey."

"I agree," Rohit nodded. "I've already talked to some third-party HR consultants about how to execute something like this properly. I want staff to feel like they're sharing their feedback in a safe space, but I also don't want this survey to set any weird precedents, like whatever they criticize will automatically be on the chopping block. We just need to get a baseline for where staff are at in terms of satisfaction with the work culture and then figure out how to address it."

Cynthia studied him for a long moment. "You really dug deep on this one, huh?" She frowned and lowered her gaze, her hand balling into a fist on the tabletop. "I guess you had to after I royally fucked things up with my brilliant idea to bring in Sahara."

"Hey," Rohit said, his hand reaching to pat hers. "It wasn't a *complete* fuckup—at least you got a funny story out of it."

She glared in response. It was likely too soon to be cracking jokes, but Rohit was still riding the high of her admiration from earlier and it made him feel daring.

"C'mon, Cynthia," he prodded. "You signed our office up for a multilevel marketing scheme. It might not have been the results you intended, but no one can say you're not resourceful."

She was silent for a moment before her lips gave in to the barest of twitches. "I better be at the top of the pyramid."

"Your future with TeamStart is just beginning. 'Work for yourself but not by yourself,'" Rohit said with a grin. "That's a direct quote from one of the pamphlets Sahara left behind, in case you wanted to know."

"You *would* read the pamphlet."

"You're going to *change people's lives*."

"Better bowel movements at Kumar Construction, all thanks to me."

"You'll be a multimillionaire by the end of the year. Maybe you'll qualify for one of those 'I Did It' Beamers or an all-expenses-paid trip to Mexico."

Then it happened. Cynthia threw her head back and laughed, and Rohit couldn't tear his eyes away from her. The unsuppressed joy in her face was something else entirely. It was a new layer he'd discovered, this beautiful lack of control wrapped in the rich huskiness of her laughter. It was as if he'd chipped away at a flawless diamond only to find something more valuable and precious inside.

"I'm impressed with how much work you've put into this already," Cynthia said once her laughter had died down.

"Your future at TeamStart?"

She leaned forward and lightly slapped his arm. She'd barely touched him and yet his skin heated. "I mean the issue at Kumar Construction," she said.

"I've been giving it a lot of thought," he admitted. "Because I really do want KC to be a great place to work for everybody."

Cynthia tilted her head to the side. "So *you* don't agree with any of the negative claims? No issues with any of the senior leaders or the work environment?"

For the first time that evening, Rohit's brain kicked in before he said something stupid, or, worse, obliviously glib. Thanks to the article in *The Watch* and his recent discussions with Cynthia, he was kind of ashamed of how ignorant he'd been of what was happening outside his own little bubble at work. The year he'd spent hyperfocused on ingratiating himself as everyone's best friend seemed self-centered now. Amid the fist bumps and the coffee meetings with

Rich, he'd never really stopped to look outside the protective walls he'd erected around himself.

"I think . . . I've had it easy," he said. "But I don't take it for granted, believe me. I know how lucky I am to work here." Rohit swallowed uneasily, wondering how Cynthia would react if she knew *exactly* how lucky Rohit counted himself to be.

"Well, you worked hard to get to where you are," Cynthia pointed out. "An MBA isn't easy to get."

Rohit took a long sip of water. "No, it isn't."

"So, while I run off to make billions with TeamStart, what's your next move?"

"What do you mean?"

Cynthia raised an eyebrow. "What's your end goal at Kumar Construction? You don't want to be a client manager forever, do you?"

Rohit was saved from answering right away by the server slinging their plates onto the table with a lack of grace that suited the Pipe and Straw's casual-bordering-on-careless vibe perfectly. The overhead lighting was poor, the picture frames on the wall dusty, and the food greasy but flavorful. But as Cynthia dug into her chicken pot pie, Rohit contemplated his oversized plate of fish and chips, his appetite a distant memory.

Since joining Kumar Construction, he'd never given much thought to his future. Everything he did was about the now, and *now* needed money. Supporting his family was a perpetual game of catch-up with little room for forward thinking. And he never felt like he was on the winning side; he was constantly behind and out of breath, his financial obligations fisting his lungs with a relentless grip.

"I don't have any plans," he said. To his ears, it sounded pathetic, and from the tilt of Cynthia's head, he could tell she didn't believe him.

"You don't think about your future?"

Under Cynthia's curious gaze, Rohit blushed, but it wasn't embarrassment coursing through him. Cynthia wore her ambition like a second skin, but there was zero judgment in her bright amber eyes as she waited for him to answer. Her kindness startled him, but in a pleasant way: Rohit felt like he was back on that ramp outside the office, where those few moments with Cynthia had felt like a reprieve from worrying about money, and job security, and the pressure of holding his family's world on his shoulders.

Taking the blame for her mistake negated everything he'd tried to build for himself at Kumar Construction, and yet he couldn't regret it.

"No, I don't think about my future very often. I think about my family's future and what their lives will look like. I worry about taking care of them and making sure they're provided for." Rohit shook his head, uneasy at where his words were taking him. But Cynthia seemed to have a pull on him that ran much deeper than lust and attraction; he felt the need to bare himself to her, including the parts of him he was usually so careful to keep tucked away. "Sometimes taking care of my family is all I think about. That's weird, right?"

To his surprise, Cynthia's face softened and she reached out to touch him *again*, only this time, her hand covered his on the tabletop and *stayed there*. Rohit hoped she couldn't hear his sharp intake of breath even as he willed himself to stay very, very still so she wouldn't pull away.

"I think that's very hard," she said. "It's a sense of purpose but a complicated one that, in a way, has nothing to do with you or what you want."

"What I want," he repeated with a bitter laugh. When was the last time he'd thought about what he wanted? There was no room for *want* living in a new country when his peace of mind depended on the well-being of people living thousands of kilometers away.

Cynthia tilted her head to the side and waited.

"Had things been different," Rohit said slowly, "I probably would have pursued a career in architecture."

"So go back to school."

Rohit half smiled. He didn't doubt for a second that this determined, willful person sitting across from him believed in the simplicity of making such a decision. If Cynthia wanted something, she found a way to get it.

But that wasn't his reality. And the thought of his grandmother's medical bills and the extra help his sister needed to get by in school filled him with fresh guilt, pulled him back from the edge of honesty where one could so easily stumble, fall, and lose everything.

"Maybe one day," he agreed quietly.

"Well, having an MBA under your belt opens doors," Cynthia reminded him, lowering her eyes. "And your family must be so proud of you. That has to feel good."

Momentarily distracted by his phone buzzing insistently on the table, Rohit let out a strangled laugh when he caught sight of the screen. "Their ears must be burning because they're calling me right now." Although the interruption was likely a blessing in disguise to save him from revealing too much, Rohit hesitated as his finger hovered to accept the call. "Do you mind?"

Cynthia returned her attention to her meal. "Go ahead."

"Rohit? It's so noisy! Where are you?" Maisa demanded as soon as their video connected. In the background, his parents were squished together just off to the side as they tried to peer over his sister's shoulder.

"I'm at a pub." Rohit did a quick scan of the room with the screen facing outward before turning it toward himself again.

"Ask him if they have Kingfisher beer," his father's voice urged from the background.

"Dad, he can hear you," his sister replied, rolling her eyes at Rohit.

"It's an English pub," Rohit said dryly. "Of course they have Kingfisher beer."

The sarcasm was lost on his dad, who grinned with pleasure at the news that his favorite brand of Indian beer had made its way to Canada, but Maisa knew better and smiled back cheekily.

"How's the butter chicken?" she asked.

Before Rohit could reply, his mother's face pushed forward, edging his sister out. "Who was that?"

"Who?" Rohit asked.

"The girl you're sitting with. The pretty one."

Rohit's eyes flew to Cynthia, who had obviously heard the question if her smirk was any indication.

"Just a coworker, Mom," Rohit answered.

"Well, introduce us," his sister prodded from off-screen. Rohit did not need to see Maisa's face to know she wore an impish grin. *Little sisters.*

To Rohit's surprise, amusement danced across Cynthia's face, and she waved a hand before wiping her mouth with a napkin. "It's fine. I'd love to meet them," she said.

A flutter of nerves rolled up Rohit's spine and, in an unnaturally high voice, he said, "Uh, well, this is Cynthia Kumar. We work together. Like, not *together* but at the same company. Although we are working on a project togeth—"

On-screen, his mother and sister traded glances.

"Stop rambling and turn the phone around," Maisa commanded, her impatient face squished back into the frame, doe eyes bright with amusement and curiosity.

Rohit obeyed while mouthing an apology to Cynthia, but her attention was focused on his family.

"Hi," Maisa said, her voice turning shy despite having initiated the introduction.

His mother, however, had no such issue. She never did. "I was right. You *are* very pretty."

"Yes, well, it takes a lot of work," Cynthia said with mock seriousness, earning her a round of appreciative laughs from her nosy audience, and Rohit couldn't help but sit back in his chair, a little dazed.

She never failed to knock his world off its axis. Rohit watched Cynthia listen intently as his family introduced themselves, her attention never wavering as if every single person was worth committing to memory, whether she ever talked to them again or not. He'd known that Cynthia's roster of clients and service providers adored her, but he'd never seen her in action like this. Her trademark confidence and quick mind were no surprise, but there was something else Rohit couldn't quite pinpoint except that whatever it was, it was irresistible and made him feel a little dizzy.

Every layer of this woman was more dazzling than the one before.

"It's nice to meet you all," she said once the introductions were over.

"So, tell us," his mother said. "What is our Rohit like at work?"

Rohit groaned as Cynthia plucked the phone out of his hand. He realized this was his parents' way of understanding—and being part of—his life, but the distance made it no less embarrassing. Cynthia's gaze was soft, though, when she shot him a quick, teasing glance before replying.

"Oh, I'm sure you know," Cynthia said. "Friendly to the point of being annoying. Always in a good mood, even on Monday mornings. Drinks the last bit of coffee and forgets to refill the pot."

Rohit dragged his chair around the table, so he was in the camera frame beside Cynthia. "That happened *once*."

His sister hooted. "Sounds like him! Mom used to ask him to fetch the clothes off the line and sometimes he'd only grab his!"

Cynthia gasped and shook her head at Rohit, her shoulder bumping his. "I'm not surprised in the least."

From somewhere in the background outside the camera, Rohit's father chuckled. "She's feisty. I like her."

"You think that's bad?" his mother chimed in. She twisted her long hair into a bun, as if preparing for battle. "Let me tell you about the time I asked him to go to the market during a cricket match . . ."

Rohit covered his face with his hands as Cynthia leaned forward eagerly, the motion pressing her entire arm against his. But as his mother began an exaggerated retelling of his childhood antics, he couldn't help but grin into his palms. Because he kind of liked it.

And as Cynthia let out a deep belly laugh, he realized he liked it a lot.

CHAPTER 14

This looks like a drug lord's bed in a low-budget porn movie."

"Naomi!" Cynthia shot a furtive glance over her shoulder at the densely packed furniture store before sending a quick, silent note of thanks to the universe that the owners were nowhere in sight.

Naomi grimaced and placed a hand on the ornately carved headboard of the four-poster bed. "Sorry," she murmured, tracing her fingers over the gold leaf inlay. Whether she was apologizing to the bed, Cynthia, or the store, Cynthia wasn't quite sure, but she didn't sound the least contrite when she added, "But threesomes will be had in this monstrosity."

Cynthia bit down on her bottom lip to school her expression, but a snort-giggle escaped anyway. They were surrounded by heavy, dark wood in the form of elaborate dining room sets, palazzo-inspired china cabinets, and an absurd number of velvet chaise longues. Her clients at Kashmiri Dining had sent her here because the owner of Wakeem's Furniture Gallery Superstore was a friend of a friend's nephew or cousin or something, and if anything in the store inspired Cynthia's vision for Kashmiri's newest restaurant, then a discount was guaranteed.

Her friend's description of the bed had been kind; to Cynthia, the *entire* store belonged on the set of a low-budget porn movie.

The things I do to keep clients happy. On a tired exhale, Cynthia perched on the edge of a dark purple chaise and was forced to admit, it *was* comfortable. Leaning back on her hands, she allowed herself a moment to enjoy the feel of soft, plush velvet against her palms. If only for a brief second, it felt nice to relax.

"Either that lounger is making you rethink your stance on casting couches or something's on your mind," Naomi commented as she bent to examine a gaudy chandelier lamp.

"What makes you say that?"

Naomi threw her a bemused smile. "You're literally sitting on the job, which I have never, ever seen you do."

Although Cynthia straightened, she couldn't bring herself to stand up. She and Naomi had worked together only a few times in the past year—usually to introduce each other to contacts or to use each other as a second opinion—but the observation was astute. Cynthia had always prided herself on the hustle, on doing everything and making the right impression on everyone without breaking a sweat. In heels, no less.

But the added work of her and Rohit's special project at Kumar Construction was neither quick nor light, and while Rich had delegated Rohit's other priorities to staff, he had not offered Cynthia the same courtesy—not that she had expected him to. Her father had never shown any specific or lengthy interest in her projects or clients and, likewise, she liked to keep things under wraps so the results could speak for themselves. A handful of times, Rich had congratulated her on her success—usually after her work was recognized in a local newspaper or magazine—and as offhand as her father's compliments were, they made Cynthia want to catch them in midair, wrap her fingers around them, and squeeze.

Most of her clients had graciously accepted the unanticipated shuffling in her schedule so she could focus on the inner workings of Kumar Construction, but still, she was burning the candle at both ends and her energy was tapering.

"It's been a long few weeks," Cynthia drawled, resisting the urge to kick off her shoes. Sitting was one thing, but she would never give in to the extent of her fatigue while on the clock. Besides, the owner might pop up at any moment.

Naomi plopped down on a nearby wingback chair heavily brocaded in silver thread and gestured at Cynthia's chaise. "Why don't you lie down and tell me about it?"

Cynthia looked down the length of the velvet chaise as if the suggestion had merit. When she looked back at her friend, Naomi had pulled a pad of paper from her large purse and was watching her intently, a red crayon poised between her fingertips. Cynthia rolled her eyes with a laugh, but she couldn't help but wonder, what was it like to be so casual and comfortable with oneself that you could be silly and weird and risk looking ridiculous? Cynthia was confident, sure, but she was always, *always* hyperaware of her surroundings, of how she looked, how she behaved. Even before Rohit's appearance in her life, every little thing she did had felt like a grain of sand on a scale, tipping the balance one way or another toward perfection.

Maybe that was what tired her out most of all.

Cynthia brushed her fingers over the velvet again and forced a lighthearted tone. "What kind of deranged therapist uses red crayon?"

Naomi waved the crayon in the air with a flourish. "The expensive kind. And also, I spent the day with Dev's nieces yesterday. I think half the crayon box spilled in my bag." With a careless shrug, Naomi tossed the crayon so it landed in Cynthia's tote bag at the foot of the chaise. "Seriously, though. Do you want to talk about it?"

Cynthia's answer was stalled by the persistent vibration in the pocket of her skirt. When Cynthia saw her mother's name on the screen, she held up an apologetic finger. "Sorry, but I should take this."

"Fine, but I'll be billing you for this, too," Naomi responded.

Switching her "one minute" finger to flipping Naomi the bird, Cynthia straightened, crossed her legs, and brought the phone to her ear. "Hey, Mom," she said. "I'm with a vendor right now, can I call you back?"

Her mother's voice was tinny and choppy. "Cynthia . . . We're stuck in Vancouver and it's . . . Can you . . . and then take them . . . Rohit."

Plugging her ear with her finger, Cynthia's eyebrows lowered in concentration as alarm flooded through her. Her parents had flown to Vancouver yesterday to meet with the Feirhair group to talk more about acquiring their chain of motels. Well, at least her father had. Sipra never missed an opportunity to tag along to a major city to shop and see old friends.

"I can't hear you," Cynthia said. "You're cutting in and out." Glancing at her phone's clock, she turned up the volume. "Aren't you supposed to be on a flight home right now?"

There was a bout of silence before her mother's voice returned, somewhat clearer than before. "Is that better?"

"I think so?"

"It's pouring outside, and I think it's . . . with my cell reception. Our flight was canceled, something about . . . storm."

"Okay," Cynthia said, waving a dismissive hand at Naomi, who watched with concern. "Thanks for letting me know. I'll see you tomorrow."

"Wait! I need you . . . something for me."

Cynthia's jaw tightened. Another thing to fuck with her day. "What is it?"

"It's . . . go to the house and grab the bag . . . for Rohit."

Great. It wasn't *any* old thing but *Rohit* that Sipra wanted Cynthia to fuck with. *Wait. That wasn't right.* Cynthia cleared her throat as blood rushed to her ears. "Can't it wait until tomorrow?"

"What?"

"*Tomorrow.* Can't it wait until *tomorrow*?" Behind her, Naomi smothered a giggle.

"Absolutely not . . . very important. Your father insists . . . too."

Cynthia's nails raked tufted lines on the chaise as she half listened to her mother's disappearing and reappearing voice on the line. They were stranded in Vancouver and their first thought was the Chosen One. The fact that he was on the forefront of not only her father's mind but her mother's, too, sent a sharp, cold stinging sensation through Cynthia's chest.

"I'll text you . . . address," her mother was saying. "And you can—"

"His address? Why?"

"To deliver the . . . Haven't you . . . listening?"

His apartment. This evening, Cynthia would be going to Rohit's apartment. The iciness in her stomach turned on a dime and burned hot, inflaming her from the inside out. Every inch of skin was aware of every follicle of hair on her body. She felt an erratic pulse skitter through her, toeing the line between embarrassment and something else—something that made her sit forward in her seat, her toes curling in her shoes.

Anticipation.

Dinner at a pub was one thing. She could fake nonchalance in public, but his apartment? Where he would likely be alone, maybe half-dressed, and not expecting her? Would he welcome her? Spy her through the peephole and remain silent until she left? With a sinking heart, Cynthia belatedly realized that it was Friday. Maybe he'd have someone over. Maybe he wouldn't be home. But still . . .

His apartment.

"Cynthia?" her mother asked, sounding both tired and exasperated. "Are you . . . take care of this?"

There was no getting out of it. While Cynthia wasn't one to shy away from risking her mother's displeasure by not doing precisely as asked, there was no way she could leave Rohit hanging by not following through. Not after everything that had happened in the last few weeks. Not after he'd taken the blame for her, and not after meeting his family and finding them much too easy to like.

"Okay, fine, I'll deliver the package to Rohit's place." In her periphery, Naomi's head jerked up from where she'd been texting on her phone, her eyes wide.

It was no surprise when, as soon as Cynthia ended the call, Naomi pounced, practically leaping to join Cynthia on the chaise. "What happened?"

Cynthia pointedly inched away and damn it if Naomi didn't follow, an obnoxious grin taking up the better part of her face. "It's nothing," she said, her voice short even as she fought the baffling urge to smile. "Just a favor for my mom. I have to get some kind of package to Rohit tonight—"

"At his apartment."

"I'm just going to drop it off—"

"At his apartment."

"—and leave." When Naomi opened her mouth again, Cynthia shot her a warning glare. "If you say 'at his apartment' again, I will shove that red crayon in your mouth. This isn't a big deal."

Naomi scoffed. "You had dinner with him a few nights ago."

"So?"

"You said you had a *nice* dinner with him a few nights ago. At the Pipe and Straw." Naomi wiggled her shoulders. "The food at the Pipe and Straw sucks, Cynthia, which means the nice part had nothing to do with the food but with the *man*."

"Would you calm down? All I said was that it was *nice*."

"'Nice' from Cynthia Kumar is like a five-star Google review from the queen."

"The queen does Google reviews?" Cynthia asked dryly.

"Well, if it wasn't Rohit's company, what made the dinner so 'nice'?" Naomi asked, exasperated.

Cynthia ducked her head and plucked an invisible loose thread off the seat and dropped it onto the floor. "All right, I enjoyed hanging out with Rohit"—Cynthia paused as Naomi's short, giddy little squeal ravaged her eardrum—"and I might have met his family, too." She raised a warning finger. *"Don't* scream in my ear again."

"You met Rohit's family," her friend repeated, her eyebrows practically brushing her hairline.

"They video called Rohit halfway through dinner and we talked for a few minutes. It was no big deal," Cynthia added quickly.

And it *wasn't* a big deal, not at face value. But the whole evening had been the highlight of Cynthia's week. Granted, it had been a hellish week, but once Cynthia and Rohit had placed their orders at the Pipe and Straw, everything that followed had ensued so easily, and gracefully, like the clean, clear blue calm after a rainstorm. The food had been awful, but the company had been welcome, the conversation effortless. It had been as easy as hanging out with Naomi, and even now, days later, it brought a silly little smile to Cynthia's face.

Unfortunately, it was a smile that Naomi did not miss as she eyed Cynthia critically. "When are you going? Are you going to change before? Do you have time to shower? Will you text me after?"

Luckily, Cynthia was saved from answering by a loud male voice. "You must be Cynthia!"

Both Cynthia and Naomi rose to their feet as a short, rotund man in suspenders made his way toward them, arms spread wide like a ringmaster. Well before he reached them, Cynthia stuck out her hand in case he did something weird, like tried to hug her or something—one could never be too careful as a young, female interior designer. She'd had clients ask her out on dates before, had endured men staring at her legs while she walked through concepts for floor plans.

As he pumped her hand in a too-strong grip, Cynthia was momentarily distracted by his bristly, curling black mustache and the thick gold chain bracelets adorning his wrists. In the porn set cavorting as a furniture store, he was right at home.

"Sorry I'm late," he said as he pulled a box of cigarettes from his shirt pocket. "Smoke break."

Cynthia and Naomi watched in silence as he pulled a cigarette from the box and stuck it behind his ear. He misinterpreted their staring and pulled out another. "How ungentlemanly of me. Cigarette?" he asked, proffering one in their direction.

Cynthia shook her head, but Naomi wordlessly accepted, much to Cynthia's surprise.

"This is my colleague, Naomi Kelly," Cynthia said. "And I'm Cynthia Kumar. Nice to meet you."

"And I am Wakeem himself! What do you think of my magnificent collection?" Wakeem spread his thick arms wide again, his white shirt straining at the buttons.

With a forced smile, Cynthia cast a look at the assortment of eyesores around her. "It's one of a kind."

"Worthy of a movie set," Naomi added with a straight face.

"I knew I would like you two," Wakeem said, nodding his approval. "You tell your Kashmiris that if they want a piece from Wakeem, they can have it at forty percent off! Hang on, let me grab my business card."

"God help me," Naomi murmured when he was out of earshot. "But I think I like him, too."

Cynthia looked pointedly at the cigarette clutched in her non-smoking friend's hand. "Great, well, maybe you two can go have a smoke together."

Naomi laughed and, for the second time that day, threw the item into Cynthia's tote bag. "Or maybe you'll need it after hooking up with Rohit in his apartment."

CHAPTER 15

I t was after ten o'clock when Cynthia, exhausted and more than a little frazzled after reporting back to the Kashmiris and talking them out of building a reflective, gold-plated bar in their new restaurant, finally swung by her parents' home, grabbed the large brown paper bag from their oversized fridge as per her mother's instructions, and drove to Rohit's apartment on the other side of town. She was too tired to care what was in the bag.

After being let into his building by a tenant returning from walking her cat, Cynthia swallowed nervously and located the unit number her mother had sent her via text, well aware that half past ten was much too late to be dropping in unannounced.

He's just your coworker, she reminded herself after hesitantly knocking on the forest-green apartment door. *It'll be a quick drop-off.*

She was debating knocking again when the door swung open, revealing Rohit, clad in a dark blue hoodie and sweatpants, his eyes wide and mouth slack in surprise.

"Cynthia?" he asked, poking his head out the door and glancing down the hallway. "What are you doing here? Is everything all right?"

Despite having imagined this very moment the entire drive over, Cynthia was momentarily rendered speechless by the sight of Rohit in sweats, hair a little askew. He was wearing *gray* sweatpants, she realized faintly, trying not to linger as her gaze traveled down to his bare feet. Under her incredulous stare, he wiggled his toes, and she jerked her head up, suddenly breathless.

"Cynthia?" he repeated, his voice gruff.

"I have something for you," she blurted out.

"Something for *me*?" he parroted back, sounding mildly alarmed.

She wordlessly handed him the paper bag and his expression morphed from startled to inquisitive. "What is it?" he asked.

Distracted, Cynthia didn't respond as she peeked over his broad shoulder into the dimly lit apartment, illuminated mostly by a television set. She ignored the tidal wave of relief she felt upon realizing that he was alone on a Friday night.

Rohit studied her face carefully before reaching into the carrier to pull out a clear plastic container. Inside was a row of three gourmet cupcakes from her mother's favorite bakery. The one in the middle was pink and on its surface were the words *Happy Birthday* in looping white frosting.

He glanced up at her, as if shy, and quietly asked, "How did you know?"

Heat rushed to Cynthia's cheeks. "I-I didn't. My parents' flight home from Vancouver was delayed, so they asked me to bring this over." Cynthia paused. "Wait. We spent a good chunk of the day at work together talking about our project. Why didn't you say anything?"

Rohit's eyes returned to the cupcake box in his hands as he

shrugged. "I don't like to make a big deal out of it. It's the one day of the year I always hate being far away from my family. I usually take it off, but with the urgency of the project and all . . ." He trailed off and looked over his shoulder. When he looked back at her, he was biting his lip. "Do you . . . do you want to come in?"

"Yes." The word slipped from Cynthia's mouth before her brain could process it. And she didn't want to think too much on it.

It was his birthday, after all.

"Okay, uh, sorry about the mess," he said as she followed him in.

It was the opposite of messy inside. While Cynthia appreciated minimalist décor, Rohit's apartment was downright sparse. There were no framed pictures on the walls, no knickknacks or old concert tickets strewn about to give anything away about the man inside. His living space was small and tidy and smelled like citrus.

But when Cynthia caught sight of what was on the paused television set—the opening credits to *10 Things I Hate About You*—she stopped in her tracks. Memories of the night they had met flooded her senses in a rush of self-consciousness, yearning, and heat. Her pulse reverberated against the confines of a very dry throat.

Perhaps Rohit felt it, too, because he avoided her gaze and mumbled, "This movie reminds me of home. My sister and I always watch it on our birthdays."

She should leave. She'd interrupted him, shown up on his doorstep uninvited. Instead, Cynthia cleared her throat. "Can I . . . can I watch with you?"

It would've been impossible to miss the way Rohit's entire face brightened or the way his dark eyes searched her face as if anticipating some kind of punch line.

She stared back, her face expressionless and tightly controlled, and at complete odds with her heart practicing a tumbling act in her chest.

Rohit fumbled to open the container in his hands. "Cupcake?" When she accepted, he hastily placed the rest of the cupcakes on the coffee table and dashed to the kitchen. "I'll get you a plate. And napkin. I don't have anything besides water but . . ."

"It's fine," Cynthia said, quelling the laughter in her voice. "Just the cupcake is great." Tenderness tugged at the corners of her lips as she watched Rohit clumsily rush about his kitchen. When he returned, he seemed to have composed himself a bit if his sheepish smile was any indication.

"Sorry," he said, handing her a small white plate. "I guess I'm still surprised you're here. But I'm really glad you are. It's a nice surprise," he quickly added.

Cynthia sat down on the far side of the black faux-leather couch and nodded at the screen where Julia Stiles was pulling up beside a car full of prep school girls. "So, what is it with you and rom-coms, anyway?"

The question hung between them for a moment, heavy with the weight of memories from a night that was far from innocent. Tension, heady and thick, seeped into the dead air behind them, but Cynthia fought the urge to rescind. She was far too curious. As she sat in this nearly empty apartment with the most popular and charismatic guy at work, the desire to hear his answer and know him sizzled through her. Her prior feelings of discomfort, exhaustion, and irritation had disappeared the minute he'd opened the door. She felt suspiciously light and reenergized, like she could go all night. The realization made her blush and she busied herself with unwrapping her cupcake as she waited for Rohit to answer.

Despite his stilted eagerness a few minutes ago, Rohit looked cautious and uncertain as he gingerly sat on the other end of the couch. "I don't know," he mused, his eyes studying the freeze-frame on-screen. "They're an escape, I guess."

Cynthia eyed Rohit doubtfully. She might've made some incorrect snap judgments about him, but one thing remained true: he was the Chosen One. What could he possibly have to escape from? Endless opportunities? Being fawned over whenever he stepped into a room? High-powered men pausing their dick-swinging to take his opinion seriously?

Yet she had no desire to charge him with such questions as she once might have. Because finding him alone on his birthday, sitting in this small, unassuming apartment with faded carpets underfoot and the faint, earthy scent of cardamom seeping through the citrus air, she realized she didn't *really* know him.

But she wanted to.

"An escape from what?" she asked, her voice pitched low as if her vocal cords recognized the fragility of the moment stirring between them, pulled taut like strings on a violin. Cynthia herself wasn't entirely sure what it was except that whatever was connecting her to Rohit right now was so fine—so delicate—that she needed to tread carefully with a hushed voice and an open heart.

Rohit removed the *Happy Birthday* cupcake from its container and contemplated the fancy, swooping script. For a split second, the unbidden image of him licking frosting off her fingertip flashed across Cynthia's mind and she suppressed a shiver.

"I like the idea of . . ." Rohit's lips twisted wryly. "Hell, you're going to mock me mercilessly for this, aren't you?"

Cynthia held her dessert up to her heart. "I swear on this cupcake to give you a free pass on your birthday."

He smiled and saluted her with his treat before his face sobered. "Things like happiness and love seem a lot less complicated in romance movies. Despite everything that happens, when the main character and love interest get together, they become a team, and love is enough."

Rohit paused as if piecing together his thoughts while his strong, graceful fingers began to unwrap his cupcake slowly and methodically. It was hypnotic, watching the flimsy wrapper pull away under his unhurried, careful hand. He wasn't one to rush that moment of sweet satisfaction, leading Cynthia to wonder, for one ridiculous moment, whether his cupcake would taste that much better.

She licked her bottom lip. "That doesn't seem so far-fetched," she said.

"Yeah, well, that's not the real world, is it?" Bitterness threaded his words. "Real-world love is sacrifice and responsibility. It's everyone relying on you and you alone. It's . . ." Rohit trailed off as a self-deprecating smile tugged at the corners of his mouth. "I should shut up now." He raised his cupcake in the air toward Cynthia again. "Cheers."

He was about to take a bite when Cynthia blurted out, "Wait!"

"What?" he asked, slowly lowering his hand.

"Something's missing." Cynthia nodded toward his kitchen. "Do you have a candle or something?"

He smiled ruefully. "Unfortunately, I don't."

"Hang on." Cynthia grabbed her tote from the floor and began rummaging inside, aware that Rohit was watching her in amused silence.

"I didn't realize pomp and circumstance was your thing."

"It's not, but it's your birthday, it should be special," she said, keeping her head lowered even though her fingers had already found the desired item. "Do you have a lighter, at least?"

Rohit's eyebrows rose but he dutifully fetched one from his kitchen. When he returned, Naomi held her hand out for the lighter, the red crayon Naomi had thrown in her bag earlier perched upright in a napkin between her thumb and index finger.

"Is this safe?" he asked with a laugh.

"Of course it is." Cynthia glanced at the makeshift candle uncertainly. "But blow it out quickly just in case."

She plucked the lighter from his palm before grabbing the same hand and pulling him onto the couch beside her. She felt silly and foolish as she lit the red wax, but when Rohit leaned in, his eyes sparkling in the small glow of the flame, she was glad she'd taken the risk. The press of his leg against hers was solid and warm, his gaze soft, almost reverent.

He wasn't looking at the crayon. He was looking at her.

"I never sing in public," she confessed. "But happy birthday."

He blew out the candle with a heart-stopping grin, and the last bits of her self-consciousness fluttered away.

Cynthia placed the crayon on the edge of her plate before sinking back into the worn, upholstered couch. Her thigh still touched his and she made no move to shift away. She liked how he slouched back and the simple, unassuming way his left arm snaked against the back of the couch, not touching her but comfortable all the same.

It was cozy. And wonderful.

When she risked a glance in his direction, his smile was so boyish and pleased that she didn't resist smiling right back.

"Did I mention how glad I am that you're here?" he asked.

"You know what? So am I."

CHAPTER 16

Coffee, Rohit mused the following Monday, had nothing on Cynthia Kumar.

They were spending the day in the smaller and less cushy Conference Room A of the Desmond Business Center, and the way she moved around the room—confident, assertive, and graceful—was more powerful than any caffeine rush Rohit had ever experienced.

Even with their new, unspoken truce, this woman tortured him. Every time she reached past him for a pen or sidled next to him to slide another chair around the medium-sized oval table, she infiltrated his senses, and he finally had a name for it: sandalwood. He hadn't been able to resist basking in it, his nose tucked against the back of her naked shoulder that first night he'd met her, nor could he deny that he had welcomed the lingering scent after she'd spent his birthday with him.

She'd made his night—*his whole fucking year*—showing up at his apartment on his loneliest day. All because she'd brought him cupcakes.

And stayed.

With the utmost discipline, Rohit forced himself not to react as she brushed past him again to survey the room that would host a series of staff focus groups that day, but with her back safely turned, he gave in: Rohit breathed deep.

"Something's not right . . ." Cynthia said, turning to face him.

Rohit cleared his throat. "What do you mean?"

She leaned over the small side table beside the oval conference table to adjust the angle of the water pitcher just so. She frowned and edged the stack of paper cups a little closer. Bit her lip, moved it away again.

Her fidgeting inspired the gentlest tug just shy of the center of his rib cage and he tucked his hands in his pockets before he did something moronic, like reaching out to give her hand a reassuring squeeze. "It looks great," he said.

Cynthia's hands froze in midair, and she straightened with a self-conscious smile. "I know, I . . . Oh! I almost forgot."

In another act of supreme self-control, Rohit averted his eyes as Cynthia bent at the waist to open the cabinet door below the table. It took a heroic effort on his part considering she was wearing a black pencil skirt today.

When she reemerged, two boxes of Timbits were in her hands.

"Where did those come from?" Rohit asked.

Cynthia popped the top open and placed the donut holes next to the water pitcher. "I stowed them here this morning. Can't be too careful around Klepto Keer."

"Klepto . . ." Rohit grinned. "You call our head of finance 'Klepto Keer'?"

She notched her chin upward even as a faint blush crept onto her cheeks, and Rohit's heartstrings pulled tight again. "Well, yeah. Because . . ."

"He's always stealing donuts," Rohit finished with a chuckle. "Clever. Any other hilarious pet names I should know about?"

"Well, I wouldn't call them *pet* names, but . . ." The corners of Cynthia's mouth quirked upward playfully—adorably—as she counted off her fingers with mock seriousness. "Klepto Keer, Leering Larry, Sleepy Simon, Moaning Martin . . ."

"*Moaning* Martin?"

"Get your mind out of the gutter." Cynthia swatted his arm. "The guy always makes the most dramatic moans whenever he stands up after sitting for too long. Or when he bends over to pick something up."

Rohit stared at the spot on his suit sleeve where Cynthia had touched him, wondering how much longer he could survive if such an innocent, barely-there gesture could set off this kind of battering in his chest. It was a concerning affliction, one that had zero sympathy for the males in the Patel family tree who were prone to being born with narrow arteries.

He was screwed. Whenever any part of her came into contact with him—whether it was a gentle nudge because he was in her way or a friendly bump of her shoulder against his when he made her laugh—Rohit fell victim to the same series of events: his breath stuttered, a rush of hot pleasure scaled down his spine, and his narrow arteries strained to keep up with his heart's newfound momentum.

When she'd asked him what he wanted at the Pipe and Straw, he'd laughed bitterly. But now every sandalwood-clouded sense gravitated toward one very obvious answer with alarming certainty.

Her. He wanted *her.* Since the moment he'd met her.

This woman, Rohit realized as the collar of his dress shirt pressed uncomfortably against his heated neck, was a health risk.

"What about Olufo?" he remembered to croak after a long pause.

Luckily, Cynthia didn't seem to notice. She'd moved to the conference table and was straightening its chairs. "Nothing," she said, sounding distracted. "I like him."

The door to the conference room opened and Beata, the third-party consultant they'd hired to conduct the staff engagement survey a few weeks ago, ambled inside. After receiving the results of the survey, where the words *poor work-life balance* and *top-heavy* had popped up more than once, both Cynthia and Rohit had agreed that the next step of their plan—voluntary focus groups to discuss the survey's findings—would require a trained professional to guide the conversation.

Beata's eyes zeroed in on the conference table and she squinted thoughtfully. "I wonder if, for this meeting, we should move the table—"

"To the edge of the room?" Cynthia finished. "I agree completely."

"Good. Because I think rows would be more . . ." Beata's hands fluttered.

"Conducive." Cynthia nodded again.

Rohit watched as the two began dragging the chairs away from the table. "Uh . . ."

"Jump in anytime, Rohit," Cynthia said as she began arranging the chairs in neat rows facing the front of the room.

"It's too bad we can't place them in a circle . . ." Beata mused, tapping her long red fingernails against the now-empty conference table.

Cynthia didn't pause in her task. "I know, the thought crossed my mind, too. But there won't be enough room, especially since we aren't entirely sure—"

"How many people will show up?" Beata nodded. "Good point."

Rohit felt dizzy. "Okay, what are you two doing?"

Cynthia continued arranging the chairs as she answered, her voice slightly out of breath. "If one of the main concerns from the survey is that people don't feel they have a seat at the table, then we probably shouldn't hold this focus group around a table that doesn't have enough chairs."

"But there are more chairs in the room," Rohit pointed out. "We have enough seats for everyone."

Beata patted Rohit's shoulder. "Try to keep up, dear."

It was almost the exact same phrase Cynthia had thrown at him a few weeks ago, and from across the room, Cynthia's laughter momentarily distracted Rohit. Her sandalwood perfume might stun him senseless, but her laughter was a much greater problem. Her joy was addictive, could drive a man to do unspeakable, criminal things.

And when Cynthia's intelligent amber eyes met his, the corners tilted up in mirth, Rohit was happily defenseless against the fresh dose of dopamine shooting through him.

"Rohit, the table?" Cynthia said, hovering nearby with a chair cradled in her arms.

Rohit jerked to attention and grabbed the edges of the table to pull it back against the far wall so Cynthia could continue building rows for the staff of Kumar Construction. It wasn't an impressive feat by any means—especially since the table was on wheels—but at least it was a contribution to the efforts of two capable, whip-smart women whose telepathic conversation did *not* need Rohit's input.

Still, Rohit hurried to help Cynthia finish as the first group of employees trickled in. They smiled at Rohit and eyed Cynthia warily before quietly taking their seats. It wasn't long before the trickle turned into a steady flow, and soon almost every chair was filled with members of the junior and administrative staff from Kumar Construction's corporate office.

When Cynthia's assistant, Jilly, and Gaia, the afternoon receptionist, walked in, Rohit hurried toward the door. "I'll grab more chairs," he said.

Beata stepped to the front of the room with a warm smile. "Thank you, everyone, for coming. It takes a lot of courage to partake in something like this, and I think the number of staff in attendance shows just how important this meeting is today."

As Beata began introducing herself, Rohit felt a gentle tug at his elbow and his heart thudded as a fresh wave of sandalwood assaulted him all over again.

"C'mon," Cynthia whispered, pulling him toward the door.

When they were outside the room, she removed her hand from the crook of Rohit's elbow, leaving him strangely bereft. "I saw the way people looked at me when they walked in," she explained. "If we're present, people might be scared to speak up."

Rohit's eyebrows shot up. "Good thinking."

With a short laugh, Cynthia led the way into the elevator. "I may not be able to read people like you do," she said, "but I can pick up on a few things at least."

It wasn't quite a compliment, but Rohit's insides warmed anyway. "I'm kind of blown away by how many people showed up," he commented. "There weren't *that* many dissenters in the survey results—maybe people were holding back."

"Looks like Melanie Burgos wasn't exaggerating after all."

Rohit turned to face Cynthia, but her gaze was trained on the numbers above the elevator door as they descended to the lobby. "What's up with the two of you, anyway?" he asked.

"What do you mean?"

Rohit thought back to the afternoon Melanie had cornered him and Cynthia outside. The reporter had put him on the defensive, too, but the tension between her and Cynthia had crackled with something more complicated than a surprise confrontation. "There was this animosity between you and Melanie or something."

"You felt that?" When Rohit nodded, Cynthia sighed and folded her arms across her chest. "We've known each other for a long time, and we've always rubbed each other the wrong way."

"Were you two ever close?"

"Not at all, but it's pretty obvious that she is very, *very* ambitious." With a little laugh, Cynthia gestured at her own body to draw the parallel, and Rohit made a point of keeping his eyes locked above her chin. "Maybe we're too similar."

Not possible. There was no one like Cynthia.

"I mean," Cynthia added in a distracted tone as she quickly checked her phone, "she's even dating my ex."

The elevator doors opened to the lobby of the business center, and Rohit hurried after Cynthia. "Your ex?"

She waved her hand dismissively. "He and I never even made it to a three-month anniversary, so he barely counts."

Although Cynthia sounded detached, Rohit's mind hooked on to two little words with a level of ferocity that made him grit his teeth: *Cynthia's ex*. His thoughts leaped over tall buildings, and he couldn't help but wonder if there were any lingering feelings there. Cynthia wasn't the type to pine over losers, but defeat also wasn't her style.

"So it doesn't bother you at all?"

They'd reached the front doors, but Cynthia paused, handle in her grasp. "What doesn't bother me at all?"

A slow heat crawled onto Rohit's cheeks, but his embarrassment was no match for his curiosity. "Your ex. Does any of the animosity stem from Melanie dating your ex?"

"*Eddie?*" Cynthia said.

So the loser had a loser name, too. "Yeah, him."

Cynthia's laugh was one part incredulity and two parts scorn. "God, no. That was years ago. When we broke up, I was barely tolerating him as it was."

Good. Rohit's stomach righted itself and he tactfully decided not to dwell on the fact that prior to about a week ago, it had seemed that Cynthia barely tolerated him, too.

There was no need for privacy today; it was cool outside, the overcast sky threatening one of Kelowna's infamous spring downpours. And yet, as if by some unspoken agreement, the two of them headed toward the ramp on the side of the building, and much like the other times, Cynthia—impatient, fast-walking, restless Cynthia—seemed perfectly content lingering in their spot.

The realization wrapped around Rohit like a pleasant hug that no chill could ever touch.

Cynthia leaned back against the safety railing and braced the sole of her high-heeled shoe on the lower bar, drawing Rohit's attention to her shapely legs. The hem of her dress had ridden up only the barest of inches, and yet Rohit could practically feel his pupils expanding outward as he took in the glimpse of soft, smooth skin above the curve of her bent knee.

She had a dark brown beauty mark just above her right kneecap, he noted forlornly. In the dark of the motel room, there hadn't been enough time to chart the constellation of beauty marks and scars that dotted her gorgeous body. Rohit would give anything to trace their pattern if she let him.

With a brusque cough, he cracked his knuckles and shifted his weight, prompting Cynthia to cock her head in his direction.

"Did the results of the survey come as a shock to you?" she asked.

Leaning against the side of the building so he faced Cynthia, Rohit crossed his arms over his chest and thought of Cynthia's dad. A flicker of guilt belied his answer: "The senior leadership team tries to look out for everyone's best interests . . ."

"In a secluded boardroom that staff are never invited into."

"Yeah, but they're nice people at heart—"

"They're old-fashioned and selective. This place feels like Greek Row sometimes. And no offense, but sometimes you fit right in."

Rohit squinted. "What's Greek Row?"

"It's the part of university campuses where all the fraternity houses are. What I mean is that sometimes the leaders here—who are all *men*, by the way—act like this place is a frat." Cynthia's smile was bitter as she slipped her feet out of her shoes and hoisted herself onto the top bar. "No girls allowed."

Rohit opened his mouth to argue, but when he looked at Cynthia again, his mouth slammed shut. One long look at the vulnerable downturn of her chin, the slight hunch of her shoulders pulling forward, was enough to erase any arguments or wayward thoughts from his mind.

It was time to listen.

"I work harder and longer than half the members of that leadership team, but do they notice?" Cynthia shot Rohit a furtive glance. "Does *he*?"

Rohit swallowed. "You mean your dad."

She averted her eyes. "I might as well be invisible around here.

And clearly, I'm not the only one who feels that way." Cynthia shook her head with a scoff. "I don't know if I should feel comforted that there are others who feel the same or . . ."

"Or?"

"Heartbroken."

It was a word he'd never expect to hear from Cynthia's mouth, and the look of wariness on her face after uttering such an admission drilled into Rohit's chest, resulting in a quick, sharp pinch just left of his sternum. Unable to help himself, he pushed away from the wall to approach Cynthia where she sat on the safety railing. He didn't second-guess himself as he braced his hands on either side of her body and leaned in so her bent knees were inches away from his chest.

Under any other circumstances, it might've been an intimate moment, but romance was the last thing on Rohit's mind. All he could think about was willing some of his warmth and admiration for Cynthia from his body to hers to ease at least a little of her heart's pain. He'd do anything, he realized, anything she needed.

"Have you ever talked to your dad about this?" he asked.

Cynthia's voice cooled. "I'm not going to ask for a pat on the head. Besides, that's not what I want. What I want is—" Cynthia stopped herself abruptly with a slight shake of her head. "Never mind. It's not important."

Everything about you is important, Rohit wanted to say. *Everything about you matters.* But in just a few subtle motions, Cynthia's entire demeanor changed. With her chin lifting slightly and her shoulders pressing back, Rohit was confronted by the Cynthia he knew—whom everybody at Kumar Construction knew—all too well: proud, aloof, and fiercely independent. *Stay away*, the steeliness in her eyes warned.

Still, he'd glimpsed her vulnerability, as fleeting as it was, and couldn't resist inching forward with caution. "I'm sure he doesn't *mean* to make you feel this way."

Cynthia cocked her head to the side and despite the fraying edges of tension between them, Rohit was struck by how unbelievably beautiful she was. Had he any money to spare, he'd bet half a year's salary that an artist would swell with pride to capture her glossy black hair, rippling like an inky, silk curtain on her shoulder, the elegant line of her long, smooth neck. But no paintbrush could truly capture the essence of this regal, mysterious woman.

Rohit himself had only glimpsed the rawness inside, the softer, more fragile parts that could reach right into him with the barest tilt of her chin and scrape away at the inside of his chest cavity, leaving him pleasantly breathless and gasping for more. She was a million unknowable pieces and Rohit feared he was a baffled Matthew Macfadyen staring at Keira Knightley across a crowded dance floor. He was too far gone.

"Well, this isn't about me, is it?" Cynthia said. "This is about the staff at Kumar Construction and that's what we should focus on."

At the finality in her tone, Rohit swallowed his protests and nodded. "So, what do you think we should do?"

Cynthia treated him to a genuine, no-holds-barred smile, and pleasure spilled through Rohit, filling his chest back up again, re-inflating his lungs.

"I have ideas," she replied, leaning forward and bringing her knees in contact with his chest. *Finally.* "Let's go grab a coffee and I'll tell you about them."

A thousand times yes, Rohit thought, as powerless against the smile spreading across his face as he was against his hands finding the sides of her waist to help her off the railing. He couldn't bring himself to let go right away; under the guise of steadying her so she could slip on her shoes, he stayed as still as a statue as he stared at her red-tipped toes.

Her head was bent to the task of finding her footing but in those too short precious seconds, Rohit's imagination went wild: how easy it would be for him to place his fingers on the soft underside of her chin and tilt her head up so he could kiss those perfect lips, parted in surprise. He wanted to. Badly.

But he knew he shouldn't. After the year they'd had, he could never be the one to make the first move, no matter how much every single nerve ending—from the tips of his hair to the ends of his toes—begged to taste just a little bit of this strong, gorgeous woman whose mind ran laps around everyone she encountered. He wanted to share her breath, feel her skin against his again. The imprint from their first time had nearly faded, and his skin itched for her to mark him again.

When Cynthia turned to lead the way off the wheelchair ramp, Rohit's hands reluctantly let go, but he couldn't help but indulge in the selfish luxury of a deep, quiet inhale that sent his senses in a flurry of teasing, comforting, tantalizing, and mystifying sensations.

Sandalwood.

CHAPTER 17

Cynthia was sitting in the center of a domestic hurricane and trying her very best not to get sucked in.

"I thought when you said you'd be coming early, you'd be helping with dinner," her mother said, moving gracefully from a burbling dishwasher to the seven-burner stove where she expertly flipped sizzling eggplant slices in a white Le Creuset frying pan before floating back to the kitchen table to wipe an invisible speck off a gold-rimmed serving platter.

Perched on a barstool at the oversized kitchen island, Cynthia's head spun as she watched her mother whirl about, and she gripped the edge of the granite countertop for good measure. "I put out the dinnerware and set the table," she pointed out. "Besides, you know I don't cook."

Sipra was already back at the stove, her arm deep in a pot of biryani. It was always a shock to Cynthia's system, watching her mother, the wife of a millionaire, toil away in the kitchen when so many of the affluent clients she worked with relied on hired cooks or had food delivered daily. But for all her parents' luxury vehicles, teams of gardeners to tend to their sprawling lawn, and monthly trips to Vancouver to shop for the designer brands they loved, nothing could beat the taste of home.

And while Cynthia appreciated the home-cooked meals, she'd never desired to learn how to make them, much to her mother's disappointment.

"It's not too late to learn," Sipra said. "Who knows . . ."

"Spare me," Cynthia interrupted with a flippant wave of her hand. "I don't need *another* lecture on how cooking is an important wifely duty."

Her mother's back stiffened but she didn't turn away from the stove. "I wasn't going to lecture you. I think we both know you're not interested in what I have to say."

The dullness in Sipra's tone took Cynthia by surprise. She was used to razor-edged disapproval, sharp reprimands. "What *were* you going to say?" Cynthia said tentatively after an uncomfortable silence.

"What I was going to say," her mother said, "was that you never know when learning how to cook will come in handy."

"How so?"

"Well, these are the foods you grew up with, that you enjoy." Her mother's voice was soft over the clatter of a wooden spoon against metal. "And I won't be around forever to make them for you."

"Is that why you learned to cook?"

Sipra flashed her daughter a quick, faint smile. "My mother and I were very close. Cooking was an interest we both shared."

Cynthia studied the hypnotic rhythm of her mother's arm moving in smooth counterclockwise circles. She'd heard similar words before, from both her mother *and* grandmother, but in the past they'd often been part and parcel of the interrogations about who she was dating, when she would get married, and at what age she planned to have children. But right now, the words seemed different, loaded with something as indecipherable to Cynthia as the spices in her mother's most complicated dishes.

They doused Cynthia in the same kind of sad longing that washed over her whenever she inspected the collection of framed family photos her mother kept on the mantel over the family room fireplace. Those pictures were arranged chronologically and told the story of a young couple who had decided to move across the world in search of a better life together. After that first sepia-toned wedding portrait of a serious groom next to his wide-eyed, beautiful bride, Cynthia was clearly the star of the story, from pictures of an animated little girl, looking happy and carefree with a golf club in one hand, her father's hand in the other, to an awkward teenager, looking stiff and uncomfortable standing alone under a tall oak tree in a plum-colored sari.

A part of Cynthia wanted to stand up and bridge that weird, impenetrable gap that seemed to hold her and her mother at arm's length. She tried to picture herself at the stove, at her mother's side, her hands clumsily reaching for the wooden spoon. Given her impatient nature, she would probably burn dinner but at least she could learn. Or, at the very least, listen.

Cynthia still felt like that stiff, awkward teenager and she just couldn't bring herself to do it. Oh, she wanted to but that wasn't her. Besides, even if she did, they'd probably end up arguing as they often did. Or her mother would make some veiled, passive-aggressive comment and Cynthia would storm out, leaving it up to Sipra to recount the story of why their headstrong daughter was skipping family dinner. Cynthia could just picture her father shaking his head, his eyebrows lowering like the standards he had long ago set for his daughter. It was hard to get it right with her parents, to be herself with them without upsetting invisible lines drawn shakily in the sand.

With a little sigh, Cynthia ducked behind her phone as the sharp pinging of the timer sent her mother hustling to the oven. When Cynthia let out a little squeak, her mother glanced around wildly, trying to locate the second timer she'd forgotten about.

"What? What happened?" Sipra asked when Cynthia squeaked again. She hurried to the counter, her eyes lasering onto the phone in a death grip in her daughter's hands.

But Cynthia was heedless to the questioning slant of her mother's eyebrows, the way she braced her hands on the other side of the large kitchen island, palms pressed into its granite surface, as she leaned forward expectantly. Cynthia saw none of that, so shocked was she by what was on her phone.

"I . . . I . . ." The words trailed off as Cynthia's brain cells fought to formulate lucid thoughts. "Where's Dad?"

Her mother pulled back, her face pinching for a fleeting second before her usual cool mask was back. "In his study."

Phone clutched in hand, Cynthia slid off her stool and hurried to the entryway, where her father's office sat to the left of the front door. His door was cracked slightly, just enough to give Cynthia pause.

As a child, she'd spent countless hours in her father's office, playing with Hot Wheels cars at his feet as he single-finger-tapped on an ancient computer, or sitting across from him at the glass-topped desk, completing her homework, her chest puffed up at the thought of doing something as important as "working" with Daddy. She'd been his little shadow; he'd been her best friend.

Until she'd allowed teenage hormones and the thrill of having a hot *older* boyfriend cloud her judgment, prompting her to abandon everything she'd worked so hard for. Hanging out with Jimmy after school had been much more tempting than fighting to keep her number one spot on the track team, late-night phone calls more satisfying than studying for perfect grades. For three and a half lovesick months she'd ditched her father, and after that, time spent with him depended on her mother's presence, family events, and the odd, quiet car ride. For all of Cynthia's affinity for getting right to the point and speaking her mind, she'd never known what to say to her dad, whose admiration she'd lost as quickly as Jimmy Reilly had dumped her via text message.

Cynthia glanced down at the phone cradled in the palm of her damp hand and reread the last line of the email her father had forwarded to her just a few minutes ago. **Let's chat about this together**, it read.

Together.

That one little word propelled Cynthia forward on feet numb with anticipation and enough nervousness that she didn't poke her head through the crack in the door as she initially planned but practically fell in, the crown of her head charging forward as if busting through a finish line.

Wonderful.

Her father's head snapped up at her fumbling intrusion, eyes blinking owlishly. "Cynthia! Are you all right?"

Cynthia's cheeks burned as she straightened and swiped at a clump of hair that had found its way into her mouth. Holding her phone aloft, she pointed at the screen. "You wanted to chat? Together?" The last word sounded pitifully hopeful, and she wondered if he'd even heard her over the thundering of her heart as it tried to escape the confines of her chest.

Rich stared at her phone blankly for three long seconds. When he finally spoke, his voice was incredulous. "I didn't mean we needed to chat *tonight*."

The phone slipped a bit in her palm's sweaty grip, prompting Cynthia to fold her hands together in front of her. "No time like the present," she said brightly. Moronically. "Your email said you have a client you wanted me to work with?"

"Ah, yes. Ben Schaffer. He's an old friend and client of mine who owns a chain of luxury spas. They're located in Kelowna, Kamloops, and . . ." Her father trailed off, squinting at the ceiling as he tried to remember.

"Invermere," Cynthia blurted out. She could have listed the names of all three spas, which one was the most expensive to visit, and the names of all of Ben Schaffer's three daughters, two of whom Cynthia had gone to school with. As far as Cynthia was concerned, knowing her father's business—understanding every nook and cranny of Kumar Construction—was her duty if she was going to take over one day. Staff morale might've slipped through the cracks but as far as the bottom line went, Cynthia knew her shit.

But her father never seemed to notice or appreciate that, so she refrained from reciting everything she knew and waited.

"Right, Invermere." Rich's nod of approval hit Cynthia right in the solar plexus in the most pleasing way and she fought back a wide, goofy grin. "He's looking to rebrand and so I thought . . ."

Cynthia pressed her lips together.

"Well, naturally, I figured you'd be the best fit."

The best fit. Not a good fit. The *best*. Cynthia wanted to squeal. Jump up and down, clapping her hands like a deranged seal. But CEOs didn't do that, nor did they pump their fist in the air with a resounding *fuck yeah*. But, oh, the temptation was strong. There was nothing "natural" about it; her father rarely complimented her in this direct, personal way, and she couldn't remember the last time *he'd* passed along a client to Cynthia.

"I agree," she said in a voice that belied the Mardi Gras–level celebration whipping through her insides. She sounded calm, confident, and in charge. To her own ears, she'd never sounded more like her father at the head of the boardroom table, running the show. "I'll get in touch with him first thing Monday."

Rich nodded, his eyes flitting down to his phone, a subtle but classic dismissal Cynthia was all too familiar with. Her feet, however, remained rooted to the spot. The thrill of his approval—of her father *noticing* her and acknowledging her worth—was a high that she wanted to ride for as long as possible. Her eyes roamed to the console at the left side of the room where three gold photo frames sat in a tidy row, angled so precisely that it was clear Sipra's hands had played a role in styling the room.

Cynthia wandered over and picked up the nearest frame. It was a picture of her as a toddler, taking what looked to be first steps toward her father's waiting arms.

"Wow, I was one chubby baby," she commented.

Her father made a noncommittal sound in the back of his throat.

Cynthia picked up the second frame. Her again, this time maybe seven or eight years old, in a soccer jersey and long black braids, her foot balanced on a soccer ball.

"Soccer was not my sport," she murmured to herself. She'd never excelled in team sports. Even as a young girl, she'd wanted to be everywhere at once, play all the positions, and excel at every single thing on the field.

"You were the fastest runner on the team," her father interjected.

When Cynthia turned in surprise, he had abandoned his precious phone and had swiveled his chair to face her, eyes on the frame in her hands. Belatedly, Cynthia remembered that her father had coached her team through those two short years of outdoor soccer.

She half smiled. "Yeah, that's why I developed an interest in track," she said, replacing the photo carefully so it lined up nicely with the others again.

Cynthia picked up the last frame, unsurprised to find yet another picture of her. It was taken a few years after the soccer photo: she and her dad standing next to their bicycles, matching grins on their sun-kissed faces.

"We tried to do every trail that summer," her father said, joining her at the console. With a great deal of tenderness, he took the frame from Cynthia's hands and examined the picture. "Some of them were very challenging for an eleven-year-old, but you were determined."

Cynthia studied her father, but he wasn't looking at her. His soft gaze was for the picture in his hands, for a moment in time they could never get back.

"My ambitious little girl," he murmured.

Cynthia took a small step back from the onslaught of memories lined up neatly on the tabletop and wondered why her father's hands had been so quick to catch her first wobbly steps as a baby but not as a teenager. Why he couldn't look past those mistakes to see that she had learned her lesson and had worked to make herself the best version she could be.

Why the mistakes of a young woman had set the blueprint for the rest of their relationship.

Without realizing she was doing so, Cynthia's hand tightened around her phone. Whether she was grasping for that high that had occurred only a few minutes ago or grounding all her frustration and desperation into the poor, defenseless smartphone pressed uncomfortably tight into her skin, she wasn't sure exactly what to say. She wished more than anything she could change the past, change her father's mind.

But he'd passed a client—no, one of his *old friends*—on to her. It wasn't much, but it was something.

And it meant the world to her.

CHAPTER 18

Four twenty-five in the afternoon was quickly becoming Rohit's favorite part of the day because it meant he would see Cynthia soon. It was a little routine they'd wordlessly fallen into in the last few weeks, checking in with each other at the end of the day, sometimes to discuss how their special project was progressing, sometimes just to talk. Once, after an arduous day of leading team-building activities, he'd run out and grabbed them ice cream sundaes and they'd spent the hour not talking at all. Instead, they'd sat side by side spooning their desserts—caramel for him, chocolate fudge for her—and watching cat videos on her computer.

When the clock showed he had one minute until golden hour, Rohit didn't even pretend to play it cool; he bolted from his seat, his inner compass guiding him to where her office was located at the end of the hall.

He slowed to a stop, however, when he realized that Gayle from HR was parked outside Cynthia's office, leaning against the door-frame as if she'd been there for a while.

"I know you and Rohit have things covered but I couldn't help myself," Gayle was saying. "I drafted a list of where we might host a company social for employees and their families."

The comment brought a small smile to Rohit's face. Since they'd conducted their staff survey and held focus groups, there had been a notable increase in staff engagement at Kumar Construction. Cynthia and Rohit might have driven the introduction of regular team-building meetings and policies to protect employee work-life balance, but more and more staff were trying their hand behind the wheel.

Rohit's lips pulled into a puzzled frown, however, when he heard Cynthia's voice.

"Oh . . ." she said faintly. "That's great. Really . . . great."

It wasn't a lack of enthusiasm Rohit detected but an uncertainty in Cynthia's voice, or perhaps it was apprehension. Whatever it was, it was a far cry from the cool, unshakable confidence he was used to.

Luckily, Gayle didn't seem to notice. "I think so, too!" she agreed, clapping her hands and stepping back into the hallway. It was then that she noticed Rohit lingering a few feet away and beckoned him forward. "Oh, Rohit! I was just telling Cynthia about my research for the staff picnic."

"I heard," Rohit said, smiling back and ambling forward as if he hadn't just been caught lurking outside Cynthia's office. "We welcome the ideas. Maybe we could assemble a group of interested staff to help plan the event."

Gayle nodded. "That would be wonderful! I know several people who would be interested in sitting on a planning committee for these kinds of activities."

Rohit peeked into Cynthia's office, waiting for her to chime in, but when she simply stared back in silence, he turned his attention to the older lady. "Why don't we run it up the flagpole? Cynthia and I can propose the idea at the next leadership meeting." He couldn't help but inch his way past Gayle to shuffle into Cynthia's office—four thirty was his time, after all.

She nodded back. "That's perfect." She threw a wary-looking Cynthia a little wave. "I'm heading off. You two have a nice evening."

Rohit barely noticed her departure, his gaze locked on Cynthia as he closed her office door and took the seat across from her desk. Regardless of the day he'd had—whether a disgruntled client complaining about labor costs or a disorganized site visit or a bad falafel—at four thirty P.M., everything felt right in Rohit's world.

But not for Cynthia today, apparently. She was staring at the spot where Gayle had just been, her eyebrows drawn together, forehead adorably crinkled.

"That's happening more and more," she murmured, almost as if she was talking to herself.

In the past, he might've read her low, trancelike voice as a cue to back off or change the subject. But if there was any sliver of this formidable woman opening up to him, there was no way in hell Rohit wouldn't try to wedge his foot in the door. At this point, he'd happily surrender his heart as a doorstop if it meant gleaning just a little more of what lay beneath Cynthia's flawless, ice-smooth surface.

"What is?" he asked.

"People dropping by my office randomly to share their ideas or offer feedback on some of the initiatives we've launched." Her eyes met his. "It's . . ."

"Overwhelming?"

The tension on her beautiful face eased and a light blush seeped onto her cheeks. "Yeah. I'm not used to . . ." Cynthia cleared her throat. "I'm usually doing my own thing around here."

Rohit cocked his head, considering. He was receiving similar visits but since starting at Kumar Construction, he was used to staff at all levels of the organization dropping by to say hello or ask for his help on a proposal or offer him the first sample of whatever they'd baked to bring in to work that day.

But it was no secret that Cynthia's reality at Kumar Construction hadn't been that way and as her cheeks steadily darkened, Rohit's insides filled with the warmth of soft, aching tenderness. She looked so unsure about something that most people took for granted that part of him wanted to kneel before her feet and assure her that time spent with her was a damn *privilege*.

It would be a cheesy and ridiculous move on his part, and she'd probably hate it.

Before he could think of something adequate to say, Cynthia spoke first. "Rohit?" she asked quietly.

"Yeah?" he rasped. Dear God, he sounded *breathless*. But how else could a man sound when Cynthia Kumar hit him with wide, trusting, liquid-amber eyes?

"Can we . . . I mean . . . Can you . . ." Cynthia took a deep breath. "Can you take on dealing with . . ." She lowered her eyes, heat rising to her cheeks again.

"The people?" he finished gently.

Her head snapped up, relief and embarrassment vying for ground on her pink face. "It's stupid, I know. I *should* be able to handle this. It's just, after everything, I'm not . . ." Cynthia shook her head and smiled bitterly. "I guess I'm not cut out to win the popularity contest around here."

It would've been easy to force a chuckle and move on from what was clearly an awkward confession on Cynthia's part, but Rohit knew her well enough by now to understand the slight hunch in her shoulders, the self-deprecation twisting her lips, and it made his heart swell for her.

"Change is hard," he said. "And right now, people are excited. It'll die down. But," he hurried to add when Cynthia opened her mouth to speak, "I'm more than happy to be the go-to guy for their feedback and suggestions." He didn't add that it would be an *honor* to help her in any way he could.

He had some pride, after all.

And maybe she already knew because her lips lifted in a small smile—the first real smile he'd seen since stepping into her office this afternoon. "Thanks, Rohit." She pushed her chair back. "I'm ready to get out of here. Want to walk out together?"

Rohit nodded. "Let me grab my stuff."

They were waiting for the elevator when a familiar voice caught their attention.

"Cynthia, Rohit! I was hoping to catch you two before you left for the day," Rich said, coming up behind them.

Rohit's heart sank as he glanced at the stack of unsealed envelopes in Rich's hands, but when the sound of the elevator doors sliding open reverberated behind them, neither he nor Cynthia dared to turn around.

"What's up?" Cynthia asked, her voice uncharacteristically cautious, and Rohit couldn't help but shoot her a surprised glance. She was usually the first to welcome additional tasks in her already jam-packed days, without ever uttering a word of complaint about the long hours.

"I've been meaning to ask you . . ." Rich glanced down at the papers in his hand, momentarily distracted, and Rohit resisted the urge to shuffle his feet impatiently. "Sorry," Rich continued, looking up again. "I've been meaning to *tell* the two of you, great work."

"Great work," Cynthia repeated.

"Yes. We may have had a bumpy start"—Rich paused to cock an amused brow in Rohit's direction—"but I think you've both done an excellent job with the task I assigned you and I'm very proud of you."

When Cynthia seemed at a loss for words, Rohit smiled while reaching behind to press the button that would summon the elevator again. "Thank you, sir."

Rich nodded. "Have a great evening," he said, swiftly turning on his heel and heading in the direction of his office.

The elevator opened right away this time and Rohit eagerly stepped inside beside a shell-shocked Cynthia. He shot her a teasing glance. "Guess it's not so bad being Mrs. Rogers after all, right?"

She turned to him, confusion clouding her beautiful eyes. "What?"

Rohit's grin faltered. "That day on the ramp outside the building? You called me Mr. Rogers?" He grimaced. "Did I not use it right?"

Cynthia burst out laughing, and before Rohit's brain could register more than the rush of sandalwood hitting his nostrils, her arms were around him. Cynthia Kumar was hugging him in the elevator, her body still shaking with mirth, her hair silky against the underside of his jaw. Beneath the glare of a too-bright overhead light, even with so many layers between them—blazers and buttons and laptop bag straps—it was the most perfect hug Rohit could remember ever receiving. There was nothing to do, he realized as his arms belatedly returned the embrace, but hold on and feel like the luckiest man on earth.

It was over all too soon. "No, that wasn't right," Cynthia said, pulling away as the elevator reached the lobby. "But I needed that." She fell silent as they walked toward the exit of the Desmond

Business Center and Rohit gave in to the sheer pleasure of stealing glances at the side of her face. Her eyes were still bright, the remnants of a good laugh lifting the corners of her lips in the most captivating way.

And just as they reached the doors, she shocked the hell out of him again.

"Do you want to hang out tonight?" she asked.

CHAPTER 19

Air conditioner on, check. Innocuous background music, check.

From where she leaned against her kitchen island, Cynthia surveyed the rest of her apartment and nodded to herself. Immaculate. Everything was in its place, tidy and gleaming, and thanks to her keen eye, it could've been the spread of an interior design magazine. But when her eye roved to the island countertop, she grimaced.

The meat rosette she had researched online and painstakingly put together was unfurling before her eyes, petal by petal, into an unappetizing pink-red lump of rumpled salami.

"Shit," she muttered, pushing herself away from the island and the charcuterie board she'd been obsessing over for the better part of the hour. She stalked to the fridge for fresh slices of meat, noticing with dismay that her sweaty palms had left streaks on the shiny metal handle of her stainless-steel fridge. Cynthia changed course and yanked a new dish towel out of a drawer, dried her hands, and cleaned the fridge handle.

And the handle of the dish towel drawer for good measure.

When there was nothing left to wipe, Cynthia took a quick lap around her minimalist living room, fluffing a throw pillow here, straightening a stack of coffee table books there. Thanks to her monthly cleaning service, there wasn't much to do, and her feet wandered back to the kitchen. It wasn't until her hand was reaching for the refrigerator door handle once more that she realized what she was doing.

Zero chill, check.

Cynthia shook her head in disgust. She was acting as if she'd never invited anyone to hang out at her condo before. Granted, her work schedule didn't leave much room for entertaining, but Cynthia knew how to host. She was well-versed in wine and the perfect food-serving-to-guest-number ratio. Photoshoot-worthy presentation was her *thing*.

Failed meat rosette notwithstanding.

But the thought of *Rohit* coming over had her reaching for the dish towel again if for no other reason than to wipe down the spotless island with rough, jerky swipes. When a knock sounded at her door, a nervous yelp popped out of her mouth.

When Cynthia opened the door, Rohit took one, long look at her and froze in the hallway.

"What?" she asked, unsure how to adopt a casual pose when he looked so good standing in her doorway. He still wore what he'd worn to work that day, minus the suit jacket, and had rolled up his shirtsleeves as if he knew exactly how much her palms longed to feel the solid curves of his strong forearms again.

Rohit's eyes traveled down her oversized, off-the-shoulder cream sweater and loose black lounge pants to her feet. When he met her gaze again, his half smile made Cynthia want to hide behind the door, but the twinkle in his eyes held her hostage.

"I don't think I've ever seen you in anything but heels," he said.

Cynthia's toes wriggled in her fuzzy open-toed slippers. "Who wears heels in their home?"

Rohit eyed her feet again. "Right. But I didn't expect . . ." When he finally tore himself away, there was a noticeable shift in his gaze, something hard to read but intense enough that a delicious frisson of awareness tap-danced up her spine. "Can I come in?"

Wordlessly, Cynthia stepped aside, watching as Rohit took in her clean, airy home.

"Now, this apartment? Not a surprise," he commented. "Although the orange is unexpected."

Cynthia considered her surroundings. The neutral palette boasted mostly warm grays and soft whites with the odd pop of burnt orange to catch the eye. "It's my favorite color," she admitted, embarrassed by the delicate heat creeping between her collarbones.

"I like it," Rohit said, his eyes catching the charcuterie board on the kitchen island. "Is that for us?"

Cynthia hurried to the cupboards and grabbed some small plates. "If you want." When she caught Rohit's pleased smile, she hastened to add, "Or whatever. I mean, if you're hungry."

When Rohit joined her side, the plates slipped from her hands and clattered onto the table. "You can ignore that," Cynthia said, pointing to the lump of Genoa salami in the middle of the board.

"Why?"

"I tried to make a meat rosette."

"A . . . a what?"

"A meat rosette. Like a flower." When Rohit's forehead wrinkled in confusion, as it often did when she threw unfamiliar slang or colloquialisms his way, Cynthia glanced around for her phone, wondering if she still had the tutorial tab open. But when she spotted her phone across the room on the docking station, she opted to show him what she meant instead, joining her hands together in front of her chest, fingers clawlike, in a poor imitation of a rosette.

"It's a flower made of—" When Rohit chuckled, she slapped his arm. "Shut up. I found it online and thought I'd try it out. Sorry I'm not Martha fucking Stewart."

"So, you googled 'meat flower'?"

"Yes."

"And weird, fetish sites *didn't* pop up?"

Cynthia fought to keep a straight face. "Maybe. It was mostly meat."

The word *meat* plopped heavily between them, and they stared at each other in silence for approximately five seconds before cracking up.

"I'm touched," Rohit said between peals of laughter, "that you'd go to the trouble of making me a meat blossom."

"Meat flower," Cynthia said, trying to sound haughty and failing miserably. "It's a meat *flower.*"

"Meat flower," Rohit wheezed. "A *meat flower.*"

Cynthia wiped her eyes and turned toward the wine rack built in the end of her kitchen island. "Do you want some wine?" She stopped short. "Wait, do you drink?"

It was a stupid question and fully deserving of the burn of mortification—and something else—that weaved through Cynthia as she remembered the night they met. The beer bottle she'd pulled out of his hands. Inexplicable heat.

The look that flashed across Rohit's face told Cynthia he remembered, too, but his voice was deceptively neutral when he answered. "Wine would be great," he said, accepting the bottle Cynthia handed him.

The moment of levity over, the sound of Rohit pouring the dark red liquid into *her* wineglasses in *her* home rushed against Cynthia's eardrums and she couldn't resist shuffling her feet again.

"Okay, what's up?" Rohit asked as he filled his own glass. Cynthia couldn't tear her eyes away from his hands. Her baser instincts remembered the slide of those clever hands exploring the dips and planes of her body. Every reverent touch had been a slow, seductive performance for her alone.

And now, even the fucking hair on his knuckles made her skin flush.

"Cynthia?" he prompted before bringing the glass of lush, deep ruby liquid to his mouth.

"S-sorry?"

"You look . . ." Rohit paused to study her, and once again, his eyes lingered half a second too long on her slippers. "You're not acting like yourself. I feel like you're nervous or anxious or . . . something."

She was *burning*, but Cynthia cleared her throat and opted for a safer response. "I'm a little weirded out. You're in my apartment, Rohit. You're in my apartment, drinking wine, and I tried to put together a charcuterie board for you. For us." Cynthia's arms lifted helplessly. "A month ago, this would've been the backdrop of a crime scene and I'd be standing over your dead body with a bunch of black garbage bags in my hands, but now we're, like, hanging out. Voluntarily."

"I'm going to skip over the garbage bag part and point out that you've been to my apartment before."

"That was for a special occasion. This is different."

Popping a cube of cheese into his mouth, Rohit looked less concerned, but his dark eyes were watchful, and he remained silent, as if he knew there was more.

And there was. A month ago, Rohit's uncanny ability of knowing when something weighed on her mind and stepping back to give her the space to work through her thoughts would've had her reaching for the sharpest tool in her knife block, but now a sweet feeling drizzled through her when she glanced at his patient, observant face.

This man, she thought as she expelled a long, silent sigh. "Everything feels kind of surreal lately. My dad . . ." Cynthia's breath caught because she couldn't bring herself to revisit her father's words to her earlier today. *I'm very proud of you*, he'd said. Granted, he'd been addressing them both but still . . . The moment was still too fresh for close inspection right now.

Instead, she tilted her head and shared another small, strange success from last Sunday night. "My dad recently referred an important client of his to me because he thinks I'd be a good fit to help with the rebrand of his chain of spas."

She had to pause to fight against the thickening lump in her throat. "He's never . . . I've never . . . I've always had to bulldoze my way into his business. I've spent most of my career feeling like I've had to claw for scraps. But suddenly, it's like I have something to offer. *Finally*." Cynthia raked her fingers through her hair. "This is what I've been working for my entire life, what I've dreamed working with my father would be like. And now that it's in my lap and . . . I don't know, I feel stressed and excited and weird . . ." She shrugged helplessly. "I don't know how to deal with it all."

"You're tense."

"I'm always tense." Cynthia's lips twisted into a wry smile, gesturing at the neat, perfect living room behind her with a flick of her wrist. "I mean, have I ever known how to relax?"

Rohit drained his glass before grabbing Cynthia's full glass off the countertop and handing it to her.

"I get it," he said, his eyelids lowering to half-mast as he watched her take a long sip. He leaned back against the kitchen island, arms crossed over his chest, body loose and relaxed, but his gaze was intense. "Even though you're getting what you want, it's still going to rock your world. I felt that way when I flew here for the first time. I'd wanted to come to North America my entire life, and while I was ecstatic to finally be here, it was a lot to take in. It was a shock, and it took a long time for things to sink in and for me to find my footing."

"You immigrated, by yourself, across the world while I'm freaking out about making headway at work. It's not comparable and I'm an asshole."

"No, you're not. It's change," Rohit said simply, reminding her that he'd said something similar earlier that day when she'd asked for his help. It had been mortifying, admitting her weakness, trying to contain her agitated nerves over something as ridiculous as being on the receiving end of her coworkers' interest and excitement.

But he'd understood and she hadn't felt weak, stupid, or incapable. She couldn't resist moving a little closer to him as if drawn forward by a force much stronger than her will.

Or maybe she was just done fighting it.

"Change is hard, and unexpected even when you're expecting it," Rohit added.

"So, what do I do?" Cynthia reached around Rohit to put the glass back on the counter, trying not to notice the press of his arm against hers. She didn't linger but she didn't edge away from the contact, either.

Rohit inhaled deeply. "I don't have an answer for you," he said, his voice a little strained. "But I do know you deserve all these good things. That you've earned them."

Something swelled against the inner walls of Cynthia's heart and the lump was back in the base of her throat. She'd worked her whole adult life to believe those words, and hearing them said out loud by Rohit of all people robbed her of the ability to speak. It was like a gift she was afraid to touch, dared not look at too long.

But it pulled her in as if her body had detached itself from her brain completely in favor of living on instinct alone. She moved closer and searched his dark, distended pupils for an answer she wasn't surprised to unearth: desire, mirrored back and beckoning.

"Do you really believe that?" Her voice was husky.

Rohit's lips parted, his body so still as she slinked even closer. Even through the thick material of her sweater, Cynthia felt the firm planes of his chest against the subtle, hardly-there brush of her breasts.

"Yes," he murmured, his lips barely moving.

Although Cynthia's heart pounded, the tension and heat in Rohit's body beckoned her forward and unleashed something in her that echoed the woman she'd embodied in the bar on a night that suddenly didn't feel that long ago.

Fueled by tequila and disappointment, that woman had been reckless and greedy, even while out of her element in that bar. That woman had worn red.

"I thought I was the Ice Princess," Cynthia teased, her body following suit as she risked another barely-there brush against his chest.

Rohit's eyes flew down to her mouth and he shook his head. "I was wrong when I called you a princess," he said, his voice pitched low, his head curving toward hers. "You're a queen."

Cynthia caught the tail end of Rohit's words when she pressed her lips against his. She was rewarded by those slow, steady hands rising to caress the bottom of her rib cage before sliding to her back and splaying wide, like an anchor.

While her mouth remembered his with unabashed enthusiasm, it was the insistence of his arms pulling her closer that let her body revel in his, a welcome return to warmth and defined muscle that she'd explored over a year ago. Physically, she remembered him well, and yet her brain was mesmerized anew. Had his chest always been so wide? Had the push of his hips against hers been so wonderfully persistent?

The tightening in her core thought so.

Rohit's tongue gliding over hers was the smooth slide of their wine, full-bodied and intoxicating. Every cell in Cynthia's body was wrung dry for him, and *this kiss* that walked the line between familiarity and raw, unabashed relief quenched every thirsty nerve ending. He explored everything her mouth had to offer, the bow of her top lip, the eager slide of her tongue. His fingers flexed against the middle of her back as if he was reminding himself to maintain control, to not burn himself on the lick of fire Cynthia always kept at bay.

But she wanted to give it to him. Wanted to pull Rohit into her, feel his strong, steady hands on her heat. Cynthia poured herself into their kiss. She wanted to goad him, challenge him for all he was worth.

How wet could he make her? How desperate?

Her hands were pressed against his chest and Cynthia couldn't resist slipping the index finger of her left hand in the slim space between the buttons of his shirt. A part of her brain cautioned against this decision, that she was trespassing into dangerous territory. For the past year, the two of them had been separated by suits and boardrooms and the eyes of others judging their worth.

This was more than crossing a line—her touch might scorch

him, send him running. But when the pad of her finger made contact with his bare skin, Rohit responded with a full-body shudder and pulled her even closer, his mouth hard, hungry, and impossibly hotter. His tongue grew wild and unpolished against hers, the hands on her back possessive.

And still she wanted more.

Cynthia wasn't sure if she had voiced her desire out loud, but Rohit pulled back roughly, his breathing uneven and his eyes heavy-lidded. "I want to kiss you everywhere."

Cynthia's mind was three steps ahead of Rohit's, already picturing them in her bed, half-undressed in twisted sheets. "Then do it," she challenged, taking his hand and leading him down the hallway.

CHAPTER 20

"Can I go down on you?"

Cynthia froze as the words penetrated her cloudy senses. They were a tangle of limbs, half-unbuttoned pants, and sliding bra straps, when Rohit's question brushed against the sensitive skin just below her earlobe. He punctuated the request with a gentle bite and Cynthia shivered.

"What?"

Rohit propped himself onto his elbow and tenderly brushed a lock of hair back from Cynthia's face. "I want to eat you out until you faint." His solemn face broke out into a half smile. "Or until I do. Until whoever has less stamina passes out."

"Probably you," Cynthia retorted on a gasp as his fingers traced the band of her underwear, patiently awaiting permission.

Rohit's eyes trailed downward to his waiting fingers and, as if he couldn't resist, his hand slid down to cup her. But Cynthia couldn't be embarrassed by the wetness seeping through her panties, not when Rohit inhaled sharply, his hand tensing against the proof of her desire before squeezing her gently.

She wanted this too much.

"Can I go down on you," he repeated in a raspy voice, dragging hooded, lust-drunk eyes back to her face. "Please?"

"Yes," she replied because what other response was there when he looked at her like that?

Rohit's answering smile was so much more than the charm and charisma Cynthia knew so well—there was relief there, too, and an eagerness that made her center pulse and *ache* to be touched. Cynthia arched her hips upward and tugged off her pants, aware that Rohit watched her every move as if committing the slide of fabric down her legs to memory. When she hooked her fingers on the sides of her panties, he stopped her.

"No," he said, his voice tight and hoarse. "Please, let me."

Cynthia's heartbeat pounded in her ears as she slowly pulled her hands away to rest above her head, palms up, surrendering. When Rohit didn't move, her fingers gripped the bedsheet and she cleared her throat.

"What's wrong?" she asked.

Tipping his head back, Rohit closed his eyes and exhaled on a rough chuckle, and Cynthia made a mental note to lick the column of his throat later. "Nothing. I've just fantasized about this moment an embarrassing number of times and now that it's happening . . ." He met her gaze and a small, self-deprecating smile quirked his lips. "I need a minute to calm down."

Cynthia laughed as Rohit moved between her thighs and, once again, traced the top of her underwear with his finger. Back and forth, back and forth, the tip of his index finger scorched a teasing line against her skin. When Cynthia's hips began to shift restlessly, Rohit smiled wickedly and moved his finger to trace the outline of her underwear against her right thigh.

Back and forth, back and forth.

"Get on with it," she ordered, inwardly wincing at how impatient she sounded. Not sexy.

But Rohit's eyes smoldered. "Damn. Why does that voice always turn me on?"

"You like when I'm bossy?"

He nipped the inside of her thigh. "Since the start."

Before she could unpack that one, he leaned forward and pressed a lingering, closed-mouth kiss to her covered slit and breathed her in. Cynthia dug her heels into the mattress, forcing herself to stay still as Rohit's tongue lapped her through her underwear. This was a new experience for Cynthia, but the damp pressure where she needed it most coupled with the friction of her black cotton underwear against her clit was surprisingly pleasing.

It felt good and it made her hot, but it wasn't enough for the tightness she felt there—that she felt everywhere. She wanted to unravel and she wanted it *now*.

As if sensing her impatience, Rohit pulled off the barrier with rough, undisciplined hands and *yes*, that was what Cynthia needed. She wanted him as frantic as she felt. Before the air could cool the wetness between her thighs, Rohit's mouth was there, tongue exploring every soft fold.

Cynthia closed her eyes, enjoying the sensation of Rohit's mouth on her, his grip firm where he held her hips. The sound of his wet tongue on her even wetter flesh was the only sound in the quiet room and the realization made her feel downright sinful, her body loose and pliant under his attention. But it wasn't until his tongue flicked her clit *hard* that Cynthia was powerless against her hips bucking upward as a spasm of raw pleasure shot up her spine.

Perhaps she'd been wrong about Rohit's stamina because he began feasting on her anew, his tongue forceful and merciless, flicking and swirling in a dozen wonderful patterns that wound Cynthia so impossibly tight that her toes began scratching at the sheets, her fingers curling into tight fists.

For once, she couldn't analyze or anticipate his next move. She could only succumb to pleasure and let someone else take charge for a change.

Not just *someone*. Rohit.

Even as her entire body thrummed with the heady desire for release, a persistent thought vibrated in the back of Cynthia's mind: she had only ever felt this way with Rohit.

She was as sure of this as she knew, despite his ministrations feeling so, *so* good, they wouldn't be enough to send her over the edge. He had brought her close to that delicate, splintering place, but it wouldn't be enough to free-fall.

When her hips eventually slowed and sank back into the mattress, Rohit's head popped up. "What's wrong?"

The note of uncertainty in his tone made her breath hitch and Cynthia squeezed her eyes shut, willing her body to do what she wanted it to do. To get the job done.

"Cynthia," he prodded in a gentle voice. "Tell me what you need, and I'll do it."

Her voice was breathy, just shy of a needy whine. "What you're doing feels great but . . . I need more . . ."

"More . . . ?"

When she didn't answer right away, Rohit's left hand came to rest on her upper thigh as he waited. But it wasn't the gentle patience on his face that beckoned this difficult truth forward. It was the quiet assurance of his large, warm palm against her skin: he wouldn't pull away because she was being difficult or complicated or uncertain.

"Pressure," Cynthia admitted quietly. "I need more pressure."

She couldn't help but close her eyes, just in case she was wrong about him. In the silence that followed her painstaking admission, Cynthia mentally coached herself not to react if frustration was splashed across Rohit's face, if he walked away without a second glance.

But when she dared to open her eyes, another wicked smile was slanted across Rohit's face.

"I have an idea," he said, sounding peculiarly cheerful for someone who had just received the news that he was failing to bring his partner to orgasm. He flipped onto his back beside her. "Climb on."

Cynthia raised herself onto her elbows and glanced at his lower half, still in dress pants and obviously erect. "What?"

Rohit was grinning at the ceiling in anticipation. "Sit on my face," he said. "Ride me until you come."

"Are you serious?" Cynthia looked down at her thighs and then his face, her neck heating. She'd never done anything like that before, had certainly *never* received an offer like this.

"Very."

"I don't think . . ." She trailed off and bit her lower lip.

"You don't need to think," Rohit assured her. "I've thought about this enough for the both of us. Many times."

Cynthia remembered Rohit's earlier confession of fantasizing about her, and a rush of potent awareness rolled over her, hot and *almost* strong enough to overcome her uncertainty. "What if . . . What if I suffocate you?"

"I can't think of a better way to die."

Her shyness dissolved and she couldn't help but laugh as she moved to scoot up the bed. Gingerly, she straddled Rohit's face, her hands resting on the top of her headboard for balance as she hovered above him on her knees.

"Cynthia," he said from beneath her. "I want nothing more than for you to use my face to make yourself come. Please." His hands rose to cup her hips and with subtle pressure, he coaxed her downward until, with a groan Cynthia could feel vibrating between her thighs, his lips made contact and he began devouring her.

Unsure of what to do, Cynthia tried to relax but her knees began to hurt, her thighs straining to stay upright in this position. Maybe she'd just hold still for a few more minutes and fake it for Rohit's sake. It wouldn't be one of her prouder moments but at least he was trying. He deserved *something* for at least noticing her discomfort earlier and offering an alternative.

Cynthia swallowed a sigh and, to relieve the increasing ache in her knees, leaned forward on her hands so the headboard could bear some of her weight and—

Oh. *Oh.*

This position was *interesting.* The subtle shift forward pushed her clit into his upper lip, bringing her in direct contact with the delicious friction of his stubble. It felt *fucking* good, and Cynthia couldn't suppress a whimper as a jolt of pleasure shocked her core. The coarse texture was similar to the rasp of cotton when Rohit had licked her through her underwear, but this was next level. This was hard, and rough, and as Cynthia subtly ground her hips downward, she could feel herself growing even wetter on Rohit's eager tongue.

Despite Rohit's reassurance, the fleeting thought that she might actually be suffocating him threaded through her brain and Cynthia looked down.

Oh, shit. Rohit was looking right back at her, his dark gaze roving over her face as if drinking her in. His eyes moved from her half-lowered lids to the flush on her cheeks and, lastly, her parted lips, and his irises completely disappeared into the black, inky depths of his dilated pupils. When he met her eyes again, he looked so utterly devoted to her—to her pleasure and satisfaction—that any inhibitions that were holding Cynthia back flew away. For a moment, it was like she could see herself through his point of view, and the picture that flashed before her eyes wasn't messy or difficult or unapproachable.

She was beautiful. Her black hair falling forward, curtaining her face from everything but his appreciative view, one of the straps of her black bra sliding temptingly down her arm. Her back muscles flexing with every roll of her hips. She was disheveled and wild and powerful.

Cynthia felt inordinately sexy sitting on top of this man. A man who made friends wherever he went and whose every word, action, and success seemed effortless. A man who looked at her now like he was hers to command. In that moment, Cynthia knew, without a doubt, that he would lie here and pleasure her with his mouth for as long as she needed—no, *wanted*—and then thank her for it afterward.

And she would believe him. That realization was all Cynthia needed to press her hands more firmly onto the headboard and hold on.

She began riding his face in earnest, mindless to everything except the swelling of her clit and the hard grind of her greedy hips as she sought fulfillment. With every downward press and forceful, upward drag, the pleasure inside her coiled more tightly. Sharpened. Her hamstrings burned deliciously as she ground against him, and she was vaguely aware of Rohit's hands tightening on her hips, encouraging her to do it again. And again.

And again, until she was shamelessly chasing the sweet splendor of crashing over the edge. So intent was she on her just-out-of-reach climax that she didn't care that she was outright moaning now, barely noticed that one of Rohit's hands had detached itself from her body, unbuttoned his pants, and was stroking himself with rough, uneven pulls.

In this moment, Cynthia had zero concern for how she looked or sounded and it felt fucking amazing.

Although she had, to a certain extent, orchestrated her own orgasm, it still shocked the hell out of her. This was no sharp, delicious burst followed by a hot, preciously short moment of release. The climax was devastating. Her entire body shuddered and her core throbbed like a winded heartbeat for what felt like endless minutes. Her skin glowed with sweat and she was out of breath, chest actually heaving as she willed her boneless, satiated limbs to get moving so she could climb off him.

In the end, Rohit's chuckle teased her clit one last time before he lifted her off him and gently deposited her to his side, leaving her nothing to do but enjoy the wake of tremors still fluttering through her. Her heart felt like it might burst. Cynthia wasn't sure if she wanted to climb back on or pass out, nor was she sure if the warmth flooding her cheeks was elation or mortification because, only moments ago, she had lost control of everything but the selfish desire for pleasure.

Pressing a kiss to his shoulder, Cynthia snaked her hand down his stomach. "Your turn."

Rohit grabbed her wrist, stopping her. "Too late."

"You . . . you came?"

"Cynthia Kumar was riding my face," Rohit said with zero traces of embarrassment, and Cynthia's toes curled in delight. "Of course I came."

Cynthia moved her arm upward and hugged his chest instead. She couldn't stop herself from squeezing tight, nor could she help but laugh when she heard Rohit's dreamily murmured words:

"Yes, I would gladly die that way."

CHAPTER 21

The scent of sandalwood teased Rohit awake the next morning as the first notes of daybreak crept through the window. Cocooned in some *very* nice, high-quality bedsheets, he turned onto his side, ignoring the pleas of his lazy, sated body that would happily welcome another hour of sleep.

But, for Rohit, there was no better reward than a glimpse of the most impressive woman he'd ever met lying beside him, fast asleep. Even now, peacefully at rest, Cynthia projected strength. She lay on her back, one arm curved over her head, her hand in a loose fist, the other flat on the mattress, a few inches from his own. He was careful not to brush against it, or do anything, really, that would rob him of the opportunity to watch her like this, unguarded and peaceful.

He'd always found her beautiful—even when she had seemed to hate his guts—but he realized now that she might always be a bit of a mystery to him. He'd seen her hard and he'd seen her soft, had witnessed her uncompromising will as well as her shy vulnerability. He'd been on the receiving end of her blunt impatience, but he'd basked in her warmth and humor, too. Cynthia was that undefinable moment between the tentative, hazy dawn and a bright, bold morning.

In the year they'd worked together, she'd always been too damn smart for her own good—except when it came to him. She was completely unaware that he couldn't keep his eyes off her. That, despite her antagonism, she was a force to be reckoned with, one he didn't want to stay away from.

She was unpredictable and he'd be content just trying to keep up for the rest of his life. Carefully, Rohit rolled to look over the side of the bed and reached into the pocket of the pants he had discarded right before falling asleep. Pulling out his phone, Rohit hunched his shoulders to shield Cynthia from the glare of the screen and was greeted by two unwelcome realizations: one, it was only five fifteen in the morning; and two, he had three missed video calls—one from his mother and two from his sister.

Damn it. Counting back, Rohit tried to recall the last time he'd talked to them. The last few weeks were a blur of introducing new changes at work, analyzing the outcomes, and, well, spending time with Cynthia. It was all too easy to forget his obligations when Cynthia's smile had become a recurring gift in his life.

Rohit placed the phone on the mattress, screen down, and tapped his fingers on the back of its case. Missed calls from home were not usually jarring, even during sleeping hours. His family was more likely to call him whenever the mood struck rather than according to time zone etiquette. But uneasiness nettled against the back of Rohit's neck and he picked up the phone again, unsure of what to do.

"Everything okay?" The question was thick with sleep and satisfaction, and the better part of Rohit's brain felt the immediate tug toward more pleasing things like buttery, sandalwood-scented sheets wrapped around a luscious, sandalwood-scented woman.

Leaving his phone behind, Rohit turned and almost groaned at the perfection awaiting him. Propped on her elbow, head in her palm, Cynthia was watching him, her hair soft and tangled, sheet pulled just high enough to offer a glimpse of cleavage that Rohit unabashedly enjoyed, much to her amusement.

"Rohit?"

"Yeah?" he asked, scooting closer.

"Is everything okay?" Cynthia asked again.

Rohit stopped midscoot, rolled onto his back, and palmed his phone again.

With a little shake of his head, Rohit held the screen up to show Cynthia. "Three missed calls from my family." When he noticed Cynthia squinting against the glare of the phone screen, he winced. "Sorry," he said before tossing it farther down the bed between their bodies.

"You can call them back if you want to," Cynthia said, again burrowing under the covers, and Rohit forlornly eyed the disappearing expanse of soft, tawny skin.

"Nah, I'm sure it'll just be the usual rundown of what am I doing and what am I eating from my dad followed by Mom's detailed report about each of her three sisters, filling me in on the gossip and their passive-aggressive behaviors. Then my sister will grab the phone and tell me about school and complain about the hardships of living at home even though she's still a teenager. And just when I think the call is almost done, Maisa will then ask about my job, and my parents will run back into the room because they love hearing about their big, important son who is living the dream in America."

Although the last little bit sounded bitter in Rohit's ears, Cynthia didn't seem to notice.

"You mean Canada," she corrected with a yawn.

"It's all the same to them," Rohit joked with forced cheeriness that masked the sudden hollowness in his chest. "Land of tall people, dry weather, and unseasoned food."

Cynthia's smile didn't quite reach her eyes. "That's nice, though," she said in a quiet voice.

"Their stereotyping?"

"That they check in with you. That they care enough to ask you about your life."

At the pensiveness in Cynthia's tone, Rohit contemplated what his life might've been like had he never left India. As a bachelor, he'd probably still be living at home in his family's small two-bedroom flat. And even though he was thirty-one years old, he knew his father would still go to the market every morning to buy jackfruit—because it was his son's favorite—and his mom would insist on tidying his room for him because he "worked too hard." And near the end of the week, Maisa would start bugging him to treat her to a movie on the weekend, always a rom-com because it was their thing.

Homesickness washed over Rohit, surprising him. Ever since Cynthia had asked him about his career goals, he'd never felt so grateful to be living in Canada. Sure, he had a mountain of responsibilities keeping him in limbo between two very different countries, but at least they weren't staring him in the face every time he sat down at the breakfast table or returned home from work. And yet, he was so lucky to have a family like that. Sure, they were nosy, loud, and financially stressed, but they cared about him and never stopped showing him they did, even when he failed to answer or return their calls for days at a time.

"Yeah," he said, eyeing his phone guiltily, "I take them for granted. I should do more for them." *And stop whining about their financial needs*, he added silently to himself.

"I don't think any kid living overseas who sends money back every month to help his family is taking anything for granted," Cynthia said. It was as if she'd read his mind; her voice was so matter-of-fact that Rohit blinked in surprise. When he shot her a questioning glance, her lips quirked apologetically. "My dad mentioned it once."

"Your dad talks about me with you?"

Cynthia snorted in response. "He talks about you to everyone."

"I owe your dad a lot, too," Rohit said.

"No, you don't. You're smart, driven, and good with people. That's all you."

The words were complimentary, but there was an edge to Cynthia's voice that made Rohit turn on his side again so he could study her face. What he saw there was yet another mystery. Cynthia was staring at the ceiling, her lips pulled down in a slight frown. Not displeasure, necessarily. Troubled, maybe. A quick, sharp but unobtrusive pain, like a paper cut.

He couldn't be certain nor was he sure he could ask, but Rohit knew he would do anything to wipe that expression from her face.

"Are you complimenting me?" Rohit joked, hoping to alleviate the tension. "Should I write down the date and time?"

The corners of Cynthia's lips lifted. "Don't make me answer that. Saying the words was soul-destroying enough."

Under the covers, Rohit slid his feet closer to hers and playfully nudged her ankle with his toes. The way she immediately swatted back with her feet was a new but interesting form of seduction.

"There's also that MBA of yours," Cynthia pointed out wryly. "That opens a lot of doors, too."

Rohit's feet froze mid-footsie. It had been a while since anyone had brought up those nauseating three letters, but when he heard them from Cynthia's mouth, his stomach reeled and he abruptly flipped onto his back again. He couldn't be lying next to her, body and soul bared after last night, and not tell her.

She needed to know all of him if he was ever going to be able to love her the way he wanted to. And, possibly, earn her love in return if he was so lucky.

"About that . . ." Rohit cleared his throat.

"Yeah?" As if it were the most natural thing in the world, Cynthia moved closer and rested her head on his chest, her leg wrapping over his. The hug was almost enough to chase away the chill seeping underneath his skin.

Almost.

"Rohit?" Cynthia prodded when he didn't answer. "Are you about to tell me you've been headhunted by another company?" Her arm tightened around his torso, as if bracing herself for the punch line.

Rohit wanted to grab Cynthia's wrist, keep her anchored to him as he delivered the blow, but he forced his arms to lay still where they were. "I never actually finished my MBA," he said. It was the first time he'd ever said the words out loud—to himself, never mind in front of someone else—and for an alarming moment, Rohit's lungs seized, and he felt like he couldn't breathe.

Cynthia didn't immediately pull away, but she did raise her head, gently clipping his chin on the way up. "You never actually finished your MBA," she parroted back. Although her voice was flat and emotionless, her thick black lashes framed wide, startled eyes as she studied his face. "Are you serious?"

He couldn't meet her stare. "Yes."

A part of him regretted saying the words out loud—to his boss's daughter, of all people—but a larger part of him was in a state of shock at the power of his admission. It had silenced the room, frozen them in time, quite possibly ruined one of the best mornings of his life. His entire body stiffened, primed for a fight, rejection, disgust, or all of the above.

But she hadn't pulled away—yet. "So . . . you lied to my father? To get the job?"

The lump in Rohit's throat took him by surprise. Admitting the truth to Cynthia had frightened him, but the reminder that he'd deceived the man who was keeping him and his family afloat was worse. Shame flushed through him and he tried to roll away.

But Cynthia's arm tightened around his torso, holding him captive. In this, too, she was stubborn and strong, and Rohit wasn't surprised in the least. "Why?" she asked.

In a low monotone, Rohit walked Cynthia through the sequence of events that had led him to abandoning his MBA program early in its second year. There was no emotion in his voice, no bitterness or sadness, not even as he described the gravity of his grandmother's stroke. He felt like a tired patient describing his medical history to the seventh doctor in two months. He'd revisited the events too many times in his own head already, turning them this way and that, looking—unsuccessfully—for a cure that might alleviate his burdens and soften the sharp edges of what Rohit was beginning to fear was resentment.

Cynthia pulled her arm away to prop her head on her hand, and Rohit held his breath. Would she throw him out, never speak to him again? Would she threaten to tell her father?

"If your family needs access to healthcare and government programs, why don't they immigrate like you did?" she asked.

Rohit exhaled shakily. It was far from a sigh of relief, but, at her curiosity, hope curled inside his chest. "I can't afford to sponsor them. Besides, I'm not sure they'd want to." It was a thought Rohit, too, had mulled over before. His sister would likely jump at the opportunity to come to Canada, but his parents had never broached the topic—their entire extended family resided within walking distance of where they lived now. And his frail, aging grandparents? He couldn't imagine them hobbling through the snow or navigating public transportation with their broken English.

"You don't have any other family members who could help?"

Behind closed eyelids, Rohit could practically see the black edges of his resentment growing, slinking inward like whisps of smoke. "My uncles and aunts back home help with physically caring for my grandmother, but . . ." He swallowed. "My parents worked so hard to send me abroad—I owe them everything."

"Is that what they told you?"

"They didn't need to." Rohit could feel Cynthia's gaze on the side of his face, but he didn't dare turn his head to look into her eyes, fearful of what he might find in their amber depths. Probably judgment, maybe pity. His heart squeezed painfully. He wouldn't blame her if there was regret given that she was now skin to skin with a man who had built his career on a lie. Who had, for over a year, lied to her and her father.

"There's no one else that could help you?" she asked.

Now Rohit did meet her eyes, unsaid words between them. He would never ask her father, *could* never. His mouth was dry but his words were firm: "No," he said. "I can't."

Something unreadable clouded Cynthia's eyes, and Rohit's brain flashed forward to what would happen next. He should pull away, gather his clothes, and leave. Beg her to keep his secret, at least until he could find another job. He prepared himself for her anger and disgust. He deserved it.

But she laid her head back on his chest, her arm around him tighter than ever, anchoring *him* to *her*. "You were in an impossible situation," she said softly, her lips whispering kisses against his chest, inches above his racing heart. "Sometimes I hate the world."

The words were said so quietly, half-muffled and completely unexpected, and yet they were everything. Rohit squeezed her back and let Cynthia drive some of the dark, curling smoke away.

CHAPTER 22

"Good afternoon, Ms. Kumar."

"Malik," Cynthia returned as she slid a takeout container—strawberry cheesecake with extra white chocolate drizzle—onto the security desk.

A grin spread over Malik's deeply lined face when he opened the lid and saw what was inside. "You spoil me."

"It's our little secret." Cynthia was about to move toward the elevator bay, but her departure was waylaid by a chorus of voices passing by her right.

"Hey, Cynthia," Filomena from sales chirped.

"I love those shoes, girl," Louise in accounting added.

Cynthia barely remembered to smile as several other members of the small group of junior and administrative staff from Kumar Construction echoed various greetings as they made their way past. Like her, they were obviously returning from a lunch break, but unlike Cynthia, they weren't floored by the innocuous act of exchanging pleasantries.

Would she *ever* get used to it? Coworkers were stopping by her office for a quick hello, showing her pictures of milestones in their lives like the birth of a grandchild or a pet dog at a graduation ceremony from obedience classes, and inviting her out for casual after-work drinks.

Cynthia wasn't sure what to make of the newfound attention except that it made her feel stiff and uncomfortable every time. Even if she was tempted, she always found an excuse not to join in and often had to resist glancing over her shoulder to make sure they were indeed extending the invitation to *her*.

Years of coaching herself to be Cynthia, Kumar Construction All-Star, and she could barely manage to react like a human.

Yannis from sales hung back as the rest of the group headed for the elevators, his gaze fixed on the takeout container sitting in front of Malik.

"Beezley's," he read from the lid. "Fancy!" He tilted his chin expectantly in Cynthia's direction. "Leftovers?"

Malik winked at Cynthia. "Dessert," he replied for her, opening the container so Yannis could see.

"Whoa. Is that cheesecake?" Yannis's eyebrows rose. Again, he directed the question to Cynthia, and under his stupefied gaze, she couldn't help but take a small step back.

"Strawberry," she confirmed in a quiet voice. Malik grinned before scooping up a huge bite.

"This one's got a heart of gold," Yannis said to Malik, jerking his thumb at Cynthia before he turned to catch up with his colleagues. "Who knew, right?"

Cynthia wasn't sure if the last comment had been directed at himself, to her, or to Malik, but she shifted uncomfortably on her feet as she watched him depart into a waiting elevator.

"I knew it all along," Malik said around a mouthful of cheese-cake, oblivious to her discomfort.

Although she could feel a faint blush spreading across her cheeks, Cynthia stayed rooted to the spot as she waited for the elevator filled with Yannis's lunch group to close and carry the staff away. She even silently counted to fifteen, feeling foolish the entire time, before she shot Malik a parting wave and claimed her own ride up.

When she found a spot at the back of another crowded elevator—thankfully, with zero employees from Kumar Construction as far as she could tell—Cynthia wondered where Rohit was, what he was doing. If she crossed his mind in this way, like the faint, catchy notes of a Top 40 song that nudged the recesses of one's headspace all day.

If, like her, his heart swelled a little bit with each replay.

When the elevator doors slid open on the fourteenth floor, Cynthia instinctually backed into the corner to allow for the newcomers to enter. As if she'd conjured him, Rohit and her father stepped in, so deep in discussion they didn't even notice her, squeezed in the back behind three men, two in identical black suits and one food delivery guy carrying a stack of pizza boxes. Rohit seemed preoccupied, his head bent over a thick report in his hands.

Her dad's obliviousness came as less of a surprise. And, for once, Cynthia had no desire to dwell on this sad, predictable fact. She was too distracted by the broad width of Rohit's back, the short hairs at the nape of his neck that tickled her fingers in the most delightful way. She could practically feel her chest expanding in the confines of her structured, black shift dress as she looked at his shoulders, which, she now knew, bore the weight of so much.

He'd kept his secret this entire time. She had loathed him for the better part of their acquaintance, while having *no idea* of the depth of his loyalty and devotion to his family. She'd grossly overestimated the size of his ego and had been oblivious to the incredible magnitude of his heart.

"You did great in there, son," her father said as he punched the button for Kumar Construction.

"I don't know," Rohit responded, tucking the report under his arm. He cracked his knuckles and Cynthia immediately knew he was nervous. "They didn't look like they were buying into the projections."

Rich patted Rohit on the back and Cynthia's spine stiffened when her father's hand lingered on Rohit's shoulder. "Don't underestimate yourself, you nailed it. This is going to be huge for us and I have complete faith in you leading the charge."

"You want me to *lead* the project if they sign with us?" Rohit asked with disbelief, and Cynthia made a mental note to check the building directory to see who occupied the fourteenth floor.

"You're more than ready," her father replied.

As the elevator climbed higher and slowly emptied itself of lawyers, engineers, investment bankers, and pizza guys, Cynthia stayed plastered to her corner, quietly inhaling the lingering smell of pepperoni and mentally debating if she wanted them to turn around and see her.

They didn't.

"I think I'm out of my league," Rohit murmured when they finally reached Kumar Construction.

Her father chuckled as they stepped off the elevator. "I'll coach you through it."

Cynthia watched their departure as they made their way down the hallway to their offices. With their wide-set shoulders in dark, tailored suits and their short black hair, they could've been mistaken for father and son. They even walked the same: confident and with purpose.

"Did you need something, Cynthia?" Jilly asked from the front desk.

Startled, Cynthia stumbled out of the elevator. Jilly sometimes covered lunch breaks for the receptionist, and to have her assistant catch her slack-jawed and lifeless flooded Cynthia's face with heat. Cynthia shook her head weakly.

"Are you sure?" Jilly was already half standing, her forehead wrinkling.

"F-fine. I'm fine." Cynthia cleared her throat and managed a feeble wave before making a beeline to the safety of her quiet corner office. There was no time to untangle the tightness knotted in her chest, however, because seconds after she took her seat behind the desk, Rohit breezed in and plopped himself in the chair across from her.

The cut of his black suit hugged his frame and emphasized his trim waist, but Cynthia couldn't appreciate the perfect lines or the sexiness of Rohit's open collar where he'd already ditched his tie because painted on the backs of her eyelids was their departing backs—her father's and Rohit's—and how they had looked, even to her, so similar despite not sharing any genes.

A match made in heaven. The son her father should've had instead of a daughter he couldn't be bothered to understand. "Did you want to grab dinner tonight or . . ." Rohit trailed off when he got a good look at her. "What happened?"

Cynthia purposefully turned toward her computer and assaulted the spacebar to wake up the monitor. "What do you mean?"

Rohit's eyes widened at the defensiveness in her voice but unlike before, he didn't retreat with a departing shot about her being an Ice

Princess. Instead, he leaned forward in his chair, worry flooding his eyes. "Cynthia. Tell me."

"Can you close the door?" she asked, and when Rohit rose immediately to do her bidding, she tried to compose herself. The ache in her chest clawing for freedom was *not* something Cynthia wanted to share with the entire office. Learning how to be more human with her coworkers was one thing—vulnerability and angry crying were something else entirely.

When Rohit returned to his seat, Cynthia crossed her legs and tried to lighten her tone. "You and my dad were looking pretty chummy back there."

"Back where?"

"In the elevator."

Rohit's raised his eyebrows. "Did you bug the elevators or something?"

Cynthia scowled. "I was *in* there, dummy."

"You were? We didn't see you."

Although she had lived it, the words stung. "What a shock."

"I'm sorry about that. It's been a stressful day. Your dad asked me to present in front of potential investors today and—" Rohit stopped when he caught Cynthia's answering scowl. "What?"

"You never mentioned that you were working on that."

Rohit shook his head in confusion. "Do I need to?" When Cynthia's frown deepened, his eyes narrowed. "What's this really about, Cynthia?"

"Don't you find it odd that since our efforts to boost morale around here, you've been busier than ever?"

Rohit shrugged. "Business is booming. Isn't that a good thing?"

"Maybe for you. My dad has been handing you projects left, right, and center."

"You've been busy, too," Rohit pointed out. "You've worked late both Monday and Tuesday of this week."

At Rohit's observation, Cynthia sat back a little in her chair. Along with her newfound popularity at Kumar Construction, getting used to Rohit's attention was also new ground for her, but she welcomed the light sprinkling of warmth it caused, fluttering from the pit of her stomach into her chest. It was an unfamiliar and new, but so pleasant that it made her want to wrap her arms around herself to preserve the feeling and keep it safe.

And then open her arms right back up to accept more.

"I'm the same kind of busy I've always been," she admitted. She didn't add that the return to hustling her ass off was tiring her out like it never had before.

"And didn't you say, a few nights ago, that your dad had copied you onto that email with one of his high-end contacts?"

"Well, yeah." But there hadn't been much more after that.

"So . . . ?"

Rohit's obliviousness sharpened something inside Cynthia, and she sat forward again, careful to curb the steeliness in her voice. "*You've* become my dad's right hand." *Even more so than before.*

"Didn't your dad mention he had a special assignment for you at the last senior leadership meeting?" Rohit asked, his brow wrinkling as he thought back.

"Snacks." Cynthia finished for him, her voice flat. "He asked me to coordinate ordering healthy, organic snacks for the break room as part of the wellness initiative we proposed."

Rohit winced. "At least it'll help you turn a profit with Team-Start?"

"Rohit."

"Okay, it's not great." Rohit paused. Opened his mouth and then shut it, uncertainty flitting across his face.

"What? What is it?" Cynthia couldn't disguise the reedy note in her voice, or the disgust she felt with herself for prodding Rohit for information about her own father. She had had a lifetime with him, felt like she'd studied him for decades, and yet here she was, desperate to hear whatever insight she could glean from a guy who'd known Rich for sixteen months. A guy who had the privilege of knowing her father behind the closed doors of daily coffee catch-ups. Who shadowed him to big investor meetings and received the congratulatory clap on his oblivious shoulder for a job well done.

While she sat in her cushy, lonely corner office and excelled at the art of being invisible.

"Cynthia, you run your own show around here," Rohit finally answered. "Your dad must look at you and think you don't need the extra attention or the assignments."

So Rohit thinks I'm alone and thriving, too. "Awesome."

"I'm not just saying that. You're the most self-sufficient person around here and everybody knows it."

Rohit's assessment should've filled her with pride, but she felt hollow. Maybe she'd done *too* good a job, had orchestrated her own demise. She'd been going above and beyond for so long, but the suggestion that she was beyond her father's realm of praise and recognition failed to fill that hollowness.

From the depths of a place she wished would just dry out already, twin tears slipped out of the corner of her eyes, prompting Rohit to hurry to her side and crouch beside her. "Rani, what's wrong?"

Queen. The combination of the endearment and Rohit's proximity and earnest expression were too powerful for Cynthia. His hand was too comforting and too warm on her bare skin just above her knee and suddenly, Cynthia was too damn tired to keep her humiliating insecurities under lock and key.

"It just feels like he hasn't seen all the hard work I put in with you over the last month. It's like I wasn't even here," she said. The words were those of a lost little girl wanting a pat on the head, but Rohit's gaze was soft with understanding.

"That's bullshit," he said. "There is no way we would have accomplished everything we did without you. And there's no way your dad doesn't know that."

Glancing down at her lap, Cynthia fiddled with the hem of her dress. "If you're sure . . ."

"I am. Just the other day, Leering Larry told me he was looking forward to your plans for off-site team-building activities." Rohit paused to search Cynthia's face, and when he spoke, his voice was cautious. "Do you want me to say something to him?"

"No," she said quickly. "Definitely not." Cynthia straightened her shoulders and tried to ignore the mortifying flush spreading across the back of her neck. Forcing a smile felt too fake and, knowing Rohit, he'd see right through it anyway, so she settled for levity.

"So Larry's forgiven me for his two-year subscription to Team-Start's life-changing smoothies?" she asked.

With a quiet laugh, Rohit moved his hand to clutch her free one, and, in a spontaneous gesture that both supercharged her heart and made her want to look away bashfully, he brushed a kiss across her knuckles. His lips were soft, his gaze worshipful, and Cynthia's entire hand tingled afterward.

"Your dad knows your worth," he said. "We all do."

CHAPTER 23

Sitting at a wobbly high-top table, Rohit ran his palms along its scuffed edge and looked around the downstairs game room of the Leprechaun Trap. He'd never ventured into the basement before, but the same nondescript, classic rock music drifted through the speakers, perfectly offsetting the yellowing, wood-paneled walls and the scent of stale beer.

Yet Rohit felt like he was in a parallel universe. Unlike the last time, when he'd wandered in and decided to shoot his shot with Cynthia, this time, *she* had invited *him* out—with *her* friends, no less. From across the room, Rohit watched Cynthia sink another dart a fraction of an inch away from the center of the board's target before raising her arms in triumph at an amused Naomi.

Cynthia, too, was the same but different. She was relaxed and easygoing—the polar opposite of the woman to whom he'd felt an instant attraction. But as she hit a bull's-eye with effortless grace, he experienced that same rush that had ricocheted through him the first time he'd seen her. She was still so fierce.

He tugged at the collar of his shirt before downing the rest of his now-tepid beer. Was there anything this woman could do that *wouldn't* turn him on? Because he was seriously contemplating dredging up some more stolen movie lines and taking her home.

"Do you want another drink?"

Rohit barely heard the question coming from somewhere to his left as he lifted his empty glass to his lips while watching, riveted, as Cynthia carefully angled herself, her lips pressed together, fingers expertly cocking the dart as she studied the target. The intensity on her face struck a deliciously familiar chord—it was the same one she'd worn, head thrown back, as she'd ridden his face, just moments away from—

"Rohit, do you want another drink?" The voice was more forceful this time.

Startled, Rohit turned to find Naomi's fiancé, Dev, looking at him, eyebrows raised knowingly.

"I'm sorry, what was that?" Rohit asked. He cleared his throat with a nervous chuckle when he realized he was holding an empty glass to his lips.

Dev gave him a long look that was equal parts commiserating and amused before sliding off his bar chair. "I'll take that as a yes. Be right back."

"Thanks," Rohit called to Dev's departing back before his eyes were unable to resist sliding back to where Cynthia was showing Naomi how to improve her throw. As if she could feel his eyes boring into the side of her delectable neck, Cynthia glanced over her shoulder and gave him a wicked little half smile, as if she knew exactly what was running through his mind.

Rohit forced himself to look away as Dev made his way back to their table. It was his first time hanging out with Cynthia's friends, and it was important that he make the right impression. She was obviously very selective about whom she spent her free time with, and it made this invitation seem all the more significant. Besides, the last thing he wanted was to be known as the date who sported an erection in the basement of a tired Irish pub.

When Dev passed him his beer, Rohit barely finished mumbling his thank-you before taking a much-needed swig of the icy liquid.

"So how long have you been seeing Cynthia?" Dev asked.

Rohit choked on his drink. "Uh . . . Well, we've worked together for a while," he hedged. He wasn't sure how much Cynthia had told her friends about him or how much she wanted them to know. It didn't feel like they were hiding anything, both in and out of Kumar Construction, but he felt tentative, the trust between them hard-earned and delicate. The potential to create something beautiful that would withstand the test of time was there, but the bonds between them were too new: still pliable and easily shattered by one clumsy misstep.

He'd never wanted to be more careful in his life. "When's your wedding?" he asked Dev instead.

Dev scowled at his beer bottle as he picked at the edge of the label. "Not soon enough."

"Isn't it the bride that usually stresses about wedding planning?"

"Yeah, well, Naomi doesn't have to live with my mother." The response was delivered with such deadpan, Rohit felt bad for laughing until he caught the slight upturn of Dev's mouth. "Seriously, though," Dev added. "She's wedding-obsessed and is driving Naomi up the wall, too. She's been really patient with Mom." When Dev turned to look at his fiancée, his dour expression softened, and Rohit couldn't help but smile.

At least he wasn't the only one who found it hard to look away. Rohit considered Naomi, who, next to a skilled player like Cynthia, had been throwing lemons all night and didn't seem to give a damn. She was optimism personified, especially next to Dev's seriousness, and yet anyone in their vicinity could see that she and Dev were well matched. They fit together in that comfortable way only a couple who had learned to curve around each other's sharp edges could. Every time Naomi stole a fry off Dev's plate or playfully cuffed his shoulder, he looked at her with a level of adoration Rohit had only seen in rom-coms.

"The girls are headed back over here," Dev said. "Don't mention the wedding. Naomi spent all afternoon going over seating charts with my mother—she needs a break from the madness."

Rohit nodded distractedly while trying not to linger on how Cynthia tugged at the hem of her black work dress once she'd taken her seat next to him at the small, round table. She'd invited him to meet with her and her friends right after work, and whether it was a date or not, it hadn't crossed Rohit's mind to say no. He'd say yes to whatever this woman wanted for the rest of his life if she allowed him the privilege.

God help him, the spirit of Dev's wedding-obsessed mother was trying to get him, too.

"Okay, Rohit, I think I need to ask the question everyone wants to know," Naomi announced after helping herself to a drink from Dev's bottle.

Rohit braced himself and shot a nervous glance at Cynthia.

"And, spoiler alert, we've already discussed this behind your back," Naomi informed him so cheerfully he couldn't take offense.

"Naomi," Cynthia said warningly.

"What . . ." Naomi paused to take another sip, and whether it was for dramatic effect or she was really that thirsty, Rohit wasn't sure, but the sweat beading his neckline indicated that it was effective nonetheless. "What," Naomi repeated, with a mischievous glance at Cynthia, "do you use in your hair to make it look so shiny and thick?"

"I . . ." Rohit shook his head as the words registered. "Wait, what?"

"It's true, dude," Dev said with that seriousness Rohit was never sure he should take seriously. "Your hair is unreal."

With Dev's, Naomi's, and Cynthia's eyes on him, Rohit wasn't sure how to react until a small smile cracked Cynthia's face and she reached out to brush the hair at the nape of his neck. The moment was as fast and fleeting as the faintest whisper of a breeze on a hot summer day, and yet it was enough to set Rohit's nerve endings crackling.

"It's soft, too," Cynthia informed the table.

"Can we touch it?" Naomi teased.

"She's kidding," Dev hurried to add.

"My mom used to massage coconut oil into my scalp when I was a kid," Rohit said, ducking his head. "I don't know if that does anything."

"Maybe Cynthia could carry on the tradition," Naomi said with mock innocence, earning her a narrowed glance from her friend.

Rohit cleared his throat and tried to think of anything but pointed, black fingernails digging into his hair to work the sensitive skin of his scalp. He would not, in the middle of this bar, imagine how damn good the pull of strands through those hands would feel. Just like he wouldn't let his mind wander to how amazing it had felt when she'd done the same thing when his head had been between her thighs.

Clearing his throat, Rohit took a hasty pull from his beer, aware that everyone's eyes were on him, tracking his every move. The knowing look was on Dev's face again and Rohit couldn't bring himself to care, not when Cynthia's hand had drifted back to the nape of his neck to gently play with the hair there.

Rohit was saved from uttering a pornographic groan and never being invited out with her friends ever again when the universe finally took pity on him and his phone vibrated on the tabletop.

His sister's face flashing across the screen indicated a video call, and Rohit automatically swiped up to answer. "Hey, little sister," he said, unable to mask the relief in his voice. "Say hi to the group."

Rohit flipped the phone to face the other members of the table, and everyone waved in return. He couldn't help but linger slightly longer on Cynthia than the other two as if proving some kind of point. It felt suspiciously like pride, and when he realized that he was actually bragging to his sister about hanging out with Cynthia, Rohit hastily turned the phone back to himself.

The smile on Maisa's face was strained, the corners of her eyes drawn tight. "Hang on," he told her, sliding off his stool. With an apologetic look at Cynthia, Naomi, and Dev, Rohit excused himself. "I'll be right back," he said, before heading outside into the late evening and slipping around the side of the bar, away from the main street.

Rohit leaned back against the red brick wall and eyed his sister through the screen. "What's wrong?"

"I'm so sorry, Rohit," Maisa said in a rush, as if she had been rehearsing her lines. "I didn't want to bother you with this, but . . . I really don't know what else to do."

A chill spilled through Rohit's veins. "What's wrong. Are you okay? Is it Mom or Dad?"

"It's Dadi."

At the mention of his paternal grandmother, Rohit straightened away from the wall. The last time he'd received a call about a grand-parent, it had been to inform him of his maternal grandmother's stroke. His father's mother was much heartier for an elderly woman. She made the best rotis.

"Is it a stroke?" The assumption scraped out of Rohit's throat where an invisible hand had him in a choke hold. Suddenly, he was transported right back to his second year of graduate school. He'd been on his way to an operations strategy class when his mother had informed him of his nana's stroke. It had been mid-January, and he'd dropped his overloaded backpack with a thud on the frozen, snowy ground.

And now, in the middle of spring, he felt the same icy, January air pierce through his skin. His lungs burned.

"No," Maisa said, shaking her head vigorously. "Dadi is okay."

Rohit's pressed a hand to his chest, careful to keep it out of Mai-sa's eyesight.

"But . . ." Maisa added, and Rohit's hand clenched into a fist. "Dad recently found out that she hasn't been taking her diabetes medication."

"What? Why?"

"She can't afford it."

Rohit clenched his jaw and tried not to show any reaction, but the urge to slam the back of his head against the side of the building was strong. He barely heard Maisa's explanation of how their dad had found out over the rising fire of something sharp and darkly acidic in the pit of his gut. It swirled inside him, gaining momentum as it spread, igniting everything in its path.

Another medical bill to add to the list. Great. Would his family even notice if their needs burned him to a crisp? Probably not if it left a stack of cash in its wake.

That's not fair, Rohit admonished himself. *Your family loves you.* The self-reassurance doused his resentment, reminding him, as always, that their needs must come first: thousands of miles away, his family struggled to make ends meet while he sat in a bar, on a Wednesday, sharing after-work drinks with friends, regretting the decision to answer this damn phone call. He was a terrible person.

"I'll take care of it," Rohit blurted out.

"Oh, no, Rohit, I just wanted to talk about—"

"It's fine."

Maisa's mouth snapped shut and her eyes widened.

"It's fine," he repeated, more gently this time.

"That's not why I called." Her voice was meek, but Rohit couldn't bring himself to apologize for snapping at her. If he did, the resentment would build again and Maisa didn't deserve it.

"Yes, but it's what needs to be done," he said instead.

"I'm sorry, Rohit," Maisa said in a small voice. "I just . . . I didn't have anyone else to talk to about this stuff."

"You did the right thing. I'm glad you told me. I'll call you later, okay?" He barely waited for his sister's goodbye before he ended the call. He didn't want to go back into the bar, not when the weight of another responsibility—another call from home, another bill, another obligation—scraped against the pit of his stomach like broken glass. In the barely lit alleyway between the Leprechaun Trap and an all-you-can-eat sushi joint that had closed hours ago, Rohit felt trapped. The warmth of new friends, laughter, and Cynthia's fingers toying with his hair felt universes away now, thanks to the problems of a world he was no longer a part of closing in on him, permeating every single part of his life. At this rate, he'd be stuck here forever.

"There you are."

Rohit heard Cynthia's husky voice before he saw her cautiously making her way toward him in the feeble light, her arms crossed over her chest. He was vaguely surprised to realize that the temperature had dipped with nightfall, or perhaps it was Maisa's phone call that had left him so numb. When Cynthia came to a stop in front of him, he immediately slipped off his suit jacket and wrapped it around her shoulders.

"I came to check on you," she said. "Is everything all right?"

Tipping his head backward, Rohit looked up at the sky. He loved that he could always see the stars in Kelowna—there had been too much light pollution in Toronto and smog in India. But the twinkling lights seemed impossibly far away in this moment, reminding him of his limits and the places he'd never reach.

"My life is always going to be like this, isn't it?" he murmured, more to himself.

"Like what?"

"Everything I do is for a home I left behind. It doesn't even feel like home anymore, but I can't escape it," he said. "Maybe my obligations to them would feel like less of a burden if I moved back in with them."

When Cynthia didn't respond for a long moment, Rohit looked at her and hated the worry lines that creased her forehead. He'd put them there. Had he kept his secret to himself, she'd never know the weight that was his to bear alone.

"I think we all wind up in situations that seem impossible to crawl out of," she said slowly. "But eventually, we will. *You* will."

"How do you know?"

"Because you deserve good things," she said, parroting the lines he'd said to her the first time she'd invited him to her apartment.

Rohit's insides warmed as he reached for her, pulling her in so their foreheads touched and the sweet scent of sandalwood, strength, and Cynthia could blanket his senses and offer him a bit of a reprieve if not the freedom from his burdens.

"I probably don't deserve you," he said.

"Haven't you figured it out yet?" A sly smile pulled at the corners of Cynthia's lips, even more wicked and seductive in the dim alleyway. "'Sasha Tran, I want to hold your purse for you.'"

Rohit couldn't help but grin. He'd introduced her to *Always Be My Maybe* just a few nights ago and it was the most perfect thing she could have said to him in what, up until she'd found him, had been a horrible, devastating, and imperfect moment.

Even if she'd gotten the line wrong.

CHAPTER 24

T*his* is your house?"

Cynthia glanced at the passenger seat of her white Audi, where Naomi sat, her eyes wide, mouth slightly ajar as Cynthia maneuvered the vehicle into her parents' curved driveway.

"My parents' house," she corrected. "You've been to my apartment before."

"Right." Naomi nodded as she unbuckled her seat belt. "But you know how your parents' home always feels like your own?"

Folding her arms over the top of the steering wheel, Cynthia looked at the dwelling that was, and would always be, an extension of her father's success. The house was the immigrant dream personified: located in a nice, quiet neighborhood, with a large and immaculately tended lawn, the pool in the backyard shimmering and clear. Her parents had designed and built this house to make a statement. The Tudor-style home, complete with overlapping gables and an arched overhang above the front door, boasted that they had successfully found their place in upper-crust society, while the modern touches—the heated driveway and motion-sensor-lit walkway—confirmed that the Kumars had money to spare.

The house had always been a point of pride for Cynthia, but in her mind, it was a testament to her *father's* hard work, and now more than ever, it didn't feel like hers.

She sidestepped Naomi's question by swinging her car door open. "C'mon, let's go." Her voice sounded unnaturally bright to her own ears, but Naomi didn't comment as she followed Cynthia up the peony-lined path that her mother took full credit for even though a gardener came weekly.

Once inside, Cynthia led the way upstairs to her old bedroom. Her mother had preserved her childhood room despite her daughter moving out more than five years ago. Whenever Cynthia stepped back into the space—usually for access to the closet full of saris, lehengas, salwar kameezes, and other garments she had worn only once or twice before—the room, like the house, did not feel like her own.

Sipra had decorated the room in rose gold and white with fluffy-slash-furry everything and rose-patterned fabrics. As a child, Cynthia had tossed the pink, oversized rose pillow on the floor every night with no intention of retrieving it in the morning. And yet, every day, when she returned from school, there it was, greeting her from the center of her frilly rose gold pillows.

To this day, Cynthia abhorred roses.

Despite interior design being a large part of her portfolio now, teenage Cynthia hadn't spent a lot of time customizing her bedroom aside from a small collage of teen heartthrob pictures torn from magazines arching over the curve of her tufted cream headboard and a ridiculous number of now-expired perfumes lining the dresser.

"Whoa . . ." Naomi's eyes were even rounder than they had been on the driveway. "*This* was your room?" She gingerly sat on the bed and fingered the pink duvet embroidered with roses. "I never pegged you for a girly girl."

"I wasn't," Cynthia said flatly, crossing the room to the wall-length, mirrored sliding-door closet. "Unfortunately, my mom didn't care much for my tomboy ways."

"I was a tomboy, too!"

In the mirror, they exchanged grins, but Cynthia broke the connection by sliding the closet open with a briskness that belied the rush of pleasure spiraling through her. The onslaught of human connection at work was still overwhelming for her, making her feel like an overfilled sponge burdened by the weight of everything it had absorbed with no clue how to wring itself dry. With Naomi, though, the feeling was different—light, easy, and, most importantly, *comfortable*.

The closet was filled with neatly lined-up outfits, arranged by style, in a flurry of colors and textures. Seeing them tugged a fragile thread in Cynthia's chest: every ensemble told a story, sometimes taking her back to specific moments in time like spending an entire evening playing hack-and-slash video games with the boys when visiting a family friend's home while the girls played Barbies in the corner.

Sometimes Cynthia's heart squeezed for her younger self, who couldn't have known what shoes she would try to fill one day, zero inkling of the impossible tasks that would one day be in front of her.

Naomi's squeal cut through Cynthia's trip down memory lane as she pushed past her to finger the exquisite clothes. "These are gorgeous! Are you sure you're okay with loaning me one?"

With a careless shrug, Cynthia took a seat at the vanity table from Pottery Barn and waved a dismissive hand. "Help yourself."

"This is so generous of you," Naomi said, her words muffled by her head being halfway in the closet. "I'm attending a puja with Dev's family and I can't afford to buy something new every time we get invited somewhere."

"It's totally fine, but I thought Dev's sister-in-law was lending you stuff, too?"

"Oh, she does." Naomi paused to pull out a flashy pink salwar kameez and study its design work. "Priya is really amazing. But she also has two toddlers at home, and she works full-time at the library. I feel bad always bothering her for clothes."

Cynthia opened a random drawer at the table and pawed through its contents as if Naomi's ability to bond with anyone and everyone didn't fill her with a faint glimmer of envy. She'd never been able to forge easy friendships with people; even her relationship with Naomi had started off rocky.

But she was friends with Naomi now *and* she had Rohit. And as Cynthia fingered the handle of a wooden hairbrush, she knew, without a doubt, she would kill for them if the situation called for it.

Naomi shot Cynthia a mischievous smile in the mirror as she held an orange outfit in front of her body. "You, on the other hand, I have no guilt about bothering."

Cynthia rolled her eyes and joined Naomi at the closet. "Not this one," she said, taking the outfit from her friend's hands and returning it to the closet. "It's too much for a puja. Are you going to a temple or someone's house?"

Naomi's eyebrows shot up. "Does it matter?"

Cocking her head, Cynthia rifled through the outfits with a decisiveness she usually reserved for steering clients in the right direction. Except lately, if she was being honest with herself, she felt a little unsettled in the driver's seat. Cynthia still knew her shit, was committed to going over and above her clients' expectations, but something had changed. The urge to floor the gas pedal and crow her victory at the finish line had faded.

It was like someone had thrown her map—wrinkled and marked up from years of planning and plotting—out the window. A year ago she could've redrawn that map from scratch, but now?

She wasn't sure she wanted to.

"Where they're having the event doesn't matter, but the event itself does," Cynthia replied, clearing her throat and returning to the task at hand. She pushed a few outfits into Naomi's hands. "I mean, you wouldn't wear something really sparkly or gaudy to the temple—or someone's house—unless it was a big engagement party or something. Religious-type events, unless it's a big festival type of occasion, are a little more subdued and modest."

Naomi dropped her gaze. "Sometimes I feel so stupid not knowing all this stuff. It's like there are a ton of rules that everybody knows but me."

"You're smart. You'll pick it up." Cynthia grinned and elbowed her friend. "You'll have to once you're Mrs. Mukherjee."

A rosy blush seeped onto Naomi's cheeks. "Shut up."

"Namashkar, Mrs. Mukherjee." Cynthia pressed her palms together and bowed as she delivered the greeting that was traditional to Naomi's and Dev's shared Bengali heritage.

"You're hilarious." Naomi elbowed her back. "Seriously, though, I might need your expertise in this area when it's time to plan what I'm going to wear to all the wedding events. All of which your presence will be mandatory, by the way."

Her hands still pressed together, Cynthia fought the urge to hug herself, similarly to when Rohit had casually tossed an unexpected endearment her way.

Rani. He thought she was a queen.

It was ridiculous how these simple, barely perceptible moments affected her and yet she wanted to preserve them. They spread a wonderful warmth in her chest, one that Cynthia knew, despite the limited number of relationships in her life, was precious and should be protected. And she would protect them.

She reached into the heap in Naomi's hands and pulled out a soft green anarkali with a swirling white design embroidered down the front. "This one." She cringed when she heard how thick her voice sounded, and she hurriedly moved toward the dresser to hide her face. "Try it on and I'll find accessories to match."

As Cynthia rifled through the drawers where her mother—or a professional organizer—had arranged her jewelry sets in rows worthy of a display in an upscale boutique, Naomi's sly tone gave her pause.

"The real question is . . ." Naomi paused for dramatic effect, "whether or not I should include a plus-one on your invite."

A silver necklace skittered out of Cynthia's hands to clatter back into the drawer, and from Naomi's cackle, she knew her friend had witnessed her clumsiness. Cynthia turned to see Naomi in the green outfit with an impish smile on her face.

"You've been spending a lot of time with a certain someone if I'm not mistaken," Naomi added.

"It's nothing." The protest was hollow, barely half-hearted.

Naomi's voice took on a singsong quality. "You liiiike him."

Cynthia turned back to the dresser and tried to curb the silly smile pulling at her cheeks. "Fine. I like him."

"You *really* like him."

Cynthia couldn't bear to face her friend even as the acknowledgment came easily to her lips from a place inside her that knew its truth with absolute, soul-grounding certainty. "I really like him."

Naomi's shrill squeal provided a nanosecond of forewarning before she hurled herself across the room and threw her arms around Cynthia. Although Cynthia, with a good four inches over Naomi, stayed firmly rooted to the spot as the shorter woman bounced on her toes, she couldn't help but grin because Naomi's over-the-top exuberance was exactly how she felt inside.

"I knew it," Naomi said into her back. "You're in loooove!"

Maybe. But Cynthia wasn't ready to say it out loud.

Naomi didn't need confirmation, nor did she ask for permission as she grabbed the silver necklace from Cynthia's hands and sashayed back to the closet mirror to inspect it. She swayed side to side with the necklace held up against her neck while loudly, and obnoxiously, humming "Love Will Keep Us Together" by Captain & Tennille.

"You couldn't think of a more modern reference?" Cynthia said, trying to look indignant as she plopped back down at the vanity.

Naomi pursed her lips in concentration. "Would you prefer Dua Lipa's 'Love Again'?" With a wicked grin, she wiggled her hips. "Or perhaps '34+35' by Ms. Ariana Grande?" Naomi licked her top lip like an oversexed cartoon character before throwing her head back and cackling.

With a glare, Cynthia threw a pen that Naomi failed to dodge. If this was what having girlfriends was like, then maybe Cynthia hadn't missed much. She watched Naomi wearing *her* clothes and *her* jewelry while unapologetically laughing at her expense like a hyena.

Okay, it was annoying *and* kind of awesome and Cynthia couldn't help but smile to herself.

"Stop pretending you're annoyed," Naomi added. "So far today we've talked about our childhoods, clothes, my wedding, and now dating. We're friends, whether you like it or not."

Friends. Cynthia didn't bother to resist this time; she wrapped her arms around herself and squeezed the moment into her heart. Her arms grew slack, however, when her mother appeared in the doorframe.

"I heard laughter," Sipra said by way of greeting. She looked from Cynthia to Naomi—dressed in Cynthia's clothes—and then back to Cynthia.

Cynthia caught the discomfort on Naomi's face and stood. "Mom, this is my friend Naomi," she said.

"Pleased to meet you," Naomi said as Cynthia shot her mother a warning look.

Sipra ignored her daughter and strode toward Naomi, who fidgeted under her assessing gaze. After a brief moment, Sipra shook her head. "This won't do," she said, opening the closet doors. "This shade suits you, but color contrasts are trending." She pulled out a violet outfit and tugged the dupatta and pants off the hanger. "You should pair it with this."

Naomi raised her eyebrows at Cynthia. "And why didn't you inform me of this trend?"

Sipra waved a dismissive hand. "If it's not black or white, my daughter doesn't care for it."

Accepting the items from Sipra, Naomi headed for the door. "I'll go change in the bathroom. Be right back."

Cynthia frowned at her mother. "Did you interrupt us just to make me look stupid?" She couldn't quite locate why she was so offended except that her mother's casual dismissal had stung.

"You don't care about fashion," Sipra pointed out, "but I'll leave if you want me to. I heard laughter upstairs and just thought . . ."

The downturn of Sipra's eyes and the hint of longing in her voice took Cynthia by surprise. It would've been easy to shoo her mother away, as she had done so many times before when Sipra's brand of advice and helpful suggestions grated on her nerves. But a tiny wisp of something that felt like guilt but echoed of loneliness fluttered against Cynthia's sternum, and she swallowed her irritation instead.

"Maybe you could find some accessories that will work with the new color?" she said by way of apology.

Sipra brightened and offered a pseudo-apology of her own. "That necklace you picked is beautiful. But she needs earrings. And a bindi."

Cynthia joined her mother at the dresser and watched as her mother snapped the organized, glass-topped boxes open and shut with practiced hands that left neat, pin-straight rows in their wake. When she didn't find what she was looking for, Sipra moved on to the next drawer with a determination that kept Cynthia silent beside her.

"Aha!" Sipra said quietly, pulling out a small black box. "These." She opened the case to reveal two small, bell-shaped earrings.

"Are those mine?" Cynthia commented. "I've never seen them before."

Sipra smiled sadly down at the earrings. "I bought these for you when you were sixteen. You pitched a fit because you didn't like dangly earrings, and thought these were too old-fashioned-looking."

Cynthia reached forward to finger the fine silver but found herself pulling away. She had no memory of scorning the gift, but she could picture her teenage self yelling and pushing them away, for no other reason except that doing so might bring her closer to her father. He'd loved her best as a tomboy, after all.

But it hadn't worked then and it wasn't working now.

"Obviously, I wasn't as mature as I thought I was," Cynthia murmured.

With a little laugh, her mother closed the case and placed it in Cynthia's hands. "Neither was I. We had a huge fight about them." She shook her head and clasped Cynthia's hand with both of hers for a long second before letting go.

Cynthia examined the earrings. "They're beautiful."

Her mother's lips lifted in a soft smile. "Did I tell you that your old friend Henna Sharma is getting married? Maybe I'll get her a pair for her wedding."

"Who?"

"Henna Sharma."

"I have no idea who that is, Mom."

Sipra sucked her teeth impatiently. "We visited them once when you were nine. *Hen*na *Shar*ma."

Cynthia couldn't help rolling her eyes as she placed the earring box back in the drawer. "That's hardly a friend."

"Well, her mom is a friend of *mine* and called me with the good news a few days ago, and I'm thinking of heading down for the wedding a week or so early to help with the preparations."

It wouldn't be the first time her mother would make this kind of trip. Traditional South Asian weddings were weeklong events and required a village of willing women to pull it together. With many immigrant families living overseas with their relations so far away, friends often pitched in to help celebrate the happy occasion.

Although it had been a while since her mother had broached the topic of marriage with her, Cynthia pressed her heels into the floor, steeling herself for how this conversation would predictably go.

But Sipra surprised her. "You should come with me."

"What?"

"They live in a different province. It could be a nice little mother-daughter trip."

"We've . . . we've never done something like that before."

"I should've tried harder when you were younger," Sipra said with an apologetic shrug. "I think sometimes I pushed too hard in the wrong direction."

"Well, I pushed back."

"Different but the same." Her mother shrugged.

As Sipra turned to the dresser, Cynthia took the unguarded moment to study her mother's profile. Throughout her childhood, her likeness had always been compared to her dad, from their ambitious, competitive personalities to their tall, slender height, and thick black hair. Cynthia hadn't minded the slight aquiline dip of her nose or the square shape of her nails because they matched *his*.

But as she watched her mother sort through the drawer with a sharp eye and decisive touch, Cynthia wondered if she'd overlooked the subtle, yet meaningful, similarities that were reflected in her mother, too.

What else had she missed, ferociously chasing one impossible dream her entire life?

"I'm going to call your father and see when he'll be home for dinner," her mother said, shutting the drawer. "Tell Naomi I said goodbye, okay?"

Cynthia managed a nod, but she couldn't help the unsettled feeling stirring in her chest as she watched her mother depart with her trademark walk: graceful and confident. Almost regal.

In that short exchange, it felt like her mother had been trying to tell her something—multiple things, maybe—but Cynthia wasn't exactly sure where to begin deciphering the coded messages. It might have been one of the most civil conversations they'd ever had, as brief as it was, and yet loaded in a way that left Cynthia no less tense than their usual interactions. Or sad.

She was saved from falling down a dangerously murky rabbit hole by Naomi walking back in, looking much more vivid and eye-catching with the violet bracketing the mint-green dress.

"So?" Naomi didn't bother looking in the mirror; her eyes were focused on Cynthia as she waited for her approval.

Cynthia nodded as she tried to swallow past the confusing lump that had taken residence in the base of her throat. In just a few minutes, Sipra had recognized the exact right thing to bring everything together. She'd run circles around them.

Maybe she always did and no one ever noticed.

"You look perfect," Cynthia told her friend with a smile while wondering why a small part of her wanted to cry instead.

CHAPTER 25

Rohit gently shook a trio of ants off the handle of the cooler he'd packed before opening the lid and peering inside.

"More sparkling grape juice?" he offered Cynthia, who sat beside him on the blue plaid blanket.

She leaned back on her hands, her legs stretched out in front of her, and shot him a quick, distracted smile. "No, thanks."

"Apricot?"

"I'm good."

"Sandwich?"

She didn't even bother to respond this time, only gestured with a slight tilt of her chin at the half-eaten sandwich nestled in a napkin on her lap.

Rohit hesitated, his hand hovering awkwardly over the lid of the cooler. Packing a picnic and bringing Cynthia to Harmony in the Park had been his idea, and he was starting to think it had been a bad one. She'd been distant all night: picking at her food, slow to respond to conversation, accepting his affection but not initiating. He'd grown accustomed to her touch—was hyperaware of every caress and playful cuff—and without it, Rohit's heart felt bereft.

Still, because it was Cynthia, he tried again. "Meat flower?"

When Cynthia didn't respond, Rohit gave up and pushed the cooler aside. Planning a picnic in the park for the daughter of one of the wealthiest families in Kelowna had been a stupid move on his part. Cynthia was used to luxurious thread counts and fine dining, and he was trying to court her at a free community music event on a blanket he'd found in a thrift store.

Stupid, stupid, stupid.

"Do you want to head out?" he asked, hoping she'd decline despite himself and this disastrous evening.

"Sure," she said, hopping to her feet, grabbing their garbage, and heading for the nearby garbage can. It was the most life force she'd shown all night, and Rohit slowly followed her lead.

They walked to his seven-year-old two-door gray Toyota in silence, Rohit carrying the cooler with the rolled-up blanket tucked under his arm, Cynthia scrolling through her phone. She barely looked up as he stashed the items in his trunk, but when he opened the passenger door for her, Rohit snagged her attention by grabbing her hand before she could slide into the car.

"I'm sorry," he said.

Her head snapped up and she pocketed her phone. "For what?"

"This was a terrible date idea," he said.

Her forehead wrinkled. "No, it wasn't," she replied, pulling him toward her and kissing him on the cheek. "It was great."

Drawn into her nearness for the first time this entire evening, Rohit didn't pull away immediately. With her silky black hair teasing his jawline and her reassuring hand on his shoulder beckoning him forward, closer, into her, how could he not indulge? This was home. Rohit palmed the delicate space between her shoulder blades and leaned in, breathing deep, relieved, ecstatic, and grateful when she seemed content to linger in the embrace.

It wasn't enough to erase all the insecurities he'd felt just a few minutes ago, but once he'd settled himself in the driver's seat, the urge to survey the interior of his secondhand car through her eyes was waylaid by Cynthia speaking again.

"I know I've been off," she said.

Rohit looked out into the grassy green expanse ahead of them where, the concert having ended, people were packing up their belongings. "You deserve more than a picnic in the park."

"Rohit, stop it." Cynthia leaned over to squeeze his knee. "I've just had a lot on my mind lately. I'm sorry."

He wanted to pry—discovering every inch of her brilliant mind was becoming his favorite hobby—but when she turned her head to look out the passenger window, Rohit slid his hand to the back of Cynthia's headrest and focused on reversing out of the parking lot instead. It was slow going as the parking lot was flooded with headlights and parents carrying sleeping children to their vehicles.

Maybe Cynthia's mind was as heavy with the weight of learning his secret as Rohit's had been since telling her. At the time, she'd reacted better than he could've hoped for, but the last time they'd spent real quality time together had been at the Leprechaun Trap— the night Maisa had called to talk about their grandmother's diabetes. If it had been enough to scare Rohit, then surely it was enough to scare Cynthia away.

Because, as far as Rohit could see, picnics in the park and free entertainment was not just a temporary phase for a guy one year into his career in account management in a new city. At this rate, he would always be just hanging on to the tail end of a fraying rope, pulled taut by a dark secret and worn down by the burden of financial responsibility.

She could change her mind about him and he wouldn't blame her. The sight of her in a designer dress, sitting in his less-than-impressive vehicle, hurt his eyes.

"I don't know if you've noticed," Cynthia said, "but I've been working off-site a lot lately."

He'd noticed. "Was it intentional?"

"Was what intentional?"

"You . . ." But he couldn't bring himself to ask if she had been avoiding him, or worse, *why*. "You working off-site a lot."

Her response was quiet but crushing. "Maybe. I just feel I need some space from the office," she added.

And space from me. Rohit couldn't bring himself to say the words out loud. Funny how his ability to mask his thoughts and true feelings behind charming words and an affable smile—something he had always believed to be one of his greatest strengths—suddenly seemed like a curse. Hiding his irritation from his family harmonized his relationship with them, and being the easygoing guy at work promised job security. But with Cynthia, it created an uneasy sense of space between them when all he wanted was to breathe her air and sink into her skin.

"I've been playing a lot of catch-up, too, with clients," Cynthia continued, drumming her fingers on the center console. "All that extra work at KC really set me back."

Rohit turned to study Cynthia. Her gaze was downcast, emphasizing the faint shadows under her eyes and his chest twisted. "You need to take care of yourself, too," he said.

"That's first on my list as soon as I get on top of things."

"Maybe you need some help playing catch-up," he ventured softly.

Cynthia's chin snapped up and Rohit would've been more taken aback had Cynthia's eyes not looked so . . . lost. She abruptly turned to look out her window again. "I just need to catch up on sleep," she said.

As Rohit pulled out of the parking lot, he saw a child on the sidewalk bawling in agony over an ice cream cone splattered in the dirt, and he had never identified more with another human being. Or ice cream. "Do you want me to take you home, then?"

Cynthia turned back to him, and to his surprise, a smile tilted her soft, perfect mouth.

"Actually, I'd like to go back to your place," she said.

"Seriously?"

"Don't make me invite myself over again, Rohit."

Rohit grinned. It was the sweetest reprimand she could have said to him.

His high spirits, however, were short-lived. With every twist and turn toward his neighborhood, Rohit found his throat closing as he fought against the urge to throw nervous glances in Cynthia's direction. Even though she'd been to his apartment before, it was far from a point of pride that they were driving away from the vibrant, urban part of the city. There was no way that Cynthia's sharp eye was overlooking the increasingly dated architecture and the boarded-up businesses that had failed to attract new tenants as they drove down the road.

It was a far cry from her living situation; her condo was in a newer building surrounded by boutique stores and quaint local cafés and bakeries. Rohit lived in an older neighborhood, lined by single-story homes, sidewalk chalk, and children's bicycles littering the yards.

"Home sweet home," Rohit said, nervousness coating his bravado with a shaky lilt as he maneuvered his vehicle along the sidewalk across from the building. He saved fifty bucks a month on a parking stall this way, even if it sometimes required a lengthier trek if someone was throwing a party nearby.

He killed the engine and studied the back of Cynthia's head as she looked at his building through her passenger window. He didn't bother removing his hand from his keys, still jammed in the ignition, in case she took another look at his building's dull concrete exterior and faded awning over the entrance and changed her mind.

But she unbuckled her seat belt and swung the car door open. "I may have invited myself over, but I can't let myself in," she said over her shoulder before stepping out of the vehicle.

Rohit led Cynthia to his unit on the first floor and tried to see the modest living space through her eyes. Like Cynthia, he preferred minimal clutter and functional living, but his place lacked the tasteful, eye-catching coordination of someone who understood interior design.

His apartment was a lot smaller, too. His entryway led both into a small kitchen and the living room, where an overstuffed black leather sectional and flat-screen TV took up most of the space. To the right were two doors that led to the bedroom and the bathroom. The windows were curtainless, the walls bare.

And while Rohit was glad something embarrassing, like a poster of a bikini model, wasn't greeting Cynthia now, he was struck by how his home looked somewhat nomadic. Like an exchange student setting up residence for the school year only.

"You know, I'd always expected fancier digs for the most popular guy at work," Cynthia teased as she crossed the short distance between his kitchen and the living room.

He knew she was teasing but the words were jarring. "We're not all blessed with your sense of style," he said half-heartedly.

Or financial freedom, he added silently to himself.

"You're so close to your family," she mused. "Maybe some photos would cozy up the place." A mischievous little smile quirked the corner of her mouth. "Or would that be a turnoff in your bachelor pad?"

"You're the first woman I've brought here," he admitted quietly. After a brief internal debate, Rohit took a deep breath to quell the uncertain flutter in his chest, and he added, "You're the *only* woman I want here."

Maybe Cynthia heard the urgency in his voice, because she grabbed the front of Rohit's shirt and jerked him forward. He caught a glimpse of her smiling lips before his mouth was on hers, the touch of her wet, welcoming tongue against his.

Rohit pulled away. "So you're not sick of me?"

Cynthia's eyebrows shot up. "What?"

"We haven't seen each other in a while . . . I thought you were avoiding the office because . . ." Rohit felt his cheeks flush, but still he searched Cynthia's wide-set eyes for even a glimmer of regret.

"I *have* been busy with work. We both have." Her eyelashes swept downward for a full second, and when she looked back up, Rohit was sure tenderness shone there. "You're the only thing I miss at Kumar Construction. Trust me. Besides . . ." Her face softened. "No one has ever taken me on a picnic before."

Their next kiss was one of relief and pure heat as Rohit tried to show her, with his lips, teeth, and tongue, just how much he needed this. Needed *her*. The hands clutching the front of his shirt splayed wide on his chest, and when his fingers cradled her jaw, she practically purred.

Lord, this woman. In public, she ruled everything and everyone around her with a cool kind of confidence, edged with a startling intelligence that snapped a person to attention. But behind closed doors, she was something else. Still regal and poised, but soft and sweetly pliant, like a cat arching its back into someone's touch.

Hot or cold, there was no guessing with Cynthia. She told him what she liked and took what she needed; she was a queen and every part of Rohit's lovesick spirit wanted to worship her. Even now, in his apartment, Cynthia broke the kiss first and tugged him in the direction of the two closed doors.

"Bedroom?" she asked.

"On the right," he managed to croak.

It didn't take long for them to undress each other down to their underwear, and Rohit's breath stuttered when his hands came into contact with Cynthia's soft skin. He touched her carefully, as if she were uncovered treasure that no human was meant to find. Invaluable and incomparable. His hands shook ever so slightly as if they, too, were in awe of her.

Cynthia pulled away to sit on his bed. Unlike hers, there was no bedframe bracketing his mattress, which sat on a box spring directly on the floor, but Cynthia didn't seem to mind. Her eyes were focused on the front of his straining briefs, which was conveniently now at eye level. Rohit's stomach muscles tightened at the gleam in her beautiful amber eyes.

"Take it out," she said.

"Wh-what?"

With a smirk, she leaned back on her hands and tilted her chin at his waistband. "You heard me."

Rohit swallowed and felt warmth seep onto the tips of his ears as his hands fumbled to follow her command. He was acting like he'd never been with a woman before, which was only heightened when, under her contemplative gaze, his erection jerked upward. He moved forward to join Cynthia on the bed, but she shook her head to stop him and leaned forward instead. Her hands came to rest on the backs of his thighs.

When her lips parted and she moistened her lips, Rohit's heart stopped. "You don't have to," he blurted out.

Cynthia looked up at him under an arched eyebrow. "Do I strike you as the kind of woman who does anything she doesn't want to?"

Whether because she had just admitted to wanting to taste him or because her confidence always set him on fire, her words were an aphrodisiac and his cock jerked again. A coy smile crossed Cynthia's lips a scant second before she took him in her mouth in the same way she did everything in her life: passionately and with no holds barred.

Rohit's knees buckled and he couldn't resist digging his fingers into her hair but not to set the pace or direct her as he flirted with the limits of his self-control. With every long, languid lick of her playful tongue and the shameless way she gazed up at him while sucking him deep, it was more than obvious to Rohit that he was hers to lead whichever way she wanted. He tried to calm his harsh breathing, but focusing on the wet, erotic sound of her mouth pleasuring him had him careening toward the edge.

"Okay, you have to stop," he said, pulling away.

The look of disappointment that crossed her face made Rohit squeeze the base of his shaft in warning. *Don't think about how she might have wanted you to come in her mouth*, he told himself sternly. *Don't or this is going to be over in three seconds.* Still, Rohit couldn't ignore the heady rush of pleasure and incredulity that this gorgeous firecracker of a woman was *naked* on *his* bed and she wanted *him*.

Cynthia removed her last bit of clothing before scooting backward and biting her swollen bottom lip expectantly. Rohit climbed up beside her, his eyes locked on hers as she swung her leg over his hip so they faced each other, the entrance of her perfectly positioned over him. He could feel the heat of her on his tip, the lush wetness there, and he closed his eyes to collect himself.

"Hang on," he said.

"What's wrong?" Her breathlessness scorched the already frayed edges of his self-control, and he squeezed himself again.

"I should get a condom."

"I have an IUD," Cynthia informed him, her trademark impatience simmering below the surface, and Rohit couldn't help but smile fondly despite *aching* to sink into her. "And I haven't been with anyone since . . ." She trailed off and pressed her lips together.

"Since when?"

"Since you."

Rohit's heart banged at the walls of his chest as if building momentum to rip through his skin and launch itself at her. The first time they'd slept together, so many months ago, had been everything and still nothing like this. They'd enjoyed each other's bodies—multiple times—but they'd been near-strangers. He'd been in awe of her then, but now . . .

Now he knew she was intelligent, caring, compassionate, hardworking, and a million other things that made Rohit want to worship every inch of her. She was honey and heat, and with her, he was home.

"Me either," he said, his voice as solemn as the certainty grounding him to this moment. To her. "I haven't been with anyone since you."

Cynthia smiled, leaned in, and gently bit his earlobe. "I need you."

All of Rohit's altruistic intentions deserted him and he sheathed himself in her with one forceful, upward thrust of his hips. He chased her moan with another long, slow pump, hell-bent on driving Cynthia to her limits as she had when she'd taken him in her mouth. But when he snaked one arm under her leg to spread her wider to accept more of him, she retaliated by pulling his hand to her lips and sinking her teeth into the palm. He twitched inside her, making her laugh and gasp at the same time.

"Let me take care of you," he said, before flipping her onto her stomach and sliding into her again. She was so tight like this but that wasn't why he'd positioned them this way. He might chase the workings of her beautiful brain for the rest of his life, but Cynthia's body was becoming familiar to him—a wonderland of planes, curves, and treasures that welcomed all of his five senses and beckoned his sixth.

He knew what she liked, what she needed to come. With one arm propping his weight above her, his other slipped between her heated body and the scratch of well-worn sheets to find where she would need his touch to find release. His girl liked dry, firm pressure just left of her clit in tight little circles that made her whimper, writhe, and fist the sheets. For good measure, and perhaps in playful vengeance as well, he scraped his teeth against the back of her neck and was immediately rewarded with a gasp of satisfaction.

"More," she said, her voice muffled but demanding.

He obliged and then soothed the spot with a gentle lick. *God, she tastes so good.*

As if on their own accord, his hips sped up and the slap of skin on skin warred with Cynthia's moans of satisfaction in the sweetest symphony Rohit had ever heard. His fingers between her legs never ceased their rhythm as he leaned forward, his lips against his ear, to whisper, "I *want* to take care of you, rani."

She shivered under him and came, pure liquid heat squeezing

him indescribably tight, and still Rohit held back. He wasn't done with her—would never be done with her, if she allowed it.

He rolled her onto her back and hooked her leg over his shoulder, angling himself so he drove upward in search of her perfect spot. When Cynthia closed her eyes and trembled under him, he knew he'd found it and began fucking her anew, the mattress squeaking beneath them.

"I'm going to come again," she breathed.

He was right there with her. "Open your eyes," he breathed back. "Please."

As soon as her potent, liquid amber eyes found his, raw pleasure shot up Rohit's spine and he came to the tempo of Cynthia squeezing him as she found her climax again.

Her orgasm lasted longer than his, allowing Rohit the luxury of studying her face as she came back down. With half-masted eyes, lips parted, and a faint, rosy blush on her cheeks, she was a seductive femme fatale, but when her gaze met his, the adoration Rohit felt was reflected back and his chest tightened wonderfully.

A small laugh rattled between them, from her chest to his. Suddenly, Rohit didn't give a damn about the lack of thread count under their bodies or that the overhead lighting might begin to flicker at any moment thanks to the fading bulb he was pushing until burnout. All he cared about was the woman in his bed and in his arms.

"Thanks for letting me invite myself over," she said with a sweet little smile.

Rohit ducked his head into the nape of her neck and inhaled her intoxicating scent, one dizzying thought surfacing above the rest.

I need you, too.

CHAPTER 26

"Jeez, Cynthia, does every project you work on begin as the set of a low-budget porn movie?"

Cynthia managed to elbow Naomi in the ribs before her friend stepped deeper into what would, one day, be Kashmiri Palace after *a lot* of work.

Because whomever had chosen the décor for the previous business—an after-hours cocktail lounge if Cynthia remembered correctly—must have been inspired by a BDSM dungeon complete with studded red leather booths and red-and-black damask wallpaper.

Regretting that she'd chosen a leather, military-style blazer for this particular site visit, Cynthia crossed her arms over her chest and bit her lip nervously as Naomi drew a squiggle on the dusty bar with her finger.

"It would be a complete renovation," she said, hurrying to Naomi's side and tapping through the screen of her tablet until she found the blueprint for the Kashmiri Dining Group's new restaurant. "Like your work on Gia's Bazaar. You'd be starting from scratch." When Naomi didn't respond, the first stab of disappointment sliced through her. "I know it's a big job," she added, pushing the tablet into Naomi's hands. "And I know it's a tight timeline but . . . I just need . . ."

Cynthia forced her mouth shut and took a step back. It wasn't like her to hover or ramble. But as she watched Naomi purse her lips as she flipped through the specs, Cynthia could admit to herself— even if only silently—that she very badly needed Naomi's buy-in.

Collaboration was *not* on Cynthia's very long list of professional strengths and yet here she was, hope churning in her stomach that Naomi would agree to take on fifty percent of the contract for this new restaurant. She'd brought Naomi in today under the same pretext she'd told Rohit after their picnic in the park—that she was currently slammed with playing catch-up after tackling an important internal task at Kumar Construction.

And while this was all true, Cynthia knew there was more to it than that. It was as if a new heaviness had settled in her bones, one that pulled her back from being the first to speak up when Leering Larry said something stupid and borderline sexist, and slowed her pace as she raced the clock to meet with her many, many clients.

Kashmiri Palace, with its sex dungeon beginnings, wasn't the only thing that felt like too much these days. What a strange feeling it was, confronting her growing feelings of fatigue and burnout. And asking for help.

Not that she *needed* Naomi's help. She could do it on her own. She was more than capable of—

No. Cynthia admonished herself with a quick shake of her head. *Look what happened the last time you thought you were better off without help.* And yet the word alone left a funny taste in her mouth. Years of conditioning herself to do and be everything so no one would think twice about a woman's place at the head of the table, and here she was, hope, anticipation, and disappointment competing for real estate in her insides. She wanted nothing more than for Naomi to say *yes*.

It was enough to push Cynthia to go for broke. "I just need help," Cynthia finished. Although the words made her throat feel tight and her mouth dry, she was surprised that they tasted much better when said out loud. They were more than palatable; they were *necessary*. It was okay to need help.

Cynthia licked her lips. "I know that you're busy planning the wedding and that your plate is already full, but—"

"Cynthia." Naomi's voice was gentle. "It's not that or any of things you're worried about. I'm trying to figure out what my contractor might say."

"Your contractor?"

Naomi's eyebrows knitted. "Well, yeah. I figured, when you explained why you'd want to bring me on, that you'd want me to oversee the demolition and rebuild, too."

Cynthia could practically feel every single muscle in her body expand and relax, relief pulling her shoulders away from her ears. "So, are you in? You'll do this with me?"

"Well, yeah, this is a great opportunity . . ."

"But?"

"But I think we should hear Nick's opinion first. That's my contractor's name, Nick Santiago. I meant for you to meet him this morning but of course, as usual, he's late. I swear, that man—"

As if on cue, the entrance of the restaurant swung open and a tall, handsome guy strolled in.

"Nick!" Naomi said, her hands on her hips. "I *hate* when you do that."

"Do what?"

"Your sense of timing is *so* annoying." Naomi glanced at Cynthia and hastened to add, "But his timing is impeccable, too. I swear, he will work miracles in the time he's given to complete the job. I've known this guy professionally for years and—"

"You're rambling," Nick sang in an impressive and surprisingly melodious tenor.

Cynthia wasn't sure if it was the number of rom-coms she'd watched with Rohit or not, but, to her, Nick looked like a stereotypical contractor from a Hallmark movie. Tall, fit, and with linebacker shoulders, he was wearing a flannel shirt with sleeves rolled up to his elbows, to boot. He looked relaxed, with just a touch of mischievousness, as he ribbed Naomi with a glint in his dark green eyes. All he needed was a small town and a family farm to save.

"Shut up, Nicky." Naomi's hip bumped him back. "He's very professional," she assured Cynthia. "I promise. With the timeline and budget you indicated, I think he's the right person for the job."

Cynthia quirked her eyebrow as she eyed Nick. "You did Gia's, too, didn't you?"

With a wink, Nick quirked his eyebrow right back. "Yep."

"I love the finish of the countertops there," Cynthia said. "Honed, right?"

"Yes!" Nick said with a delighted grin. This time he nudged Naomi. "See? I told you matte would be worth the splurge."

Naomi rolled her eyes. "Cynthia is the queen of interior design. Of course *she'd* notice."

Despite the playful exchange, Cynthia could feel her shoulder blades pulling tight again as she waited for Nick's response to Naomi's decree. Her friend's compliments were one thing, but Cynthia had dealt with contractors before, had jumped through hoops many times in the past to prove to them she knew what she was talking about, that she knew more than what colors were trending and which fabrics were the most stain-resistant.

All those contractors had been men who did not take too kindly to a woman—especially a younger one—making calls and reviewing their work with a fine-tooth comb, or, in Cynthia's case, a compact leveler that she kept in her purse.

But Nick surprised her. "I can tell she knows her shit," he said, wandering deeper into the dining room. "You don't rock a blazer like that if you don't know what you're doing."

He was probably kidding, but the throwaway compliment leaped straight into Cynthia's chest cavity and did absurd, mortifying, wonderful things there. She wanted to laugh with relief. Or maybe cry. She wasn't sure.

Was this what it was like working with people who accepted her insight and applauded her intelligence? For the first time, maybe ever, the knot that normally sat behind Cynthia's sternum—the one that pulled her posture ramrod straight and urged her to stay three steps ahead of everybody in the room or risk having everything she wanted unravel—eased. She could relax.

She could relax at work and just be herself. It was an odd feeling and Cynthia couldn't help but eye the room, contemplating if she should sit down for a moment.

Better not. Who knew what had happened in those studded-leather booths?

"You want to gut the entire place?" Nick called from the rear of the dining room, stooping to examine the undersides of the floating shelves on the back wall.

"The whole thing," Cynthia confirmed, wincing before adding, "in a month's time."

She waited for Nick to scoff, to laugh that patronizing contractor laugh she'd heard many times before when she mentioned a tight turnaround. What followed was usually a condescending breakdown of why her demands were unachievable, forcing her to reevaluate her schedule and, in most cases, bend over backward trying to accommodate everyone else to get the job done.

But Nick tilted his head, considering, and jerked his thumb over his shoulder. "Is the kitchen back there?" At Cynthia's confirmation, he headed around the corner.

Once he was out of sight, Naomi handed the tablet back to Cynthia. "I know, he seems way too laid-back, but he's the best I've ever worked with, I swear."

"I trust you," Cynthia said simply. "And your judgment."

"Could've fooled me."

As if on instinct, Cynthia's stance widened ever so slightly, and she braced herself. "What's that supposed to mean?"

Naomi made her wait three long, excruciating seconds as she traced another line down the bar with her fingertip before answering. "Oh, I don't know," she finally said, her tone nonchalant. "You don't trust me enough to mention that you . . ."

"That I what?"

"Had sex last night."

Cynthia gasped. "How'd you know?"

Her friend's face brightened. "I'm right, aren't I? I knew it! A married woman always knows."

"You're not married yet."

Naomi raised her left hand, fanned her fingers, and wiggled them obnoxiously so her engagement ring sparkled under the room's task lighting. "It was Rohit, wasn't it? How was it?"

"I'm not answering that." Cynthia fought the telltale grin spreading across her face.

"I knew it!" Naomi squealed and grasped Cynthia's shoulders. "Your face is practically glowing! Even your hair looks shinier. Was it good?"

A slow heat curled through Cynthia's body, unfurling through her with the lazy grace of a cat stretching in the sun. It was a pleasant warmth, one that had the power to seep into one's veins so that everything felt cozy and secure.

Cynthia stopped trying to hide her smile.

"*That* good, huh?" Naomi's eyebrows lifted in excitement.

"Again, I am not answering that," Cynthia repeated.

Nick strolled out of the kitchen, a measuring tape in his hands. "Not answering what?" he asked. "Questions about the fantastic sex you had last night?" He grinned. "Naomi, you are *so* inappropriate."

"Nicky!" Naomi slapped Nick's arm as Cynthia covered her face with her hands and laughed.

"I heard everything," he admitted with zero contrition on his face. "In addition to the unmatched skill in my hands, I have excellent ears. And eyes. How else do you think I correctly predicted when Naomi and Dev would do the nasty?"

Naomi swiped at Nick's arm again and Cynthia could tell, from his slight wince, that it was much harder this time. "You did not."

"Please, you guys were so obvious." Nick threw Cynthia an exaggerated wince. "My crew was taking bets."

"I take back everything I said about this guy being any kind of professional," Naomi grumbled.

"On that note," Nick said, gesturing toward the kitchen, "we'll have to soundproof the kitchen properly so the diners don't hear what's going on in the back." He shrugged apologetically as he waited for that info—and the accompanying dollar signs—to sink in, then turned to Cynthia with an innocent smile. "So, was it fantastic?"

Her brain reeling from Nick and Naomi's rapid-fire exchange in addition to the shocking realization that she was actually having fun on the job, Cynthia squinted in confusion. "Was what fantastic?"

Nick's grin was wicked. "The sex, of course."

When Cynthia pressed her lips together and shook her head, he held out his hand with an overdramatic sigh. "Okay, let's see."

"What?" Cynthia asked, shooting an uncertain glance at Naomi.

"The guy, obviously."

"You might as well," Naomi advised. "He's relentless when it comes to gossipy things."

Cynthia pulled out her phone and swiped through her most recent photos. She was more than a little disappointed to find that despite having spent the better part of the last four weeks with Rohit, she had failed to capture more than a handful of selfies with him. She was even more disheartened to realize that most of her photos were work-related: the rows of images showed buildings, before-and-afters, furniture samples, and pictures of business cards.

The images were reminders of the work she had done and hoped to do, of the future she had been chasing for years without really realizing that, once lined up under her seeking finger, it was all just a dull, meaningless blur.

Cynthia enlarged a selfie she had taken with Rohit a few nights ago when he'd spontaneously challenged her to an axe-throwing competition at a local rec room. With his appalling lack of aim, Cynthia had done the bare minimum to wipe the floor with him. He'd laughed, then bought her a bubble tea as a reward. It wasn't a particularly special moment, but as Cynthia took in the happy crinkles in his eyes, the carefree way she pressed a kiss to his cheek, her eyes half-closed and the picture off center because perfection had been the last thing on her mind, she realized it meant everything to her.

And she wanted more of this. More of him.

She smiled proudly as she passed the phone to Nick so he could see what Rohit looked like.

Nick whistled as he studied the phone. "Damn," he said. "First Dev, now this guy. Should I be dating more brown dudes?"

Cynthia and Naomi traded grins. "Yes," they said in unison.

CHAPTER 27

Why had no one ever informed Cynthia that a mocha Frappuccino was basically an adult milkshake for breakfast?

Because this whipped-cream-topped concoction was making her day.

And it was only ten in the morning—another first for Cynthia. After a late client meeting the evening before, she'd decided to sleep in this morning, happily burrowing right back into the soft, cozy sheets after unabashedly watching Rohit dress in a crisp slate-blue suit for work. The lingering brush of his lips against the top of her head was the last thing she remembered before sinking back into a deep, satisfying sleep.

She'd needed the rest as much as she apparently needed this regular dose of Frappuccino in her life. In the past, Cynthia had always deemed the drink too frivolous, the absolute wrong beverage to be carrying while breezing into work in her formal business wear, ready to fight for her seat at the table. She couldn't remember the last time she'd slept in, nor could she ever remember loitering outside the

Desmond Business Center on one of the stone benches, reluctant to start yet another workday.

Was the sun always so generously warm and bright on a Tuesday? Were the clouds always so lush?

However, when Cynthia finally stood and turned toward the wide-set concrete staircases leading up to the building, the moment soured. Melanie Burgos was hurrying down the center aisle, her brown leather messenger bag banging against her hip. When she caught sight of Cynthia staring up at her, she slowed, her face wary, then challenging.

She stopped two steps above Cynthia and looked down at her with haughty eyes. Whatever Melanie was expecting, Cynthia's only response was to take a long, fortifying sip of her drink and stare, unblinking, right back. They were silent for several long seconds as they sized each other up, and Cynthia had to swallow the urge to laugh.

They probably looked ridiculous.

"Cynthia," Melanie finally said, eyeing the drink in her hands with a smirk. "Dessert for breakfast?"

"Isn't it kind of *early* for you to be prowling around, trolling for a story?" Cynthia shot back.

Melanie's lips pursed. "Isn't it kind of *late* for you to be rolling into work?"

"I set my own hours," Cynthia said, momentarily taken aback by the pride in her voice. It might've been the sugar coating her tongue, but the words tasted sweeter today. Until now, every move had been a calculated step forward to attain her father's role and his business. But today, the morning was *hers*.

And now all she wanted to do was enjoy her fucking milkshake in the sun.

Cynthia grinned.

Behind her very large glasses, Melanie's eyes widened and, combined with her thick lenses, she looked like an emoji come to life. "And here I thought you were all about the grind."

Cynthia's gaze drifted over Melanie's shoulder to the office tower's flawless glass exterior. It felt like a lifetime ago that the sight of the shiny, professional building filled her with a sense of purpose. She had loved breezing through the door to the rhythm of her high heels tapping on the polished floor, her mind alive and already working overtime to figure how she'd go the extra mile, cram in her never-ending slew of client meetings, and prove herself worthy to her father. Daily, she'd reminded herself that she was too busy for dating, self-care, and anything else that distracted her from her goals. She'd been convinced that all those things would naturally fall into place once she achieved the endgame.

"I was," Cynthia answered, hating the uncertainty belying her words. "I mean, *I am*, but . . ." With a quick shake of her head, Cynthia snapped her mouth shut. She was *not* going to bare her soul to Melanie Burgos of all people. Instead, she quickly hopped up the two steps so she and Melanie were on level ground, with the added benefit of her towering over the much shorter woman. There, that felt like more familiar territory for her. She pulled her shoulders back before asking, "What are you doing here? Still trying to sabotage Kumar Construction?"

Melanie quirked an eyebrow. "Why, is there something you want to get off your chest?" When Cynthia shot her a pointed look, Melanie rolled her eyes. "Believe it or not, I'm not out to get you or your dad. In fact, I've heard nothing but positive changes at your company lately."

"Is that so?"

"I've checked in with my sources and they seem quite happy about the improved corporate culture and new strategies for engagement."

These are all good things, so why don't you want to go inside? a little voice quipped in the back of Cynthia's brain. She gave her head a shake and forced herself to take another step toward the entrance of the building. "I guess you'll have to find another way to impress your boss," she told Melanie before turning to go.

Melanie's words, however, stopped her retreat. "Women like us always do."

"What's that supposed to mean?"

"Don't pretend you're not hustling as much as I am to get ahead," Melanie said. "In that, at least, we're alike."

Cynthia wasn't sure if it was the note of admiration in Melanie's voice or the comparison between the two of them that sent a sliver of discomfort down her spine, but the words gave her pause and she stepped back down so she and Melanie were on even footing again. But before she could think of an appropriate response, however, someone below them cleared his throat. Loudly.

Both women turned in unison to see two young, cocky-looking men standing below them in expensive black suits and skinny black ties. They were good-looking in a waxy, gym-bro way, but their flirty smiles were identically gross.

"Do you ladies mind *not* blocking the way?" the overgelled blond one said, his eyes assessing Cynthia's bare legs. "Not that we mind the view."

His friend leered and stroked his goatee. "Especially if you two are about to have a catfight."

"My money's on the tall one," the blond one piped up again.

Cynthia traded a quick glance with Melanie. If they were expecting her to flirt, they were dumber than they looked, and she would *not* apologize for taking up space. Cynthia spread her arms wide and gestured at the two other staircases flanking the area where they stood. "Go around," she said, purposefully channeling her frostiest Ice Princess.

"And do better," Melanie murmured loud enough for them to hear.

The men's smiles dropped as they each veered in opposite directions to climb the stairs. "Bitches," Cynthia heard the blond one grumble.

"Finance bros," Cynthia lamented when the men had disappeared into the building.

"Oh, definitely," Melanie agreed, cracking a smile while adding, "I could totally take you, by the way."

A chuckle escaped Cynthia's lips. "It would be a fight to the finish."

"I can't believe they expected *us* to move out of *their* way."

"And probably apologize for it."

"Undoubtedly." Melanie shot Cynthia a long look. "This is why we have to hustle, Cynthia. So one day we're running the show and guys like that will get out of *our* way."

Cynthia nodded dutifully. There was no doubt in her mind that Melanie would one day fulfill that prophecy and take over *The Watch*, but as she slowly made her way to work, she realized her future seemed murkier by comparison.

"THAT WASN'T A ROM-COM," Rohit announced later that night from the comfort of Cynthia's living room as the end credits for *The Devil Wears Prada* began rolling on-screen. "You misunderstood the assignment."

Drowsily, Cynthia glanced up from where she lay with her head on his lap. "You said true crime freaks you out."

"Meryl Streep was scary in this, too."

Cynthia sat up, patting her staticky hair down before reaching for the remote and turning off the TV. It wasn't the first time she'd seen this movie, but the unsettled feeling rolling through her was new.

"Do you think the moral of the story is that women who try to have it all are doomed to fail?" she asked.

"No, I think the moral is that you're not supposed to wear florals in spring." Rohit's playful smile fell when Cynthia stared at him blankly. "What? What's wrong?"

Cynthia's lips parted but she didn't know the right words to describe the tendrils of doubt curling in the pit of her stomach. She was right back on the steps outside Kumar Construction, frosty drink melting, knowing she had somewhere to be—things to accomplish—and making no move to do so.

When she didn't respond, Rohit tucked a lock of hair behind Cynthia's ear, the pads of his fingers tracing the sensitive skin before pulling away. "Hey," he said softly. "I think *you* can have it all. You're at the top of your game at work. You—" Rohit abruptly stopped himself, but when his warm brown eyes met hers, it was clear what he had been about to say: *You have me.*

Her chest grew pleasantly tight as the chambers of her heart squeezed. The space between heartbeats, Cynthia was learning, was for pining, aching, and yearning. Falling. There was no uncertainty when it came to Rohit, forever kneeling before her, hand out and waiting for her to grab on, whether she was at her worst or her best.

But who was she without Kumar Construction? She'd chased one goal her entire life, defined her life according to her father, whose shadow engulfed everything in its path.

"I always thought I wanted more," she said, noticing his crestfallen face and hurriedly adding, "at work. I always thought I'd run things."

Rohit's forehead creased. "But you already do?"

Cynthia averted her eyes as she busied herself with unfolding the throw blanket off the back of the couch and arranging it around herself just so. She didn't want to talk about her plans for her father's company right now or how often she thought about the weight of her proud, hardworking father's hand clapping *her* on the back, handing *her* the proverbial keys because she'd made it. Because she'd proven herself as worthy of his empire, that past mistakes belonged in the past, and he needed to let it go.

It would've been her crowning achievement. But the crown seemed wrong now, like it wouldn't quite fit as she'd always imagined it would. And how could she explain all of this to Rohit, who called her his queen?

"I'm not sure if I'm satisfied with everything I've worked for anymore," Cynthia said instead. She bit her lip and looked down at her hands, helplessly entwined on her lap.

"Hey," Rohit said, "come here."

Her body reacted before she could second-guess herself, and she immediately scooted closer, loving how Rohit's arms reached for her, hauling her easily onto his lap. Enveloped in his firm, steady hug, her head tucked securely under his chin, Cynthia could finally relax. Here, with his warm hands sweeping soothingly up and down her back, there was room for mistakes and imperfections. For thawing ice princesses who sometimes struggled to get along with others and maybe didn't always want to.

This, at least, Cynthia realized as she closed her eyes and cuddled more deeply into Rohit's broad, inviting chest, was easy. Effortless. She knew with absolute certainty that she wanted this. She wanted him.

But she wasn't entirely convinced it was enough.

CHAPTER 28

There were many things Cynthia was good at, Rohit mused as he cast a sideways glance at her, confident behind the wheel as she belted out the words to an old Justin Bieber song. Every day with her brought forth a new revelation to tuck away in the back pocket of his heart: along with razor-sharp intelligence and dry wit, she was on a first-name basis with all the best hole-in-the-wall restaurant owners in town, could list all the elements on the periodic table, and knew every lyric to every pop song ever written since the nineties.

But she was a terrible singer and as a snappy Christina Aguilera song burst through the speakers, Rohit wisely turned his grin toward his passenger window as Cynthia tried to hit the high note with the grace of a shrieking macaque.

His girl could not sing.

A sense of rightness settled in his chest as she smoothly backed her car into a parking stall in front of the Desmond Business Center while shamelessly butchering a complicated run. She was impossible not to love.

"What are you grinning about?" Cynthia asked, putting the car in park.

"Just in a good mood." Rohit waited for Cynthia to cut the engine, but when she made no move to do so, he nodded toward the office building. "We should get going. We're already cutting it close."

She was also surprisingly easy to read once a person got to know her because when the heated glow of Cynthia's amber gaze met his, he knew exactly what she was thinking.

They might be running a touch behind, but it had been worth it, and he couldn't stop his eyes from flicking toward her inner thighs, which likely bore the burn of his morning stubble. Maybe he was becoming ridiculously transparent, too, because under his lingering gaze, Cynthia shifted in her seat, the hem of her white dress riding up ever so slightly.

"Are you sore?" he asked in a low voice, thrilled as a light blush seeped onto her cheeks. She hadn't seemed to mind the roughness of his facial hair when he'd pulled her on top of him this morning, nor had it stopped her from grabbing the headboard and grinding against his eager mouth until she found satisfaction.

Cynthia cleared her throat. "I'm fine," she said in a firm voice even as her cheeks reddened steadily.

Rohit felt a goofy grin stretch across his face and he didn't bother to hide it. But when Cynthia's hand remained wrapped around the steering wheel, his forehead wrinkled. "So . . . ?"

"You know what?" Cynthia said, her voice unnaturally bright. "I think I'm going to hit up Starbucks or something."

Rohit didn't miss the hint of strain underneath Cynthia's words and the way her hands fluttered to the parking brake before fiddling with the indicator and tracing buttons on the head unit. Her unwill-

ingness to charge into the building and take everything on the thirtieth floor by storm nudged a hint of worry in the pit of his stomach,
and it wasn't the first time he'd experienced that cool, uncertain
sensation in the last few days.

There were some things that didn't prick his gut: her willingness
to be teased back to bed for just a few more minutes, for example,
was something Rohit was completely on board with. But in the last
few days, he'd begun to see undercurrents of avoidance when it came
to Kumar Construction, a hint of dissent that went against everything
he'd thought he'd learned about Cynthia over the last year.

She was quieter in the senior leadership team meetings, choosing
to work off-site the majority of the day, and although their project of
boosting morale had been successfully delegated to a special in-house
task committee, she seemed disinterested about its progress.

Although the two of them grew closer, he couldn't ignore that
Cynthia was pulling away from the company.

"Is everything okay?" Rohit asked, covering her hand with his
own. His chest squeezed when she responded by threading her fingers through his.

"Everything's fine. But I feel I owe Malik a special treat since
I've skipped for the last few days. Go without me."

Rohit's other hand found the door handle but still he hesitated,
unsure if he should pry. This was new territory with Cynthia, too—in
the past, pushing the Ice Princess too far would've had him on a
one-way trip to a rusty guillotine, but he chanced it anyway. "Are
you sure?"

"Seriously, go," Cynthia said with a laugh, playfully shoving him
with her right hand. But Rohit didn't miss how her hands gripped
the steering wheel afterward as if she was ready to gun the engine as
soon as he left.

As he stepped out of the vehicle, Rohit hesitated again but for a completely different reason. Not for the first time, the urge to say *I love you* rose in his throat and he had to physically swallow the words back down. This was new territory, too, but unlike second-guessing just how far he should pry into Cynthia's beautiful, unknowable brain, this uncertainty made him want to do moronic, archaic things.

Like beat his chest and lay claim, in some shape or form, to the most wonderful thing that had walked into his life.

Rohit knew Cynthia wasn't the kind of woman one laid claim to, but he was absolutely certain that she deserved to be showered with love. She was a queen, and, at least in a quiet part of his brain, *his* queen. She deserved *everything* and it was getting harder and harder to hold back those three words, especially over the simplest, most obscure things. Like now, when he caught sight of her cranking up the radio and opening her mouth to sing out through the passenger window. From the way she tilted her head back as she pulled out of the parking stall, it was obvious she was singing at the top of her lungs, and the words sprang back into Rohit's throat.

I love you, he mouthed silently as he watched her car pull out of view.

KEER WAS WAITING for Rohit outside the elevator doors at Kumar Construction.

"Where have you been?" Keer hissed as Rohit stepped out.

"What?" Rohit shot him a baffled look as he began walking to the front reception desk to see if any mail had arrived for him.

Keer's hand clamped down onto his shoulder, stopping him, and

Rohit instinctively checked his shoulder for donut crumbs. "Rich has been waiting for you," Keer said.

Well, that wasn't anything new. More and more, Rich was finding reasons for Rohit to tag along on his daily activities. Whether it was to a work site Rohit had previously had nothing to do with or to a one-on-one meeting with a senior leader, Rohit often played Rich's shadow. Although it meant putting in a lot of overtime, Rohit was flattered that Rich was taking a keen interest in him, especially because the older man never micromanaged or questioned Rohit's decision making.

Besides, impressing the father of the woman he loved couldn't hurt.

"Okay, I'll just drop off my laptop and—" Rohit was cut off by Keer determinedly steering him down the hallway.

"You're to go to Rich's office *immediately*," Keer said.

At the urgency on Keer's face, Rohit's grip on his laptop bag tightened. Was this about Cynthia? It wouldn't take much for a person to guess that they were dating, but, given that he wasn't her superior or vice versa, it didn't go against any company policy Rohit was aware of. Maybe his boss was more old-fashioned than he seemed and had expected Rohit to ask for his permission.

Rohit's hands began to sweat. Maybe he wasn't good enough for Cynthia in her father's eyes.

When they reached Rich's open door, Keer followed Rohit inside, where the other four members of Rich's senior management team hovered around the CEO's desk. Rich, of course, sat in his office chair, fingers steepled together, his brows furrowed. To his right stood Larry and Simon, leaning against the wall, hands in their pockets. Martin and Olufo had dragged in chairs from another room to flock the sides of the desk, and Keer ambled over to Rich's other side.

"Have a seat," Rich said.

All eyes were on Rohit as he crossed the room. It wasn't until he reached the last empty chair that he noticed Melanie Burgos sitting next to it with an open notebook on her lap. Rohit's thoughts raced and he stopped short behind his chair, bracing his hands against its back. Had Melanie found out about his secret and told Rich? Is that why the room was so solemn and silent?

"Sit down," Rich repeated, his face giving nothing away.

"Perhaps one of the senior leaders would prefer to take the seat?" Rohit stalled, gesturing at Simon, Larry, and Keer. When Rich shook his head, his stomach dipped. "Or I can go grab some extra chairs?"

"Nonsense," Olufo said firmly, pointing a wrinkled finger as if directing Rohit to the electric chair. "You sit right here."

"Did you see that, though?" Keer said from his spot on the wall. "Putting other people's needs first."

Rich nodded. "He respects his elders. These are the kind of values we uphold at Kumar Construction."

Rohit's head buzzed in confusion as Melanie leaned forward to write in her notebook. "Your company has executed a miraculous turnaround given the state of affairs just one month ago," she commented.

State of affairs. Rohit's trepidation eased as he scoffed inwardly, imagining Cynthia's reaction to that pretentious choice of words. He straightened in his seat and looked around the room again. Besides Melanie, he was sitting in a room with the core group of people who attended the biweekly leadership meeting, with the exception of one.

The most important one.

He was about to point out Cynthia's absence when Melanie

looked up from her notepad. "I've spoken with several employees who had nothing but good things to say about the last few weeks," she said, pushing her oversized glasses up the bridge of her nose. "I appreciate you inviting me for an exclusive interview."

Exclusive interview?

"Well, it's all thanks to this man," Rich said, tilting his chin in Rohit's direction amid the murmurs of approval from the rest of the senior leadership team. "He's responsible for pulling it all together. First, with the staff engagement survey and then . . . Tell her how you did it, son."

"Well, it wasn't *just* me—"

"So modest," Keer interrupted with a chuckle. "Of course, the staff supported Rohit with open hearts. We really are like a family around here." He punctuated this decree by reaching into his pocket and pulling out a Timbit, which he popped into his mouth like it was a stick of gum.

Momentarily disgusted, Rohit watched as Keer chewed with open-mouthed gusto. Cynthia's wry voice echoed in his head: *Klepto Keer strikes again.*

His lips twitching, Rohit looked at Melanie. "Right. But I didn't do it alone."

"Who else should I credit?" Melanie asked, cocking her head.

Samuel lifted an eyebrow. "I thought the engagement survey was your idea?"

"Well, *technically*, yes, but—"

"And, after the whole pyramid scheme debacle, didn't you bring in that HR consulting group to help lead us in the right direction?" Martin chimed in.

"Pyramid scheme?" Melanie clicked her pen rapidly. "What pyramid scheme?"

Heat crept up Rohit's neck. "Okay, so, let me explain what happened—"

"And there's more to come," Larry chimed in. "Rohit's planning an organization-wide team-building event next quarter!"

Their interruptions rolling in like thunder, Rohit suddenly had the deepest empathy for what Cynthia must experience in the presence of these men. They didn't care for his answers, nor did it appear that they could hear him when he talked.

Rohit gritted his teeth in frustration, but before he could open his mouth to speak, Rich sat forward in his seat and clasped his hands together on top of his desk, and everyone shut up.

"We owe a huge debt of thanks to Rohit," Rich said. "Which is why I have invited you here today, Melanie, to make my announcement."

Every single member of the senior team straightened. Keer grinned and shot Rohit an exaggerated wink. Melanie turned to Rohit and lifted a questioning brow, and when he shrugged in response, she swiveled back to face the CEO, her left hand tightening expectantly around her notebook.

The room was so still, save for the sound of Rohit nervously cracking his knuckles. He couldn't even begin to guess what Rich was about to say, his mind whirling with this shit show of an "exclusive interview." When Rich shot Rohit a long, pointed glance, a shock of panic worked its way back into his brain and he became hyperaware of a single bead of sweat snaking a cold trail from the nape of his neck into the collar of his shirt.

"That first article in *The Watch* really opened my eyes," Rich said, "and showed me that times are changing. That's how I realized that Kumar Construction needed a change, too."

Rohit was swiping at the sweat on his neck when a flash of white caught the corner of his eye. Cynthia was standing at the doorway of the office, a cup of coffee in each hand. Rohit inclined his head in an invitation for her to join the group, but she didn't see him. Her eyes were trained on her father.

"And thanks to Rohit's diligence, Kumar Construction *has* changed," Rich continued. "He really stepped up in the face of adversity and became the leader we needed him to be."

"Yes, and—" Keer chimed in eagerly, but Rich held up a warning hand, and the finance director's mouth snapped shut.

Rohit winced and threw a silent apology Cynthia's way. *I'll correct them*, he promised, *just as soon as Rich is done speaking.*

"He's an innovative, hardworking, intelligent young man." Rich leaned back in his seat, his hands folded on his stomach. "In just one year, I've watched him grow and successfully take on whatever challenge I threw his way. And he does it with a maturity and charisma that never fails to impress."

Rohit ducked his head as Rich threw him a proud smile. In the back of his flustered brain, a small voice reminded him that Cynthia was all those things, too, and just as deserving—possibly more so— of the praise. He needed to find a way to make sure everyone in the room knew that.

"Even now, he's so modest," Rich said. "Everyone here loves him and recognizes him as a leader. And for these reasons, I take great pride in announcing that, in a year's time, I plan to officially retire and relinquish Kumar Construction to its new CEO, Rohit Patel."

I'll tell them Cynthia also— Wait, what?

As Melanie's pen flew across the page, everyone began clapping, Rich included. Rohit's head spun as one by one, each man in the room walked over to where he sat frozen in his chair, slack-jawed and wide-eyed, and clapped him on the back with words of congratulations. Rohit couldn't register what they were saying over the white noise crackling between his ears. His stomach twisted as the room began spinning, too.

When Rich approached him, Rohit stood on clumsy legs and accepted his handshake in a limp grasp. He couldn't feel his fingers, but a lucid thought finally entered his brain: *My family is going to be okay.*

But what about Cynthia?

Rohit's eyes flew to the doorway. She was gone.

CHAPTER 29

Twenty-nine steps. That was how many were needed to reach the elevator. Cynthia knew this because counting the clip of her high-heeled pumps against the hard floor was the only way to distract her brain from replaying the terrible, *heartbreaking* scene she'd just witnessed in her father's office.

Don't cry, don't cry.

"Cynthia?" Jilly called as Cynthia stepped into the elevator.

With each hand clenching a to-go coffee cup, Cynthia swung her elbow to punch the button for the ground floor, barely registering how the tepid liquid sloshed onto her wrists. She shook her head frantically at a bewildered Jilly as the doors slid closed. Cynthia's eyes blurred with fresh tears, and she tipped her head up to the ceiling, willing them to recede.

They didn't—not even when she gritted her teeth and counted. Forty-two seconds. That was how long it took to ride the elevator to ground level.

When Cynthia stepped out of the elevator, she shoved the coffee cups into a nearby garbage can with shaky hands. She'd bought the second cup on an impulse, one that felt especially stupid now. There would be no praise from her father, no pat on her shoulder because she'd remembered he liked two creams and two sugars.

He probably would've assumed it was from Rohit, anyway.

"Ms. Kumar?" Malik's voice cut in, his chair creaking loudly as he half stood in the rush of her flying by his desk.

Cynthia tried to throw him a smile—*everything's fine, just fine.* In that horrible, fleeting second, she saw his mouth drop open as she beelined toward the sprawling glass doors. So close to freedom.

Freedom from *this place.* How come she'd never noticed how stuffy the air was in here? Would it kill them to open up the lobby doors once in a while? Actually, the whole place could use a facelift. The polished floors were ostentatious; the sun pouring through the glass walls was blinding.

I need to get out.

When she finally stepped into the fresh morning air, Cynthia broke into an uneven jog in her four-inch heels, her oversized black tote awkwardly tucked against her side. She felt the curious stares of the vapers and smokers scattered across the front lawns as she galloped past like a sick greyhound, aware of the sound of her uneven gait and the graceless slapping of her bag.

For once, she didn't care how she looked—escape was first and foremost in her mind, taking precedence over wiping the tears pouring down her cheeks or quelling the shuddering gasps escaping her chest. And when she finally reached her car, Cynthia refused to think about anything except finding her keys in one of the dozens of inner pockets in the large Michael Kors bag that she'd proudly bought after securing her first successful contract with a prominent restaurateur.

It didn't matter anymore.

"Ms. Kumar?" a tentative voice asked.

Cynthia froze, her arm elbow-deep in her bag, and turned very slowly to see Jilly and Malik standing in front of her, their eyebrows furrowed and worried. Jilly was biting her lip while Malik's quick, practiced brown eyes jumped over Cynthia's person as if checking for injury.

Trying to regulate her harsh breathing, Cynthia swallowed and tried for a smile that, against her trembling cheek muscles, felt more like a grimace. "You can call me Cynthia," she replied, the last word convulsing on a mortifying hiccup. It was as if her body was revolting against her last shreds of dignity.

Malik reached into the breast pocket of his expensive suit and proffered a blinding white handkerchief that Cynthia accepted but then held aloft in her upturned palm, as if unsure what to do with it. Jilly moved closer and, after a moment's hesitation, placed her hand on Cynthia's back.

It was a far cry from a hug, but Cynthia leaned into the touch as her shoulders hunched forward and she continued to sob in the parking lot in front of her assistant and the security guard. *Can it get any worse?* she thought to herself before noticing the splotches of caramel coffee across the front of her dress from where she'd spilled the drinks earlier in the elevator.

When Malik sidled to her other side, his much larger hand finding her back as well, Cynthia cried harder.

It took several long, agonizing minutes for the tears to slow and for Cynthia to get hold of herself. She couldn't remember the last time she'd wept like this, was certain she'd *never* made such a spectacle of herself in front of other people. *The Ice Princess is melting*, she thought after a loud, unladylike sniff, half expecting the skies to punctuate the moment with an epic downpour.

But no—there was nothing but a bright, cheerful sky above, as perfect as it had been when she'd dropped Rohit off at work, aching with the desire to tell him she loved him.

"What happened?" Jilly asked as Cynthia wiped her face with Malik's soft handkerchief.

"My dad just announced his retirement."

Jilly and Malik exchanged confused looks.

"He named Rohit as his successor," Cynthia added.

"I guess that makes sense," Jilly said, tilting her head to the side. "He's kind of young, but . . ." She trailed off as Cynthia's eyes dropped down to the pavement.

Cynthia willed her mouth shut, but the bitter words were too acrid to keep inside. "He was never going to pick me. He doesn't even know I exist."

"Rohit?" Jilly asked, perplexed.

"My father."

Jilly's voice was full of surprise. "I'm so sorry, Cynthia. I didn't realize that's what you wanted."

"I've been wanting this my entire life—" Cynthia stopped. The words sounded tinny in her ears, and she raised her head to gaze at the place where she had shaped every part of herself to convince Rich Kumar that she was worthy of his legacy.

And his admiration and respect.

She'd tried so hard to mold herself after her father that she'd become something else entirely: a steely, unyielding shell of a human who relied on ice and illusion to hide the cracked, crumbling parts of her. And still, it hadn't been enough.

"You would have made an excellent CEO," Malik said kindly. "I'm sorry, too, Cynthia."

Cynthia rubbed at her eyes again before attempting a small, wobbly smile at the two people who had followed her out here, hung on while she'd lost her composure, and now comforted her with awkward pats on her back that no longer felt so awkward. Maybe she wasn't as hard as she'd thought.

"Do you . . ." Jilly cleared her throat. "Do you want me to get Rohit?"

"Why?" Cynthia asked sharply.

Jilly flushed. "Um . . . Because you two are . . . I mean, I thought you two were . . ."

Cynthia shook her head. At the mere mention of his name, fresh pain washed over her, but this time it was different, easier in a way. This was the mild disappointment she'd felt upon stumbling into an impromptu meeting in her father's office that, of course, had failed to include her. The familiar irritation of hearing everyone heap praise on Rohit for his commendable work. The absolute slap in the face when Rohit failed to credit her.

This pain burned like July wildfire, ferocious and all-consuming.

Cynthia was honest enough with herself to admit that her father's announcement came as no surprise; a part of her had always known that he wouldn't choose her as his replacement.

But she'd believed everything Rohit had told her. *Your father knows your worth*, he'd said once on bent knee, *we all do*. He'd called her a queen.

Malik offered her one last pat before clearing his throat. "Can I grab you anything, Ms. Kumar?"

"Cynthia," she corrected dully.

"A bottle of water, maybe?" Malik continued.

"I'm okay," she replied, well aware that her voice shook. "You should get back to work, Malik. You, too, Jilly."

Malik gave her shoulder a squeeze before departing, but her assistant hesitated.

"Maybe . . . there's a silver lining here," Jilly suggested in a hopeful voice.

"Like?"

"I'm not saying you don't deserve the role, but maybe it's better Rohit got it. That job takes on a lot of responsibility and seems stressful. Your dad is *always* working, and—"

"I'm already doing all those things." The admission felt wrenched from Cynthia's chest as she scrubbed at her face. "And I've been doing them long before Rohit got here with his so-called MBA."

Somewhere in the distance, an ambulance's siren cried in warning as the two women stared at each other in silence.

"'So-called MBA'?" Jilly's eyebrows knit together.

"I— Forget I said anything," Cynthia said hurriedly, her heart pounding. The ambulance was long gone but the echo of its siren continued to replay in her ears. "I'm just angry."

When Jilly slowly nodded, Cynthia gently stepped out of her reach.

"Is there anything else I can do?" Jilly asked.

"Really, Jilly, I'll be okay." With an overwhelming sense of chagrin, Cynthia looked into Jilly's brown doe eyes. She'd often treated Jilly with brisk impatience, likening her vapid gaze to that of a flighty squirrel that couldn't hold two thoughts at once to save its life.

Before, Cynthia had chalked Jilly's decision to stay by the side of a demanding, ambitious, and impatient boss as complacency; there were worse things than getting snapped at for fifty-five thousand dollars a year and a health spending account. But Cynthia realized now how very wrong she'd been. There was no bonus or overtime to be had while comforting your teary-eyed superior in the parking lot.

Cynthia owed her an apology but all she could muster right now was a quiet and heartfelt "Thank you."

Jilly squeezed her arm before she took her leave. "I got your back."

CYNTHIA HUGGED HER gym bag tightly to her side as she made her way down the sidewalk toward her condo building, where Rohit was sitting on the front steps. She tried to ignore the lump in her throat as she took in his wrinkled suit jacket and rumpled hair, as if he'd been running his hands through it all day.

But when he opened his mouth and had the audacity to *yell* at her, the lump turned into a tightness that was more foreboding than forlorn.

"Where have you been?" Rohit stood up so abruptly his knees cracked.

Cynthia came to a halt on the path up to her condo and folded her arms across her chest. It didn't matter that she'd ditched her no-nonsense work dress and heels for black leggings and a sports bra. She'd just finished two grueling back-to-back kickboxing classes and was primed for a fight.

"Excuse me?" she said, drawing her chin up.

"I've been sitting out here for hours," he said, gesturing at the darkening sky. "You never came back to the office, and you've been ignoring my calls and texts. I was worried!"

The admission was a jab to her solar plexus, but she hadn't spent the last two hours tightening her core for nothing. Cynthia cocked her head and infused her voice with that same icy condescension she reserved for finance bros and contractors who called her "honey." "So? What's your point?"

Rohit gaped at her. "Are you serious?"

When he moved to make his way down the steps to her, Cynthia held up her hand to stop him. She should have felt triumphant when Rohit froze in his tracks, wariness pulling his handsome features downward. Instead, Cynthia couldn't help eyeing the space between them, a cold seven or so inches that pierced her heart.

Damn him for breaking down her walls.

"I want to talk to you about what happened earlier." Rohit swallowed. "In your dad's office." When she didn't respond, he continued. "I don't know how much you heard, but—"

"Oh, I heard plenty." She told herself she didn't care when his face fell. "Let me guess," she said snidely as a tall, muscular guy in shorts walked past her, headed to the building. "You didn't *realize* I was standing there until it was too late. I shouldn't *need* the praise to know how *valuable* I am. You didn't want to *interrupt* the circle jerk to remind everyone that I deserve credit, too."

The muscular guy faltered as he swiped his fob and shot Rohit a look of alarm and pity before heading into the building. Rohit's gaze, however, never wavered from Cynthia's face. He looked stricken.

"Well?" Cynthia asked, kind of hating the mocking impatience threading through her voice, detesting it even more when Rohit winced. "What shitty excuse are you going to give me this time?"

"What's a 'circle jerk'?"

"What?"

"You said I didn't want to 'interrupt the circle jerk' but I don't know what that is," Rohit said, his cheeks flushing.

Cynthia rolled her eyes and fished her fob out of the side pocket of her gym bag. "Seriously? That's what you have to say to me right now?" She moved toward the door, too aware that every step closer to Rohit seemed to squeeze the air right out of her lungs. Cynthia could practically feel panic building in her veins, rushing through her, making her both hot and cold, heightening her senses but leaving her feeling achingly numb inside.

She kept her eyes trained on the entrance of her building as if it were some kind of finish line. *You can fall apart when you're on the other side.*

"Cynthia." Rohit made no move to touch her, but that soft, solemn voice stopped her hand midswipe over the fob's panel. "You're right. That meeting was awful, and I should've said something. But everyone kept interrupting me when I tried to speak up, and—"

"Typical Rohit," she interrupted, hating how her voice cracked. "More concerned with staying in everyone's good graces than doing the right thing."

"You're not even letting me talk. If you would just listen—"

"Like I said, I already heard everything I needed to know."

"So that's it? You're back to being the Ice Princess?" he asked. When Cynthia swiped her fob again and reached determinedly for the door handle, his voice rose a pitch. "I know I didn't handle things well in there, but I was completely floored by your dad announcing his retirement and wanting *me* to take over . . ." Rohit trailed off as Cynthia began shaking her head.

Her next words slipped out, bringing with them a rush of heat to her face that she wasn't entirely sure was embarrassment or anger. "Did it ever occur to you that maybe someone else might want to be Kumar Construction's next CEO, too?"

"Who?" Rohit's eyes widened. "You mean . . . *you*?"

He sounded so dumbfounded, Cynthia wanted to throw something at him. The audacity. *How dare he.*

After everything he'd said to her, he'd never really believed in her.

"So did you accept the job offer?" she asked, propping the door open with her foot.

"Cynthia. You know about my responsibilities to my family."

"Did you accept?"

Rohit shrugged helplessly. "I'd be a fool not to."

Cynthia felt the mortifying moment her face fell, everything sagging downward to the trembling point of her chin, and she clenched her jaw hard in retaliation. *Don't cry*, she told herself in a cold, firm voice. *Don't show him any weakness.*

But it wasn't enough. She wanted to hurt him like he'd hurt her. Like he'd destroyed her and everything she'd convinced herself to be true. Anything to resurrect her walls and push him away.

"But do you *deserve* the job?" she said in a soft voice.

Rohit stepped back onto a lower step, his face aghast as if she'd reached out and slapped him. She might as well have.

"You can be so hard sometimes," he said after a moment, his voice a heartbreaking mix of dismay, hurt, and confusion. "There's never room for second chances with you, is there?"

With a scowl, Cynthia turned and forced herself to walk—not run—through the open door. "I already gave us a second chance, Rohit, and look where that got me."

CHAPTER 30

T wo days later, Rohit was sitting in Rich's office listening to the older man reminisce about his company's humble beginnings in a dilapidated warehouse thirty-odd years ago when a hard knock sounded against the open doorway's frame.

Until that moment, Rohit had been faking interest in a story Rich had told him many times before, but at the sound of that firm, decisive rap, the hairs on the back of Rohit's neck stood up.

It had to be her.

He hadn't seen Cynthia since that night outside her condo, but she'd haunted him anyway—the scent of sandalwood infiltrating his senses at the oddest moments, his gait automatically slowing as he passed by her empty office. His stupid heart stuttered whenever the clip of brisk heels echoed in the halls.

He couldn't shake her—had never been able to since that first damn night in that damn bar—but he couldn't bring himself to acknowledge that little voice in the back of his mind whispering that maybe he didn't want to.

He loved her still.

Don't turn around, Rohit coached himself. *You need to move on.* But the urge was too strong, like his bones, joints, and tendons were tethered to her aura, powerless against her pull. He'd tried to convince himself it was for the best that she'd so coldly thrown his apology back in his face, that he was better off without this impossible, undecipherable woman in his life. Once an Ice Princess, always an Ice Princess.

But Rohit's heart was dusty and parched for her. Years of watching and rewatching the same plotlines play out in countless romantic comedies and still he'd been defenseless against her.

Rohit gave in, turned around, and drank in the sight of her in a modest black knee-length dress that accentuated her purposeful stride. Her liquid amber-brown eyes avoided his, and while Rohit's heart gave a painful thump in protest, he couldn't look away.

"What is it, Cynthia?" Rich asked, tossing his empty coffee cup in the waste bin beside his desk.

"Um . . ." Cynthia bit her lower lip and Rohit forced his eyes away. "Have you seen a copy of *The Watch* today?"

Rich shrugged at Rohit. "No."

"They published another story about Kumar Construction. Maybe . . ." The tentativeness in Cynthia's voice raised pinpricks of awareness over Rohit's skin, and he leaned forward in his seat. "Maybe we should talk about this in private."

Rohit made to stand, but Rich waved him back into his seat. "It's okay," Rich said with a half smile at Rohit. "Gotta learn media relations if you're going to run this place."

Risking a quick glance at Cynthia, Rohit was surprised by her face as she approached her father's desk. She didn't shoot daggers in his direction, nor did she look pained by the reminder that her father had named Rohit his successor.

She looked like she didn't care. Whatever sustenance had filled Rohit's heart from the sheer sight of her gushed right back out, leaving a dehydrated, shriveled raisinlike lump behind. He would have preferred anger—Julia Stiles kicking a soccer ball at an unsuspecting Heath Ledger's head or Rachael Leigh Cook screaming at a speechless Freddie Prinze Jr. at the prom Rohit could handle.

Indifference, on the other hand, was crushing.

Cynthia handed her father a copy of *The Watch* before taking a seat next to Rohit, staring straight ahead as her father skimmed the article. When Rich looked back up, his face was unreadable as he stared at Rohit. "This article claims you never got your MBA."

"What?" Rohit reached forward and yanked the newspaper out of Rich's hands. The words blurred on the page as Rohit's eyes frantically sought those damning three letters. "It says *what*?"

Beside him, Cynthia made a pained sound in the back of her throat.

"This is defamation of character." Rich's voice rose. "I cannot *believe* they would print such lies. I'm going to—"

"Dad," Cynthia said quietly.

Rich didn't hear her. "—call Tim *right now* and—"

"Dad—" Cynthia said.

"I'm going to demand a retraction!" Rich muttered as he angrily scrolled through his phone.

With shaky hands, Rohit placed the newspaper back on the desk. "Stop." To his own ears, the protest sounded weak and tired, but it carried enough weight to grab the attention of both Cynthia and her father.

"Rohit?" Rich asked.

"Rohit," Cynthia echoed.

At the soft caution in Cynthia's voice, Rohit stiffened. It was his turn to ignore her now. "Everything in this article is true," he said to Rich. He pretended not to notice Cynthia's sharp intake of breath and the way her hands clamped onto the arms of her chair. She was probably afraid he'd out her for leaking the story, trashing Kumar Construction's reputation and her own at the same time.

Because that was all she cared about, wasn't it?

"Cynthia, shut the door," Rich commanded. When she'd obeyed, Rich picked up the paper again. "Which parts are you talking about exactly? Because it says here that—"

"Everything," Rohit replied. "When you interviewed me for the job, I didn't correct you when you congratulated me on getting my MBA. And I've let everyone believe I have one."

Well, almost everyone. Still, Rohit refused to look at her.

A deep crease settled between his boss's eyebrows. "Why?"

"Shortly before applying for a job here, I dropped out of my MBA program because my family needed financial help. When you didn't check into my credentials, I couldn't pass up the job opportunity." Rohit dragged a hand through his hair. "I'm sorry, Rich. I deserve every single consequence for lying to you. I'm not proud of it, but after my grandmother's stroke, I didn't see any other option. I am so sorry for bringing this on the company."

Rich leaned back in his seat, his hands folded together and stacked on his abdomen. Rohit didn't allow himself to break eye contact, even as Rich's sharp, scrutinizing gaze inspired a slow, agonizing heat to scale up Rohit's spine. His humiliation, however, was no match for his guilt, but there was no apology worthy of what he'd done.

Beside him, Cynthia cleared her throat, but as she parted her lips, Rohit beat her to the punch. "I'll resign," he said.

Although Rohit rarely found himself one step ahead of Cynthia, there was no victory in besting her. To his surprise, he felt very little anger toward her, too. He should have been livid that she would betray him this way, that everything they'd been through—the good and the bad—could amount to this kind of revenge. And for what? A CEO position?

When Rohit finally turned to look at her, he felt nothing but pity for Cynthia. "Well, I guess you'll get what you want now."

She looked stricken. "Rohit, this isn't . . . This isn't what I want."

Rohit shook his head. He knew he wasn't blameless in this, but at least he hadn't sought to hurt anyone in this whole mess. Despite himself, Rohit felt a little lightheaded. Perhaps it was the whiplash of events or the realization that he was now unemployed, but that didn't explain the newfound lightness he felt in his chest or the strange urge to laugh.

He remembered feeling this way once before. It was on that first day he'd arrived in Canada—after two days of traveling and one heinous layover, Rohit had stepped out of the Toronto Pearson Airport and experienced this same rush of relief: *I made it*, he'd thought, his eyes, ears, and heart overwhelmed in the most exhilarating way, *I can breathe now.*

Thanks to Cynthia, he was free. Sure, he'd need to find a new job quickly—perhaps even move to a new city—but at least this time, he could do it right.

Rohit met Rich's gaze again. "I'm really sorry for deceiving you, Rich," he said again.

Rich's head tilted to the side, considering. "We need privacy," he said. But when Rohit tried to stand again, the older man raised a commanding hand. "Not you," he said before shooting Cynthia a meaningful glance.

Cynthia wet her lips and reached out to touch Rohit's hand, but when he shifted out of reach, she pulled her hand back, as if burned.

Still, she asked, in a soft voice: "Rohit?"

Rohit looked at her. Funny how a face could be so, so beautiful while, at the same time, leave him so, so empty.

"You should leave," he said in a quiet but firm voice. His mind reached for the many instances over the past year where she'd shut him down, turned a frosty shoulder toward his efforts to befriend her. He didn't want to stoop to her level, but after months of working with the Ice Princess, he'd learned a thing or two.

Cynthia stood and looked at him beseechingly.

Rohit turned away. "I think I've gotten what I *deserve*," he said quietly, shooting her words right back at her. "Don't you?"

CHAPTER 31

Y ou're not A Little Seoul," Cynthia said, squinting against the fluorescent-lit hallway of her apartment building. Her grip tightened on the knob of her front door as Jilly cast an uneasy glance down the corridor before meeting her eyes again.

She made a mental note to give her assistant a raise for tactfully overlooking the literal hot mess in front of her. Cynthia was well past a disheveled state of falling apart for six o'clock on a Tuesday evening, but sheer stubbornness stopped her from belting the front of her favorite hooded bathrobe. She could pretend she wasn't embarrassed by rumpled silk pajamas, one leg of which had untucked from her fuzzy tube sock. Or the zit patch on her chin, which she raised now, defiant.

"I'm sorry for turning up here unannounced." Jilly cleared her throat. "Well, actually, I *did* try to contact you . . ."

Cynthia glanced over at her kitchen counter, where her phone sat on its charging dock, muted. With her confrontation with Rohit fresh in her mind, several voicemails from Jilly and one concerned text from Naomi asking why she had canceled their weekend dinner plans had been enough for Cynthia to stop checking altogether. There was a missed call or two from her mother, too.

Too bad the silent cell phone did little to stop Cynthia from wondering why *he* hadn't called. Or texted her. Or thought of her.

Stop it. You pushed him away, remember? Walls are safer.

"I'm sick," Cynthia said flatly. "Deathly contagious."

Jilly's eyebrows furrowed. "In the whole time I've worked for you, I've never seen you miss more than one day of work unless you were on vacation and, even then, you forwarded work emails and sent me reminder checklists every day."

Cynthia gritted her teeth. Yeah, and look at all the good that had done her. "Like I said, I'm sick," Cynthia added, slowly closing the door. "But thanks for checking in."

But then Jilly did the most un-Jilly-like thing Cynthia had ever seen her do. She stuck her foot in the entryway, thrust her face to the opening, and met Cynthia's gaze with a hard one of her own. "I need to talk to you."

Cynthia stared at her assistant's determined, size six, ballet-flat-wearing foot.

"Can't it wait until Monday?" It wasn't an outright lie for when Cynthia planned to return to work but a generous guess at best.

"It can't."

With a long sigh, Cynthia left the door ajar and withdrew back into her living room to flop onto the couch. She knew she was being rude—and aware that her couch looked like she hadn't left it for days—but right now, she didn't give two flying fucks.

And it felt good. When was the last time she had binged two seasons of a TV show in four days? Or lived in her pajamas? She hadn't shaved her legs or cleaned up after herself for days and it felt great.

A hollow accomplishment, sure, but great.

"Have a seat," Cynthia said, swinging a fuzzy-socked foot onto the coffee table.

Jilly wasn't interested in finding a place to sit among scattered throw blankets and a half-empty bowl of all dressed chips. She stood in the middle of Cynthia's living room and looked around with a dubious frown.

"Okay, so obviously I'm not deathly ill," Cynthia said, sarcastically. "But even if I were, this is beyond the call of a good assistant."

"Quit it," Jilly snapped. From the way her eyes widened afterward, Cynthia surmised that her tone had surprised them both. "Sorry. I know you're going through a tough time, but I need to tell you something. It's important."

With a petulant huff, Cynthia turned off the television. *Selling Sunset* would have to wait. She crossed her arms over her chest and leveled Jilly with a narrowed stare she'd perfected years ago and used many times to force grown men a few steps back. It had *always* put a stop to Jilly's incessant apologizing in the past, too.

But Jilly straightened her shoulders instead. "I was the one who tipped Melanie off about Rohit's lie about his MBA."

Cynthia's arms uncrossed, her hands falling like dead weights onto her lap. "*You what?*"

Chagrin colored her assistant's face. "I don't regret it," she said. "I mean, I feel guilty about it because Rohit is a nice guy, but . . . When I saw the article about your dad's retirement and how Rohit was given all the credit for *your* work, I don't know, I wanted to do something for you."

"Our work," Cynthia corrected automatically.

"What?"

"Both Rohit and I were assigned the task of fixing KC's reputation."

The words left a bitter taste in her mouth, but Cynthia wasn't going to pretend she had done it all herself. *Unlike some people . . .*

But the reminder of Rohit's stealing all the credit did not summon the righteous anger it once had. Her heart squeezed around a pointy little thumbtack instead. Four days of holing up in her apartment with the high-end real estate agents of West Hollywood as her only companions had done nothing to erase the look on Rohit's face in her father's office when he'd seen his secret revealed in austere, black ink.

Inside her chest, the thumbtack sharpened. "We did the work together," Cynthia added in a quiet voice.

"You don't have to give any credit for what you did for the staff at Kumar Construction," Jilly said. "We both know *you* did all the heavy lifting. You always do."

Cynthia couldn't deny that Jilly's staunch defense of her warmed her insides, but it was more than she deserved. She shook her head. "Not this time. It genuinely was both Rohit and me. My dad—" Her voice caught and she took a quick, steadying breath so the next words tumbled forward in a rush. "I guess my dad doesn't see it that way."

"Cynthia—"

Shaking her head again, Cynthia pulled an orange throw pillow onto her lap. "I don't want to talk about him," she said.

Whether Jilly knew if Cynthia was referring to Rohit or her father, she wisely remained silent while Cynthia pressed her head back onto the couch cushions, her eyes fluttering closed for a moment as she sorted through Jilly's admission. "Why would you want to ruin Rohit's future?"

Jilly hurried to the coffee table and perched on its edge, tactfully avoiding the scattered pile of unused takeout napkins from various restaurants. "I wasn't trying to ruin Rohit's reputation," she explained. "I mean, I didn't think that far in advance. I just . . ." Jilly shrugged. "You were so upset in the parking lot. I wanted to help. I, of all people, know how hard you work."

"But . . . I don't understand." Cynthia paused and studied Jilly's earnest face. "Melanie found out about Rohit so quickly after publishing that news article about my dad's retirement. How did you get hold of her so fast?"

Jilly blushed. "I kind of already had Melanie's contact information," she said quietly.

A chill snaked its way down Cynthia's spine. "You had her contact information," she repeated.

Jilly licked her lips. "I . . . I might've been one of the people complaining about Kumar Construction before that first article came out."

Cynthia stood up abruptly and the glass table under Jilly's butt squeaked as she scooted back, startled. "That was you?"

"It wasn't *just* me," Jilly protested as Cynthia stalked to her kitchen, unsure how to regulate the shot of adrenaline running through her. "B-but yes, I was one of the, uh, whistleblowers."

"Why?" Cynthia shook her head. Without knowing what to do, she reached into one of her cabinets, grabbed an omelet pan she'd never used, and dropped it roughly onto the stove. Its clatter was strangely comforting. "My dad gave you that job as a favor to your father. You had zero credentials and no experience when he got me to hire you."

Her assistant bowed her head but not before Cynthia saw contrition flood her face. The same shame laid siege over Cynthia's senses, too. It wasn't entirely Jilly's fault Melanie had found out; at least Jilly's intentions, misguided or not, had been kind of noble. Cynthia had been the one to blurt out Rohit's secret in a bitter moment of weakness.

Worse still, she'd sneered at the promotion to Rohit's face when he'd tried to apologize, as if a person's hard work, track record, and value should be overlooked because three letters were missing from his résumé.

What she'd done was much, *much* worse.

"Jilly, I don't mean to shit on you. I'm sorry," Cynthia said, leaning against the stove and raking her fingers through her hair. "You're just throwing a lot of information my way."

Jilly stood up and, with tentative steps, shuffled over to the kitchen. Cynthia half smiled. The squirrel-like tendencies were growing on her.

"I can't apologize for telling Melanie about what Kumar Construction used to be like. It was not a good place to work, Cynthia." Jilly averted her eyes. "No one wants to work at a place where people are quick to criticize but slow to praise, there's no room to grow, and you always feel like you have to be tied to your work phone."

A knot pulled tight in Cynthia's stomach as the mortifying truth behind Jilly's admission sank in. She was part of the problem. Hadn't she, despite her better judgment, talked down to Jilly when she failed to keep up with her? Had she spent *any* time, outside of piling on the work, coaching or mentoring Jilly?

This woman was in her apartment pouring her heart out and Cynthia couldn't remember the last time she'd thanked her for a job well done. Or, Cynthia realized as a nauseating discomfort stirred in her gut, if she had *ever* recognized Jilly for the long days or the little ways she tried to anticipate her boss's needs. She'd never been particularly kind to Jilly, but still, when Cynthia had been at her lowest, her assistant had shown up for her, no questions asked.

"And it's so much better now," Jilly rushed to add, her voice pitching a little higher in the wake of Cynthia's silence. "I told Melanie that, too."

"Jilly, I'm not mad," Cynthia said. "You were right to speak up about your feelings, even if it was to someone like Melanie. No"—Cynthia raised her hand when Jilly opened her mouth to argue—"I'm *glad* you went to *The Watch* with your complaints. Things weren't good at work and you were right, they needed to change." Cynthia paused and, after a brief hesitation, placed an awkward hand on Jilly's shoulder. "I was part of the problem, too. I didn't realize it then and I hope next time you'll feel comfortable enough to tell me, because I am sorry for playing a part in making you feel undervalued. I'm lucky to have you and I don't tell you enough."

Jilly's face flushed with pleasure and her back straightened. "Then I don't regret telling Melanie about Rohit, either. Not after what he did to you. You deserve better from KC."

Cynthia's lips quirked in a rueful smile. A year ago, Jilly's brand of a black-and-white type of justice would've made complete sense to her. Rohit had been the enemy, she the rightful heir to her father's legacy, and there had been no in-between.

It had been a simpler time. Easier in a way but lonely. So damn lonely that Cynthia wrapped her arms around herself and squeezed. Things still felt heavy inside, but at least those wonderful moments she'd etched into her heart from the last few months were still there.

They were tiny sparks in a cold, dark place and, Cynthia realized with a start, had nothing to do with her career.

On an impulse that was weird, uncomfortable, and wholly wonderful, Cynthia threw her arms around Jilly and squeezed. "I appreciate you trying to protect me," she said softly.

And when Jilly responded with a watery laugh and hugged her back, the sparks grew.

CHAPTER 32

"A re you sure you want to do this?" Naomi asked in a hushed voice as Cynthia led her into her parents' home.

Cynthia glanced over her shoulder to where Naomi was literally creeping along on tiptoes and rolled her eyes. "You don't have to sneak around. We're not doing anything illegal. This is *my* parents' home." Still, Cynthia took a quick survey of the empty foyer before leading her friend into her dad's office.

Because she did feel kind of sneaky. Normally, Cynthia relied on the printers at Kumar Construction, but having avoided the office for a whole week now, she needed to print her resignation letter. She couldn't tamp down the childish little thrill, however, over printing it in the CEO's personal office.

But there was fear there, too. She'd hitched herself to her father's legacy for almost fifteen years. It was all she'd ever known, all she thought she'd ever *have* to know to get where she wanted to go.

Without her father's company, Cynthia wasn't sure what she was anymore and although the knowledge—or lack thereof—was a tender pressure point between her shoulder blades, her hands moved determinedly as she connected her laptop to the printer.

She'd figure it out. She always did.

As the devices paired together, Cynthia looked up to see Naomi edging into her father's office. "You should probably put on some gloves or something, so you don't leave fingerprints."

When Naomi glared back, Cynthia laughed. "Seriously, if you're that uncomfortable, you don't have to be here with me," she added. "You can wait outside."

"Of course I have to be here. You're leaving your father's company, which you've been with your entire career. This is a big deal and you need moral support."

Cynthia shot her a dubious look even as her heart swelled at the words. She wasn't sure what she'd done to have inspired this level of loyalty and friendship in the people around her, but the flare of gratitude she felt in moments like these shocked her system every time.

But she welcomed them—*needed* them.

"Don't worry, I'm chill," Naomi said, sitting down on the love seat sofa in the corner of the room. She looked anything but calm as she perched on its edge, ready to bolt. "Are you almost done?"

"So chill," Cynthia teased, her words swallowed by the printer—an older model purchased at least twenty years ago—spitting out Cynthia's resignation.

Cynthia pulled it off the tray and silently reread its contents. A fifteen-year tenure ended in five lines and three sentences. It was formal and to the point, but it didn't feel complete. It was missing something Cynthia wasn't sure she could express on a standard 8½-by-11-inch letter even though the feelings were coded on the most fragile parts of her heart.

She'd held back too many things for so long. Too long.

"Cynthia?" Naomi asked.

"What?" Cynthia's head jerked up. She hadn't heard Naomi move across the room to join her behind her father's desk.

"It's okay to have feelings about this. Like I said, it's a big deal, even if you're leaving on good terms." Naomi paused. "You *are* leaving on good terms, aren't you?"

"Who's leaving on good terms?" Cynthia's mother asked as she walked through the office door. "Oh, Naomi! How nice to see you again. How was that event you went to? What earrings did you pair with the silver necklace Cynthia picked out? I bought that necklace on a trip to Toronto."

Naomi smiled politely. "It was lovely, thank you. Cynthia has excellent taste."

Sipra laughed. "I'll take that as a compliment! My daughter has never had much interest in traditional clothes. I picked out all those items in her closet."

Naomi and Cynthia exchanged awkward glances as her mother approached Cynthia's side, her eyes glancing at the paper clutched in Cynthia's hands. "You're leaving?" she asked in surprise.

When Cynthia didn't answer right away, Naomi cleared her throat. "I think I'll go upstairs and try on more of Cynthia's excellent wardrobe."

"I know what you're going to say but I can't work there anymore," Cynthia said once Naomi had departed. Her throat tightened around the admission, but she was on a roll. "I've already wasted too many years there working toward nothing and—"

"*Bas*," her mother said, her hand coming to rest gently on Cynthia's biceps.

Cynthia flinched. "Let me guess. You're happy that I'm going to finally stop fixating on my career and focus on more important things—"

Her mother tightened her grip, and, somehow, the pressure on Cynthia's arm became soothing. "I said stop," Sipra said, her voice firm. "You always think you know what everyone is thinking, how everyone will react."

"What?"

"You've always been this way, ever since you were a little girl. Always trying to anticipate everything, plan for everything, and feel in control." A bittersweet smile pulled at Sipra's lips. "I've never seen a child so observant and . . . *hyperaware* of everything and everyone around her." Pinning her daughter with a long look, Sipra added in a softer voice, "Except of herself, maybe."

Cynthia's eyebrows knit together as her mother tapped a long, square-tipped nail on the surface of the letter.

"I'm glad you're leaving," Sipra said.

"So I can focus on finding a husband?" Cynthia cringed at how bitter the attempt at humor sounded in her ears.

Her mother shook her head impatiently. "So you can focus on being *happy*."

Cynthia's mouth popped open in surprise, earning her a sad smile from her mother. "You think you know me, and I don't know you," Sipra said. "But I know more than you think. You might be intelligent, talented, and successful at what you do at your father's company, but you're not happy there."

"That's not . . ." Cynthia swallowed hard. Her mother's words stung because they were *true*. "How are you so sure?"

"You're not the only observant one, you know." Sipra moved to sit on the love seat and patted the empty space next to her.

Shyly, Cynthia joined her mother and stared down at her

clasped hands. "Kumar Construction was never going to be mine, was it?"

Sipra shrugged. "I don't know. I don't involve myself in your father's business decisions, but not for the reasons you think. I might not live the life you want, Cynthia, but I live my life on *my* terms and I don't answer to anyone."

Cynthia's eyes widened as she studied her mother's calm, confident gaze, the proud arch in her neck.

"And I think you need to start doing the same," Sipra added, lightly pinching Cynthia's chin between her thumb and index finger.

"Why didn't you tell me this earlier?"

"Would you have listened?" Her mother slid her arm around Cynthia's shoulders, softening the rebuke. "I think you've always had a singular vision of success in your head, and I'm not sure I could've changed that."

"You could've tried!"

Sipra nudged her playfully. "Cut me some slack. It took me a while to realize that pushing you to want the same things that made *me* happy—marriage, kids, a comfortable, domestic life—wasn't going to work for you. You're a smart woman, I wanted you to figure out your life for yourself."

Cynthia crossed her arms over her stomach and fought the overwhelming urge to cuddle into her mother's side. "What if I don't know what I want?"

"You don't always have to know, but be honest with yourself for a second. Is taking over for your father going to make you happy?"

It was something she'd asked herself many times, a question that had been a guiding principle to . . . Cynthia closed her eyes in dismay. *To every goddamn thing I've ever done.* Hearing the question come from someone else—her *mother*, of all people—sent a shock wave through Cynthia. It was like hearing the acoustic version of a well-known song, a little dissonant but simple and honest.

"No," Cynthia said slowly. "No. I don't suppose taking over Dad's company is going to make me happy."

"Then what will?"

Rohit.

The answer came to her in a rush of tenderness that made her chest expand and her heartbeat hum in agreement. The truth was so unbelievably obvious, as was the overpowering certainty that she loved him so much. It was belly-laughing, ugly-crying, showing-up-no-questions-asked, kneeling-before-someone's-feet kind of love, and Cynthia had never felt so certain about anything in her life.

Without a doubt, it was him.

"Rohit," Cynthia said in a voice that wasn't her own but a conviction that came from deep within. "Rohit makes me happy." The acknowledgment undid something in Cynthia, and she gave in to the temptation to lean into her mother's side. "I've been awful to him," she added. "I've shown him the worst sides of myself."

"Cynthia, you've always tried too hard to be perfect. You're always in your head, trying to stay ahead and never make an error." Sipra pulled away and placed both hands on Cynthia's shoulder, leveling her with an even look. "My smart, ambitious girl. You are more than your mistakes; maybe it's time to forgive yourself and move on."

"You're talking about what happened with Jimmy when I was a teenager, aren't you?"

"Among other things," Sipra said with a soft smile, pulling Cynthia into her side again. Her familiar perfume wrapped around Cynthia, but for once, it wasn't too flowery and feminine for Cynthia's taste. Because beneath the expensive notes of bergamot, jasmine, and a hint of peach were new aromas she'd never noticed before: courage, strength, compassion.

Love.

Her mother kissed the top of her head. "I know you've always wanted to be like your dad . . . But I think there's plenty of me in you, too. And that makes me proud."

"So, what do you think I should do about Rohit?" Cynthia gazed up at her mother, afraid to close her eyes and confront his stricken face stamped across the back of her eyelids. "He has every right to never talk to me again."

Sipra squeezed her tighter. "I think you should listen to your heart, for once."

It was good advice and long overdue. Cynthia was in the midst of relaxing into her mother's embrace again when a random thought occurred to her and she jerked upright. "Hang on a second," she said, studying her mother's serene face. "You didn't react when I told you Rohit makes me happy. Why aren't you more shocked?"

Her mother shot her a look that was brimming with an impatience Cynthia knew too well, and despite everything, she suddenly felt like laughing. "Didn't you hear what I said earlier?" Sipra said. "You're not the only observant one in this family."

CHAPTER 33

With his cell phone wedged between his ear and his shoulder, Rohit twisted uncomfortably, laptop cradled against his side with one arm and an empty food delivery bag in the other, to shut his car door with the heel of his shoe.

"Is now a bad time?" Maisa asked on the other end of the line when she heard him grunt.

"Shit," Rohit mumbled to himself as the laptop tipped precariously forward. He paused a minute to regroup his belongings before adding, "No. It's fine."

"Are you sure?"

Rohit closed his eyes in frustration when he realized he'd left his car keys in the car. It, in fact, was not a "fine" time to chat—it was a *horrible* time. He'd just completed his first shift as a food delivery driver and it had been even more exhausting and less lucrative than he'd imagined. But with Rich telling him to "lay low" for a bit while he sorted out this newest PR crisis, it had been the quickest form of employment Rohit could think of.

Rohit shoved the bag under the same arm as the laptop, retrieved his keys from the ignition, and hit the back of his head on the doorframe on his way out. "Who's sick this time?" he said between gritted teeth.

"What?"

Rohit bit back a response as he trotted toward the front door of his building, which Mrs. Smith from the top floor held open when she saw him approach.

"Thanks," he murmured to the elderly lady as he slipped past.

"Rohit?" Maisa prompted as he swung a right down the hallway toward his apartment.

The petulance in his sister's voice slid through the last remaining traces of his patience. "Maisa, why are you calling me?"

He immediately knew, from her sharp intake of breath, that he'd hurt her feelings. He was *never* short with her, *never* treated her calls as if they were unwelcome. But given recent events, Rohit's charm and levity were in short supply. Feelings of freedom from lying and guilt had been wonderful but short-lived and soon replaced by an insistent throbbing behind his eyelids, a head-pounding drumbeat keeping time as his world crumbled around him.

Right now, he couldn't pretend everything was great. That he was living the immigrant dream. That he had all the solutions, all the resources—and then some—to take care of everyone and every little thing under the sun.

"I-I'm sorry," Maisa said. "I just wanted to check in."

Rohit reached his apartment door and tightened his grip on his laptop as he unceremoniously dumped the delivery bag on the floor. "Yeah, and?"

When he turned around to close his apartment door, Rohit couldn't help pressing his forehead into the cool, textured surface, well aware he sounded like a jerk. But he couldn't help it. Was another grandparent sick? Or maybe some second cousin's uncle needed funding to send his kid to a private school?

This line of thinking was immature and cruel—not to mention terrifying since he'd made less than fifty-three dollars in tips that day—and when Maisa didn't respond right away, a thin, burning sensation snaked through the pit of his stomach. His little sister didn't deserve to be on the receiving end of a cranky older brother whose professional and personal lives were burning to a crisp.

She obviously didn't think so, either. "You know what?" Maisa snapped. "I think I'll call later when you're in a better mood."

"Wait, Maze, I'm sorr—"

"Or better yet, *you* call *me* when you're done acting like a . . . like a . . . like a bitch!"

"Maisa—"

"Rohit?" His mother's voice appeared on the line, her tone baffled. "Why is your little sister calling you that bad word?"

Rohit placed his laptop on the counter and rubbed the bridge of his nose. "Probably because I'm acting like a bitch."

"Rohit! What's gotten into you?"

Letting out a sigh, Rohit rubbed his temples. "Just a bad day, Ma. Horrible, actually."

"Do you want to talk about it?"

"Are Pappa and Maisa nearby? I think I need to talk to all of you."

His mother provided exactly zero warning before yelling for the other members of his family directly into the speaker. The pressure between Rohit's eyes intensified.

"I was about to take a shower," his father grumbled in greeting.

"I have to tell you all something," Rohit said. His voice sounded thick and he swallowed before continuing. "Something I should have told you a long time ago."

Rohit turned to lean against the counter and stared at the blank white wall in front of him. He tried to summon the feelings of relief he'd experienced in Rich's office after his secret had been exposed, but this was his *family*. They were so proud of him, of the successful immigrant son who took care of them, no questions asked.

This confession would splinter all that—everything they believed, and loved, about him—into broken shards he wasn't sure he could repair.

"Well?" his mother asked as the silence stretched between them.

"I never finished my MBA."

His announcement prompted another long pause.

"You never finished your MBA," his mother finally repeated.

"No. When Grandma had her stroke, I dropped out of school so I could start earning money to send home."

"Oh, Rohit," Maisa said in a low voice.

"Have you lost your mind?" his mother demanded.

"Her care was more important," Rohit argued. "And Maisa's schooling. And—"

"My son has lost his mind!"

"Hang on," his father chimed in, always the voice of calm if not reason. "There is nothing greater than caring for your family—"

"Have you lost it, too?" As his mother's voice picked up in both speed and decibels, Rohit shot a nervous glance at his closed front door and quickly lowered the volume on his phone. "We sent him to Canada to study! To make something of himself—to have a better life!"

Rohit's knees buckled and he sank to the floor. "Ma—"

"As I was saying," his father said again, his voice slightly louder. "There is nothing greater than caring for your family." He waited to see if his wife would interrupt him before adding, "But."

It was one of his father's infamous pauses, and despite having been on the receiving end of this particular kind of drama many times in the past, Rohit couldn't help but hold his breath.

"But what, Pappa?" Maisa asked.

"*But* your mother is right, too, Rohit. You are in Canada to build a life for yourself. We appreciate everything you've done, but we didn't sacrifice so much to send you away so you could end up like this."

"That's right," his mother said, her voice too close to the phone's speaker. "That's what I am saying."

"Ma, you're shouting," Maisa piped in.

"I am a mother and that's what we do to knock some sense into our senseless children."

"End up like what exactly?" Affronted, Rohit repeated his father's claim. "I have a degree and a good job." Well, the job part was hanging in the balance, but Rohit wasn't about to deep dive into *that*.

"Do you like your life?" his father asked. "Are you happy?"

"The last month notwithstanding, all you ever do is work or hang out at home," Maisa chimed in. "Or drive to work or drive home. Your life seems pretty boring."

"Thanks, Maze." But the truth behind his sister's summary of his existence brought a warm flush to his cheeks.

"Are you *happy*, son?" his father repeated gently.

Rohit closed his eyes and leaned back against the kitchen cabinet. The last year of his life hadn't been awful, but it had been more about feeling grateful, and scared, and anxious than happy. "I don't know. I don't even know if getting an MBA is what I really want."

It was the first time he'd said the words out loud, and he braced himself anew for his parents' disappointment, well aware that the distance would do nothing to temper the pain their reaction would imprint on his heart.

But they surprised him. "Well then, maybe that's where you need to start," his mother said. "You need to figure out what you want first."

"But Grandma's medical bills. And Dadi's diabetes medication . . ." Rohit protested.

"And my schooling," Maisa added softly. Rohit's spine straightened, the wall cool and solid pressing against his back. "That's right," he said firmly. "These things are too important. I want to help. It's my responsibility to help."

His father's voice hardened. "And it's our responsibility to care for you, too. Family takes care of *one another*. It's time we reached out to our siblings. We appreciate your help, Rohit, but our entire family's care should not fall upon you. You need to live your life, too."

Rohit hadn't realized he was crying until the first tears splashed onto his pants. He swiped at his damp face. "I—" He wasn't sure what to say, not with his voice choked up like this, the single word trembling precariously on the edge of his worst fear.

Because since that day he'd quit school, this was the moment he had feared and hidden behind congenial smiles and never-ending cheer. This entire time, he'd believed the love between him and his family was one of sacrifice and responsibility.

Well, he'd been right in a way, but he hadn't realized that this relationship with his family wasn't a one-sided affair. It was a full, perfect circle. That same sacrifice and responsibility was reflected right back.

They loved him, regardless.

"I—" Rohit tried again. "I was so scared how you'd react."

His boisterous mother's voice softened, as it always did when tears were involved. "You are our son first, no matter what country you are in or what you choose to do with your life."

"Or *whom* you choose to spend it with," Maisa added. "Because we all agree, in the last month, you've been a lot less boring."

"She's right," his mother chimed in. "Go live your life, Rohit. We support you."

"I still want to help where I can," Rohit said, using the heel of his hand to dry his eyes. "Maisa's education is important to me."

"We appreciate it," his father said. "But don't forget to put yourself first, too. We'll figure this out together."

"And I'm sorry I called you a bitch," Maisa said.

Rohit couldn't help but chuckle. "I deserved it."

Once they'd ended the call, Rohit stood, ignoring the cramps in his tired feet, and contemplated his apartment. Suddenly, it looked so stark and austere. *Boring.* He'd unknowingly resisted making this space a home; it was a budget-friendly shelter, a place to eat and sleep and convince himself that eventually, somehow or someway, things would work out for him.

But trendy décor and sentimental knickknacks were the last thing Rohit needed. Luckily, he knew exactly what he did need—or, more specifically, *who.*

Cynthia. Cynthia was home.

Rohit glanced at his phone and winced. It was almost midnight and he was overdue for a shower, but even as the thought crossed his mind, he was pocketing his car keys and stumbling for the front door. He had to see her, had to make things right. Besides, didn't rom-coms always end this way? The guy appearing at the most inopportune moment to reconcile with the girl?

If only he had a gift or something for her, he mused, reaching for the doorknob. He'd practice what he needed to say in the car or maybe he could . . . Rohit swung open the door and nearly knocked Cynthia over.

Plans for a heartfelt, hastily rehearsed speech flew into the abyss. "What are you doing here?" he blurted out.

She shifted her weight, nervousness splashed across her lovely features. "I know how much you appreciate grand gestures . . . Can I come in?"

Wordlessly, Rohit shuffled backward, trying not to breathe too deeply as she stepped past him in a heady, familiar mist of sandalwood that made his chest ache.

She stopped a few feet from his couch, hesitant. "Can we . . . can we sit?"

It was one of those rare moments where her hard, unyielding edges gave way to her softer side, and Rohit couldn't deny that he welcomed the answering flutter in his chest. That flutter morphed into wild, flapping wings when, after he'd seated himself on the couch, Cynthia didn't seek the other end.

She chose to sit only a few inches away, and it was all Rohit could do not to reach for her.

But she didn't look at him, choosing instead to stare at her lap. "I didn't leak your information to Melanie," she said.

A part of Rohit wanted to believe her, but a frisson of doubt pricked at his spine anyway. "But no one else knew."

"I'm not completely blameless," Cynthia admitted, meeting his gaze. "I accidentally let it slip to Jilly during my Kim K–level meltdown after my dad announced his retirement."

Rohit pressed his lips together, mentally filing away "Kim K–level" to research later, but Cynthia saw the confusion on his face and a smile tugged at her lips.

"I ugly-cried in the parking lot in front of Jilly and Malik," she clarified. "Anyway, Jilly thought she was doing me a favor running to Melanie with the information. Turns out Jilly was one of our whistleblowers, too."

"I spoke to her a few days ago, and she didn't mention any of this."

"You spoke to Jilly? On the phone?" Cynthia's eyebrows furrowed and Rohit was struck by how much she could resemble her father.

"No, I saw her at the office." Rohit gestured at his laptop on the counter.

"So you're not fired?"

Rohit cocked his head to the side. "Do you want me to be?"

Cynthia closed her eyes and took a deep breath. "*No.*"

The honesty in that single syllable drew Rohit closer to her, the fake leather couch squeaking under the tentative movement. "How could you let something so important 'slip'?" he asked.

"I feel horrible about it." Guilt blanketed her eyes. "I was just so upset and hurt. I was a mess in the parking lot and . . . I regretted it immediately. Rohit, I am incredibly sorry."

The last of her apology was delivered on a tremulous quiver and, despite himself, Rohit found himself inching closer again. "Well, I'm not in the clear," he said. "Your dad told me to stay away for a while and sit tight. Who even knows what that means."

"We need to fight this," Cynthia said.

We. Rohit closed the distance some more, but she didn't seem to notice. The shame was still there, but Cynthia's eyes had brightened with the passion and determination he knew so well.

He loved her—every part of her. His entire life, he'd been taught to believe a marriage lasted seven lifetimes, and before today he'd tucked that piece of information away as an old wives' tale, next to other silly beliefs like the unluckiness of black cats or the power of a lucky penny.

But in this moment, Rohit knew with stunning clarity that seven lifetimes with this woman wouldn't be enough. He was drawn to her, as if his soul were a magnet and in her was the opposite pole. She'd strengthened their magnetic field, charged it with an unknowable, irresistible force with one simple word: *we.*

"Your dad told me to stay out of the limelight for a while and I don't think his instincts are wrong," he reminded her, his arm sneaking around her waist before he could think better of it.

It was as if his body were reaching for its other half, and yet Rohit couldn't lean in fully, not when his soul needed reassurance that it wasn't the only one who had found its mate.

He needed to know that hers yearned for his, too.

Cynthia didn't disappoint. *She never does*, Rohit realized as her strong, capable fingers found his forearm and squeezed. Something new washed over Rohit, better than relief.

Love. Rohit tugged her even closer.

"We'll fix this. Somehow, we'll fix it." she said.

Again, that word: *we.* That beautiful, addictive word. His heart expanded, nudging a sigh from his lungs as her body relaxed against his, pushing what could no longer be contained from his chest in the dizzying pull between them. "I love you," he said to this unpredictable, unknowable woman who was a million different things, layered and lush, and deserved to hear these words every day. "I love you so much."

She pulled back, tears in her eyes. "No!" she said, competitive as always. "I wanted to say 'I love you' first." Twisting away, Cynthia leaned over the side of the couch where she'd dropped her purse, and when she straightened, a see-through container with a heart-shaped cupcake inside was in her hands. An adorable blush seeped onto her cheeks and her chin dipped. "I know it's cheesy," she said, gesturing to the confection, "but . . . do I still have a chance?"

Rohit half smiled. *This woman.* Here she was, his every fantasy brought to life, sitting in his living room, trying to win him over. She'd won him over long ago and she still hadn't figured it out.

"Don't you understand?" he said, gently taking the cupcake and placing it on the table. He then entwined his hands with hers, loving the way she immediately held on tight. "It'll never be too late for us."

Her eyebrow quirked. "Is that a line from a movie?"

Rohit abandoned her hands to cup her jaw. "No, that's all me."

Her face lit up and she smiled, and, finally, Rohit breathed deep. *I'm home.* And then he pressed his lips against hers.

CHAPTER 34

The urge to laugh was strong as Cynthia packed the last of her office belongings. There wasn't much to clear away, but the sheer act of cleaning out the space that had practically been a second home to her for the last fifteen years had been an eye-opener.

Kumar Construction's design was one of heavy, solid wood furniture, muted colors, pastel landscapes dotting the walls, and clunky metal file cabinets. It was a traditional, old-school environment, created by a man who, while not necessarily resistant to change, didn't chase it, either.

Cynthia's office, however, had been an outlier. She'd made it her own with cool white tones, sharp edges, and metallic lines. One oversized painting had graced the wall: an abstract piece of bold, powerful brushstrokes.

It was a wonder it had taken her so long to realize she didn't fit here, not the way she needed to.

"I can't believe it's your last day," Jilly said from the doorway. She looked around the room with an unhappy frown.

"It's time to move on," Cynthia said. There was no bitterness in her voice—working under her father's banner had been safe, but the unfamiliar was new. Exciting. She now knew that she thrived on her own, surrounded by people she liked who welcomed her opinion and listened when she spoke up.

"What will you do next?"

"I'm going to start my own business." Cynthia hadn't meant to sound cryptic, but when Jilly's forehead crinkled, she added, "I'll be doing the same things, just not under the Kumar Construction umbrella anymore."

"We . . . That is to say, I . . ." Jilly hesitated. "I'll miss you."

Cynthia abandoned her cardboard box of belongings and folded Jilly in a hug. "Don't miss me too much," she said. "I'll probably need an assistant soon."

When she pulled away, Jilly's face had brightened considerably. "I'd be honored, Ms. Kumar. You meant . . . You mean me, right?"

"Yes, Jilly. And it's Cynthia."

A half hour later, Cynthia brushed invisible wrinkles off the front of her black blazer as she stared hard at the sign for Conference Room B, her forehead oblong and distorted in its shiny, beveled surface. She tilted her head back and was slightly mollified to see that her pimple patch had worked its magic.

Had she been a heroine in one of the romantic comedy movies Rohit loved so much, this would be an iconic moment of female empowerment, set to the tune of Diana Ross's "I'm Coming Out." The part where the main character kicks down the door, guns blazing, and tears her boss a new one with biting remarks and damning evidence.

From top to bottom, she even looked the part with her hair slicked back in a low, understated ponytail, her most severe and serious pantsuit punctuated by the same don't-fuck-with-me heels she always wore for these meetings. She'd rehearsed what she wanted to say this morning, fell asleep visualizing what this moment would look like, how it would feel. She'd imagined a biting departure à la Renée Zellweger quitting her job in *Bridget Jones's Diary* or maybe she'd be coolly regal like Jennifer Lopez in *Maid in Manhattan* telling her mother she could figure out her own life, that she didn't need anyone's help.

But she knew better and had decided to just be herself.

Still, the sight of that oversized mahogany door released a flock of overcaffeinated butterflies down her sternum. *You're a queen*, she reminded herself. *And even when you don't feel like one, the Ice Princess gets the job done, too.*

Cynthia lifted her chin as she pushed the door open, pleasantly surprised to realize that when conversation came to an abrupt halt at her entrance, she wasn't intimidated or uncomfortable.

She was ready.

"How kind of you to join us," Keer said sarcastically, before lowering his voice. "Near the end of the meeting."

"Probably woman troubles," Larry mumbled with a snicker.

Cynthia rolled her shoulders back, ignoring the faint pinch between her shoulder blades. *Not today.* Still, she couldn't help but swallow hard when her father leveled her with a pointed stare.

"This meeting is adjourned," he said. "Thanks, everyone, for taking the time out of your *busy* schedules to attend."

As the senior leadership team, trailed by her father, began making their way toward the exit, Cynthia placed her bag onto the empty chair next to her and cleared her throat. "I need to speak with you."

Like a parliament of gray owls, several grizzled heads turned in unison to blink at her.

"My . . . dad," Cynthia clarified, her voice sounding unnatural and loud. "I need to speak with my dad."

With a start, she realized that before today, she'd never, *ever* referred to her father this way in front of the old men staring at her, their interest ranging from bored to mildly curious. She'd been so focused on proving to them that her value, and her future as the CEO of Kumar Construction, had nothing to do with family ties. That her ambition, competence, and relentlessness were marks of character and not just an extension of her last name. She had wanted to be the chosen heir of her father's legacy.

It hadn't worked, but in this moment, Cynthia was glad for it. After today, she wouldn't have to attend this stupid meeting anymore, nor would she have to work with this group of stodgy yes men who could not see her as anything but the boss's kid.

Good riddance. She was focusing on being happy, and if fifteen years had taught her anything, it was that happiness was not to be found in this room.

Not for her, at least.

Rich broke away from the group but not before Keer offered him what looked like a commiserating thump on his back. Cynthia rolled her eyes. *Go choke on a donut.* She waited until her father was settled in the chair across from her before pulling a sheet of paper from her bag and placing it facedown on the table.

"What is it?" her father prompted, as he pulled his phone out of his pocket and unlocked the screen.

Cynthia eyed his phone with disdain. She wasn't settling for anything less than his full attention. Today, she would be seen.

"Dad, I have something important to give you," she said.

"Mm-hm."

"I'd appreciate if you put your phone away when I'm speaking to you." The words came out more impatient than she'd intended, nervousness snapping the syllables tightly together.

Rich's head flew up, his finger frozen in midair. "I didn't raise you to talk to me like that."

Cynthia was done worrying about that, too.

"I'm not trying to be disrespectful," she said, but when her father nodded and turned back to his phone, she stood, leaned across the table and gently tugged the phone out of his grip. "But I am trying to talk to you," she said, placing his phone facedown on the table just out of his reach. "And for once, I want to talk *to* you. Not *at* you, or to everyone else in the room in hopes that you'll hear me."

Rich looked confused but he sat back in his chair, hands folded across his stomach. It was a small win but enough to both strengthen and straighten Cynthia's spine as she sat back as well. She felt strangely vulnerable, her fingers buzzing with the need to fidget. She wished Rohit, who was still laying low as per her father's instructions, were here. But just remembering him, his name at the forefront of her thoughts, gave her courage, and she blurted out the first words that rushed to her lips: "I don't think you should fire him. Rohit, I mean. If he wants to come back, I think he deserves a second chance."

Rich's eyebrows knit together, but he remained silent.

"I know he lied about his credentials," she continued, "but you and I both know that Rohit has earned his place here. *You* never got a university degree, either and look at everything you've accomplished."

"Cynthi—"

"Besides, this place needs someone like him at the helm. Your leadership team is stale and male, Dad, and I'm not the only one who thinks so—"

"'Stale and male'?" her father repeated with a half smile.

Cynthia ignored the heat spreading to her cheeks. "You know what I mean. I just think we could do—*you* could—"

"I'm not going to fire Rohit," Rich interrupted.

"You're not? But he wasn't in the meeting today."

Rich shook his head. "He needs to keep a low profile for a while, but I never intended to fire him. If anyone understands his position, it's me."

Cynthia blinked and laid her hands flat on the table. "You do?"

"You think I was an instant success when I started Kumar Construction?" Rich chuckled. "It was a struggle—I didn't turn a profit for the first three years. The only reason I was able to build all of this is because people in the community took a chance on me, an immigrant newcomer, fumbling his way through projects and red tape and about a hundred other mistakes that needed to happen." Rich's voice gentled. "That's what it was, Cynthia. Rohit made a mistake."

When Cynthia blinked again, the sting of tears greeted the backs of her eyelids. She wasn't sure if it was the relief that Rohit's job was safe or that, for once, she and her father were *talking*. Really talking. Sure, she'd had to wrestle the phone out of his hand for his undivided attention, but he was listening and, more importantly, the hot, impatient spike that normally seared a hole in her stomach lining while she waited for her turn to talk and impress and prove her point was nowhere to be found.

It was a wonderful feeling, just existing, especially in this ostentatious, gleaming room that once had the power to make her feel physically ill.

Maybe this could still be an iconic moment for her. She could be regal and cool and confident, but from now on, it would be on her own terms.

"Have you told Rohit yet?" Cynthia asked.

"I'm going to call him later today."

"With everything the company has been through these past few weeks, I'm surprised at how lenient you're being."

"Well, I'm not a fan of that tabloid parading as a newspaper anymore," her father said dryly, "but strong work ethic, loyalty, and diversity are the values I believe in for this company. These people are my family."

So am I. Cynthia lowered her gaze to her lap and bit the inside of her cheek. The tears might have receded but her father's words burrowed deep in her chest, and she dropped her chin. She didn't want his opinion to matter anymore, but it did. She didn't want to need his approval, but her heart ached to hear it.

But before she could bring herself to ask for it, her father cocked his head to the side.

"Hang on one second," he said with a wrinkled brow. "I want to go back to something you said before . . . What's this about my team being 'male and stale'?"

Cynthia shrugged. "If you want to uphold these kinds of values at Kumar Construction, then things need to change around here on an organizational level. More than half the admin and junior staff are female, and yet there are no women on your senior leadership team. Aside from Rohit, no one under the age of fifty has a seat at the . . ." Cynthia paused. "No one under the age of fifty has a seat *or voice* at the table."

Her father's eyes widened. "I can't just fire my senior leadership team."

"There are other ways to make this place more inclusive. You could bring in a board of directors made up of a more diverse group of people. You could create an actual human resources department that's more than just Gayle sitting in a room filled with file cabinets. You could hire a consultant to make this place less hierarchical and emphasize things like equal opportunity and decentralization." Cynthia licked her lips and paused to shoot her father a nervous glance. "It's not enough to talk the talk anymore. If you want people to feel valued and seen, then you have to lead by example."

Although her father's eyebrows had climbed almost to his hairline during her little speech, she didn't read judgment or disapproval in his brown eyes. His gaze was assessing, the set of his jaw contemplative. A very small part of Cynthia itched to see admiration flit across his face or, at the very least, grudging respect, but as she looked at the empty, cushy leather chairs around them and the gleaming surface of the mahogany table that, in the past, had stretched endlessly across the room, she realized she would survive without it.

"So," Rich said, nodding at the sheet of paper that lay facedown to her right. "Is that a list of potential board directors?" He reached forward, but Cynthia was quicker.

"No," she said quietly. Her hand was steady as she flipped the paper over and slid it across the table to her father. "This is my resignation. I'm ready for a change."

Rich's eyes skimmed the letter quickly before meeting her gaze. "You're leaving?"

"I don't think Kumar Construction is the right future for me." Cynthia smiled self-deprecatingly. "And surely you must know that, too. I mean, you named *Rohit* as your next CEO, so obviously—"

"Hang on." Her father leaned forward in his chair. "Are you saying *you* had hopes to become the next CEO?"

The question made Cynthia's throat feel tight and she forced herself to take a long, deep breath to chase away the tension gathering there. When it came to business matters, she'd practically strained her vocal cords trying to get her point across, but when it came to these moments, Cynthia had always resorted to tucking all the feelings of disappointment, pain, pride, and wistfulness away. She had convinced herself that she, like her father, believed that actions spoke louder than words, but she could admit now that she'd been hiding from the words that were, for her, so hard to say.

It was time to speak up for herself. And for her heart.

"Of course I wanted to be the next CEO."

Her father looked incredulous. "Why didn't you ever say anything?"

"C'mon, Appa." When the childhood moniker for *Dad* slipped from Cynthia's lips, she paused, momentarily surprised. "I've been busting my ass for the last fifteen years trying to prove to you that I would be the right person to lead Kumar Construction after your retirement. It's been my one goal all this time."

"I . . . I didn't realize."

"I should have said something a long time ago. I wish . . ." Cynthia's voice was beginning to shake but she forced herself to continue. "I might have let everything I worked so hard for slip away once long ago, but people make mistakes and deserve second chances, Dad."

Realization dawned over her father's face, and he studied his daughter in silence for a long while. Cynthia stared back. She saw so much of her features in her father and yet, right now, she felt like a completely different person and from the vertical crease between her father's brows, he might've realized that as well.

"You're right," he finally said. "Cynthia, if taking over my legacy is something you really want, I can revisit my decision. You *have* proven yourself very capable and ambitious in your field. I know you can accomplish anything you set your mind to, and I have no doubt that this company would flourish under your leadership." He cocked his head to the side. "As my daughter, you would be the natural choice for my successor. Is this what you want?"

When she had fantasized about this moment, she'd played out scene after scene, mentally fortifying herself against the fear, doubt, and regret she would feel the next day when she'd hand her father her resignation letter. She'd never pictured *this* happening. Her main goal had been to find closure or, at the very least, relief.

Reality was much, *much* better.

"No." Her answer was softly spoken but firm and powerful. *She* felt powerful. "This isn't the best fit for me or for what I want."

To her surprise, her father's eyes misted over. He reached across the table, but instead of grabbing his phone, he placed his hand gently on hers. "You've done a lot here to help me build my legacy," he said. "But I think it's obvious that you were destined to build your own."

CHAPTER 35

Rohit stopped short on the sidewalk in front of the Desmond Business Center when he caught sight of Cynthia, trailed by Jilly and Malik, approaching the parking lot with cardboard boxes in their arms.

He shot Jilly and Malik a friendly wave but when Cynthia stopped in front of him, his smile faded. Cynthia waited until Jilly and Malik had made their way past before she placed her box on the ground and shook out her arms.

"What's in there?" he joked half-heartedly. "Bricks you'd hidden under your desk to throw at my head?"

Cynthia's lips quirked. "That and years of underappreciation and bitterness. They can weigh a girl down."

"Hey." Rohit pulled her into a hug. "You're not weighed down anymore, though, right?"

"Not anymore." She tipped her head back and grinned at him. "But I will keep the bricks. Just in case."

"I can't believe it's your last day."

Cynthia turned to stand by his side and examined the office

building with him. "I know. I considered this place a home away from home for almost fifteen years."

With its reflective glass exterior, the building had always seemed imposing to Rohit, but now, in the brilliant afternoon sun, it looked cold, too. Inhospitable. He supposed he'd believed this place to be a home of sorts, too, and he couldn't deny it had served an important purpose for him, as a newcomer to Kelowna. He'd met most of his friends and acquaintances here. His mentor, too.

But it wouldn't feel the same without Cynthia. He'd always liked going to work, but she'd been the real draw, even when she'd hated his presence. She'd been an exasperating, addictive, complicated fixture in his work life. That life seemed decidedly lacking without his Ice Princess burning hot one minute and spearing him with icicles the next.

"I can't believe we're not working together anymore," he murmured.

"Don't go soft on me now."

But they both knew that between the two of them, he *was* the soft one. And because he knew she loved him all the more for it, he allowed himself to speak from the heart: "I think I've loved you every single moment since the night I met you. I don't know what I'll do without you."

Cynthia turned to him, her face solemn. "You still have me," she told him, grabbing his hand and squeezing, "for as long as you want me."

Forever, he thought, squeezing back. But he didn't need to say the words out loud. If she didn't already know, then he would show her for the rest of his life.

Rohit raised their joined hands to his lips and brushed a kiss on the back of her hand as they stood in silence watching the steady stream of harried-looking professionals entering and exiting the building, briefcases, unlit cigarettes, and coffee cups in their hands.

"Will you miss this?" he asked.

After a few long minutes, she answered, "I honestly don't think I will." Cynthia laid her head on his shoulder. "Nervous?"

"Your dad asked me to come in today," he reminded her and, perhaps, himself.

"Maybe it's to celebrate my departure."

Rohit rolled his eyes. "You know it's about everything that went down these last few weeks. For all I know, today might be my last day, too."

"You won't know until you go in there," Cynthia sang off-key, reminding Rohit how much he loved her.

And now he could say it. "I love you."

Cynthia's face softened. "You better," she said. She pulled him into a tight hug and pressed her lips close to his ear. "And if you forget, I have the bricks to remind you." She waited until he'd finished laughing before adding, "I love you, too."

STEPPING ONTO THE thirtieth floor was like sliding under a microscope that morning, but Rohit ignored the faint buzz of speculation around him as he made his way to Rich's office. It wasn't so much the curious glances thrown his way but the knowledge that no one, it seemed, knew what lay in store for Rohit today. He'd received plenty of private messages and texts in the last few weeks from colleagues checking on him and railing against the unfairness of it all.

The outreach had warmed Rohit's heart, reminded him that although the future of his career was uncertain, his second family was a sure thing. He belonged at Kumar Construction, and while he wasn't proud of how he'd gotten his foot in the door, he was glad he had. But when he found Rich's office empty, his hopeful spirits cooled considerably and, on leaden legs, he headed toward his own desk instead.

Rich was waiting for him there, standing at the window and looking out into the city, his hands clasped behind his back.

"I . . ." Rohit cleared his throat. "I thought we were meeting in your office." *As we have, almost every morning, for the last nineteen months.*

Rich didn't look surprised to see him as he gestured for Rohit to take a seat at his office chair before claiming his own across Rohit's much less impressive desk. "I felt like a change in scenery," the older man said.

When he didn't elaborate, Rohit shifted in his seat. "Change can be good . . ." he ventured uselessly, and when Rich didn't respond, he cleared his throat again. "And change can be . . . bad?"

Rich's face split into a grin. "You can relax, Rohit."

"I can?"

"You're not fired." Rich paused and stretched his legs out in front of him. "But also, I've decided not to retire."

Rohit knew he had no right to feel anything but gratitude and relief, but he couldn't help his shoulders slumping forward.

"I've decided not to retire . . ." Rich repeated, "yet."

"What do you mean?"

"It's recently come to my attention that there is a lot more work to be done around here. I love my company and I'm proud of what I've built, but I can do better. I *want* to do better."

It was the one of the first times, while meeting one-on-one with his boss, that Rich was talking about the future. Their time together was usually spent revisiting the past, reminiscing the twists and turns that had led Rich to building an empire. But there was a glint in Rich's eyes that Rohit had never seen before, one that made him sit forward in his seat, every nerve ending on high alert.

"I think that's very commendable," Rohit ventured. "And I'm grateful that you're allowing me to keep my job."

"Oh, you won't be a client manager anymore."

He was being demoted. Rohit forced a polite smile as his heart dove into the pit of his stomach. "Well, still, I'm very grateful—"

"No, son. I still want you as my successor, but I want to spend some time making sure you're equipped to be successful. I'm going to spend the next few years closely mentoring you to take over, and we're going to make changes in that time so the staff here are equipped for success, too."

"What kinds of changes?"

"I'm bringing in a board of directors. We're going to restructure." Excitement threaded Rich's words as his eyes took on a faraway look. "I built something great here, something that some immigrants only dream for themselves. But I'm not done building my legacy yet. There's still more I wish to do." His gaze refocused and he cocked his head. "There's more work to do for *you*, too. If you're interested, I'd like to arrange for you to finish your MBA during this mentorship. The company can help with the expenses."

Again, Rohit knew he should be thankful, but something else was squirming its way into his heart, only this time, his shoulders pulled back. During his entire career at Kumar Construction, he had adopted a go-with-the-flow persona in order to make himself indispensable to his superiors and popular with the rest of his staff. And while he'd reaped many benefits in this role, he'd been oblivious, complacent, and, like Rich, too comfortable with a problematic status quo.

He'd allowed his family's financial needs to dictate the course of his life, but he was the one who'd taken it too far and that ended now. He couldn't keep putting everyone's needs and desires before his own. "Or maybe I can pursue architecture," he said. The words sounded tentative to his ears and Rohit momentarily closed his eyes, reaching deep for the confidence and strength he'd seen Cynthia show so many times before when she stuck to her beliefs and went against the grain. He found himself lifting his chin, and when he reopened his eyes and met Rich's gaze, his voice was much more assertive. "I've always wanted to be an architect. And with the company's backing, I think it could help build your legacy and make this place better."

"An architect?" Rich leaned back in his chair, a surprised but pleased smile spreading across his face. "It's certainly something we can discuss," he said.

"Thank you, sir."

"I forgot how exciting change can feel," Rich mused.

While it sounded like the older man was talking to himself now, Rohit couldn't help but ask, "What brought on this need for change anyway?"

"Cynthia." There was no small amount of wonder in Rich's voice. "This is all her."

"Well then, it makes sense," Rohit said. Realizing it sounded like an underhanded shot at the man who had secured his future, he tried to backtrack. "What I mean is—"

Rich lifted his hand to waylay him. "My daughter is really something, isn't she?"

Rohit was in full agreement. "She's incredible."

"So, son," Rich said. "Before we move forward, I have to ask: is there anything else about you that I should know?"

"Well, actually, sir, you should probably know . . ." Rohit reached for courage again, but this time, it was all his own and, to his delight, the words that followed were strong and firm: "I'm in love with your daughter."

EPILOGUE

Leaning against a mound of throw pillows, Cynthia admired the bold yet delicate henna adorning the back of her hand: below a mandala, the henna artist had drawn a thick, intricate pattern of vines and lace around her wrist like a cuff. The same lacey flora swirled around her fingers. Gorgeous. Maybe she'd get her other hand done, too, once all the guests had gotten a chance to receive theirs.

Cynthia turned to look at Naomi, who lounged beside her, her feet, ankles, hands, and arms already stained with the dark brown paste. She was about to compliment her friend's bridal henna when she realized Naomi was humming along to the song playing faintly through the speakers with a suggestive smirk on her face.

"34+35" by Ariana Grande.

Cynthia grabbed a small velvet cushion and with careful, gentle precision, bopped her friend over the head.

"Hey!" Naomi yelped, her eyes widening in alarm until she realized her drying henna remained untouched.

Cynthia fingered the soft edge of the throw pillow. "How did you even get this song in?" The playlist, so far, had been mostly Bollywood music, and the number of oldies but goodies hinted to Cynthia that Naomi's future mother-in-law, or someone of that age group, had curated the song selection.

"I may have slipped in a few." Naomi grinned and notched her chin at the gathering in Dev's childhood home's backyard. "You know how I like to mess with tradition." All around them, guests sat at tables, chatting and admiring one another's henna. Kids ran around on the available green space and a steady stream of people kept spilling out of the house, plates piled high with snacks.

Cynthia and the bride-to-be had stationed themselves at the luxurious, glamping-style nook set up specifically for Naomi by her mother-in-law and aunt, and Cynthia was honored to be in this chosen spot.

A bride's henna party was a time-honored ritual, usually reserved for the bride and female guests only, but Naomi and Dev had elected to invite everyone, and the groom had even grudgingly allowed one of the henna artists to create a small design on his inner wrist with Naomi's name hidden inside.

She'd done the same for Naomi, too, but with Dev's name, and Naomi was being suspiciously tight-lipped about its placement as, per tradition, it was Dev's responsibility to find his name marked somewhere on her body on their wedding night.

"Besides . . ." Naomi added, reclining back onto her little throne of pillows. "How could I resist when I found out you were bringing Rohit with you?"

It was Cynthia's turn to grin—try as she might to hide it—as her gaze found Rohit almost immediately. He was surrounded by a small contingent of aunties by the coolers, and from the way they fluttered around him, it was obvious they were charmed.

Cynthia's grin deepened.

"Should I have added 'Hopelessly Devoted to You'?" Naomi asked.

Cynthia bopped her on the head again.

"Hey, stop beating up my wife," Dev's voice called as he made his way toward them.

"She's not your wife yet," Cynthia reminded him.

Dev angled his intense gaze on Naomi. "Two days," he said, a dimple flashing in his cheek as his lips lifted in a smile.

Cynthia's heart flooded with something deeper and more robust than happiness for her friend, whose face turned several shades of pink that easily rivaled the rich magenta of the bridal sari she would wear two days from now. But Cynthia couldn't tease her or laugh at Naomi's expense, not when she understood why, even as Naomi ducked her head, she couldn't tear her eyes away from her fiancé.

Cynthia understood it all too well, and when her eyes found Rohit again, her heart skittered in anticipation when he broke away from his fans to join them.

"My mom wants to introduce you to some out-of-town friends," Dev said to Naomi as he carefully helped her to her feet.

"See you later," Naomi called as Dev led her away, but Cynthia barely registered their departure.

Because Rohit had found her.

He nodded easily at Dev and Naomi before gingerly taking a seat beside Cynthia.

"What's wrong?" Cynthia asked, raising her eyebrows.

"What do you mean?" Rohit asked innocently as he slowly stretched his legs in front of him.

"You're moving like an old man. Are you hurt or something?"

Rohit grinned and reached down toward his left pant leg and

slowly eased the hem upward. Cynthia gasped as the edges of a simple but familiar henna design came into view on the inside of Rohit's ankle. Her name written in script, surrounded by the same style of vines that decorated her wrist.

Cynthia's chest squeezed and she gave in to the desire to wrap her arms around herself by wrapping her arms around *him* instead, careful to keep her henna-stained hand away from his clothing but holding him tight all the same.

"Is this more romantic than stolen pickup lines, or what?" he asked.

"I like them both," Cynthia said, her lips brushing his earlobe, prompting Rohit to shiver. Cynthia held on tighter.

The urge to confess that she'd like—no, love—moments like these with Rohit for the rest of her life was strong. That she never wanted to let go of him, that for so long, she'd been empty and hadn't even known it and now, she was full. Deliciously, wonderfully, perfectly full. He was her beginning and her end, he'd be everything in the middle, too. And whether that middle was soft or hard, shaky or easy, if they were together, she'd always feel whole.

But she didn't bother to say any of these words. For now, it was enough to hold on tight and press the feelings close to her chest.

Besides, he'd had her name etched on his ankle. He already knew.

ACKNOWLEDGMENTS

At the risk of losing popularity points in the writing community, I'm going to be completely honest: writing this book was a dream. Writers generally fear the second novel—creativity and motivation can feel a bit tapped out after the whirlwind of debuting—but writing a fierce, assertive character like Cynthia next to a romantic simp like Rohit was a delight. And there are so many people who added to this unforgettable experience:

First, I have much love and gratitude for my agent, Jem Chambers-Black, and my editor, Sareer Khader, who are, arguably, the best people to work with. Thank you for your kindness, generosity, and support. I'm in awe of both of you!

I would also like to thank the hardworking team at Penguin Random House, including Kim-Salina I, Chelsea Pascoe, Natasha Tsakiris, Monika Roe, Monica White, Amy J. Schneider, and the many other superstars who work behind the scenes to put books out into the world.

Thank you to the early readers of *Honey and Heat*, especially Mae Bennett, Swati Hegde, and Alexandra Kiley, for helping me find my way through the first draft. I also owe a debt of thanks to the many wonderful writers who patiently held my hand in the "do I even know what I'm doing?" phase of writing a book, including Noreen Nanja, Jessica Joyce, Heather McBreen, Regina Black, Kate Robb, Shannon Basnett, Amy Buchanan, and Bhav Bansi. (If I forgot anyone, I am so sorry [and, as I'm an apologetic Canadian, you know I mean this].)

A heartfelt thanks also goes to the loving people in my life who help hold me down: Sreepati and Dipti, Marcel and Evelyne (who might hold the record in buying copies of *Sunshine and Spice*), Sarah (who would likely come in second for that record), the best communications team in the world (Sarah, again, and Sharon, Sheryar, and Caroline), Chelsea, the Comeback Tour crew, and my kids. Thank you to the Canada Council for the Arts for supporting this project.

To the readers who reach out with messages and take the time to post about my books, thank you for being a light in the dark. Putting words out into the world is a very scary experience, but your responses make it worth it. A special shout-out to those who make it their mission to uplift BIPOC writers and stories: you are amazing!

Finally, while this book is dedicated to the women who do it all, I must acknowledge my spouse, Christopher, who also tries to do it all so I can do the things I love, like writing these books. Thank you for loving me, even when I'm cranky. Also, I'm sorry I never get your movie quotes.

Honey and HEAT

Aurora Palit

READERS GUIDE

DISCUSSION QUESTIONS

1. Would you call Cynthia an unlikable heroine? As a romance reader, are you drawn to stories featuring characters like her?

2. Aside from the fact that Rohit is practically head over heels in love with Cynthia from the moment he meets her, why do you think they're drawn to each other? Do they share similarities with each other, or is this a case of opposites attract?

3. Both Cynthia and Rohit are struggling with inner demons when it comes to confronting conflict with their families. Why do you think it's so difficult to talk about what's in our hearts with the people we want to feel closest to?

4. Rohit loves romantic comedy movies, and they offer him comfort when he's missing home. What genre of movie/literature offers you comfort, and why?

5. After watching *The Devil Wears Prada* (chapter 27), Cynthia wonders if "the moral of the story is that women who try to have it all are doomed to fail." Why do you think that is the conclusion Cynthia comes to? What are your thoughts on women who try to do/have it all?

6. At the end of the novel, Cynthia's father finally offers her exactly what she's always wanted from him: to inherit Kumar Construction. Do you think she made the right decision in declining? What type of career path do you think is right for someone like Cynthia?

7. How is Cynthia's definition of success affected by gender stereotypes? Does her understanding of what it means to be successful change throughout the novel?

8. Both Rohit and Cynthia grapple with life-defining mistakes they've made in the past (i.e., Rohit lying about his credentials, and the consequences of Cynthia's first time in love). Do you think men and women are held accountable for their mistakes in different ways?

9. Rohit often compares his relationship with Cynthia to those of the couples from the romantic comedies he loves to watch. Who are some of your favorite couples from romance books, movies, fanfic, or television?

BOOK RECOMMENDATIONS

As a tribute to Rohit, who comfort watches romantic comedies, here is a list of some of Aurora's most reread romance novels:

1. *Lord of Scoundrels* by Loretta Chase (femme fatale meets beast!)

2. *Ravishing the Heiress* by Sherry Thomas (level-ten yearning)

3. *Faking It* by Jennifer Crusie (swoony con artists)

4. *The Fastest Way to Fall* by Denise Williams (one of my favorite female main characters)

5. *The Kiss Quotient* by Helen Hoang (one of my favorite male main characters)

6. *Wicked and the Wallflower* by Sarah MacLean (level-twelve tension)

7. *Unmarriageable* by Soniah Kamal (my first *Pride and Prejudice* retelling—you never forget your first time)

GABRIELA CRUZ PHOTOGRAPHY

A first-generation Bengali Canadian, **Aurora Palit** grew up in rural Alberta, where she was always the only South Asian student in her class. Her love of reading began at age four, but it wasn't until high school—when she wandered into the romance section of a bookstore—that she realized happily-ever-afters are her jam. Flash forward [an undisclosed number of] years and Aurora is now writing those stories with her own unique brand of humor, perspective, and belief that people of color deserve love stories, too. During her time pursuing a master's degree in English literature, Aurora was drawn to discourses on diaspora and identity, racism, and multigenerational immigrant experiences, topics she now explores in her writing.

VISIT AURORA PALIT ONLINE

AuroraPalit.com
🄾 AuroraPalit

Ready to find
your next great read?

Let us help.

Visit prh.com/nextread